"Presidential darling, America's sweetheart, national rebel: Teddy Roosevelt's swashbuckling daughter Alice springs to life in this raucous anthem to a remarkable woman."

—Kate Quinn, *New York Times* bestselling author of *The Alice Network*

"Epic in scope and rich in immersive detail, *American Princess* is a compelling and poignant tribute to one of America's most colorful, unconventional, and trendsetting women. . . . Highly recommended read!"

—Laura Kamoie, *New York Times* bestselling coauthor of *America's First Daughter* and *My Dear Hamilton*

"A fascinating account of the life of the daring and adventurous Alice Roosevelt Longworth. Brimming with political history, scandal, and insight into some of America's most influential figures, *American Princess* is a must-read for historical fiction fans."

—Chanel Cleeton, *USA Today* bestselling author of *Next Year in Havana*

"Thornton skillfully brings to life the incomparable and unapologetic Alice Roosevelt, whose scandalous life was at the center of American politics for nearly a century. Fast-paced and written with verve and sass, this book is a treat and a treasure for history lovers. Fabulous!"

—Stephanie Dray, *New York Times* bestselling coauthor of *America's First Daughter* and *My Dear Hamilton*

"Skillfully woven and impeccably researched, *American Princess* brims with scandals, secrets, and the complexities of love in all of its wondrous, maddening forms. . . . A vividly imagined portrait that mesmerized me from the first page to the last."

—Kristina McMorris, *New York Times* bestselling author of *The Edge of Lost*

"Witty and poignant, chock-full of secrets and scandals, and richly researched, *American Princess* has everything you could want in historical fiction."   —Renée Rosen, bestselling author of *Windy City Blues*

WRITING AS STEPHANIE THORNTON

The Secret History
Daughter of the Gods
The Tiger Queens
The Conqueror's Wife

AMERICAN PRINCESS

A NOVEL OF FIRST DAUGHTER ALICE ROOSEVELT

Stephanie Marie Thornton

BERKLEY
NEW YORK

BERKLEY
An imprint of Penguin Random House LLC
1745 Broadway, New York, NY 10019

Library of Congress Cataloging-in-Publication Data

Names: Thornton, Stephanie, 1980- author.
Title: American princess : a novel of first daughter Alice Roosevelt /
Stephanie Marie Thornton.
Description: First edition. | New York : Berkley, March 2019.
Identifiers: LCCN 2018023615| ISBN 9780451490902 (trade pbk.) |
ISBN 9780451490919 (ebook)
Subjects: LCSH: Longworth, Alice Roosevelt, 1884-1980—Fiction. | Children of
presidents—United States—Biography. | Politicians' spouses—United
States—Biography. | Roosevelt, Theodore, 1858-1919—Family. |
Biographical fiction. | Historical fiction.

Classification: LCC PS3620.H7847 A84 2019 | DDC 813/.6—dc23
LC record available at https://lccn.loc.gov/2018023615

First Edition: March 2019

Printed in the United States of America
3 5 7 9 10 8 6 4 2

Photo of woman © Lee Avison/Trevillion; photo of the White House by
American Photographer (20th century)/Private collection/© Look and Learn/Bridgeman Images
Cover design by Katie Anderson
Book design by Kelly Lipovich

For Hollie Dunn and Heather Harris,

My sisters who, like Alice Roosevelt,
have both been known to break a rule or two

Prologue

WASHINGTON, DC
1970

Given the choice, I'd have preferred a sudden heart attack in the Senate audience gallery to this mundane death by surgery.

I squint in vain against the garish hospital lights, the walls a phosphorescent white that blur painfully into the nurses' sterile uniforms. Perhaps even something as dull as dying warm in my own bed would have sufficed. But the villainies of age continue, and I find myself instead subjected to the injustice of a starched hospital gown and the impending threat of a scalpel.

"Are you comfortable, ma'am?"

I'm about to be drugged and butchered. Of course I'm not comfortable, you moonbrain.

I wave away the nurse's inane question with a hand so spotted and gnarled it might have belonged to a Pharaonic mummy. Sometimes I scarcely recognize the white-haired biddy I've become; I miss the hedonistic hellion who smoked foul-smelling cigarettes on the roof of the White House, feted mustachioed German princes and an iron-fisted Chinese empress, and inspired the rage for the color Alice Blue in the spring of 1902.

"I'm fine," I lie to the nurse. "After all, I'm about to become Washington's only topless octogenarian." My voice trembles with age and, if I admit it, a hefty dose of fear even as my pulse thuds in my ears.

I shouldn't be afraid. After all, I've been through this before, almost fifteen years ago—not to mention all the other painful procedures I've undergone over the years—but the cancer returned so now the other breast has to go. I shouldn't be attached to a lump of sagging flesh, or even life itself now that I'm just an old fossil. But I've always drunk greedily from the cup of life, even when it was its most bitter.

At eighty-six years old, I'm not done living.

A warm hand in mine banishes a fraction of my fear. "I'll be waiting outside, Grammy." Joanna's pale brown hair is loose around her face; she looks so like me when I was her age. "I'd sit with you in the operating room if they'd let me."

I pat her hand. "I know you would, darling," I say as the nurse gives the intravenous needle an efficient tap and swabs the inside of my elbow with a cool pad of alcohol. "And if this is the end . . ."

"I'll have you buried wearing your Cuban pearls, in the plot you picked out right next to her. I swear it." Joanna kisses me on the forehead as the needle pricks the thin flesh of my arm. "But that's not going to happen. Not today."

"If you say so."

I recall as if through a haze receiving those pearls before my wedding day, but then my mind tilts drunkenly as the nurse wheels me into surgery. I think of my father, barrel-chested and booming-voiced even after being shot by a would-be assassin, brandishing the bleeding, undressed bullet wound to a worshipful crowd. My earliest memory pushes its way in, of trying to clamber onto his lap, me frocked in a pink dress while he still wore leather chaps that smelled of the dusty Dakota Badlands. Train whistles shrieked and engines roared as he'd brushed me off and handed me back to my aunt.

"I can't," he'd said even as I reached up empty arms for him. "She has *her* eyes . . . I just can't."

Oh, Father . . .

I've seen sixteen presidents come and go—including my father with his spectacled face chiseled on Mount Rushmore, and my crowd-pleasing, fedora-toting cousin Franklin. Yet, they're all gone and I'm still here, the *other* Washington Monument.

Where on earth did I even get that name? I scowl, unable to jar loose which journalist dubbed me with the title. I suppose it doesn't matter now.

The terror of the surgical theater brings me back to reality, with its glaring lights and swarm of white-garbed physicians. "We're going to start your anesthesia in a moment, ma'am," one says to me. "Can you count backward, starting from ten?"

I scoff, for I won't waste my final moments with counting numbers. I count memories instead, with crystal clarity: burying a bad little idol of Nellie Taft in the White House gardens, calling President Harding a decaying emperor, and comparing cousin Franklin to Hitler. (Not my finest moment, that.)

Merry hell, but my tongue has gotten me into trouble.

Perhaps I might have swallowed some of the things I said and protected feelings here and there, but it's too late to undo things. And as the world begins to blur with a heady mix of sedative and memories, I muse that at least if I die on the operating table in this goddamned hospital, I'll never regret grabbing life by the throat and refusing to let go, despite the mistakes I've made.

But then, if you live as long as I have, you're bound to make a few mistakes here and there. They say that it's the mistakes that make life more interesting.

If that's the case, then I've led the world's *most* interesting life . . .

Part 1

THE PRESIDENT'S DAUGHTER

*I can hardly recollect a time when I was not
aware of politics and politicians.*

—ALICE ROOSEVELT

Chapter 1

ADIRONDACK MOUNTAINS, NEW YORK
SEPTEMBER 1901

I peered through the rain coursing down the cabin's front window and frowned at the frantic Adirondacks park ranger who rapped hard on our door, water dripping from his hat onto his drab uniform that was already drenched. "Mr. Roosevelt!" he hollered, his bushy brows drawn together like late-season caterpillars. "Mr. Theodore Roosevelt!"

Edith, my stepmother, hadn't finished unpacking her bags from an overnight campout and swung open the door mid-bang, stopping the ranger with his meaty fist still raised. "I'm afraid the vice president isn't here," Mother informed him in her most mollifying voice, smoothing back her damp hair even as I shoved deep my jealousy at the mud that stained her skirt's hem and the fragrance of a jolly campfire that still clung to her.

Mother doesn't even like *camping. Whereas I . . .*

I made a face behind her back before resuming the task of adjusting my hairpins in the hall's tiny mirror, expertly stabbing them into the coiled plait of brown hair twisted atop my head while imagining the party I planned to attend tonight, where I might happily forget there were such things as parents, presidents, or politics. I'd turn eighteen this February and had been experimenting with various hairstyles for my debut ball, none of which met my approval considering that Mother refused to buy me the pearl combs I craved for my pompadour. Too expensive, she claimed, forgetting that a girl comes out only once, and thus deserves the most lavish accessories that money can buy.

As always, I tried not to let it bother me that all my younger half siblings were granted whatever pets and toys they set their hearts on, further evidence that I would forever be *other* when it came to our family. I supposed I could always use my inheritance from my mother if I couldn't live without the hair combs.

"Mr. Roosevelt isn't here?" the ranger parroted back to Mother, sweeping off his unfortunate hat to wring it in his hands, so I doubted whether the waterlogged leather would ever recover. "Where is he?"

Archie and Quentin's cowboy rodeo down the hallway involved much whooping and hollering, interspersed with an angry crowing; my brothers had recently adopted a foul-tempered, one-legged rooster that enjoyed chasing the younger children. "Alice?" Mother asked suggestively, inclining her head toward the children's rooms, but I pretended not to notice.

"My father is hiking Mount Marcy today," I answered for her, tossing myself into a leather-slung chair and plucking a red apple from the bowl on the sideboard. Its crisp taste exploded in my mouth in a burst of autumn as I idly kicked the flounced hem of my dress, much to my stepmother's horror. I'd watched Father depart at yesterday's sunrise with her, Archie, and my little sister Ethel for an overnight trip to Lake Colden and had hoped to join them, even though they'd planned to turn around early to allow Father to hike Mount Marcy in peace today.

"Can I come too?" I'd asked, but my father had only shaken his head, a rare shaft of sunlight glinting off his spectacles, his gaze not on me but on the craggy mountain in the distance.

"You won't be able to keep up, Sissy."

The truth hurt, for despite being fully recovered, I was still wobbly on uneven ground after spending years in metal leg braces (more like medieval torture devices) to correct a mild bout of childhood polio. He saw my disappointment and sighed. "Perhaps next time."

That's what he always said, but there was *never* a next time.

When I was six years old, I'd been chastised for trying to walk like Father, mimicking his mix of cowboy-boxer swagger that Mother deemed entirely unladylike. At ten, I'd been reprimanded for trying to talk like him, peppering *dee-lighted* into every other sentence and grinning in a way no gently bred girl ever should. Now, at seventeen, I'd have hiked to Canada barefoot if it meant spending an afternoon alone with him.

Instead, it's the same as always, any excuse so my own father doesn't have to spend time with me.

For no matter how Father romped and played with his five other children—*Mother's* children—I was always the child who carried his first wife's name and blue-gray eyes.

And nothing I did would ever make up for that crime.

"I'll have to ride to find him," the ranger said, wiping the rain from his face before stuffing his mangled hat back onto his head.

"Perhaps you could leave a message?" Mother motioned for one of the maids to check on the children. A real humdinger of a fight seemed to be breaking out between Archie and the rooster.

"I'm afraid not, Mrs. Roosevelt," he said. "For it pertains to President McKinley."

His words threw a sudden chill into the air. Only a week ago, the entire nation had been stunned when an anarchist shot President McKinley at the Pan-American Exposition in Buffalo. The wound was a nasty affair—as I suppose it always is when a man is shot twice in the abdomen at point-blank range—but McKinley seemed to improve after a gynecologist found on the fairgrounds performed emergency surgery to remove the first bullet. The president rallied so much that my father, America's vice president, had insisted that we keep our scheduled trip here in the Adirondacks.

A little chaos was no match for my father's well-laid plans, not when there were mountains to conquer, rivers to ford, and wild game to shoot. Plus, Father had no desire to seem as if he were hovering over the president, waiting for him to die even as the newspapers and a constant stream of telegrams reported that McKinley had been growing sicker over the past days. Mother's fingers fluttered to her mouth, as if to trap the impertinent question on her lips.

I, however, had no such qualms. Perhaps it seemed callous, as if I had no pity for the dying McKinley, and I *did* feel a pang of grief for him, but I could feel the surge of history in the making, beating in my blood and carrying me with it.

"Is the president dead?" My feet were firmly on the floor as I leaned forward in my chair, all thoughts of tonight's party forgotten as Mother came to stand beside me.

The ranger shook his head in a manner almost reverential.

"Not dead," he answered. "Dying of blood poisoning. They say he won't last the night."

Mother clutched my hand as the ranger tipped his hat to us and mounted his sorrel horse, kicking the animal's ribs and tearing off in the direction of Mount Marcy, to fetch my father back to Buffalo in case he suddenly became the most important man in America.

"Lord help us." Mother crushed my palm as if a handful of my bone fragments would give her strength. I extricated myself and left her in the hall.

"What's happening, Sissy?" My little sister Ethel poked her head out of the room we shared, her blond hair parted after a fresh bath following her camping trip and combed to gleaming perfection around her ten-year-old face. Skip, our feisty rat terrier, yipped at my feet, but for once I ignored him.

"Father's going to be president," I said slowly, staring out the window as my mind raced ahead to what this meant for us. I'd always resented the fact that Father had been shoved unwillingly into the token position that was the vice presidency, but had never really considered that he might one day be president.

That I might be the president's daughter.

. . .

President McKinley died at two fifteen the following morning, plunging America into a shocked grief and rousing us remaining Roosevelts from our sleepless beds to begin the long trek by buckboard and train to the nation's capital.

I gaped when the carriage finally turned onto Pennsylvania Avenue and allowed me my first glimpse of the Executive Mansion's stately white pillars, its curved portico shrouded in deep autumn shadows, and the dark velvet curtains in all the windows drawn as if the entire building was asleep and waiting for us.

"Which room do you think will be ours?" Ethel murmured from beside me, but I didn't answer, struck speechless for perhaps the first time in my life.

This was our new home.

My father was now president of the United States of America.

And that meant I was now First Daughter.

Chapter 2

WASHINGTON, DC
OCTOBER 1901

A girl was given only two opportunities in life to really shine: her debut and her wedding. With the way things were looking, my funeral was going to be livelier than my debut.

"Mother, it will be a terrible sockdolager to host a debut without champagne and cotillion favors." I did my best to keep my voice level while I paced the musty-smelling Red Room. Above me on the burgundy silk walls hung an implacable portrait of George Washington with his arm outstretched, as if urging me to charge forward into battle. "It simply isn't done."

Mother scarcely glanced up from her inspection of my debut gown, still creased from its wooden delivery crate. The dress had arrived today from New Jersey—not from Paris's House of Worth as I'd hoped—and been delivered to the parlor for Mother's approval, not mine. I'd have draped myself in black just for the sensation it would cause, but Mother had insisted on a singularly repulsive number with its cascades of white taffeta and silk rosebuds.

"Cotillion favors are too expensive," she repeated for the third time that afternoon. "And we'll offend the teetotalers if we serve champagne. Every move we make reflects upon your father now, Alice. You must remember that."

As if I could ever forget.

I flopped back on a threadbare crimson settee in a huff, ignoring the loose pieces of horsehair while trying to convince myself that the gossip rags might still swoon rapturously over my debut's flat lemon punch and austere lack of favors. These were only the latest in an ever-lengthening list of problems with my debut.

I grimaced at George Washington and switched tactics. "I still don't think I should come out with all my cousins," I said. That was a bit of an exaggeration, as prim cousin Eleanor was still at her English boarding school. One less cousin to worry about, I supposed. "It's provincial to share a debut with four other girls. And more young people could attend if the debut came after New Year's. Otherwise I'll be lucky to dance with anyone other than Feather Duster."

Mother *tsked* under her breath. "Alice, I told you not to call your cousin that name."

"It's not my fault Franklin prances and flutters just like a duster." In fact, he was the sort to sail a boat instead of sweatingly rowing it in the hottest weather as Father would have insisted on doing. "I thought the whole purpose of a debut is to attract eligible young bachelors."

"It is." Mother pursed her lips, whether because she was displeased with me or my gown or the shabby state of the hideous dark parlor, I couldn't guess. Probably all three.

"You never know," I said, rising to give her a peck on the cheek. "Maybe I'll fall madly in love with some dasher after my first quadrille, make an early marriage, and be out of your hair forever."

It was a tack I'd tried more than once, only Mother didn't realize that I had no intention of marrying for a little while. I'd give myself plenty of time to dance at balls, vacation at Newport, and read my name in the society columns before I settled down with a husband and the children that would inevitably follow. I wasn't sure how I'd reconcile all that with Mother's interminable list of old-fashioned dos and do nots that all well-bred young ladies must follow, but where there was a will, there was bound to be a way.

After all, I was a Roosevelt, and as Father always said, a Roosevelt could do anything he put his mind to.

Or in this case, anything *she* put her mind to.

Mother was saved from having to reply as Archie and Quentin pounded down the hallway on stilts, shrieking while our menagerie of dogs yapped after them. She gave a deep sigh, yet I'd have sworn her brown eyes sparkled with some sort of secret laughter. "Ask your father about all the debut business during his usual four o'clock appointment with you children. He has the final say in this."

I couldn't wait hours for Father's standing appointment that would inevitably devolve into a pillow fight with my siblings, not to mention that I might also have to compete for his attention with the official dignitaries he sometimes invited along. So I burst into the presidential study just a few minutes later, breathless with anticipation and holding our terrier Skip squirming in my arms, whom I'd rescued from a near trampling by stilts in the corridor. "Father." I interrupted midsentence the conversation with Owen Wister, his longtime friend from the Dakota Badlands. "Mother says I should talk to you about my debut. Right now."

Wister's pointed mustache twitched with annoyance, yet I ignored him.

"Hello to you, too, Alice." Father removed his round spectacles to polish them with a kerchief from his vest pocket. "Owen here was just informing me that he's dedicating his next book to me."

His chest puffed out a little as he spoke, and I had a sneaking suspicion this wouldn't be the last thing named after him now that he was president. "That's lovely," I said, even as I mused distractedly that perhaps I might finagle having something dedicated to me too. Maybe a book, a song, or even a hairstyle . . . I wasn't picky.

"But, Father," I said. "My debut? Mother really was quite insistent that the details be decided. Today."

"Was she now?" Father asked as he crossed the frayed taupe carpet. He wasn't an overly tall man, but he filled every room with the sheer magnitude of his presence. In his dapper suit he seemed entirely out of place in the Executive Mansion, whose interior seemed to have come straight from a hundred-year-old Victorian novel, one that was dog-eared and creased around the edges. "Then I suppose you don't know that your mother and I discussed your debut over breakfast while a certain lazybones was still abed."

I cursed myself for sleeping in and missing my chance to make my case for why the president's daughter needed a spectacular debut. With bated breath, I set down Skip, who made a beeline for my father. "And?"

Father tucked Skip under his arm and idly scratched behind his floppy ears. "Your debut will be in January, after your mother's New Year's reception."

I shrieked in delight. "January? Not December with the rest of my Roosevelt cousins?"

"January," my father repeated. "And you shall be the only girl dressed in debut white."

"And where will it be?" I asked, breathless with anticipation.

"Here in the Executive Mansion, of course."

I flung my arms around him—and Skip—with a squeal, but Father only offered me an awkward pat with his free hand. His wooden response recalled the many train station embraces from my childhood, him still smelling of the leather, horses, and the wide-open plains of the Dakotas. My real mother—Alice Hathaway Lee—had died of Bright's disease on the same day that Father's mother had died, leaving him so grief-stricken that he'd abandoned me, an infant of only a few days, to be raised by his sister until I was four. Today he smelled of tallow from his Williams' shaving soap, but his hug was as stilted as ever.

"Thank you, Father," I said, trying to recover my jubilee as I made a show of smoothing my skirt.

"You may thank Mother," he said. "She seems to believe more young men can attend the festivities after their college exams and Christmas."

I smiled, for Mother had picked up the trail of bread crumbs I'd sprinkled about for days, hints of more eligible bachelors being available after the holidays, all in the hope that I might have my own debut. And yet she'd sent me to Father so I might hear the good news from him instead.

Don't ask questions. Just accept the gift.

Father tugged the bottom of his vest, his attention already shifting from me. "Now, Alice, if you don't mind, I'm going to finish my conversation with Owen. We shall continue discussing your debutante ball another time."

"All right," I said, recognizing that I'd finally worn out my welcome.

Anyway, my debut would be the perfect opportunity to impress him with my newfound poise and maturity. Yet not everyone seemed to view me that way.

"Your daughter Alice seems a bit wild," Wister said a bit too loudly as I departed, halting my jaunty steps. "Perhaps you could rein her in somewhat?"

I pivoted on my heel to glower at him, but he and Father had already turned to peruse a dusty pile of maps.

"My dear friend," I heard my father say, his voice laced with exasperation. "I can either run the country or I can control Alice. I cannot possibly do both."

I closed the door silently behind me, my euphoria draining like air from a rubber balloon pierced by a needle. Why, oh why, couldn't Father just be proud of me?

I straightened my shoulders, deciding there was only one thing left to do.

Just as Father had taken first New York and then all of America by storm, I'd become the talk of Washington by becoming the most successful, witty, and lively debutante of the season. I'd prove that this apple hadn't fallen far from the tree.

Then maybe, just maybe, Father would look at me the way he did all my other siblings, grinning that toothy grin while his ice-blue eyes warmed with pride.

And love.

After two months of quibbling over details, I pulled a sour face at the mirror before going down to greet my six hundred guests, half surprised at the girl—no, woman—who mimicked me. Mother had been occupied with the debut preparations since dawn so Auntie Bye—my father's eldest sister Anna, although no one ever called her that—had helped prod, cinch, and stuff me into my traditional white taffeta gown.

"Why, Alice, I've never seen a more perfect debutante, not even when your mother came out," she said now, drawing me into a hug that smelled of the bread she loved to bake. I returned the fierce embrace before she released me with an awkward shuffle, a result of her permanently hunched spine after a bout of infant paralysis. "Your only job tonight is to enjoy yourself; do you understand?"

I bit my lip, adjusting my white elbow gloves as I worried the tiny diamond pendant at my neck, a gift from Father and Mother earlier that night. It was Auntie Bye who had taught me to walk and tie my shoes when Father was in the Badlands and had given me my first diary while Mother was busy birthing and caring for all my half siblings: first Ted, followed in quick succession by Kermit, Ethel, Archie, and Quentin, each of whom arrived on schedule almost every two years. In fact, it was my aunt who had finally told me that I had a different mother than my siblings.

"Your father won't speak of Alice Lee," Auntie Bye had said while she cuddled me one night as Mother recuperated from a long delivery with one of my brothers—Archie, I think. I'd snuggled closer, tucking my feet into the warmth under her legs. "But your mother was more lovely than Gloriana the Faerie Queene, too beautiful for this world, I fear."

I had no memory of Alice Hathaway Lee—she'd died only two days after my birth—but I learned from Bye's scrapbooks that she'd been a beautiful socialite who shared my blue-gray eyes. I'd begged my aunt to tell me more, and she had, that Alice Lee had been as charming and frivolous as child bride Dora from Dickens's *David Copperfield*, which she'd then set about reading to me. Because Aunt Bye firmly believed that the answers to most of life's questions could be found in books.

Yet no amount of reading had ever convinced me that Father could truly love me, not when my existence was a painful reminder of the love he'd lost.

Perhaps there truly is no hope for me.

Auntie Bye's praise tonight soothed my ragged nerves, but there was one last thing I needed. I grasped Bye's wrist as she turned to leave. "Do you think Alice Lee would be proud? If she could see me tonight, I mean?"

"Oh, Alice." Auntie Bye reached up to touch my cheek with her gloved hand. "Don't you know? Your mother would be near to bursting if she were here."

I'd never been a namby-pamby and I wasn't about to start snuffling now, but I had to blink hard to keep my vision from blurring. "Thank you, Bye," I whispered.

"I'll see you in the receiving line, my blue-eyed girl."

I took a long moment to collect myself, for it wouldn't do to have a blotchy face for my own debut. When the door creaked I expected to see Mother ready with an admonition against my lingering, but instead Ethel stood in the corridor in her pink satin nightgown and her hair in papers so she might have passed for a child version of Medusa. Her eyes widened and her mouth turned to a perfect O of surprise. "You look like a princess," she breathed.

I laughed and dropped a kiss on her forehead. "Would you like to carry my train to the stairs?"

She gave an eager nod and so I heaved a final breath—as much as my Edwardian corset would allow—and walked out the bedroom door to the staircase, measuring my pace just as Mother had instructed. I hesitated on the top step until the United States Marine Band picked up the notes of one of Beethoven's violin concertos to announce my arrival. In a moment Father would see me, and he'd beam with pride before introducing me to Washington's elite.

This is the moment I've waited for my entire life. This is when my life begins.

All eyes swiveled toward me as I descended slowly into the assembled crowd, taking the time over my pounding heart to enjoy the polite applause mingled with excited murmurs. This was the first time in my life I could recall being the absolute center of attention, and I was surprised to discover that the weight of everyone's gazes made me feel powerful, as if my very skin crackled with excitement. The surge of energy and pride made me tilt my chin a little higher. Was this how Father felt when he addressed a crowd of thousands, so wonderfully alive that his blood *sang*? I hesitated only to glance back to where Ethel was still watching. She ducked behind the banister and I smiled, continuing my descent until I reached the receiving line in the Blue Room and, beyond that, the East Room's makeshift ballroom.

"You look lovely, Sissy," Mother whispered as I took my place in the receiving line. It was high praise from my stepmother, but I only stood on tiptoes to find my father, spotting him with head bent in conversation with portly William Howard Taft, his new secretary of war. All of Taft's three hundred plus pounds had been stuffed into a tuxedo whose white vest threatened to pop its ivory buttons at any moment, but my father was dressed fashionably in a black tailcoat and white silk tie. I yearned for him to bellow across the room how lovely I looked now that I was all grown up, and felt a surge of disappointment when he only smiled and nodded at me from his vantage near the ballroom doors. His tiny nod of approval would have to be enough.

For now, at least.

Aunt Bye's admonition to enjoy myself was easier said than accomplished. I'd thought my debut would mean simply outshining all the other guests while I feasted and whirled about like a dervish; I hadn't counted on all the social niceties.

I *loathed* social niceties.

"Alice, the satin rosebuds on your gown are just delicious," enthused one Astor matron who smelled like she'd rolled in a decaying rose garden.

"You're too kind." The smile I'd been wearing for the past hour nearly cracked my face.

"Chin up," Auntie Bye murmured when she made it through the line. "The torture is almost over and then the fun can really begin."

"I hope you're right." My whisper was a bit too loud as I glanced around at the flawless tailoring of the men's peaked lapel dinner jackets and the bouffant hairstyles that pegged the women as members of the Four Hundred, the group that included New York's richest and most fashionable families. "Because from what I've seen tonight, most of the Four Hundred are awful stiffs. Ugh!"

That prompted Mother to level a glare at me that might have frozen the Potomac in July. "Alice . . ."

Now I'm really in for it.

"I'm sorry, Mother," I said hastily, realizing from the way everyone—including Father—was staring at me, that this wasn't the best way to become the season's most successful debutante. "My mistake."

For I was a connoisseur of mistakes, everything from riding bikes with boys back home in New York to causing my mother's death when I was born. Yet, surely I could subvert my natural liveliness for this one evening, for my parents' sake, if not for my own.

So I continued curtsying to society dames whose mothballed lace made my nose twitch and greeting their stiff-lipped politician husbands who yawned as much as I wanted to. Gouging my eyes out might have been more enjoyable.

Sadly, the gong rang to announce the opening of the banquet long before the receiving line had trickled away. My stomach growled in a most unladylike manner as the tables were laid with so many of my favorite foods: oysters Rockefeller and breaded lamb cutlets, quivering towers of currant jelly and coconut custard pies.

"I've asked the maids to send a coconut pie to your room tonight," Mother whispered during a momentary lull. "I'm afraid you'll have to open the ball and may not have a chance to eat."

She was right, for the plates were already being cleared when I thanked my final guests for attending and opened the ball on the arm of a Lieutenant Gilmore of the artillery (with a mustache that rivaled the tail of a coonskin hat) who had won my first quadrille. After months of eager anticipation, I found the entire soiree a bit disappointing, although I did love the way everyone orbited around me, like small planets to my glowing sun.

"The men around you are seven deep," said a male voice at my elbow. I turned to see smooth-faced cousin Franklin wearing his customary grin and a pair of gold-rimmed pince-nez glasses identical to my father's.

Destined for the drudgery of sitting for the New York bar exam, I thought to myself, *but he idolizes Father, so I suppose he can't be all bad.*

"Seven might be a bit of an exaggeration," I said as Feather Duster offered his hand for the next dance.

"Seven is dead-on, fair cousin," Franklin said with a wink. "I counted."

My cousin's future as a dully competent lawyer looked brighter with each passing moment. I expected him to be a heeler on the dance floor, but his step was lively and his timing impeccable as he guided me about the linen crash laid over the East Room's hideous mustard carpet, although a proficient waltz was hardly going to make me the star of the society columns tomorrow.

"I'd claim the next dance, if the debutante doesn't mind a turn with her father, that is."

I grinned like a Cheshire cat to see Father offering his hand to me. My cousin was quickly claimed by Maggie Cassini, the flamboyant daughter of our Russian ambassador. She was striking in an ivory evening ensemble spangled with black velvet swirls and tiny mirrors that called to mind a Romany caravan so I could almost hear the crash of Gypsy cymbals. I knew Maggie only by sight, but her flowing black curls and barking laugh seemed far too exuberant for the likes of Feather Duster. I was right, for we'd scarcely started moving before Franklin bowed a hasty departure and left Maggie smirking after him.

"You've done admirably well this evening," Father said. I remembered once—I think it was Christmas, or perhaps the memory was just tinged with such wonder that it may as well have been Christmas morning—when I danced with Father, my tiny patent leather shoes atop his own big feet as he twirled me around the floor. Now I strained to listen while I studiously avoided stepping on his feet. "Your mother and I are passably pleased."

Admirably well. Passably pleased.

My mouth went suddenly dry at this colossal failure, worse than if I'd tripped us both in the middle of the dance floor. "Thank you," I mumbled, unable to meet his eyes. "And thank you for tonight."

"You're welcome, Sissy," he said, as if I'd merely complimented him for passing me the bread at dinner. I forced a smile as he handed me off to his graybeard attorney general.

Playing the proper young lady is an utter bore, I thought as I excused myself and fled to the powder room, *and it made me invisible to Father. Face it, Alice, you balled up this time.*

Back in my room later that night, I kicked off my satin Louis heels, too distraught to eat a bite of the coconut pie the maids delivered, before collapsing onto my narrow bed. I snuggled down under the pink patchwork quilt Auntie Bye had made me ages ago, willing myself to forget Father's lukewarm praise. Instead, I remembered the feel of everyone's attention as I'd walked down the stairs, a memory that made me warmer than if I'd quaffed a whole bottle of champagne.

I'm doomed to be a bitter pill for Father to swallow, but I won't let that stop me from having a little fun. More than a little, actually.

If I played my cards right, there would be many more magnificent balls, operas, and garden parties to make my head spin in the months to come.

Unfortunately, my parents had other plans.

I found myself trussed into my debut gown again and posed in the corner of the Yellow Oval Room one week later, the hundreds of debut roses and hyacinths used to decorate the Blue, Red, Green, and East Rooms long since donated to Washington hospitals. I wrinkled my nose at the haphazard pile of newspaper headlines and autograph requests that had accumulated on the Louis XIII writing table just out of reach, for I'd read them all at least ten times already.

ROOSEVELT DEBUT CHARMING, LACKS COTILLION FAVORS.

FIRST YOUNG LADY OF THE LAND DEBUTS WITH EXTREMELY SIMPLE DECORATIONS.

"Perhaps one with your hand on the back of the chair?" Frances Johnston adjusted her box camera while she directed my pose. I liked that my photographer was a woman, and even more that I had cause to be photographed. For despite the bland reviews of my debut, the press had dubbed me with a new title.

Princess Alice.

Overnight, I'd become America's favorite daughter, hence my being dressed up again like a life-size doll and arranged in stiff positions all morning, accompanied by the acrid smell of sulfur and the boom of exploding chemicals while I twitched with impatience.

"This is the last one," Frances said, just as Rose, my favorite of the White House's Negro maids, and my mother bustled in. Rose and her brother Ike—a White House usher who possessed an unfortunate parish pickax of a nose—had helped all my siblings and me find the largest tin trays in the pantry to slide down the staircases on our first night in the White House. "More autograph requests," Rose said, setting them on the desk. "Soon you're going to need a secretary to answer all these letters."

Mother's lips took on a decidedly pinched look. "At least you'll have appropriate photographs now to placate this brief fascination with America's 'first young lady of the land.' Neither your father nor I are keen on your newfound popularity."

Because heaven forbid either of you be keen on anything I might enjoy.

The camera's deafening crack of sound and blinding flash of light saved me from responding. "That was the last one," Frances said. "There should be some excellent shots once they're developed."

"Do you know, Miss Alice," Rose said, handing me an ivory-handled letter opener with which to attack the envelopes now that I was free to move again, "I was walking home yesterday and passed Miss Vincent's dress shop. You'll never guess what she had in her front window."

"A dress?" I quipped as I tore open the first letter.

"Alice," Mother said, her very tone a warning. She grimaced at the pile of envelopes as if they were vermin to be swept away while Frances packed up her equipment. "Don't be pert."

Rose started humming as if neither of us had spoken, a testament to the unflappable composure common among the White House staff. "At least three day gowns, all in a color advertised as Alice Blue." Rose squinted at me and shook her head. "Miss Vincent claims this season's color is the same shade as your eyes, but they're not nearly so gray."

"I've never met Miss Vincent," I said. "How could she know the color of my eyes?"

Rose didn't answer, but I suddenly recalled a snippet from one of the society articles I'd read shortly after my debut.

Miss Roosevelt's lively eyes are a lovely shade of gray-blue . . .

I couldn't recall greeting any newspapermen face-to-face at the ball, but I'd been introduced to over six hundred people that night. I might have met Abraham Lincoln and not noticed.

I filed away the realization that my every sneeze might now potentially wind up as news to be discussed over American breakfasts. It was a daunting thought, but perhaps one that I might somehow use to my advantage, although I wasn't sure how just yet.

Still, a color of my own was something to celebrate. Only a few months in the White House and already I had something named after me, just as I'd hoped. Maybe tomorrow I'd have a song or a new dance . . .

"I'm all done here." Frances hefted her case with one hand and her wooden tripod with the other. "I'll send word as soon as the cabinet cards are ready."

"I'll approve all the photographs before we decide which ones to purchase," Mother said before turning and showing Frances out with a swish of crinoline skirts. "Then Alice may sign them."

Perhaps Mother should hold my hand while I sign the damnable pictures, too, in case I spell my name wrong, I thought as I glared at her retreating back. *Heaven forbid I should do anything on my own.*

"Help me out of this dress?" I asked Rose after Mother and the photographer left. "I'm off to see Auntie Bye for tea."

Rose followed me back to my room and helped me unbutton my debut gown, so I could slip into a new striped navy day dress. I'd just finished tugging on my white gloves and adjusting my hat—a delectable creation featuring a bouffant of white egret feathers that had cost me over a month's allowance—when Rose stopped thumbing through the pile of correspondence.

"Miss Alice, you may want to read this one before you go," she said, offering me an envelope as if it were stuffed with precious jewels.

"Toss it with the others," I said. "I don't want to keep my aunt waiting."

"But it's from Buckingham Palace."

I stared at her, then snatched the letter. Rose was right—above my painstakingly stenciled name was the official emblem of Buckingham Palace, stamped on vellum so thick it might have been the cover of a book rather than an envelope. Inside were two papers, one a letter from Whitelaw Reid, my father's special ambassador, and the other . . .

"It's an invitation to the coronation of Edward VII!" I'd never been a girl to get the vapors, but a fainting couch wouldn't have gone amiss had there been one available at that moment. I fanned myself with the paper, cursing the tightness of my corset that kept me from drawing a decent breath. "Did the rest of the family receive invitations too?"

"Not that I'm aware of." Rose tried to peer over my shoulder to catch a glimpse of the invitation. "Will your father allow you to attend?"

"Of course!" I said with more confidence than I felt, kissing both her dark cheeks before skipping down the stairs. After all, surely it was fitting that America's princess attend the crowning of a king?

I didn't even make it to the front door when Mother stopped me, her face ashen.

"What's wrong?" I asked, for it was common knowledge that only a catastrophe on par with the coming of the Four Horsemen of the Apocalypse could shake the First Lady's usual aplomb.

The yellow paper of a Western Union telegram shuddered slightly in her trembling hands, the same capable hands I'd watched darn my father's socks and soothe my caterwauling siblings after they scraped their knees.

"It's your brother, Ted, at Groton," she said. "He's very ill. Your father and I must leave immediately."

With those words, the coronation of a king seemed very trivial indeed.

*   *   *

Dear Alice,

Your brother Ted lingers in his sickbed here at Groton. The physicians assure us this is only a mild bout of pneumonia, but he calls your name as he tosses and turns in his sleep between doses of warm lemon whiskey. I believe a visit from you would ease him tremendously.

   Please hurry.

Much love,
Mother

I tucked the letter back into my traveling valise and tapped my foot impatiently, waiting beside my silent father to board the train that would whisk me away to my favorite brother. Despite my best intentions, fifteen years ago Ted had weaseled his way into my heart when the nurse first placed him red-faced and mewling into his crib. I'd pulled my rocking chair alongside him and declared with crossed arms that I'd stay there forever beside my howling little polly parrot. To my dismay, his current school schedule meant I only ever saw him during holiday breaks and a few weeks every summer.

So now I traveled to Groton with a copy of our shared favorite, *The Jungle Book*, to read and recite with him. The one boon to Ted's illness—if there was a boon—was that I'd met my father for a flying moment at the Baltimore and Potomac train station and he'd lingered to see me off even as a huddle of newspapermen waited to interview him about a possible coal strike. It was always hellos and good-byes between us, rarely enough time for a breath in between.

"Ted will be glad to have you to keep him company," Father said now as he handed me into the train carriage bound for Massachusetts, his suit still rumpled from his own return journey and his Secret Service agents yawning into their hands. Father loathed having guards, but it was a necessary evil after McKinley's assassination. "Try not to get into too much trouble while you're at Groton."

I ignored his admonition. "Father, have you had a chance to decide whether I'm to attend Prince Edward's coronation?"

"We'll discuss it when you return to Washington. In the meantime, I've agreed to allow you to christen Kaiser Wilhelm's new yacht, the *Meteor*, when his brother brings it to America next month."

"Really?" I wanted to shriek with excitement, but an Associated Press reporter watched us from under the brim of his hat, so I instead contented myself with a gleeful clap of my hands. After all, I didn't want to end up in the papers for squealing like a stuck pig, even if meeting a German prince was the most exciting thing to happen since my debut.

"If we can't keep your name from the papers, we may as well have you doing something worthwhile. Which reminds me." Father dug in his pocket and retrieved a small velvet box, which he flipped open to display a gaudy diamond bracelet, its center graced with a sour-faced portrait of the grandly mustached Kaiser Wilhelm. "A gift for you from the kaiser."

I slipped the bracelet over my wrist and admired its blinding sparkle in the weak winter sunlight. The thing really was beyond lurid, but it would be my first keepsake from my time as the president's daughter. "You have no idea what that means to me!"

I meant the responsibility of the christening, but Father seemed to think I meant the bracelet itself.

"Very well then." He patted my cheek awkwardly before waving to the crowd of newspapermen and its resulting cacophony of exploding flashlamps. "Be a help to Mother while you're gone."

I bounded into the carriage before pausing to wave exuberantly out the window to the same group of reporters. After all, it wasn't just Father who could court the papers.

If only I could impress my own father as easily.

Ted recovered quickly with me at his side and even spent an afternoon helping me shatter empty wine bottles against an unlucky oak tree to practice for the *Meteor*'s christening. The day of the christening dawned cloudy but calm, the briny air from New York's harbor and the brisk breeze making my step light as I greeted heavy-jawed Prince Henry of Prussia alongside Mother and Father.

"In the name of Kaiser Wilhelm, I christen thee *Meteor*," I repeated in a crisp voice the words I'd practiced all morning, then gave a self-satisfied yip of laughter as I smashed the champagne bottle against the port bow with a magnificent spray of finely aimed golden froth. I'd fretted all the way to the harbor that the silver hatchet wouldn't sever the ropes, but the yacht slid gracefully into the water after I sawed through the final tie that held her. The celebration gala afterward included thousands of tiny electric lights and fanciful sugar-spun seashells with the American flag imprinted on one side and the German eagle on the other, and I wrote my name on stacks of menus alongside Prince Henry's, pocketing one for myself to paste into a scrapbook later.

I'm only eighteen and eating up the world. If only everything in life was this easy . . .

I was a rabid success according to the papers, several of which commented on the fact that the designer Beneson of Paris had copied the style of my beaver cloak and was selling it to fashionable Parisian ladies under the name "Miss Roosevelt's Wrap."

Beneson was no House of Worth, but still.

First a color, and now a new fashion. The acclaim was all I'd hoped for, but never in my wildest imaginings had I guessed it would happen so fast. There was no precedent for my sudden popularity, for there was no denying that I was the second most popular Roosevelt in the world.

I'd survived Father's first public test for me and was ready for the main event, Prince Edward's coronation.

That is, until Mother delivered the edict that I wouldn't attend.

"We must write Buckingham Palace with our regrets and congratulations," Mother said at the breakfast table, her eyes dark-rimmed from lack of sleep.

"Regrets?" I asked, setting down my third cup of coffee. "What do you mean?"

Mother sighed as she rubbed her temples. She'd finished nursing Ted back to health, but now Archie was abed with a bout of measles and she'd been up with him all night. The rest of the children were subdued after Quentin had brought Archie's calico pony to his bedside to cheer him up and Mother had given Quentin a scolding to make his ears bleed. (The bag of oats they'd strewn all about Archie's room hadn't improved her temper.)

Mother gave a tight frown. "I mean that your father has decided that you won't be attending Prince Edward's coronation."

"Why?" I dropped my half-eaten toast to its plate, prompting Mother to raise an eyebrow in warning.

"Because that's what the president has decided." Mother's perpetual calm was more infuriating than usual.

"I'm eighteen now," I argued, my chair scraping across the hardwood as I stood up. My siblings shrank in their seats, as if sensing that this row might overshadow the mess with the pony. "That's apparently old enough to christen the kaiser's fancy boat, despite the fact that Father believes the Germans to be one of the greatest threats to world peace. Yet I'm forbidden to attend the coronation of one of America's greatest allies?"

"I didn't realize you'd been paying attention to who our allies were these days," Mother said.

"I've sat through enough conversations with senators and princes to possess a basic grasp of world affairs." My voice was almost a growl. "I *do* listen. And I read the papers too."

"Yes, to see your name in print."

I bristled further. "And so that I can discuss the events of the day with those same senators and princes that now come my way. I'm not some empty-headed dub who cares only for the latest fashion of hat. Just yesterday I read about Father's antitrust suit against J. P. Morgan. And I know that Whitelaw Reid praised my deportment at the *Meteor*'s christening in the *New York Tribune* before he spent the rest of the article praising the event's diplomatic advantages. I fail to see how the English coronation will be any different."

Unless . . .

"You don't trust me, do you?" I asked as I leaned over the table. "You think I'll make a shambles of it, reflect poorly on Father and America?"

"Don't give yourself airs, Alice," my stepmother said as first Ethel and then the boys rose and filed double time from the room. "The Irish Americans have lobbied against your attendance, because it would be seen as a show of support for England."

"That's ridiculous," I said, but Mother only picked up two newspapers from the top of the pile—the one with the mention of *Miss Roosevelt's Wrap* and another speculating how many marriage proposals I'd receive that year. (So far I'd seen wagers of anywhere between three and ten.) She opened one and then the other, deflating my argument as she silently pointed to editorials on the subject she'd just mentioned.

There was little I could do to argue as she set aside the papers. "Anyway, your annual visit to your Lee grandparents conflicts with the coronation."

I frowned and strummed my fingers against my forearms, recognizing a lost battle when I saw it. But then I realized that visiting the Lees in Boston would get me out from under my parents' ever-watchful eyes.

"I *do* enjoy my visits with my grandparents," I said sweetly, sitting down and taking a demure bite of my now-cold toast. Mother's eyes narrowed in silent scrutiny, but I affected my most angelic expression.

And I also love the freedom they give me. In fact, my grandparents let me do whatever I want.

What I wanted was for Father to entrust me with more duties like christening the *Meteor*, to give me even greater opportunities to shine. To do that, I was going to have to get his attention, and the best way to do that was to land my name in the papers as much as possible, to make Americans clamor for more of their *princess* so that Father had no choice but to give in.

And to do that I'll need to break a few rules.

Or maybe even more than a few.

Chapter 3

"She's a beauty, isn't she?"

I beamed at the reporter's question even as Lila Paul cooed next to me, her gloved hand on the hood of her brand-new Valentine-red cruiser. The darling of well-heeled society, Lila always seemed more fulsome when there were cameras nearby, and she'd convinced me to stop in Newport so she could give me an unchaperoned ride to Boston in her new Panhard automobile, almost certainly so her name would wind up on tomorrow's front page alongside mine. "We'll drive so fast that the photographs will be blurs," she said, confirming my suspicions as she posed for the newspaperman to snap our picture next to the devil wagon. "That will give the *Times* something besides all your beaus to report on."

I ran an admiring hand over the car's sleek twelve-horsepower wagonette body, rimmed by cherry-red wheels that begged to race. The speed gauge inside went all the way to a jaw-dropping fifty miles an hour, which promised an exciting caper from the train's plodding pace. Plus, a news story covering my driving escapades might put to rest Father and Mother's hysterics over those same papers reporting my five recent engagements. (Newspaper tycoon William Randolph Hearst's assertion that my suitors were as numerous as Penelope's wooers from *The Odyssey* made me want to retch; I didn't even know one of the men the papers claimed as my fiancé, and others speculated I might end up with cousin Franklin. I'd sooner have had all my fingernails pulled off and fed to me.)

There was no doubt that this ride would get Father's—and America's—attention.

So now I shoved the last of my hatboxes into the back seat and popped a piece of Wrigley's chewing gum into my mouth before clambering into Lila's car. I slid over the buttoned crimson upholstery into the driver's side, arranging my ankle-length duster to save my lavender day dress from the weather and road grime. "Let me have a go?" I asked Lila. Women weren't supposed to drive automobiles, but that wasn't about to stop either Lila or me.

Lila glanced at the newspaperman and then shrugged, going around to the other side. "Far be it from me to deny Alice Roosevelt anything."

I grinned, chanking away at the spearmint gum, and adjusted the goggles over my eyes. "How do you do it?" I asked her.

"Just release the brake and push the throttle. Not too hard now!"

I held tight to the steering wheel and did as she instructed, mostly. The red beast found its voice and lurched forward with a primeval growl.

"Wish us luck!" I called laughingly as the newspaperman jumped back.

"May you have clear skies all the way to Boston!" he called. A sudden cloud of exhaust swallowed him as Lila and I tore away at a speed that threatened to rip the very vehicle to pieces.

Lila and I *did* wind up in the papers, although she was the one driving when we finally pulled into my grandparents' Chestnut Hill home, both of us cackling like hyenas at having topped speeds of twenty-five miles per hour and coated in road dust so thick a farmer could have planted radishes on our foreheads.

"You'll have to ask your father to nab you a cruiser of your own," Lila said as I kissed her on the cheek. "Surely the president can afford to give his First Daughter a toy or two."

Laughing, I turned to her. "My father would never do such a thing." Especially since Lila's roadster had cost a jaw-dropping one thousand dollars. "For all that Father proclaims to be a modern man, he prefers riding horses to driving, and only just installed a telephone at Sagamore Hill. He claims the bell will drive him mad."

Silly, silly Father. Didn't he know driving him mad was *my* job?

I was abed a few days later, warm and cozy beneath the down in my grandparents' guest room while rereading Father's recent letter regarding my peccadillo driving with Lila—his angry pen strokes made me wince, for they fairly scorched the White House stationery—when someone knocked.

"Come in," I said, folding the letter away as my door creaked open. "Hello, Papa Lee."

My grandfather was a dear little gentleman with silver-white hair impeccably trimmed beneath his favorite straw boater with its turned-up brim. However, at this time of day—just past noon—he should have been at his Lee, Higginson & Co. office, not standing in my doorway ashen-faced and with one hand on the doorknob as if to brace himself.

I sat up and hugged the coverlet to my chin. "What is it?" I asked.

"My dear girl, I'm afraid there's no good way to put this." He shifted his weight from one foot to the other. "Your father is in the hospital."

"What?" A cold fist closed around my heart. Father was in Massachusetts as part of a New England campaign to benefit Republican congressmen running for reelection this midterm, and he was expected at the Lees' for dinner tonight.

Now I remembered similar terrible news delivered about President McKinley and rumors of suspected assassination plots toward my father in the early days of his presidency. Surely, Father hadn't been shot—he was a lion that would outlive us all.

"An electric trolley struck his carriage at Pittsfield," my grandfather said, temporarily alleviating my fears until his next words magnified them a hundredfold. "William Craig, his Secret Service agent, was killed instantly."

The burly, blue-eyed face of William Craig clicked into focus in my mind like a photograph, for the former Scots prizefighter was Quentin's and Archie's favorite of all my father's Secret Service guards, always interpreting the comic cartoons in the papers for them and slipping crackers to Eli Yale, our loudmouthed macaw.

"Is Father all right?" I finally dared ask, slipping from bed to retrieve my shoes from my traveling trunk with shaking hands. I dared not meet my grandfather's eyes for fear of the truth I'd see there.

"I don't know. He was thrown from the carriage and taken to the Pittsfield hospital."

Panic constricted my throat and made it difficult to squeeze out my next words. "I need to see him."

"Of course you do, my dear," my grandfather said. "Let me call the driver around with the victoria."

I dressed hurriedly and willed the horses to gallop faster once seated next to my grandfather in the carriage, wishing I had Lila's cruiser instead. My hands were slick with sweat, and I'd worked myself into a panic before we finally stopped outside the brick hospital. Running up the steps, I burst through the hospital doors.

I hadn't been in a hospital since before Father became vice president, when I'd had an abscess in my jaw and the doctors had planned to remove all of my lower teeth. Mother had stopped them, but now the overpowering smell of antiseptic nearly brought me to my knees.

Merry hell, but I hated hospitals.

"Miss!" One of the nurses sounded as if she might stop me until recognition dawned on her face. "Oh, Miss Roosevelt!" she quickly amended. "You must be here to see your father."

I supposed instant recognition was a benefit to my face being constantly plastered all over the papers, but I didn't have time to appreciate it in that moment.

The white-garbed nurse ushered me to my father's private room, where a Secret Serviceman nodded me inside. My father sat propped in a hospital bed already surrounded by sympathy bouquets and stacks of telegrams, another nurse tending his bruised face while a doctor prodded his left shin. Father squinted and scowled as the door slammed; without his spectacles he was terribly shortsighted. But he was breathing, which was all I cared about.

"Father!" I rushed to his side. "Are you all right?"

"It's nothing, Mousiekins." The sound of his voice and the use of the endearment from when I still wore knee-dresses nearly made my battered heart explode. "I walked away with merely a scratch on my leg, despite the swings I took at the trolley motorman."

I blinked. "You fought the driver?"

"The man's incompetence led to William Craig's death." The cuts and bruises on Father's face made him more fearsome than usual. "He deserves to be drop-kicked from here to Sunday."

Given my father's boxing background, I had no doubt that the driver would have found himself in a world of hurt had the Secret Service not intervened. The ensuing headlines would have put even my newspaper escapades to shame.

Pots and kettles, that.

I grimaced at the wounds on Father's cheek and nose, some already smeared with foul-smelling medical ointment. "I'm sorry about William Craig," I managed to say, my voice cracking with equal doses of sadness and relief that my father was relatively unscathed.

My father's brow furrowed. "Craig was a good man and a credit to his country. I'd have endured far worse if it meant he might have escaped the brunt of the crash."

I bit my lip. "I'm glad that you escaped with no more than a few scrapes."

Father cleared his throat, wincing as the doctor sutured his leg. It was difficult to tell which was more uncomfortable for him, the medical examination or my words. "So, Sissy, what has occupied your thoughts as of late?" he said, changing the subject with the ease of a true politician. "No more car rides, I hope?"

Now it was my turn to veer the subject to safer waters. Perhaps I'd learned a trick or two from being a politician's daughter.

"I've been reading about the Pennsylvania coal strike," I said hesitantly.

I did not have then, nor would I have for some time to come, the remotest real interest in politics beyond its use as dinner conversation. But I'd have debated the merits of the Sherman Antitrust Act or recited the Constitution backward if it meant having my father's full and undivided attention as I did now.

"Oh?" he asked, replacing his spectacles as the nurse finished tending the scrapes on his face. "And what is your position on the miners' demands?"

"They seem reasonable. I don't blame them for not wanting to work fourteen hours down a dangerous coal shaft."

My father gave what passed for a chuckle, considering how tightly the physician was bandaging his leg. "So you believe the coal operators should give in to the miners?"

"I think it highly unlikely that they will," I said, wondering whether he would agree with me. This was the first time I could remember his asking my opinion on political matters, and I wondered if it was a test of sorts. "But it seems the fair thing to do."

"I agree." He rubbed his mustache. "But winter is coming and in the meantime, America may well freeze to death without coal."

"Perhaps the owners would listen if you were to recommend a course of action?"

Instead of beaming with pride at my suggestion, my father scowled at the ceiling. "The president has no constitutional power over business disputes, Alice."

"I know that." I retrieved the pocket copy of the Constitution—my birthday gift from Father—that I'd taken to keeping in my purse. "But there's nothing in here that says you *can't* intercede on occasion either."

This time my father's eyes twinkled with something I took for pride. "I've thought the same thing over the past few weeks. Always stoking the fires, aren't you, Sissy?"

"I learned from the best." A flush of pride crept up my neck as I replaced the Constitution. I reached out and squeezed Father's hand.

And he squeezed it back.

"You shot your pistol off a train?" My father's face went a dangerous sort of red bordering on purple as he let me have it with both barrels. Summer and autumn had long since passed and with them, my freedom at the Lees'. Father dropped the crumpled newspaper on his plate of Mother's famous cinnamon sand tarts, scattering a sandstorm of cookie crumbs everywhere. His game of billiards on the newly installed Brunswick table—one of the many additions to Mother's newly renovated White House—was also forgotten, a definitive sign that I was in scalding hot water. "What if you'd hit someone?"

"You taught me to aim better than that," I grumbled, my arms crossed over my chest. "And you're the one who gave me the pistol to begin with, *and* let me skip the Christmas Eve church service to practice shooting it."

Father shook an angry finger at me. "Young lady, it's the target practice from a moving platform and not the gun itself that crossed the line."

"Why is it so difficult to please you? Every time I do something I think you'll approve of, it only serves to aggravate you further!"

"Because for every one appropriate act, there's five others to counteract it." My father sifted through the day's newspapers, rolling one up to gesture at another. "This one reports on your constant chanking—"

Mother shifted in her seat in the corner, setting in her lap a pair of Father's wool socks she was darning. "I told you it was unseemly for a lady to chew gum in such a manner," she chided me gently.

My father continued his tirade, waving papers in the air and creating a rain of tart crumbs that matched the snow falling outside. "This next paper damns you for eating asparagus with your gloves on at the Assembly Ball, and a third claims Henry Cushing is in love with you."

"Henry Cushing is a fob!" I felt as if I were about to explode, like a balloon filled with too much hot air. "It's not my fault that you're the president and now the entire country knows everything about us—"

"Not *us*, Alice," Mother interrupted, glancing up from the socks. "Just you."

"I'm putting the hoof down, Alice," my father said, glaring at me through his spectacles. "It's high time you found something worthwhile to work on, a charity to support with meaningful contributions to this country, not just pouring tea and racing cars so your name lands in the papers like a common guttersnipe."

My jaw dropped at the insult. After his accident, Father had been asking my advice about the coal strike, and now *this*. How dare he!

"Your father doesn't mean that you *are* a guttersnipe," Mother said quickly, shooting Father a stern look. "Only that we want your actions to reflect well upon all of us."

One glance at my father, and I wasn't so sure.

Regardless, my father and I were back to where we started ages ago. I'd thought he was finally coming to value me and my opinions. Instead, it seemed we'd moved two steps forward and four steps back. I barely managed to swallow the urge to scream.

"There's no cause I feel passionate about," I countered mulishly, my arms crossed tight across my chest as if that might somehow keep my temper from shattering into a million pieces. I was more than willing to read the newspapers every day and study up on our nation's history in order to please my father, but the thought of taking up dull ladylike pursuits like sewing quilts for charity made me want to shout.

"Write to Eleanor," my father said, his face stony. "Your cousin has no problem helping those less fortunate than herself. She's even made arrangements to teach calisthenics to immigrants after her debut in December, once she returns from boarding school in Britain."

Eleanor Roosevelt, who was *so* good and *so* nice about everyone that she was quite intolerable. The very mention of her cut deep, as I suspected a daughter like her would have pleased my father to no end, no matter how plain her face. Whereas I . . .

I was Father's gum-chanking, cigarette-smoking, poker-playing hoyden of a daughter. Perhaps Father might finally be proud of me if I spent my days in a consumptive ward and died of the bloody flux. It suddenly dawned on me that no matter what I did to please my father, it would never be enough.

I would never be enough.

"You never get upset at Ted or Kermit or Ethel or Archie or Quentin!" I yelled, hating myself for the rare tears that spewed from my eyes. "I swear you love me an eighth of what you love all of them, maybe less!"

Turning on my heel, I burst into the corridor, ignoring my father's shouts behind me.

I almost tripped on Kermit's discarded stilts before slamming my bedroom door behind me and fumbling fruitlessly in my purse for my cigarette case. I needed to throw something, *hard.*

The nearest item at hand was a toy horse branded with a heated hairpin to make the sign of Father's Triangle Ranch on its rump.

Given to me when Father couldn't stand the sight of me. Fifteen years later, and nothing has changed. Ugh!

I hurled it at the wall with a feral roar, but it wasn't enough to douse this anger that had seeped into the very marrow of my bones.

The coast was still clear in the hallway and I barreled my way down the corridor to the newly remodeled roof promenade that overlooked Lafayette Square, the frigid night air making me wish I'd thought to grab a coat as I struggled to light a cigarette. My heart calmed as the shag finally lit and I released a long sigh of smoke.

I was eighteen and America's princess, but I'd forever be a little girl seeking her father's approval.

In that moment the entire situation—and my life—seemed entirely hopeless.

Buck up, Alice. Self-pity is dreadfully dull.

I watched the red cigarette ember burn down in the dark until the door behind me opened. "I'm coming in." I dropped the shag to the snowy bricks and snuffed it out with my toe. I stopped when I saw Mother, the froth of her breath swirling into the chilly night sky. Of course she'd had the forethought to put on the thick beaver coat my father had brought back from one of his trips west. I waited for the inevitable lecture, but she only offered me a paper doily with a lone cinnamon tart in the middle.

I took a hesitant nibble of the peace offering, ignoring the fact that cinnamon and cigarette smoke were an abominable combination of tastes.

"What are you doing out here?" she finally asked.

I shrugged. "Father told me ages ago that I couldn't smoke under his roof."

"So you're smoking *on* the roof instead?"

I only shrugged again.

She sighed. "Oh, *Alice*."

Now probably wasn't the time to mention that I'd also taught five-year-old Quentin how to smoke a corncob pipe.

Instead, I let out a single tortured groan. "I'm such a failure." I stuffed the last bit of tart in my mouth and struggled in vain to maintain my composure. "If I were a boy, I could shoot and race and spar, but I'm only supposed to dance and simper and drink tea. It's enough to make a girl explode."

Mother rubbed the bridge of her nose. "You are your father's daughter. Neither of you can help being conspicuous."

It was the closest thing to forgiveness I was likely to hear from either of my parents. I gave a wry chuckle. "Father does want to be the corpse at every funeral, the bride at every wedding, and the baby at every christening."

I stepped closer so Mother might wrap her arms around me, envelop me in the flowery scent of Pears' soap and croon that I wasn't the cretin Father thought I was. Instead, she crossed her arms in front of her chest, her shoulders stiff as if ready to march into battle, and I shrank back again.

"What would you think about traveling to New Orleans for Mardi Gras?" Mother was as warm and fuzzy as a knife-ridden cactus, but she was adept at defusing the most difficult of situations. And that's what I was right now: a situation.

"Why?" I asked.

"You enjoyed Newport and you seem to thrive on travel, just like your father," she said. "Perhaps your natural restlessness might be cured by a trip to warmer climes."

It was echoes of Newport again, and I *had* enjoyed Newport, for the most part. It occurred to me then that perhaps my family and I could only peacefully coexist with at least several states'—or countries'—distance between us.

Perhaps I should move to Europe and marry a prince, or wed an African warrior and live in a mud hut. Maybe then my parents would finally miss my company.

"I would like Mardi Gras very much," I answered. Who knew, but maybe I could persuade a voodoo queen to whip up a gris-gris charm or spirit doll to make my parents love me.

"Good." Mother reached up to tuck a flyaway wisp of hair behind my ear. "Come inside and we'll work out the details of your trip. Perhaps you can even open the Comus Ball."

I snuffled into my sleeve as we stepped back into the heat of the White House. Mother shut the door tight and rubbed her hands over mine in a vain attempt to warm them. "I want you to make me a promise while you're in New Orleans."

"I promise I'll behave—" I started, but she cut me off.

"I want you to make friends while you're down there."

I frowned. "I have friends."

But the words rang hollow, even to me. I'd fallen out of touch with my few chums from Oyster Bay and was now suspicious of anyone who professed their friendship to me, always scrutinizing whether they truly sought my friendship, or whether, like Lila and her car, they just wanted to see their name next to the president's daughter's in a *Times* headline.

Merry hell. If I couldn't find a friend, how would I ever find someone to marry one day, someone who might rescue me from my increasingly oppressive parents?

"I'll do my best," I told Mother. "But I wouldn't hold my breath if I were you."

Not for the first time, I worried that there was simply no hope for me.

Chapter 4

MARCH 1903

I was like one of those hurricanes that rips through the Caribbean every year, growing wilder and more destructive as winter loosened its grip. Heaven only knew when, if ever, I'd finally wear myself out.

Only this time I found two hurricanes to join me.

I'd done as Mother had instructed and tried to make friends while at Mardi Gras, but again encountered only flocks of eager sparrows who wanted their picture with Princess Alice and who couldn't have cared a whit about getting to know plain old Alice Roosevelt. So I spent the festivities leading up to Fat Tuesday surrounded by the entire population of New Orleans, eating crawdads and waving from ostentatious floats, yet feeling utterly alone.

It wasn't until I came back for the end of the season that I was reintroduced to the bejeweled cyclone that was Maggie Cassini.

"*Chyort*, but this is a dry little affair." Maggie yawned into her ungloved hand only ten minutes into cousin Eleanor's drab debut at the Waldorf-Astoria hotel.

I chuckled. "You could always ask Franklin to dance with you again."

"That silly little man? I think not." Maggie's every movement crackled with energy just as it had when she'd scared cousin Franklin off the dance floor at my debut, and she'd dressed with her usual verve tonight, opting for a black off-the-shoulder harem-skirt gown with a bejeweled sort of Byzantine sash. Dark curls hung loosely about her angled face, her feline eyes lined and lips rouged, and to top it all off she wore an antique gold crown probably pilfered from some Russian noble. However, it was the full-size Russian rapier she'd tied at her hip in lieu of a purse that was most outrageous. Yet, I might have outshone her with my newest accessory.

"Maggie Cassini," I said to my friend as I opened my beaded satin clutch. "Meet Emily Spinach."

A little green head popped out in answer, my scaly stowaway's forked gray tongue flicking while partygoers twittered around us. I waited for Maggie to shriek or gasp, but she only offered a hand to my new garter snake as if being introduced to a foreign duke. "Charmed," she said as she gave a deep curtsy, then giggled as Emily Spinach bobbed her head. "I must say, I hope serpents in handbags becomes a new trend. *Princessa,* your darling pet is just the thing to liven up the dullest of parties."

I encouraged Emily Spinach to twine around my wrist before I replaced her in my clutch. "Don't tell," I whispered, "but I've thought of letting her roam free in the State Dining Room during Father's next diplomatic luncheon."

Maggie gave a throaty chuckle. "Now that I have to see, *princessa.*"

The three-story Waldorf-Astoria ballroom with its yawning balconies and infinity dance floor echoed like an empty cavern as I saw Eleanor, her angular frame hidden in a lackluster white sack of a gown, and called her over. "Eleo!" I waved enthusiastically. "It's been ages, hasn't it, darling?"

Plain Eleo's mouth and nose seemed to have no future, and now she wrinkled that nose as Maggie blew a succession of perfect smoke rings in her direction. "Hello, Alice," she said as she kissed both of my cheeks in the European fashion. I supposed that made sense, as she'd spent the last few years at her English boarding school.

How is it that even plain-faced cousin Eleanor manages to make me feel positively provincial? Buck up, Alice!

Maggie removed her rapier from her sash and admired her reflection, garnering blatant stares from every man present. She slipped it into her sash with the ease of an Ottoman sultana. "I suppose dancing at least will keep me from falling asleep."

My cousin watched her go, her wide eyes bulging further to see my friend lift the hem of her black silk skirt as the musicians picked up the first tinny notes of a ragtime strut. Maggie's feet tapped out a sprightly jig and she threw her head back with an enviable peal of laughter. "I'm surprised at the company you keep these days, Alice," my cousin said.

At least I have *company to keep,* I wanted to say. Awkward, serious Eleanor might have invited every soul she'd ever met during her eighteen years and still only filled a quarter of the room. I hadn't even seen her dance yet, and this was *her* debut.

I shrugged. "Mother told me to make friends, so I did."

"I doubt whether Maggie Cassini is the type of friend that Aunt Edith had in mind." Eleanor's voice dropped. "There's a wild resentment against Maggie in Washington, you know."

"Do tell!" I already knew all the stories, but I enjoyed the idea of saintly Eleanor gossiping. Eleo suddenly picked at a loose thread on her dress under my scrutiny, but apparently dishing with me was more appealing than taking to the dance floor. "They say Maggie's the Russian ambassador's illegitimate daughter," she whispered, her wide mouth twisting as if the very words tasted foul. "Did you know that her father tried to pass her off as his niece when they first came to Washington?"

"Why should I care about all that?" I lit a Lucky Strike and smiled with satisfaction as my perfect white Os floated like tiny clouds toward the gamboling cherubs painted high overhead. I wondered what Eleanor would do if I set Emily Spinach loose at her debut. "It's not as if Maggie can help the circumstances of her birth, any more than I can help mine."

Sometimes I even wondered if Maggie's vim was her way of covering up her own insecurities. If so, hers was a story I could recite in my sleep.

I suddenly spotted my other newest friend, Cissy Patterson, her mass of red hair coming loose as she kicked up her heels next to Maggie. While sometimes the behavior of these two girls made me cringe, I was willing to overlook their most audacious behavior—and even Maggie's occasional cruelty—for the sense of belonging their friendship gave me. Eleanor stopped me from joining them with a touch at my elbow.

"Alice, Uncle Theodore told me you were looking for useful ways to occupy your time. I'd love for you to join me next week in the East Side slums. I plan to teach dancing to the immigrants there." She raised an eyebrow at the current dance floor shenanigans. "I was thinking something along the lines of the Viennese waltz."

Sadly, we can't all be angels like you, cousin Eleanor.

"I'm afraid I'm booked next week," I lied. "Maggie, Cissy, and I keep a full itinerary, you know."

Just then, Cissy stood on tiptoes from the middle of the dance floor and gave me a wild wave. "Alice, we need you!"

"Congratulations on a bully debut," I said to Eleanor, kissing both her cheeks. "Come dance with us if you'd like."

But I knew she'd rather be drawn and quartered than ruck up her dress to dance the Cakewalk. I was almost to the dance floor when I brushed shoulders with cousin Franklin. "Good evening, Alice," he said with a crooked smile and a raised eyebrow. "Keeping everyone on their toes as usual, I see."

"Always," I said, sparing a glance back at Eleo. "I know someone who'd be grateful for a dance partner, if you know what I mean."

He straightened his white bow tie. "I believe I do. And I'm happy to oblige."

"Alice!" Cissy shrieked when I joined her and Maggie. "It's about time!"

The papers called us the Three Graces, but the Three Hoydens was closer to the mark.

"This party's a flat tire. We should leave." Maggie arranged a cigarette at the end of her opera-length jade holder as soon as we finished the Cakewalk. I was impressed that she managed to juggle both her sword and such a ridiculous cigarette holder; hers must have measured at least twenty inches compared to my foot-length red theater holder.

Somehow Maggie even manages to show me up when we smoke.

"The party's just started." Cissy's voice was full of effervescent champagne giggles, but as always, Maggie overruled her.

We were already shrugging into our fur coats when Knickerbocker James Hyde pushed his way through the crowd toward us. Hyde had recently inherited the Equitable Life Assurance Society and was reputedly worth a billion dollars. Sadly, he was drier than the carriage collection he droned on about at every party. "Ladies," he exclaimed, panting a little when he finally reached us. "Don't tell me you're leaving!"

"We have other engagements to attend." Maggie flipped her long curls over her shoulder with the tip of her sword, and I admired the way she told the thumper smoothly, for we had nowhere to go and nowhere to be, so long as it wasn't here.

"Well, I'm relieved I caught you," he said, regaining his composure. "I'm throwing the final dance of the season next Saturday, a costume ball like those held in Versailles in the days of old." He beamed at us. "And it's in honor of the Three Graces!"

He said it in such a manner that it was clear he expected us to fawn over his largesse, but Maggie scarcely glanced his way before sauntering wordlessly out the front doors, pulling Cissy with her.

"We'll try our best to attend," I said. My eyes strayed to their disappearing backs. I wanted to follow, but Mother's and Father's admonitions about my behavior echoed in my mind and made me linger.

"You'll try?" Hyde asked, so taken aback that I actually felt bad for him. "But it's all for you."

"That's so very kind of you to think of us. I'm sure we can squeeze it onto our calendars."

I escaped into the night air and almost collided with Maggie as she waited for her car. "I think you might have just broken Mr. Hyde's heart," I said, but she only smiled like a she-devil.

"Ah, *princessa*, I thought perhaps if I left you two alone for more than a minute that Mr. Hyde might propose to you." She and Cissy looked at each other before bursting into strident peals of laughter. "It's obvious he's desperate for feminine attention. I'm sure you could finagle at least a ten-carat diamond out of the deal."

I gave a tight smile and ignored the insinuation that I, too, was somehow desperate.

"Now we have to find some excuse to avoid his miserable ball," Cissy moaned dramatically, still hiccupping with occasional laughter. "I'll bet you both five dollars he comes dressed as a horse."

"Or a barouche," I forced myself to add, prompting fresh chortles of laughter from them both. I was accustomed to pushing all of life's limits, but sometimes it was exhausting trying to keep up with these two.

"We already have the perfect excuse." Maggie checked to ensure that her rapier was still securely fastened to her sash. "Nick Longworth invited us to dine with him next Saturday at the Alibi." She waggled her eyebrows. "*Alone.*"

I vaguely remembered Longworth from a dinner a while back, my father claiming that the witty freshman representative from Ohio might amuse me. That had been almost a year ago, but I remembered the newly elected congressman introducing me to the dark-haired beauty sitting next to him . . .

I frowned. "Isn't Nick Longworth engaged?"

Maggie only waved her hand, her foot tapping with impatience as the car had yet to appear. "He broke it off with Miriam Bloomer. She was a vapid little Ohio girl who set her sights too high."

That wasn't quite how I remembered the tall, queenly girl at Nick's side, but Maggie continued without missing a beat. "Nicky's a *man*," she said, "not one of those Groton boys with peach fuzz still clinging to his lip. He's the most gorgeous bloom after dark, as familiar with the role of Romeo as he is with politics on the floor of the House. Cissy's thoroughly swizzled over him."

"So what if I am?" Cissy asked, even as her cheeks flushed a pretty shade of pink. "He *did* kiss me when we saw him at the Vanderbilts' ball last week."

Another twinge of envy at that, for I'd been forbidden from attending that particular ball *and* I'd never been properly kissed. How was it that I was the president's daughter, yet I was so hopelessly out of my league with these two?

"But if he's from Ohio," I said to Cissy, tugging my beaver wrap tighter as fresh raindrops prompted servants to appear with umbrellas, "then I doubt he has a plush title to give you, unlike your Austrian count."

"I *do* love a man with a title." Cissy giggled and batted her eyelashes, for she'd informed us in excruciating detail how she'd kissed an Austrian count during her European tour, and how she hoped he'd sweep her away to his castle in the Carpathian Mountains. "Although, I haven't heard from Count Gizycki since I returned from Europe last year. A man like Nick could persuade me to forgo a coat of arms."

"So we'll skip Mr. Hyde's ball?" I could only imagine how my ears would bleed from the rip-roarer Father and Mother would give me for neglecting to show at a ball thrown in my honor.

Then there was the larger scandal that dining alone with Representative Longworth would cause, potentially a bigger brouhaha than I'd yet weathered.

Still, all three of us Graces would be there, so one couldn't really call that *alone*.

Maggie only shrugged as her four-cylinder convertible pulled to a stop before us, the lights gleaming like molten gold on its cherry-red hood. I found myself staring jealously at Maggie's car, for an automobile of my own would offer the measure of independence that I craved. "We'll cable Hyde with our regrets," she said. "He can't expect us to give up a perfectly good evening listening to all that insufferable horse talk."

I cast a glance over my shoulder to where I'd left Mr. Hyde, thinking of how I'd recently run over my allowance by a thousand dollars. A man worth his staggering sum would go a long way toward keeping me in furs and jewels and cherry-red roadsters, but I could never spend my life with a man whose idea of scintillating conversation was discussing carriage mounts and horse withers.

Cissy pulled me along as Maggie slid into the driver's seat, and we scrambled in next to her as hearty raindrops plinked on the windshield, me holding tight my handbag with Emily Spinach.

At least a clandestine dinner with Representative Longworth at the Alibi was guaranteed to provide better merrymaking than another ball, regardless of the hell I'd surely pay later.

You only live once, Alice. Surely a dinner isn't the worst mistake you'll ever make.

We girls huddled together against the cold the following Saturday night and craned our necks at the pre–Civil War three-story brick row house that was the mysterious Alibi Club, aptly named for its penchant for providing alibis to its illustrious members.

It's not too late to turn back, hightail it to Mr. Hyde's Versailles masquerade like a good girl. Because I can be good, when I want to.

And then I'd soldier my way through dancing the selfsame waltzes, eating the same overcooked beef Wellington, and giggling at the same tired jokes from behind my fan when what I really wanted to do was jump out the first available window.

So much for being good . . .

"Poor Mr. Hyde will never speak to us again." Cissy fidgeted with excitement, her cheeks flushed in the night air.

Maggie glanced down the empty block, then patted her dark curls into place. "I'm surprised the president and your mother let you come here tonight, *princessa*. You did tell them, didn't you?"

I turned my shiver into an artful shrug. "When Father's not up to his eyes in recommendations about the Anthracite Coal Strike Commission, he's hammering out a treaty with Colombia to excavate the Panama Canal." I tugged my mink stole—borrowed from Auntie Bye—a little closer. "I told Mother a bit of fimble-famble about going to Auntie Bye's."

And eased my conscience by reminding myself it was mostly true since I'll return there after the Alibi.

"Why, aren't you a little minx," Maggie said, admiration shining in her dark eyes.

"Who else is a member here?" I asked as I scrutinized the nondescript—and, frankly, almost shabby—building, its only distinctive features its turquoise door and louvered shutters, the curtains all tightly drawn as if hiding forbidden state secrets.

"No one knows for sure." Maggie removed a mirrored compact from her handbag and pursed her lips in a perfect moue to touch up her scarlet lipstick. "It's a secret society, only fifty of Washington's most elite. Nick Longworth is the real deal."

"It's more fun if it's covert," Cissy added. She squared her shoulders, but her white-gloved hands fluttered like nervous doves. I supposed it wasn't every day that a girl meets the man she's decided to marry.

"It's not covert if he invited us," I reminded them both. "Shall we?"

I led the way inside, feeling like a fish in a tree as we approached the antique front desk at the end of a narrow hall, a haze of cigar smoke layered with the scents of old books and men's cologne. Gasolier lights lit the mahogany walls, a throwback to more genteel times. "Ah, yes." The snowy-haired butler looked up slowly, as if he hadn't been disturbed in years. "You must be Misses Cassini, Patterson, and Roosevelt here for Mr. Longworth. This way, please."

I wasn't sure if the butler had a predilection for alphabetizing, but being placed after Maggie and Cissy set me to scowling as we passed a hodgepodge of pewter plates, rusty swords, and signed correspondence that covered every available section of wall.

I lagged behind as we mounted the creaky stairs to a private room on the second floor. Inside, floor-to-ceiling bookshelves were packed with leather-bound volumes from Virgil to John Locke that somewhat made up for the overall gloom. The walls here were a mismatched assemblage of Japanese scrolls and yellowing caricatures of frowning men whom I assumed were, or had once been, members of the club.

"It's all donated by members: the books, the scrolls, the whole lot of it," a cultured voice answered my unasked question. Its owner belonged to a man boldly inspecting us from the oval table at the center of the room. "I think there's even a signed copy of *Uncle Tom's Cabin* in here somewhere," he continued as he snuffed out his cigarette in an ivory ashtray. "Stowe's publisher was one of the Alibi's founders."

"Washington's secret flea market," I muttered, although, in truth, I was somewhat awed.

Our host arched an arrogant eyebrow—and I arched one back— before he rose with a swashbuckling sort of grace to greet us.

"Thank you, Aggasiz," he said to the butler, who nodded and discreetly disappeared. "You must be Miss Roosevelt," he said to me. "Maggie and Cissy I already know."

Representative Longworth was a good height for a man, scarcely an inch taller than Father, which put him just a smidge over me in my Cuban heels. He wasn't ancient like most congressmen, either, perhaps in his early thirties, with penetrating copper eyes that distracted from the way his dark hair thinned a bit at the front. Cissy might have been dotty over him, but that didn't stop my breath from catching at the sight of him in evening togs.

"Hello, Nick." Maggie easily redirected his attention. "I hope you don't mind that we're fashionably late."

To which Longworth only quirked a smile. "I'm pleased you ladies could accommodate my invitation, what with your bustling social calendars. The Three Graces are in high demand."

Nervous heat radiated from Cissy even as Maggie sidestepped us in a cloud of bergamot and rose Divinia perfume that made my nose twitch. I refused to follow in her wake, but instead veered left to her right, claiming the Windsor chair across from Representative Longworth and leaving Cissy to make up her mind whether to stand quivering in the doorway or follow after one of us. After a moment's hesitation, she traipsed after me, looking like she might swoon from nerves.

"I was worried the Hyde ball might prove more interesting than a dinner with a lowly freshman representative," Longworth said, gesturing for us to sit as he prepared to pour four flutes of champagne.

"None for me," I said, receiving a raised eyebrow in response. "My spirits are high enough that I avoid the liquid version, so no one can claim my gaiety comes from a bottle."

Truth be told, that was Father's advice. But he was right, so I'd claimed the idea for my own.

Nick poured three glasses, then filled the last with punch and handed it to me. "I'll remember that for next time."

He really did have a marvelously warm voice, like melted caramel, and I suspected a man like Nick Longworth rarely worried that his invitations would be turned down by any woman.

"We'd rather be here with you, Nick, than at the Hyde ball," Cissy proclaimed, a bit too loudly. She reached for a glass of champagne so fast that the golden liquid sloshed over the rim and stained her swan-white glove. Maggie and I exchanged a meaningful glance.

"Do you have any cigarettes?" I asked in an attempt to draw Nick's attention away from Cissy's crimson cheeks.

"Of course." Longworth withdrew a silver case from his pocket. I leaned close so he could light it, then puffed out a link of perfect circles as Maggie had taught me.

"So, Nicholas Longworth of Cincinnati," Maggie drawled, lighting her own cigarette perched on her trademark ivory holder. "What brings you to the District?"

"Boredom," he said. "It was either become a politician or collect paintings like my father and grandfather. Collecting art seemed awfully pretentious, even for me."

"It *is* pretentious," I agreed. "But only if it's French art."

"I love art!" Cissy exclaimed. We all waited for her to expound further or say something, *anything*, but she only shrank into her chair under the full weight of all our gazes.

"How long do you plan to remain in Congress, Mr. Longworth?" I asked before shooting Cissy a look that begged her to pull herself together. Honestly, Longworth *was* handsome in an older-man sort of way, not to mention wealthy and smart enough to have been elected to Congress, but from the way he ignored Cissy's cow-eyed simpering, I'd never have known they'd exchanged names before this moment, much less the impassioned kiss Cissy had told us about, over and over.

"Hopefully you'll stay at least a few seasons," Maggie practically purred, crossing her legs in a way most certainly discouraged by *Godey's Lady's Book*. "Washington has been positively bleak, at least until you arrived."

Nick's eyes followed those long legs, and a grin tugged at his lips. "I suppose I'll stay until I grow bored or until America elects me president," he said. "But I doubt anyone stays bored for long when you're around, Miss Cassini."

Cissy sat up straighter in her chair, her expression fairly spitting broken glass at Maggie, who acted as if Cissy was no longer in the room.

I sat back, content to smoke my cigarettes and watch my two best friends haggle for Longworth's attention as Aggasiz served the first course of steaming oyster soup. "Do either of you play music?" Longworth asked.

Maggie leaned forward, effectively blocking Cissy from view. "Only the Russian *balalaika*, and that very poorly, much to my father's chagrin." She sipped her champagne even as Cissy pursed her lips. "What about you?"

"I've played the violin since I was a boy," he answered. "One day I'd like to own a Stradivarius."

"You'll have to treat us to a private concert sometime," Maggie said.

Cissy chose that moment to interject, rather too loudly, "Well, I, for one, enjoy Mozart. He's my favorite composer."

To which Maggie and Nick only began discussing the note scale of the Russian *balalaika*. "Honestly, Cissy," I whispered. "Could you even recognize *Eine kleine Nachtmusik* if the bells of the National Cathedral started tolling it?"

"Shush," she said, fanning herself even as Maggie commandeered the conversation from the moment the duck confit was served to its eventual clearing away by the uniformed staff. I tucked my feet up under me and lit an after-dinner cigarette, content to lounge ringside.

"Well, ladies." Nick surprised me as he stood and pushed in his chair. Were we being dismissed? "I'm afraid you'll have to follow me to the kitchen for your dessert."

"The kitchen?" Even Maggie looked caught off guard. "You can't be serious."

"I've never been more serious in all my life."

Which left us nothing to do except follow him.

"Good evening, Mr. Longworth." The uniformed chef in his white toque greeted Nick before filing silently out the kitchen with the rest of the staff and abandoning us to a forest of copper pots and pans, the oak icebox, and a Hoosier cabinet with its built-in spice rack and flour sifter.

A platter of strawberry shortcake sat forsaken on the Hoosier's counter and I swiped a generous finger of whipped cream. The Alibi chef could give those at the White House a run for their money. "I take it you've annexed the kitchen here before?" I asked.

"A few times." Nick shed his dinner jacket and donned a white apron over his pleated tuxedo shirt before offering us three more. Cissy gave a nervous giggle, but Maggie only lifted her hands. "I eat the food; I don't make it." She made a great show of leaning over the counter to pluck a strawberry from the shortcake. I rolled my eyes as she gave a theatrical shiver of pleasure when she bit into the berry. "But I'm happy to be your taster."

"Alice?" Nick held out the apron and I took it, noticing the way his eyes lingered on Maggie even as I caught a discreet hint of spice from his cologne.

Of course. Because everything about Nick Longworth is decadent, from the sheen of his vicuña dinner jacket to his tapered musician's fingers. No wonder he's intrigued by Maggie; a man who has everything must become apathetic easily.

But from what I'd seen, he certainly wasn't apathetic about Maggie.

Nick showed me how to simmer the milk and crush almonds until we'd whipped up a batch of almond pudding that had Maggie and Cissy cheering for more. Longworth might be a man of many talents, but recognizing feminine infatuation wasn't one of them, or perhaps he'd only ever wanted that one kiss from Cissy. My poor friend grew more despondent as the night went on, until the mantel clock struck one o'clock in the morning.

"It's been lovely," Maggie said, her voice softer than the velvet stole Longworth helped her shrug into. "We really should do this again, with a violin concerto next time, of course."

"It would be my pleasure," Nick said smoothly before turning to me. "It was a delight meeting you, Miss Roosevelt." Cissy preened beside me as she waited for her turn, but Longworth seemed to have forgotten her as he opened the door and addressed one of the staff. "Could you please ask for Miss Cassini's car to be brought around?"

Next to me, Cissy wilted like a daisy out too long in the sun. We hadn't even hit the pavement outside when she whirled on Maggie. "Just what exactly were you doing in there?" she hollered.

"Whatever do you mean?" Maggie searched her handbag for a matchbox. She might have sounded innocent, but I caught the smirk on her lips.

"I mean you throwing yourself all over Nick, so I could scarcely get a word in edgewise!" Cissy actually stomped a foot so hard I feared she'd break off a heel. "When you knew I'd set my cap at him!"

"Nicky never would have noticed you," Maggie drawled, letting her vowels soften into a false Russian cadence. "Considering you were so swizzled that you could scarcely speak."

"How dare you!" Cissy started, then whirled on me. "Are you going to let her act like this?"

"You *did* bungle things in there," I said, unsure whether to laugh or cringe as Cissy's face turned twelve shades of purple.

"You're as bad as her!" she said, jerking her chin toward Maggie. "God help you if you ever introduce her to one of your beaus."

If I ever had a beau, which was looking less and less likely these days.

"Please," Maggie said, rolling her eyes. "You'd scarcely even met Nicky until tonight. He certainly wasn't your beau, or your *anything*, for that matter."

"Well, I never want to see Nick Longworth, or you, ever again!" Cissy shouted at Maggie as the car pulled around. Cissy took one look at it as the valet exited, let out a pent-up scream of rage that scared the poor man half to death, and stormed away in the opposite direction. Maggie, however, slid into the driver's seat as if nothing had happened, and peered through the window at me.

"Are you coming, *princessa*?" she asked.

Leaving me to choose between following after Cissy in a sympathetic dudgeon or saving my feet an aching walk to Auntie Bye's by riding with Maggie.

I sighed, wishing Maggie hadn't been so *Maggie* tonight. "I'd better make sure Cissy's all right. I'm sure by tomorrow she'll have forgotten Nick Longworth and will be swooning over her Austrian count again."

I hoped that Maggie would acquiesce, maybe even apologize to Cissy, but she only smiled in a way that seemed far from altruistic before she tipped her chin at me. "As you wish," she said before she drove off, leaving me to scowl after her before I chased after Cissy.

Despite Cissy's temper tantrum and my prediction to Maggie, that wasn't the last we'd see of Nick Longworth.

Not by a long shot.

Chapter 5

After the dinner at the Alibi, Cissy had her own alibis for not seeing Maggie—not that I could blame her—and thus, the Three Graces were reduced to two. Maggie hadn't batted a single Rimmel-blackened eyelash at Cissy's departure, leaving me to wonder what she'd do if I stopped answering her late-night phone calls or jumping out of bed to meet her for a lunch of borscht at her father's embassy.

I went to visit Cissy a few weeks after the disastrous dinner and dared broach the subject of Nick Longworth over scones and tea in her family's conservatory, but Cissy only waved me off.

"Maggie can have him," she said, wrinkling her nose while sipping from Wedgwood porcelain. "It was a silly infatuation."

I set my cup in its saucer and scrutinized her for evidence of tear-swollen eyes or some other sign of listless melancholia. A beau had always seemed more trouble than he was worth, but it had also occurred to me that my eventual—and inevitable—marriage would free me from my father's rules and restrictions. Cissy had had her heart broken, but now seemed the picture of health, glowing even, as her frown smoothed. Perhaps a suitor wouldn't be the hardship I'd imagined.

"Don't tell me you've found another man to fawn over," I said, yet I could already guess the answer from the simpering smile she gave me.

"If I tell you a secret," she said with a glance at the open conservatory door, "will you promise not to tell, especially not Maggie?"

"Genghis Khan's horses couldn't drag it from my lips," I promised.

She stood with a rustle of crinoline and latched the door, then turned back and leaned against it with a positively feral grin. "Count Gizycki is coming to America," she whispered.

"So you've set your sights on a title again?" I asked, but she only put her hand on her heart as if ready to swoon.

"It's more than a title." She crossed the room to kneel beside me, resting her forearms on my chair. "It's love."

"Does your mother know?" I asked.

"Mother claims he's gambled away all his money and is looking for a rich young heiress." Her voice dropped so I had to lean in despite our close proximity. "She rants that he's a gal-sneaker bent on seduction, but I think she just doesn't like him because he's foreign."

"A foreign rogue." I tapped a finger to my chin. "He sounds like a keeper to me."

"That's what I said!" Cissy said with a giggle. "And I hear you have your own foreigner these days."

"Charly isn't *my* foreigner," I said, despite the fact that I'd drawn a silly little heart next to his name in my diary only that morning. The new secretary at the French embassy had entranced me with his quick wit, vast interest in all things fun, and an accent that set my heart aflutter. Nick and Maggie were fast becoming a matching set, and Nick had introduced us to Charly just after the Alibi debacle, so he'd become the fourth to round out our new quartet. Since it appeared Maggie had her eyes set on Nick, that left me free to draw hearts around Charly's name and flirt mercilessly with him at every opportunity.

"Watch out for Maggie," Cissy warned me again. "You can be sure I won't introduce her to Josef until I wear his ring. Even that might be too soon."

I only hugged Cissy. "I can't wait for the wedding invitation," I said as she saw me to the door. I was due in half an hour at the Russian embassy, and from there Maggie and I were going to dress to meet Nick and Charly at the Alibi before attending the annual naval ball.

I walked the few blocks to the Russian embassy, reveling in the warm sunshine on my face and the even warmer thoughts of Charly's adorable blond mustache and clumsy, endearing walk. *Does he like me at all? Can he, with Maggie at my side? Maggie will probably strap a Winchester rifle to her back or enter atop an elephant, but still . . .*

A stiff-lipped butler draped in a Russian military sash and a dizzying array of medals answered the embassy door. I snapped a stiff salute and took the stairs two at a time, sniffing my way to the room that reeked of a bower of dying roses from the Divinia perfume Maggie was spraying onto her wrists and décolletage.

"You're not dressed yet?" I picked my way around the mess of feathered hats and tulle-bowed dresses that lay strewn about the floor as if a typhoon had recently hit. Maggie only lounged like a lazy tiger, a diaphanous Chinese silk wrapper imprinted with flying white cranes tied at her tiny waist.

"Not yet, *princessa*." She stretched her arms overhead. "I thought I might attend *au naturel*."

"It's not *that* warm out," I said. "Goose pimples would mar the look."

"I suppose you're right." Maggie chuckled and motioned me toward an armoire crammed into the corner. "Then be a dear and find my new Cuban heels, the black ones with the diamond buckles. I think they'll be just the thing for the new frock I picked up today."

But I only unbuttoned my own dress, eager to change into the shimmering gold Driscoll evening gown I'd had sent over. "Get them yourself," I said. "I hope they're made for dancing though. I plan to caper with Charly all night."

"Do you?" she asked, in a way that made my eyes narrow. "And here I thought I might get in a dance or two with our favorite Frenchman."

Perhaps I was overly sensitive after listening to Cissy's warnings, but something about the idea of Maggie dancing with Charly made me wish she'd sprain an ankle during dinner. Maybe both ankles, just to be safe.

I feigned nonchalance as I let the gauzy silk skirt fall over my hips, the material shot through with metallic gold thread that turned molten with my every movement. "I'm sure I could spare him for a reel or two. If you're willing to trade for Nick, that is."

She gave me a sharp glance, but I only gestured for her to button me up. After all, we could both play her little game.

Yet it wasn't Maggie who ruined my fantasies of Charly that night. At least not on her own.

As we approached the Alibi's second-floor kitchen, I was brought up short by the rumble of male laughter from within. "I thought it was just us and the boys," I said to Maggie, who peered inside.

"Just us and the men," she corrected me with a wink and an artful flick of ash from her Lucky Strike cigarette. I stubbed out the ember with my toe so it wouldn't ruin the Turkish carpet. "So *many* men."

"So this giglet is Miss Alice Roosevelt," said one I recognized as a junior senator after Nick introduced us to his tuxedoed colleagues. Charly was nowhere to be seen, which only left me further tongue-tied.

These are Father's cohorts. To them, I'm the president's daughter, not just Alice. So how on earth do I act tonight?

The silence had stretched on too long, and now Junior Senator and his ilk were watching me. I searched for something outlandish to distract them from my awkwardness—a bet to place or a joke to crack, but my tongue looped itself into a veritable Gordian knot under the weight of their stares.

Merry hell, I'm worse than Cissy. Pull yourself together, Alice.

It was Nick who came to my rescue.

"So," he said, tying a white butcher's apron around his waist. "Who shall be my *sous chef* tonight?"

"I had no idea you were such a housewife, Nick," Junior Senator said, effectively distracted from my gaffe. "You cook, you clean . . . maybe you can polish my shoes when you're done washing up."

Or maybe he can wash your mouth out with soap, I thought as my hands curled into fists. Yet the retort died on my lips as Nick gave a good-natured laugh and rolled up his French cuffs. Junior Senator faded away as I struggled to tear my gaze from Nick's well-defined forearms, so unlike the gangling arms of boys my own age.

But then Nick was different from every other man I'd ever met, self-assured and more worldly, I supposed.

"Grab the nutmeg and sherry wine, will you, Alice?" he asked after he'd tied an apron over my gold ball gown. Was it my imagination, or did his hand linger at the small of my back? "You can assist with my masterpiece while these loafers slouch about."

"Your masterpiece?"

"My famous Toothsome Terrapin." How had I never noticed the way his hazel eyes sparkled, surrounded by a dusting of pale lashes? "You haven't lived until you've tasted it."

While Maggie entertained the congressmen with a spot-on impression of her father and every other foreign ambassador in Washington, I hummed to myself while zesting lemons and tried to keep from crying as I chopped the onion. "Sorry," I said to Nick when his hip bumped mine as he scrubbed the turtle shell with boiling water.

He only winked. "Don't be. Soak the onion in cold water before you cut it next time."

I grinned—that is, until I felt Maggie's gaze scalding my back. Still, Nick's terrapin might have been mixed with turpentine for all I tasted after speaking to Charly, who was more than fashionably late.

I was irked when he failed to acknowledge me after I finagled a place next to him at the Alibi's thirty-person formal dining table, a room that might have been romantic with its massive fireplace and heavy beams, and that resembled a sixteenth-century tavern. Instead of laughing at my jokes as he always had, tonight his eyes followed Maggie's every move until I'd decided there was nothing to do but confront him between courses.

"I'm afraid Maggie's not on the menu tonight," I said, after she'd risen and claimed the need for the powder room, prompting the men to stand even as their gazes clung to her swaying backside. Normally I'd have joined her, but not this time.

"Hmm?" Charly blinked, having barely managed to drag his attention away from her retreating figure.

"You're staring at her like you want to eat her." I tried to keep my tone playful when my fingers itched to dump my water over his pretty blond head. Only then did I realize that Longworth was listening, not even attempting to be discreet as he swirled his wine in his glass.

"Alice." Charly's hand clasped mine in a way that made my pulse thrum in my ears. "May I give you a secret?" His thick French accent made my toes curl despite being shoved into a new pair of rhinestone shoes. Charly could have told me that my face was green then, so long as he kept holding my hand. I managed to nod, tilting my head in a way I'd seen Maggie do that drew men like flowers to a heavily perfumed sun. And it worked; Charly leaned so close I could smell his musky aftershave.

"I think I am in love," he said, and my heart exploded in a dangerous display of holiday fireworks. Until he finished that thought. "With Maggie."

"You're in love?" My voice came out an octave too high. *How could I have been so blind?* I thought, even as I wanted to melt under the table in mortification. "With Maggie Cassini?"

Don't let them see you bleed, Alice. Disguise this as you have every other disappointment in your life. But two thoughts clanged loudly in my mind. *What in the devil is wrong with me that Charly would choose* Maggie *over me? And how could I not have noticed?*

I realized then that Maggie and I had never actually discussed who we were interested in. Had I just assumed she wanted Nick because of how she'd acted in front of Cissy? Had she been chasing Charly all along?

"Your Maggie is so enticing, so alluring." Charly rubbed his freshly shaven chin. "Everything a woman should be. And she always smells so, so . . . good," he finished lamely, as if his English had finally failed him.

"I thought . . ." My voice trailed off as I fumbled for my cigarette case. If ever a girl needed a cigarette, this was the time. "I thought I was your best girl," I said, forcing myself to laugh as if his admission was the funniest thing ever.

"You I love like a sister," he said, squeezing my hand before letting it go. "Any man seeking your affections would need more courage than I, considering . . ."

"What?" I asked.

"Considering who your father is."

"Oh," I said dumbly.

He brightened, oblivious to my agony. "But Maggie . . . Does she ever speak of me?"

"No more than she does about her favorite hat." I rummaged harder in my reticule to avoid Charly's eyes. Where *were* those damn cigarettes?

A lighter clicked and I glanced up to see a cigarette offered by Nick Longworth.

"Thanks." I forced myself to balance it delicately between my lips instead of gulping down its calming smoke as he lit the end. I might have gnawed the thing whole—paper and all—if it would have made my hands stop shaking. "You're a godsend."

He winked. "That's what all the girls say."

Maggie reentered then, and I was forced to watch Charly moon over her as the Welsh rabbit was served following Nick's terrapin. And the night wasn't over when the empty plates were taken away, for we still had the naval ball to attend.

Fortunately, my parents were absent, but Auntie Bye stood in the receiving line next to her husband, ashen-haired Commander William Sheffield Cowles, one of the most senior officers present tonight. He was terribly solicitous of my aunt, patting her hand in his arm every so often, and I found myself jealous of their easy affection.

"Alice, dearest." She clasped my hands and pressed a kiss onto my cheek. "I feel like I scarcely see you anymore."

I could never hide anything from Auntie Bye. Regardless of the line behind me, she held both my hands so I couldn't dash away. "Whatever is the matter, dear girl?"

"Nothing," I said too brightly. "Merely the travails of youth."

She frowned and patted my cheek with her gloved hand. "You can tell me all about it tomorrow. I need help picking out a new day hat and will trust no one save you with such an important task."

The thought of browsing the millinery shops might have cheered me had Charly not immediately swept Maggie onto the floor, leaving me standing on the sidelines. I glanced up to find Nick leaning against a wall with boneless grace, surrounded by a gaggle of chiffon-clad officers' daughters. No matter where he went, Nick drew pretty girls to him like flies to a honeycomb.

He nodded to me and then the dance floor—we'd stepped out a few reels at every ball we'd attended—but right now I didn't care to be anywhere near Maggie.

She hadn't purposely stolen my beau as Cissy had warned, but she'd poached Charly all the same.

I waded my way through Nick's flock of feminine admirers and grabbed his arm. "Let's see how good you are at poker," I said, dragging him toward the tables.

"I'll rob you dry," he boasted with a grin, his wallet already in hand.

"Challenge accepted." But then my gaze fell on Auntie Bye and I skidded to a stop. "Damn! I forgot about my aunt."

Nick raised his eyebrows.

"What?" I asked.

"Nothing." He shrugged. "Only who knew America's favorite daughter was such a saucebox?"

"Please," I said irritably. "Haven't you ever heard a girl curse?"

"I don't mind." Nick held his hands up in surrender. "In fact, I like a bear-garden mouth. It tells me the girl in question is made of sterner stuff than most wilting roses."

I might have been made of Carnegie steel, but I couldn't get Auntie Bye in trouble for my gambling right under her nose. I explained as much to Nick, who seemed sympathetic, even as he replaced his wallet.

No Charly, no dancing, and no poker. Surely *something* at this ball might prove a distraction.

"Are you up for some unconventional gambling?" I asked Nick.

"What do you have in mind?"

"Something that won't land my aunt Bye in a bind come morning."

"You're on." Nick scanned the hall intently. "See Walter Luckerman over there?" he finally asked, nodding across the way to a middle-aged lieutenant whose paunch was now serving as a convenient sort of table on which to hold his cards. "I've always wondered if old Walter wears a wig or not. I'll bet fifty dollars you can't find out before the end of the night."

Fifty dollars could buy me at least three new evening dresses. I was suddenly impressed that Nick Longworth had that much spare cash to throw around.

Never make a bet you don't intend to win, Nick.

"Deal." I wanted to cackle with glee as I offered my hand and my best poker face. Nick took it, the pressure of his fingers against mine making my breath hitch before I tugged him closer so I might whisper in his ear. "Rest assured that when you've lost all of your hair, Lieutenant Luckerman will be happy to give you the name of his wig-maker."

Nick pulled back, his hand still in mine. "And just how do you know that?"

"He joined Aunt Bye and her husband for a seaside holiday a while back." I rocked on my heels with excitement. "I may have witnessed a rogue ocean wave carry away the unfortunate hair in question."

Nick gave a hoot of laughter as he slapped his leg, his handsome face alight. "I'll bet you know more about Washington than the entire Secret Service combined." He pressed a kiss to the back of my hand with lazy, unhurried grace. "I do adore you, Alice Roosevelt."

I was stunned deaf and dumb, even as he let my hand drop to riffle through his leather wallet. My poor battered little heart perked up at his words, despite the trampling it had taken from Charly tonight. Surely Nick spoke in jest?

He's a skirt chaser, Alice. Don't get swizzled over a little throwaway comment.

"And how do you know I haven't already interrogated the Secret Service to uncover state secrets?" I quipped, impressed at my own insouciance.

"It wouldn't surprise me if you had." Nick handed me a fifty-dollar bill with a flourish. I folded it and slipped it up the back of my glove, wishing every night could be this profitable.

And enjoyable.

Somehow, Nick Longworth had taken a miserable evening and turned it around, whether he meant to or not.

"Let's dance." I didn't wait for him to answer, only pulled him onto the floor while waving at Auntie Bye and ignoring the angry glares from the officers' daughters who'd been hoping to stack their dance cards with Nick's name.

"You and Nick are quite a pair tonight," Maggie noted between dances while Nick hunted down some punch. "You're downright flushed."

"Have you set your sights on him?" I asked, fearing the answer. Either way, I wanted this settled once and for all.

"Who, Nick?" she asked with a high trill of laughter. "Never, darling. American men are pleasant diversions, but Father would have kittens if I married someone who wasn't Russian. He's all yours," she added, a bit too loudly for my tastes.

My heart did cartwheels at the very idea that I might have a man like Nick on my arm, sophisticated, debonair, and utterly charming. If I wasn't careful, I'd find myself head over heels for him this very night.

"Who is all yours?" Charly asked me, and my heart gave a final pang at that delectable French accent. *Adieu, Charly. Adieu.* "He must be a lucky man."

"Nick is all mine," I said. "For this dance."

There I went breaking conventions again, for it was highly improper to dance more than one reel in a row with the same man. Fortunately, I wasn't the only one planning to break the rules.

Charly turned to Maggie. "Then I hope you will be mine."

"Of course, darling," Maggie said, winking. "At least for this quadrille."

The evening ended on an even higher note when I heard Charly proclaim that he was to return to France before the season ended, hardly enough time for us to have properly fallen in love. But . . .

Well, well!

Nick!

"You look absolutely divine," I told Cissy as I embraced her in the receiving line, having to maneuver around the small jungle of white hothouse roses that made up her bouquet. The Patterson family library was bedecked with enough lilies to choke a funeral parlor, but not even the drab flowers of death could have diminished Cissy's white chiffon gown trimmed with liberty gauze and duchesse lace. Nor had they detracted from the blush on her cheeks as she'd repeated her wedding vows to her Polish count.

Poor Emily Spinach had recently died, but I reached into my beaded purse to withdraw a linen handkerchief to hand Cissy in the receiving line. "The first Grace to marry!" I congratulated my friend as she dabbed her eyes. Cissy looked so happy that I had to wonder if perhaps marriage really was a blessing. "Bully for you, wrangling Cupid and bending the chubby imp to your will."

"I'm so happy, Alice," Cissy whispered, her eyes shining with tears of joy as she waited to greet the rest of her thirty-five guests.

Only thirty-five! I thought as I glanced around. *I'll have at least a thousand, whether I want them or not. More likely not, although a thousand is bound to land me in the papers.*

However, one peek over Cissy's shoulder at her glaring father and scowling mother made me wonder what sort of threats she'd made to force them to consent to her marrying the philandering Count

Gizycki, especially as I watched Mr. Patterson refuse to shake Gizycki's hand.

"Did you hear that Gizycki demanded a dowry to marry Cissy?" a doughy matron whispered to another, loudly enough to be overheard. "I certainly hope he was refused. After all this, is 1904, not 1504."

Go back to sipping your scandal water, you old cat, I wanted to yell aloud. *It's Cissy's wedding day, for crying out loud, or didn't you notice the white dress and bouquet?*

"Well," I said, making my smile even wider as I kissed both of Cissy's cheeks. "I heartily approve of the dashing rounder you've married. He may as well have sprung from the pages of *Anna Karenina.*"

Cissy flushed, stealing a glance at her groom. Count Josef Gizycki *was* handsome, if a girl liked a Gypsy sort of man with roving eyes. Not quite my style, although I did appreciate the ornate cigarette cases he'd given as wedding gifts. But now Gizycki's gaze was fixated on Maggie across the room, which certainly wouldn't do.

Cissy had been kind enough to extend an olive branch by inviting Maggie to the April wedding. Or perhaps she just wanted to rub Maggie's nose in her triumph. Either way . . .

"It is time to go," Count Gizycki suddenly announced in his thick accent. The silence that fell could have drowned half of Washington, for Cissy hadn't even changed out of her wedding dress yet.

"The count must be eager to begin married life," said Gizycki's best man, Count Ivan Rubido-Zichy, making a crude gesture with both his hands. "Who can blame him, with such a pretty young bride?"

Cissy blushed a painful scarlet and the guests fluttered with shock.

"I can't wait to see your traveling costume," I said to Cissy. My voice echoed off the library walls as the guests looked at her with sudden pity. "I'm sure it's lovely."

"It's a Worth." Her voice trembled as I ushered her toward her mother. "Just arrived from Paris."

And so Cissy went upstairs to change into her frothy House of Worth creation and Gizycki excused himself, ostensibly to the Willard Hotel to collect his belongings before taking his bride to Union Station.

The library clock ticked off each awkward second as we waited and fidgeted on the hard wooden benches set up for the ceremony. And waited and fidgeted some more.

But Gizycki didn't return.

In the meantime, a pale and wretched-looking Cissy descended in her lavender traveling dress amid the scandalized guests. (Who knew thirty-five people could whisper so loudly, despite the bride's eyes brimming with tears?)

"Are you sure you don't want to wait upstairs?" I asked, but Cissy shook her head.

"He's only been held up." Yet her lower lip quivered and she dabbed at her eyes with a lace handkerchief embroidered with her husband's initials. "Just wait—he loves me so much, Alice. He'd never do anything to hurt me."

"Tell me every detail about your plans for the honeymoon tour," I said, one ear taking in Cissy's list of spring visits to London and Paris, Prague and Krakow, while listening with the other ear as a livid Mr. Patterson sent Count Ivan to locate the groom. Only when Ivan returned some half an hour later did Cissy cease babbling about Prague's many castles. An expectant hush fell over the room, as if we were waiting for the casualty report from some nearby battlefield.

"He demands a dowry," Count Ivan reported of his absent friend. "Without which, he will leave his bride and return to Poland."

"A dowry to fix his ruined chateaux." Maggie flicked her hand with its waterfall of antique Italian lace at the wrist. "It's a fair deal considering that Cissy is Countess Gizycki now. That's how things are done in Europe, you know."

My glare sent her away with a careless shrug, even as Mr. Patterson grabbed Count Ivan by the lapels and dragged him into the private study across the hall. Mrs. Patterson followed and shut the door behind the trio. Cissy made to follow, but I shook my head, beckoning for her brother to keep her company.

"I'll see what they're up to," I said, and pretended to peruse the flower arrangement closest to the study, the better to hear the ruckus inside.

"Not a cent for him!" Mr. Patterson snarled from the other side. "I didn't want this marriage to occur in the first place, remember? But I sure as hell thought it would take longer than an hour for it to fall to pieces!"

"Rob," came Mrs. Patterson's even voice. "Perhaps we might appease Josef by raising Cissy's yearly allowance to $20,000?"

It was too late to back out of the marriage, and so the Pattersons would have to buy their way out of this mess or see Cissy—and their family name—ruined for all time.

Merry hell, but this is enough to put a girl off marrying forever. And poor Cissy caught in the middle . . .

"I think that would be sufficient," Ivan answered for his friend so smoothly that I wondered if he and Gizycki had discussed amenable terms before this depressing fiasco.

"Fine!" Mr. Patterson barked, making me jump on the other side of the door.

I put on my brightest smile and turned, coming to clasp Cissy's hands. "It's off to Union Station with you," I said, trying to sound happy. "Your count awaits *and* your parents just increased your allowance to more than you can possibly spend. I'm beyond green, darling!"

My farcical happiness did the trick, and Cissy allowed herself to be herded into the wedding carriage waiting on Massachusetts Avenue. I hugged her and wished her good luck before she ducked pale-faced into the carriage. Mrs. Patterson moved to follow her daughter, but I stopped her with a hand on her arm.

"Will Cissy be all right?" I asked.

Her mother only shrugged. "Only time will tell. If not, she can always come home."

Back to her childhood home, to live under her parents' roof and rules after a failed marriage? Is there a worse fate?

As I watched the carriage pull away from the scandalized guests, somehow I doubted it.

Spring turned to summer and love was in the air that year when the autumn social season started. But where love goes, heartbreak follows.

I rang Maggie one sunny autumn afternoon filled with cheery birdsong and scudding clouds, both my foot and my fingers tapping impatiently.

"Hello?" I said to the embassy secretary. "I'm trying to reach Maggie. She was supposed to be at the White House an hour ago to meet me for a riding appointment."

"Who is this?"

"Alice Roosevelt," I said, wishing I could add, *Perhaps you've heard of me?*

"Of course. I regret to inform you that Miss Cassini left over an hour ago to meet Representative Longworth at the Alibi."

I couldn't recall the two of them going anywhere without me, and I thought I'd made my interest in Nick perfectly clear at the naval ball. *That's odd . . .*

"Well, please have her call me when she returns," I said, but Maggie didn't call that day. Or the next.

Finally, I telephoned again after Maggie neglected to show for our theater plans several evenings later. I'd been eager to show off the flashy new four-cylinder touring car I'd gleefully purchased with a portion of my mother's inheritance after Father had finally capitulated, but had been left in the cold.

"Miss Cassini is at the Boardmans' with their daughter Josephine," the embassy secretary's nasal voice informed me. "Would you like to leave *another* message?"

I ignored her to phone the Boardmans, but Josephine only chortled, an obnoxiously breathy giggle. "Maggie's out walking with

Nick," she said. "Nick *Longworth*. Can you imagine the scandal, walking with a man at night, much less a man with his reputation?"

I *could* imagine the scandal. And I could also imagine Maggie reveling in it.

I don't care a fig for Nick's reputation, but I do *care that Maggie is hanging on his arm in the dark right now.*

"Well," I said to Josephine, "tell Maggie when you see her that it was terribly rude of her not to let me know she wasn't coming to the opera tonight."

I slammed the earpiece against the receiver and then slid down the wall, laying my forehead against my bent knees and feeling only somewhat better when Skip came and nudged me with his wet nose. First Charly, and now Nick.

"I didn't even *let* myself fall for Nick, not really," I said to Skip as I scratched behind his ears. He rolled over and I idly rubbed his black belly. "There must be something wrong with me, that I'm the president's daughter and still can't entice anyone to love me. I don't seem very adept at attracting suitors. Or true friends."

Skip sat up and cocked his head at me. "I don't know what I'm going to do, Skip," I answered. "Maggie's toying with me exactly as she did Cissy. But a Roosevelt is never defeated, not in the polls and not on a battlefield."

And there was no doubt that Maggie and I were now at war.

My stomach flailed like the Stars and Stripes that flapped in the breeze on the White House roof as I watched Maggie's roadster crawl up Pennsylvania Avenue a few days later, drifts of dirty snow melting on either side of the road after an unseasonably early snowfall. The high clouds and wind hadn't deterred the steady stream of pedestrians, carriages, and even a carefree couple on skis from enjoying the November afternoon. Yet I stood alone, waiting for my impending doom to arrive on a cloud of cigarette smoke and Divinia perfume. I swallowed a dry rattle of laughter to realize that I now stood in the exact same spot where Mother had once admonished me to make friends.

Would that I'd ignored her and never said more than two words to the Russian Judas that is Maggie Cassini.

I watched Maggie hand off her keys to a liveried attendant and paced like a caged wolf to keep my nerves from getting the best of me. *Two minutes to promenade through the Entrance Hall—making sure everyone looks her way so they can admire her ridiculous hat—thirty seconds to the top of the Grand Staircase, one minute down the hall to burst into my empty bedroom and wonder where I went . . .*

Only when I heard the succinct *click-click* of her heels on the wooden floor did I cease pacing and straighten, my shoulders thrown back like a military general.

Right on time . . .

Maggie might have passed for a Romanov empress as she swept onto the roof, dressed with her usual verve in a solid black walking dress and an Ottoman turban stuffed with quivering peacock feathers. My hair was coming loose from its pins in the wind; I'd thought I was prepared to do battle, but now that Maggie was here, I felt like a back-alley mongrel aside an exotic pedigreed showstopper. How had I ever thought I could compare to her? Or that we were the same at all?

"Hello, *princessa*." She offered me a cigarette in one of her impossibly long holders, but I ignored the shag with its thin flag of fragrant smoke and lit my own.

"What the hell are you doing?" I asked, doing my best to punch my insecurity deep inside myself. Instead, I scowled. I snarled. I hated.

Maggie choked in surprise and bent over in a coughing fit, her cigarette with its stain of crimson lipstick falling to the roof. "What do you mean?" she gasped out. I took some small satisfaction in the way her eyes watered, making her flawless mascara run just a tiny bit on her left eye.

I had no pity, even as she continued retching. "Don't play games with me," I said. "I know you're toying with Nick."

My battle plan was decimated with the grenade of Maggie's next smoke-scented words.

"Nick proposed to me last night," she said. Now it was my turn to choke, the smoke scorching my lungs right next to where my heart should have been. I couldn't breathe, couldn't *think* through the burning red mist that suddenly clouded my vision.

You only noticed Nick because Cissy and I both showed interest in him, I wanted to scream. I wanted to lunge at her, to tear at her flawless skin and claw the smirk from her lips. Instead, I stood petrified by the flames of rage that licked my very bones. *I hate you, Maggie Cassini, and I'll go on hating you until the end of my days.*

Yet I could never say that without giving her even more power over me. And that was something I would never, *ever* do.

I was still searching for words I could hone into a weapon as Maggie smoothed her face into an inscrutable mask and stretched her long legs out in front of her. The Russian viper had the nerve to laugh then, a high trill of a giggle as she lit a new cigarette. "You'll be happy to know I rejected him, *princessa*. Just for you."

I felt the unmistakable urge to press the burning end of my shag into the pale skin of her exposed wrist. "I don't care what you do with any man, much less a congressman with thinning hair. I won't see my friendship dumped at the last minute so you can go running off after a man like a bitch in heat."

Maggie's perfectly nonchalant smoke rings came to a stuttering halt as she gaped at me. "Nick's just a fellow I like to toy with," she said. "You're my dearest friend, Alice."

"You're no one's friend, Maggie. You're just a catty backbiter who cares only about herself." The words felt like glass in my throat, for I'd once believed Maggie *had* been my friend. One of my *best* friends. Yet I refused to let her see how much she'd hurt me. I stood, looking down my nose at her from my full height and pointing toward the roof access. "Leave. Now."

"What?"

"Surely you remember the way out. Or you can jump and break your neck if you prefer."

Maggie rose with such fluid grace that I wanted to scream, yet her expression was far from placid. "Be rational about this, Alice."

I'm perfectly rational. If I never see you again, it will be too soon.

"First it was a competition against Cissy, and now me. That's not friendship." I threw down my cigarette and ground it hard beneath my heel. "Get out, Maggie, and don't ever come back."

She stared at me for so long a moment that I thought I saw tears welling in her eyes before she gave a delicate sniff. "And here I thought you were going to be such fun, Alice Roosevelt." And with that, she turned and walked out of my life, trailing a cloud of cigarette smoke and Divinia perfume.

I managed to count to twenty after the roof door slammed behind her before letting loose a lone scream of anger, frustration, and so much hurt that it seemed my very bones were full of it.

Nick was playing his violin when the butler ushered me upstairs at the Alibi the next afternoon. I felt a pang to hear such melancholy notes, and paused only to wonder whether I should leave even as the butler announced me. Nick glanced up when I entered, ending on a final tremulous note before he set the violin aside. His suit jacket was off and his satin puff tie was undone, but he made no move to right either.

"Hello, Alice." The ugly circles that rimmed his eyes drained the fight right out of me. For that was why I'd come, although I still wasn't sure whether it was to fight *with* him or *for* him. "I'm afraid I'm not the best company today."

Too bad, darling, for I didn't put on my best frock and new toque hat just to retreat straight back to the White House.

"I thought I'd join you for lunch," I said brightly.

Ever the gentleman, Nick pulled out one of the Windsor chairs and even managed a bow. "Far be it from me to deny Princess Alice anything."

Yet I could tell his mind was elsewhere from the way he pulverized his watercress sandwich into his plate.

"It's no use beating around the bush, Nick." My stomach churned with nerves so that I could scarcely think of eating the deviled eggs he dished out to me. "I hear you proposed to Maggie."

"Word travels quickly," he muttered as he abandoned all pretense of eating to kick his feet in their expensive Italian leather loafers up on the table and light a cigarette. To my surprise, he offered it to me. "Then you must also know I was soundly rejected."

I *tsked* under my breath, but claimed the cigarette. "I could have told you she'd refuse."

"That might have been helpful to know *before* I proposed to her."

I gave an elegant shrug. "You didn't ask."

"Do you know *how* she rejected me?" He didn't wait for an answer. "We went for a sleigh ride down to the Potomac and I jumped out of the box to fix the horse's harness. When I looked up she was so beautiful with the snowflakes in her hair and on her eyelashes, so I asked. The words just fell out of my mouth. And do you know what she did?"

"I can't imagine." What I *could* imagine was how I felt this very moment, like I was going to be ill. I smashed the cigarette into the Venetian glass ashtray, unwilling to meet his gaze.

"She laughed and told me she'd give me an answer, then grabbed the whip and took off with me standing in the snow. I had to walk miles to get back."

That was heartless, even for Maggie. Yet I refused to show him any sympathy.

So I folded my arms in front of me. "Better luck next time."

Nick made some sort of feral noise lodged between a growl and a laugh. "*If* there is a next time, you mean. I'm of a mind to swear off all women."

"That might be a wise decision," I said. "Considering your track record. You throw around marriage proposals like the Vanderbilts toss around spare cash."

Nick gaped, but only momentarily. Then his eyes sparked and I'd swear he almost smiled. "That's hardly the sympathy I was hoping for."

I shrugged. "You should go elsewhere if you want sympathy."

"As I recall, *you* came to *me*."

I shook a finger at him. "You've already broken off an engagement with Miriam Bloomer, and now Maggie's rejected your second proposal. A girl with your record would find herself facing the yawning chasm of spinsterhood, but no one even blinks when it comes from a man like you."

"A man like me?"

"Yes. An infuriating fool of a man. You need to find a woman who will keep you on your toes, unlike Miriam, and someone who actually still possesses a heart, which Maggie misplaced long ago."

"Are you volunteering?"

Now it was my turn to gape. "What?"

"Are you volunteering? To be that woman?"

"No." I shook my head. Vehemently. "Absolutely not."

You are a liar, Alice Roosevelt. A yellow-bellied liar.

This time I shook my head as if to clear it. "We wouldn't last even a week before we killed each other."

Nick caught me suddenly off guard by leaning across the table and clasping my hand. I tried to ignore the jolt of heat that spread from his fingertips up my arm, but might have had better luck ignoring an electrical storm crashing over my head. "Promise me that you and I can still have bully fun, Alice. Cissy, Charly, and Maggie have all gone by the wayside until only you and I remain. Whatever our souls are made of, yours and mine are the same."

"Brontë," I mumbled to myself.

"What?"

"'Whatever our souls are made of, his and mine are the same.' From *Wuthering Heights*."

He gave that slow smile that made my toes tingle. "I knew you'd catch that."

I reminded myself that Nick Longworth was a self-described *bon vivant*, and one who had chosen my friend over me. Still, it would have been impossible not to be affected by his bold intellect and dangerous smile. The way he looked at me made me feel as if I were the most important person in the world, as if I alone held the key to his happiness.

It was easy to see how so many girls had fallen under his spell, yet I refused to do so. I'd once entertained the idea, but not again.

I withdrew my hand and affected my most bored expression. "We'll see, Nick," I said. "I suppose it all depends on how long you spend being a rotten old misery-guts over Maggie. I don't find a man pining away over another woman to be very entertaining."

"Then I must aim to remedy that. For above all else, Alice Roosevelt should always be entertained."

I couldn't tell whether the twist to his mouth was humorous or hurt, but I told myself I didn't care. Somehow I survived the rest of lunch before finding an excuse to duck out early.

Men who played the field were desirable, sending women aflutter. And men had always fallen over themselves for Maggie, who acted like a man when it came to love. *So I'll be like Maggie*, I thought as I walked away from the Alibi, *and leave a trail of broken hearts in my wake*.

And Nick Longworth would be my first victim.

Until Christmas Eve, when I lost control of my little experiment.

That was when the mayhem started.

Chapter 6

DECEMBER 1904

"You have a telephone call, Alice," Mother informed me that crisp and cold Christmas Eve morning. Father had won his reelection in a veritable landslide the month prior—just before my falling-out with Maggie—and we'd been enjoying relative peace and plenty of holiday cheer ever since. I groaned and rolled over, a careless arm thrown across my eyes as I breathed in the glorious smell of baking gingerbread from the White House kitchens. It was around eight o'clock, judging from the meager winter light breaking through the curtains, a truly ungodly hour. Mother cleared her throat. "I'll have Rose inform Representative Longworth that you'll return his call after the holidays."

I sat bolt upright, a soldier waking to the din of battle. "I'll take the call."

I wrapped a thick woolen robe around me and hurried on bare feet into the hallway. Mother's hand on my arm stopped me.

"Alice." The stern lines between her brows furrowed with her frown. "Nicholas Longworth is a cad with a terrible reputation."

"That's part of his allure," I said, but the lines between Mother's brows only deepened.

"He's fourteen years older than you and drinks too much," she said. "I don't approve of him and neither does your father."

Which only makes me want him more.

"Your concern is duly noted," I said. "But Father introduced me to Nick. And Nick *is* a good Republican."

I sauntered down the hall to the telephone, waiting for Mother to call me back, but for whatever reason, she let me go. This time at least.

"Nick, dearest," I said into the receiver. "I do hope you're dead or dying to be calling at this obscene hour."

Nick chuckled on the other end, the slight crackle over the line doing nothing to mar the wonderful sound. Despite his faults, he *did* have a delectable laugh in all its variations.

"I might keel over if you don't join me for breakfast this morning," he said. "The Alibi in, say, an hour?"

I knew I should reject him with some excuse of a family breakfast or charity event, but the thought of laughing with Nick over buckwheat cakes brought the most senseless smile to my lips.

"Only if you promise to serve baked apples." I leaned against the hall table and twined the telephone cord around my finger. "With a mountain of cinnamon and sugar on top."

"For you, anything," he said.

"See you in an hour," I said, hanging up.

It was an hour and a half before I traipsed through snowdrifts into the silent Alibi, for I'd taken my time getting dressed, and I smiled now as I caught my reflection in the window, chic and stylish in my new Alice Blue walking suit that complemented my eyes. A girl like me could make a man like Nick wait a while, even if it did mean that my baked apples might go cold.

"Blow me down, but you are a vision," Nick exclaimed as he rose to take my coat and gloves. "A cold vision with hands like icicles," he said when my fingers brushed his, "but a vision nonetheless."

He clasped my hands between both of his and blew warm air onto them. His lips touched my wrist for the briefest of moments, and his gaze snagged mine. It took all of my willpower to roll my eyes and withdraw my hands. "That trick may work with your other girls," I said, exhaling in supposed exasperation when really it was to calm my nerves, "but I came here for breakfast, remember?"

He grinned like an utter bounder—which I suppose he was—and then rang the dining room bell. A tall butler with enormous side-whiskers pushed in a wheeled breakfast cart, and I sighed with real pleasure at the comforting scents of steaming buckwheat cakes drenched in maple syrup, sugary baked apples, and a carafe of steaming black coffee.

"I made the apples myself," Nick said in that deep, sonorous voice of his, spooning one onto my plate and pouring my mug of coffee. He knew just how I liked it, black with two sugars.

"You're a man of many talents," I drawled. He smiled and I reminded myself to toss a few insults into the conversation just to cancel out the compliment.

"So," Nick said as I poured maple syrup over my cakes and added a dollop onto the baked apples just for the fun of it. "I'm afraid I had an ulterior motive in asking you here today. I have a most dire question to ask you."

I almost choked on my apple.

"And what might that be?" I managed to squeak out. Surely he wasn't going to ask after Maggie or some other woman? After all, that did rather seem to be my lot.

"It's what everyone in Washington is dying to know." Nick took a bite of buckwheat cake and chewed until I thought I might scream. Finally, he swallowed and waggled his empty fork at me. "Will the Roosevelts have a Christmas tree this year?"

I gulped my coffee so fast it scalded my tongue.

"No tree." I laughed far too long, almost giddy with relief that Nick hadn't asked about Maggie. "Unless Archie pulls a fast one on us again."

Two years ago, Father had banned a Christmas tree in the White House while he lobbied for more forest conservation, so Archie had cut his own tree—closer to a twig, really—and stashed it in his closet. My role in the subterfuge had been duly reported in the papers as I'd wrangled one of the electricians into rigging the tree with tiny white lights so Archie could hang presents on it for all our dogs and Algonquin the pony.

It never ceased to amaze me how much the press knew about our family, whether we willed it or not. I much preferred to feed them the stories I wished them to report.

"Surely the president won't deprive his family of stockings and presents?" Nick asked.

"Never. Father is the biggest child of us all. I think he loves opening presents more than even little Quentin."

"Anything in particular you hope to find in your stocking?"

"Another pistol would be nice." I took a bite of the baked apple now that my nerves had calmed somewhat. Nick Longworth might be an insufferable cad, but there was no denying he was a gourmet cook. "A girl can always use another barking iron. A Colt .45 rimless would be divine."

"You know, most women ask for pearls and perfumes."

"Bah," I said, waving a hand. "I have plenty of both. It's either go shooting or watch Father play singlestick again this year on Christmas. I wouldn't mind singlestick if I were allowed to play, but Father and Mother won't budge from their stance that the game is unsuitable for girls. Ghastly unfair, that."

Nick looked at me as if I'd suggested we dine on puppies. "You'd brave black eyes and broken wrists?"

It was no idle question, for Father's arm had been bandaged for weeks following a particularly nasty match last year. But I only narrowed my eyes in mock outrage. "You're assuming I'd lose," I said. "Which I wouldn't."

"You are a rare woman, Alice Roosevelt." Nick leaned forward as if to tell me a secret. "In fact, I think I might be falling in love with you."

This time I choked on my coffee, so badly that Nick had to come and thump me on my back. "You're a libertine, Nick Longworth," I managed to croak out. "And a liar too."

Thank God that Nick waggled his eyebrows at me and broke the spell. "It was worth a try."

I was able to laugh, although my voice trembled in a most undignified manner. "Keep talking like that," I said, "and I swear I'll stop coming to see you, regardless of all the baked apples you ply me with."

"That's what I adore about you," he chuckled. "You know how to put a man in his place. Please tell me you'll see this poor, lonely bachelor tomorrow."

"Tomorrow's Christmas," I said, thankful for the ready excuse. "I'll be with my family the entire day."

I won't *see Nick on Christmas,* I promised myself later as I stood in the Alibi's foyer, Nick helping me into my wool coat and me doing my utmost to ignore the spicy scent of his aftershave as he did up my top button. I'd have been made of marble to ignore the way his thumb brushed the sensitive skin at my neck, or the way his lips turned up as I shivered. *I won't see him alone ever again, not unless I want to find myself in a whole heap of trouble.*

I'd keep Nick at arm's length, for I'd seen how romantic love had ravaged my father after my mother's death, and done its best to ruin Cissy.

Yet, Christmas Day was a lackluster affair after my unexpected Christmas Eve breakfast. The gifts and stockings from Father and Mother were laid out like a fairyland in the White House library, but the train sets and new dresses lost their sparkle whenever my thoughts strayed to Nick spending the holiday alone.

The British embassy threw a Boxing Day party on the day after Christmas, and I chafed when Mother tasked me with keeping an eye on the younger children after a dinner of mincemeat pie and Lancashire fruitcakes while my brother Ted ran off to join the older boys for a game of rugby outside in the filthy winter weather. The smell of cigar smoke and talk of the most recent tariffs permeated the air as Father and the other men remained at the dining table with their brandy while sleet pelted the windows.

Not *all* the other men . . .

Was it the way Nick's copper eyes crinkled at the edges as he found me guessing children's shadows from one side of a white sheet that made the room suddenly too warm, or had the fire in the fireplace suddenly grown hotter?

My pulse thrummed in my ears as I studiously ignored him, but I had to pat my cheeks to make sure they hadn't burst into flames when he sat so close that our knees might have touched.

"Who let a cowboy into the party?" I exclaimed, recognizing Auntie Bye's son William from the tops of his snakeskin boots—a Christmas present from my father—peeking out from beneath the sheet. My cousin giggled and clamped shadow hands over his mouth.

"Don't tell me Wyatt Earp is here." Nick rubbed his chin, giving me a wink. "Or is it that rascal Billy the Kid?"

"It's just me." William peeked around the sheet with an infectious grin, pure Auntie Bye shining through. "And I'm a *good* cowboy, not an outlaw."

"Of course you are." I ruffled his thick mop of hair.

"William, I'm wondering if you can help me answer a very important question," Nick said as he crouched down next to my cousin.

William pulled himself to his full height, suddenly serious. "I'll do my best, sir."

Nick drew him near, glanced around as though to see if anyone might overhear. "Do cowboys like taffy?"

My cousin nodded sagely. "It's their favorite, specially the maple kind."

"Then you'd better hustle, because they just brought out the taffy pull. I'd bet my violin they have maple too." Nick gestured to where my younger brothers crowded the metal contraption, and William took off without so much as a farewell, abandoning me to Nick.

Which I supposed had been Nick's goal all along.

Sit with him a few minutes, Alice. Prove to him that he means nothing to you.

"I trust you had a happy Christmas?" Nick magically produced a handful of tiny paper-wrapped packages from his pocket. "Molasses taffy, fresh from the kitchen. Your favorite, if I'm not mistaken."

Nick Longworth, I'd eat rocks if you thought they were my favorite. Merry hell, but I'd drink cyanide if you asked me to.

Yet I only arched an imperious eyebrow as I unwrapped a piece. "What else are you hiding in there?"

"Nothing much," he said. "Just a Saint Nicholas suit and eight magical reindeer."

"Best keep the suit hidden from my father." I caught a glance of my father taking the first pull at the taffy, flanked by my brothers Archie and Quentin. It didn't matter that he was president; sometimes my father really was just an overgrown boy. "He's been known to dress up a time or two for the children in Oyster Bay."

"He must enjoy that."

"Playing Saint Nicholas?"

"Doing whatever he wants." Nick followed my gaze as he unwrapped another piece of taffy and handed it me. "One of the benefits of being president, I suppose."

"Being president isn't all fun and games, you know."

"I know. I've thought about having that job myself one day."

I'd known Nick was ambitious, but this was the only time since our initial meeting at the Alibi that I'd heard mention of possible aspirations for the White House. "Really?" I popped the taffy in my mouth and then regretted it as I tried to speak around the sticky mass. "Are you sure you'd want all that responsibility?"

Nick leveled his gaze at me so it became impossible to swallow. "There are a good many things I want, Alice Roosevelt, and although I haven't yet decided whether becoming America's executive is on that list, there's one thing in particular I *know* I want." He stood and offered me his hand. "Walk with me?"

I remember thinking that walking with Nick in full view of my family surely wasn't the worst mistake I'd make in my life, or probably even that day. So I, being an idiot, agreed.

How was it possible that no one saw my flushed cheeks or heard the drumming of my heart? How was it that Nick managed to make me feel as I might implode with just a look and a few careless words in his deep voice, when I'd planned all along to pull the strings of *his* emotions?

We wended our way along the buffet table with its ice sculptures of Christmas trees and snowmen, Nick greeting various dignitaries and pages along the way. He scarcely glanced at me when he next spoke. "What if I were to tell you that I was intent on winning you, Alice Roosevelt?"

"I'm not a stuffed bear at a carnival ring toss," I managed to eke out, rapping him on the forearm with my gloved knuckles and feeling as if the entire embassy was listening to our every word. My brother Ted and his friends burst inside at that moment, laughing as they shook water from their hair and muddied jackets, and my father's great laugh boomed from across the way.

Nick took advantage of the distraction to pull me around a corner into an empty side hallway that led to the embassy offices. The sleet lashing against the paneled windows muffled the sound of the party we'd left behind. Nick turned to me, his expression more serious than if he were debating the entire House of Representatives. "Alice, you are the most charming girl I know and I'm utterly devoted to you, whether you wish it or not."

My plan had worked too well, for against my best intentions, I *did* wish for Nick's devotion. All other thoughts flew from my head even as I struggled to resist the siren's call of his words.

I *would* resist. I would *not* lose my heart.

"I don't wish it," I managed to say.

"Good thing it's not up to you," he murmured.

Then to my shock, he kissed me.

My first kiss.

The casual brush of Nick's lips against mine made my stomach leap strangely. His touch was soft and welcoming, and although I knew I shouldn't be in this dark corner with him, I found myself swaying into him as if this was the most natural thing in the world.

I'd later claim I'd never kissed a man before my wedding day, but I kissed Nick back, my fingers tracing the exposed skin at the nape of his neck. Before I knew what was happening, my entire body felt like a Fourth of July firecracker, exploding with joy.

But only for a moment.

I broke off the embrace, breathless with shock and my lips feeling like they were on fire. "That was . . . unexpected," I croaked.

I could see Nick's grin even in the dim light. "Was it?" His voice was taut with unspent laughter. "I'd have thought we were heading in that direction since that first night at the Alibi."

I scoffed. "Now you're being ridiculous."

But I wanted to believe him. Every instinct told me to throw caution to the storm outside and kiss him again and again and again, but something else—Mother's steady stream of admonitions against Nick or perhaps my own gun-shy nature when it came to love—made me step away even as Nick clasped my hand.

"I love you, Alice Roosevelt." His expression looked the same as it did when he played the violin, as if he were entirely entranced. "I can't get you out of my head, no matter how I try. Please tell me there's a chance you might feel the same way."

"I do," I said before I could think. "I mean, there is. A chance, perhaps . . ."

And perhaps, I mused as I struggled to regain my composure, agreeing to walk with Nick *was* the worst mistake I'd make today.

But Nick only pressed a finger to my stuttering, idiotic lips, and followed it with yet another kiss, his body so tantalizingly close that I wanted nothing more than to cling to him. Instead, I pushed him far enough away that I might string together the thoughts tumbling through my head.

"No," I said. "We can't do this. I *know* you, and I'd bet my roadster that you've said these exact same words to a dozen other girls in a dozen dark hallways."

A dark hallway that I desperately needed to exit before Mother and Father discovered me. Yet part of me wanted to stay right where I was for as long as I possibly could.

Why had I allowed myself to get all tangled up like this?

"You mistake my intentions entirely if you think me such a rake," Nick said. He tugged down the bottom of his vest, then straightened his tie. "I have long-term plans for us, my darling girl."

Long-term plans.

If I'd been a fainter, which I wasn't and never would be, I'd have swooned dead away right there. Instead, I planted my fists on my hips, trying to imagine how cousin Eleanor with her ossified morals would extricate herself from this situation. Of course, Eleo would never have found herself in a dark hallway with someone like Nick to begin with, but that was beside the point.

"Well," I said, clearing my throat. "I'll be interested to hear those plans one day. But for now I have other matters to attend to."

And with that, I sauntered off, refusing to look over my shoulder even as Nick's low rumble of laughter chased after me. "I adore you, Alice," he called, just loud enough to be heard over the storm outside. "And now you'll never be able to shake me."

I forced my gait into a measured pace and paused only to smooth my hair and draw a deep breath before returning to the banquet hall as if nothing were amiss.

I'd scarcely made it to the punch bowl when Auntie Bye shuffled up next to me. "Was that Nick Longworth I saw you sitting with a bit ago?" she asked.

A panicked glance at her placid expression told me she hadn't witnessed my disappearance with Nick. There was no ounce of connivance in Auntie Bye, and while I might have made an excuse to anyone else, I'd never lie to her. I nodded, feeling my cheeks flush.

"Good." She gave a sly smile. "I like him, even if your mother's none too keen."

"Mother's none too keen on anyone," I said, resisting the urge to roll my eyes. "If it were up to her, she'd probably have me marry someone like cousin Franklin."

But Franklin had proposed to Eleanor of all people, and they were to be married in a few months, with me serving as a taffeta-wrapped bridesmaid. Would I be the last in the family to marry? Or worse, become a dried-up old spinster?

Yet, according to Nick, all I had to do was say the magic words and I could have him. The only question that remained was whether I trusted him not to break my heart.

But Nick Longworth was a force to be reckoned with, a man who knew what he wanted. And now it seemed he wanted *me*.

Bye chuckled, oblivious to my turmoil. "Nick Longworth has the wit and wherewithal to face not only you, but your father and stepmother too. You'll need a man like that, you know."

I knew then that I could confide in Aunt Bye, that she alone could help me.

"He told me that he loves me," I admitted, my breath coming fast again. "But what if he changes his mind? What if everything falls apart?"

Auntie Bye grinned and nudged my shoulder. "Let him love you," she said. "And love him back, my blue-eyed girl. You deserve to be loved."

"Do I?" Sometimes I didn't think so, for I lacked Father's drive, Eleanor's goodness, and even Maggie's zest for life. No matter how I tried, I was just plain old Alice.

"Of course you do. Love is the greatest part of the human experience." Bye's gaze wandered to where her husband stood, and I flushed at the way her eyes softened. "I went a long time without the sort of love Nick is offering you, Alice. Seize it." She crushed me in a hug that threatened to squeeze tears from my eyes. "You deserve much love in your life, and don't you forget it."

With that, she left to join her son William, whose face was smeared with sticky brown taffy. I felt rather than saw Nick when he reentered the hall from our secret tryst, nonchalant as he effortlessly joined in conversation with several Southern senators. When his gaze flicked briefly in my direction, he winked so fast I thought I'd imagined it.

Nick's attention, kisses, and proclamations of love had once been all I'd dreamed of. Yet, despite Auntie Bye's advice, the very idea of letting myself fall in love with Nick made me want to bolt to the embassy's roof and smoke an entire case of Lucky Strikes to calm my nerves.

Perhaps Nick and I would fall madly in love, marry in a splendid ceremony on the White House lawn, and live happily ever after.

Or he might spurn me as he had Miriam Bloomer and I'd be left to pick up the pieces of my shattered heart. And something told me that I'd be forever broken if I ended up jilted by Nick Longworth.

I was given a brief respite from my romantic woes in the form of Father's inauguration. His landslide triumph was of such a magnitude it was hard to grasp—two and a half million popular votes, the largest margin in American history—which meant he no longer feared going down in history as an accidental president; thus, we'd celebrate in style.

Franklin and Eleanor joined the family procession this time, both of them so flush with love and happiness at their recent engagement that I wanted to retch. Dressed in her usual plain style, Eleanor might have passed for a common shopgirl, but I reinvented the part of America's princess in a soft white toile dress and a hat the size of a not-so-small wheel edged with black satin. Together we jostled our way behind Father to the presidential viewing stand, the very air buzzing with joyous anticipation. The crowd burst into wild cheers the moment he finished swearing the oath of office, and I waved to every friend I saw until my arm threatened to fall off, most especially when I spied Nick.

"You're making a spectacle of yourself," my father growled to me while he nodded and smiled at the writhing mass of people. "Sit down and cease waving."

"Well, you do it," I said, still waving. I couldn't help myself, for I'd kept Nick at a distance since Christmas, but seeing him now opened up the floodgate of emotions I'd done my best to plug up. Thank goodness Father didn't know about kisses in a dark embassy hallway, or he'd have done more than growl at me. "Why shouldn't I?"

Father gave me a warning glare that told me I'd gone too far. "Because this is *my* inauguration."

I sat down in a crush of toile and disappointment.

Well, with a little luck I might one day sit in this same stand as First Lady. Then I can wave and carry on however I deem fit.

I realized with a start that I was already envisioning a future with Nick at my side. Somehow I suspected then that my heart was going to win this argument, no matter how good a fight my mind gave.

Eleanor leaned in from her place behind me as Father began a rousing speech about how much had been given to America and thus how much would be expected of us. "America loves Uncle Ted," she whispered, beaming. "You're so lucky, Alice. Do you know how often I've wished he was my father too?"

"Really? Why?"

She shrugged. "Mother died from the diphtheria when I was young, and Father . . ."

She didn't have to finish that sentence, for it was a family secret that Eleanor's alcoholic father had jumped from a sanitarium window and snapped his neck, leaving behind three small children.

Cousin Eleanor is jealous . . . of me. I hardly knew what to say, having spent my entire life being compared to Eleanor and always coming up far short.

For the briefest of moments, I forgot all of my animosity and angst toward my father as he grinned his oft-caricatured grin at the roaring crowd and shook his fist over his head. America couldn't help but love him, and neither could Eleanor, nor I.

"It's not easy having such a famous father," I said to Eleanor, swallowing around the sudden lump in my throat.

"No." She smiled benevolently as the inaugural parade kicked off with a regiment of saluting Rough Riders. "But Uncle Ted once told me to never envy anyone who has led an easy life, that nothing in the world is worth having if it doesn't mean effort, pain, or difficulty."

"That sounds exactly like something Father would say, probably after riding thirty miles on horseback in the middle of an asthma attack or storming a hail of bullets with his Rough Riders during the Spanish-American War." My laughter mingled with Eleanor's, but still, I felt a bitter pang of envy to hear that he was sharing such life lessons with Eleanor instead of with me.

That little twinge of envy over Father's advice to Eleanor was nothing compared to the raging green hydra of jealousy I felt two weeks later toward my angelic cousin.

"Your mother and I want to give Eleanor everything we plan to give you when you marry." Father had scarcely looked up from his letter to the emperor of Japan when I confronted him over rumors that he'd offered to host their wedding at the White House. "But your cousin claims she wants a simple ceremony."

Of course she had, for far be it from Saint Eleanor to cause anyone a single ounce of trouble.

I'd breathed a tremendous sigh of relief to realize she wasn't going to commandeer the White House, that is until Eleanor arranged the date and time of her wedding to coincide with Father's appearance at the New York Saint Patrick's Day parade so he might walk her down the aisle.

I was older than Eleanor and the president's daughter, yet she'd managed to marry before me while making my father so proud that I thought his buttons might burst off his jacket.

Still, I put on a brave face while I held her foul-smelling lily bouquet after the ceremony. "You look like a proper princess in all this Belgium lace and Tiffany's pearls," I gushed. "And you were so thoughtful, asking me to be a bridesmaid."

It took every shred of equanimity I possessed not to scream when Father pumped Franklin's hand and kissed Eleanor on the cheek, beaming as if *he* were her proud papa.

I could well imagine my altruistic Hyde Park cousins happily spending their honeymoon touring filthy New York tenements with plans to alleviate the plight of America's destitute immigrants, further earning my father's accolades.

I wasn't happy, yet I suspected more and more that I—or Nick, rather—held the key to my own happiness.

Except Nick was linked with some new debutante named Beatrice in the society columns a few weeks after Eleanor's wedding, along with speculation that their engagement would soon be announced. It was my sister Ethel who brought me the paper, along with a disconcerting question. "But last week the papers said Nick was *your* beau, Sissy. What did you do?"

I fled to my refuge at Auntie Bye's, where I was in the backyard smashing Father's singlestick into an unfortunate oak tree when I recognized Nick's signature knock at the front door, three hard raps followed by three staccato taps. I almost snarled aloud to hear Bye offer him tea and the two of them sit down to discuss Father's plans to establish a national forest service, all while I remained hidden outside with my teeth chattering against the cold.

It was Bye who came for me, with a peace offering of piping hot Earl Grey and a plate of paper-thin crusty bread she'd made herself that afternoon. "Nick has asked to take you driving. I said it was your choice—"

"I don't want to see him." I gulped down the tea, wondering if I'd ever feel my fingers again. "Ever."

She sighed. "You haven't heard his side of the story, my most stubborn of girls. Newspapermen have been known to bend the truth now and then. There may be a perfectly reasonable explanation for why Nick's been seen about town with that other chit."

"Probably because Nick Longworth is one of the devil's minions, sent to ruin my life."

"Alice . . ." Her voice held a hint of warning. "Don't throw away your chance at happiness."

Auntie Bye had never asked anything of me, had instead given me much by raising me after my mother's death. Yet I could see she was asking this of me now.

So it was that I stepped into Nick's carriage even as winter's final snowflakes floated down from a darkening sky, although I refused to take the hand he offered to help me up. "I don't know why I'm even speaking to you." I sank my hands deeper into a mink muff as I took my carriage seat, the better to keep from slapping him. I knew I should break it off with him, yet I couldn't find the courage to speak the words.

He only wrapped the reins around his hands with a jaunty smile. "Because I'm utterly charming and you can't help yourself?"

"Ha," I said without humor. "You're a cad and the entire capital knows it."

"A cad passionately in love with you."

The way he looked at me, with that mesmerizing stare that made me feel like the only girl on earth, I found I wanted to believe him so badly that I could taste it. But I refused to give in so easily.

"In love with me and every other passably handsome woman within a fifty-mile radius, maybe more," I said. "To think that I actually let you kiss me, only to read about you in the papers this morning . . ."

"You mean Beatrice?"

I curled my muff-hidden hands into fists. "First Miriam, then Cissy, Maggie, and me, and now Beatrice." And those were just the ones I knew about. I thought back to all the parties and balls, all the times I'd seen Nick surrounded by a gaggle of women. It was an alarming pattern.

"My darling girl." He flicked the reins and eased the mare to a patient trot that matched his tone. "Don't be put out by the mention of dull old Beatrice. She's the daughter of my mother's friend."

"So?"

"So I love you and only you."

"I don't believe you."

"You don't believe what?" He tugged the reins and we stopped so fast my teeth jarred. "That I'm not involved with Beatrice or that I love you?"

"Both."

"Don't be a child, Alice."

It was a reminder that Nick was fourteen years my senior, and more experienced than me in every definition of the word. I stood so fast I almost toppled out of the carriage. "Don't be an ass!"

Nick stared at me, then burst out in laughter as he tugged me back into my seat. "By god, but you're *jealous*! All this time I feared you were indifferent toward me—"

"Indifferent?" The word came out strident. "Because indifferent girls let you kiss them in dark hallways?"

Nick leaned forward, the reins held loosely in his gloved hands. "Oh, I know you enjoyed the kiss, but how many times have I told you I love you? And how many times have you answered back?"

None.

Because I wasn't sure what I felt, or if I wanted to give name to the emotions that had kept me up so many sleepless nights since Christmas. Sitting there in the cold, our breath curling around us while the snow fell in lazy spirals, I knew I'd never felt like this about anyone else before. Surely that meant this was love?

So I took a steadying inhale to gather my courage and speak the words that terrified me.

"I do love you, Nick." Yet I wasn't brave enough to leave the words hanging alone in the air. "But usually I want to throttle you with equal measure."

He laughed again, then caressed my cheek. "That's how you know it's real, my darling girl."

I ached to lean into that hand, to feel his lips on mine. But he wasn't off the hook yet.

"I'm still livid, you know," I said. "You might have told me about Beatrice so I didn't hear about you and her from the papers."

"I apologize for that." He bumped my shoulder with his. "It's just you for me, Alice. I'll swear on whatever you want me to, the Bible, my mother's grave—"

"Your mother's still alive."

"My great-grandmother's grave then. You're the only girl for me."

"I'd better be," I said. "Or you'll live to regret it."

And so it went, our tempestuous courtship.

We'd kiss, argue about trivialities—or some other girl he'd been seen with—and then make up with declarations that we were wrapped up in love for each other, only to rinse and repeat the whole blasted cycle a few weeks later.

And I allowed him such liberties that we might as well have been engaged—that soon we'd *need* to be engaged—but nothing formal was set, no ring offered or warning that he planned to speak to my father, so that I became in turn both incensed and choked with doubt.

What *had* I gotten myself into?

I checked the headlines compulsively every morning, worried that I should quit it all as the society columns speculated over my attachment to Nick. Sooner or later, the papers—and my father—were bound to catch wind of my inappropriate conduct, and that would be the end of me. Yet, a day without Nick was as drab as a winter rainstorm while even a fight with him brought the world into vibrant clarity. This was no schoolgirl crush like the one I'd had for Charly.

This was something more real. And far more dangerous.

And then came the day that Father called me into his office.

My knees wobbled like orange marmalade as I knocked on the door of the Executive Office, dreading the drubbing—or worse—I was about to receive.

Guttersnipe. Charlatan. Whore.

All these and more did I deserve. Worse still was the knowledge that I'd disappointed my father. Truly, there was no hope for me.

"Enter," came my father's voice. I hung my head, knowing exactly how convicts felt as they mounted the scaffold for their own hanging.

"Sissy." He rose and gestured for me to sit in the armchair across from the presidential desk, an impressive piece of woodworking that looked as if it had been carved wholesale from an ancient redwood. Our massive Saint Bernard, Rollo, lay curled next to it, but he only offered me a somber nod before replacing his head on his paws. A sort of salute for the doomed, I supposed. "I'm so glad you're here."

I startled at that. "You are?"

"Yes. In fact, I have a little request to make of you. Well, not so little, really."

I shook my head as I lowered myself tentatively into the armchair. "I don't understand. Does this mean I'm not in trouble?"

Father actually looked pained at that. "No, Sissy. In fact, I'm hoping you'll do me a favor. I want you to act as goodwill ambassador and accompany a delegation to the Far East with my secretary of war. Secretary Taft was at your debut, if you recall."

"What?" I was really having a hard time keeping up with all this.

"Just listen a few moments before you refuse. The delegation's main purpose is for Taft to pave the way during backdoor meetings for me to negotiate a treaty between the Japanese and Russians to end the ongoing Russo-Japanese War." I could tell Father was just warming up, as if I were a high-ranking senator or some illustrious diplomat he had to convince. "I can't tip my hand that I favor the Japanese—I tell you that czar is a preposterous little creature—which means that I can't travel there myself. I need to send someone who will distract the press from all the political machinations Taft will be organizing."

"And that someone . . ."

". . . is you. You'll be my eyes and ears in the East, Sissy," he said, and I immediately imagined myself incognito, hiding behind oriental screens to eavesdrop on state secrets. "You'll be the public face of the tour while Taft is seeing to the political side of things. *If* you're interested, that is."

From the look of hope on his face, I could see he actually believed there was some chance I might refuse. I shattered those worries when I leaped to my feet, stooping to drop a kiss on Rollo's furry head. "Of course I'm interested!" I rocked on my heels with excitement and just barely kept from squealing with joy. "You can count on me."

"Then I'll have an aide send a copy of the itinerary up to your room." Beaming, Father planted a hand on each of my shoulders, so that for a moment I thought he might kiss *my* forehead. Instead, he only gave my shoulders an awkward pat. "This will be a trip you'll never forget, Mousiekins."

He was right, for as soon as I received the itinerary, I realized this would be a trip like no other, departing from California for months spent touring the exotic locales of Hawaii, Japan, and China. I hoped to gather my thoughts while I was away, to sort out my muddled feelings for Nick and restore my spirits, which felt like someone had trampled them with my roadster. After all, Nick had professed his love, but not yet proposed. Who knew if a self-proclaimed bachelor like himself even would? With the way we fought—and with the way pretty young women flocked to him—I wasn't sure I should accept even if he did. These months apart would be a test of Nick's love, to see if his declarations held any weight or if I was simply a girl *du jour* for him.

All my well-laid plans imploded with the force of a Hotchkiss cannon when Rose delivered a stack of books I'd requested on the Far East along with the day's newspapers. I was almost done deciding which hats I'd take on the trip: definitely the Parisian plush tricorn edged with grosgrain ribbon and ostrich feathers, but not the beaver fur boater. It was a headline in the *Cincinnati Enquirer* that caught my eye as I tossed aside the beaver fur.

ALICE IN WONDERLAND: How First Maiden in the Land Will Travel to the Orient.

The brief article reported that Father would pay my expenses and pondered whether I'd make a speech to the Chinese empress. Yet it was the last line that made me groan aloud . . .

Representative Longworth to go along—Tropical Romance Anticipated.

"So much for solace and self-reflection," I muttered as I crumpled the paper and tossed it at the fur boater, hard. I wondered if perhaps some part of Father had arranged this to settle the merry-go-round of speculation about which man I'd finally end up marrying.

This trip would either make or break my relationship with Nick. I, for one, was terrified that I wasn't strong enough to withstand the coming hurricane.

Buck up, Alice. Remember, you are *a hurricane.*

I would have to be.

Chapter 7

JULY 1905

"Alice Roosevelt, you are the ugliest princess the world has ever seen," I muttered to my reflection in the restroom mirror of the train station, pinching my cheeks in vain to persuade some color to my wasted complexion. I'd suffered from nerves and indigestion in the weeks leading up to the departure for the Far East, so now my newly ordered dresses all hung loose, and my cheeks looked positively sunken. Worse was the constant toothache and sudden outbreak of eczema on my hands. Yet the cheering crowd on the platform outside didn't care about my maladies, so I yanked on white kid gloves to cover the evidence of my distress.

Come what may, it was time to join Secretary Taft and hop a rattler for Chicago, and from there to California, Hawaii, and the Orient.

I was blinded by impertinent flashlamps and deafened by the cheering crowd, but my smiles felt wooden as I walked alongside Taft and his wife. My family had left for Oyster Bay in late June and scarcely bothered to wave good-bye to me. Between Mother and Father, I received a peck on the cheek and a handshake, as if I were to be gone six days instead of six months. This station of waving strangers seemed to care about me more than my own parents.

So while newspapermen and even the conductor offered me a pleasant journey, the platform may as well have been empty.

Save one man.

Nick gave me a jaunty wink and tipped his hat as he boarded so that I had to swallow hard against the flutter of happiness that jigged up my throat.

The trip started off so well . . .

"You're quite the shot, Alice," Taft said as he chortled with laughter somewhere outside Chicago. It was the Fourth of July and my fingers still smelled of the celebratory firecrackers we'd set off from the train's rear platform. Then the party had started to lag, so I'd hauled out my Colt .45 for an impromptu bout of target practice.

"I'll bet you can't hit five in a row," Nick said, leaning so close my very skin tingled at the scent of his spicy aftershave. Didn't he know it was folly to rattle a sharpshooter, unless you wanted a hole in your foot?

I pretended to check the barrel, nonplussed. "What's the wager?"

He leaned down to whisper in my ear, onlookers be damned. "Five kisses."

"Deal."

My hand shook with nerves, but I adjusted my stance and took aim at the glass switches atop the electric poles. I exhaled and fired off not five but six shots.

And hit every single one.

Taft—whom I'd taken to calling Uncle Will—whooped his approval even as I stood on tiptoe to whisper to Nick. "Make that six kisses. I'll collect after dinner." To which Nick only gave a devilish smile while the senators and their wives frowned their censure. Fortunately, I knew I'd found an ally in my father's friend. Uncle Will clapped a hand against his massive thigh. "I'd wager good money it was your father who taught you to shoot, wasn't it?"

I nodded, flush with pride. "To shoot and hike and swim. I daresay I could even skin a bear if I set my mind to it."

He howled with pleasure. "Let's hope it doesn't come to that, shall we?"

Days later, when we finally reached California, crowds in San Francisco rubbernecked to see me drive down the broad cobblestone avenues as if I were the president instead of merely his daughter. I overheard sour-faced Nellie Taft mutter to her husband from the back of the trolley, "Why, it seems Alice *is* the party."

To which I turned and smiled sweetly. "Yes, in fact," I said, twirling my parasol, "I am."

"You know, Alice," Taft said under his breath while his wife's glare bored holes in my back, "you may want to consider hosting regular teas for the ladies on the junket."

"Really?" I whispered. "Why?"

"Think like a politician, my dear."

"Because I never know when I'll need their good opinion and support?"

"Exactly."

Listening to the congressional dames flap their jaws over their scandal water might have been a necessary evil, but I nearly fell asleep in my cinnamon scones the next day at the Palace Hotel as they worried about the depravations we'd experience in the East.

"I hear they eat insects," one said, her eyes practically rolling back in their sockets. "Raw!"

"Now *that* would be uncivilized," I said ruefully as I set down my cup. "Fortunately, I have it on good authority that they cook them first. I can't wait to try the grasshoppers—I hear they're delectable with a little salt and lemon juice."

At which point I excused myself and burst into the hall in a torrent of repressed giggles.

Only Nick saved me from death by sheer boredom.

"Care to slip your chaperone and take a spree into Chinatown tonight?" he asked on our final evening in San Francisco. We were standing too close together on the Palace Hotel's balcony overlooking its grand entrance foyer and famed glass ceiling. Since leaving Washington we'd been surrounded by the others, and I found myself yearning for a single hour alone in his company.

I arched an eyebrow at him. "And just what would we do in Chinatown?"

He shrugged, but his eyes twinkled with mischief. "Something sinful. Perhaps visit a gambling hall. Or an opium den."

"You are an impropriety waiting to happen, Nick Longworth." I cleared my throat, realizing that I should spend the evening learning a new knitting technique from Nellie Taft, but also knowing that the innermost circle of hell would freeze over before that happened. "In fact, that brings to mind something I read once, by Molière, I think."

I'd never received even a day of formal education, but I had a simian ability to catch on, so I'd been tutored at home and educated by reading and rereading every book in Father's extensive library. Nick was a Harvard graduate—just like Father—and extremely well read, but he frowned in puzzlement. "And what did Molière have to say on the subject of sins?"

"That it's the *public* scandal that offends; to sin in secret is no sin at all."

Nick gave me a little bow as my gray-haired chaperone, Mrs. Newlands, approached. "Make no mistake, Alice Roosevelt," Nick murmured. "I have grand aspirations to commit many public scandals with you. But tonight, if you prefer, we shall sin in secret, and thus, be absolved of our crimes."

I'd later promise my father that I never stepped foot in Chinatown or frequented its debauched gambling halls or opium dens (even though I knew from studying the schematics that our ship, the *Manchuria*, had both belowdecks), but nothing would have stopped me from hoodwinking Mrs. Newlands that night so I might see Little Shanghai. And I didn't lie, for Nick and I only skirted its borders.

I forced myself not to gape at the Chinamen with their loose trousers and long braids, some pulling rickshaws and others yoked to giant baskets of dirty laundry about their shoulders. A parade of four little boys trouped past walls plastered with yellowing Chinese papers, each child topped with a white cap and holding each other's braids like some sort of miniature human train. A mound of stained blankets in a doorway shifted when we exited the trolley car, revealing a man with the face of a corpse and skin the color of a rat, a mangy patchwork cat in one arm and a cold opium pipe in the other. I instinctively reached for my purse; I'd planned to bring my revolver tonight, but Nick had made me leave both behind, citing pickpockets.

The corpse mumbled something, his clawed hand reaching out for the promise of opium, and I breathed a sigh of relief when he fell back after realizing there was none to be had.

I'd thought myself a woman of the world with my travels to Boston and New Orleans, but Chinatown might have been on the far side of the moon, and I found myself wondering for the first time what the Far East would truly be like, whether the dowager empress of China walked on her hands or Emperor Meiji of Japan ate with his feet. I wasn't afraid of those things like the disapproving old cats at my tea parties who whispered of yellow celestials eating cockroaches and shook in their shoes at the thought of seeing anything *different* over the rims of their teacups. I ached to see the sights of a strange new world, even if they made my stomach clench with fear or horror. I *burned* to see more than the White House lawn over a flowered china teacup.

Right now I thrilled with liquid excitement to smell woks of sizzling chicken (or at least what I assumed to be chicken but might have been bow-wow mutton) from rickety street carts set up beneath red paper lanterns. Nick pulled me to a chow-chow, a hole in the wall marked with a yellow cloth triangle that faced an unsavory alley. Laughing, I struggled with a pair of wooden chopsticks, finally using my fingers to eat the chop suey and wiping the sauce from my lips with the back of my hand.

"Not bad," I said as I sucked down the last of the rice.

"You have a bit of egg there," Nick said and used his thumb to brush the corner of my lip. I pulled him to me and kissed him then, feeling suddenly, and gloriously, alive. If this could be my life, travel-

ing the globe and experiencing the world, I'd seize Nick Longworth
with both hands and never let go.

We were still on the outskirts of Little Shanghai when a woman who
could only have been a prostitute waggled her grime-streaked fingers
at Nick through the thin bars of what appeared to be a cage facing another alleyway. I'd expected Chinatown's street women to be redolent
in cheap sandalwood and dressed in garish silks, but this woman was
a pitiful specimen. It only took only a moment for her to realize that
Nick wasn't interested before she called out to a Chinaman who quickly
disappeared into her den as my cheeks flushed a violent crimson.

I'd thought to see the foreignness of Little Shanghai, but perhaps
there were some details I might have lived without.

"We should be getting back," Nick said as if reading my mind.
"Before it gets dark and the highbinders come out to play."

"Highbinders?"

"The Chinese mobs," Nick said. "They pimp out these unfortunate women, arrange hits on rivals, and rule the black market here.
I'd hate to have to explain to your father how I lost you to them."

"He might just thank you for taking me off his hands," I said, only
half in jest.

"I plan to do exactly that one day," Nick said, his arm tight around
my waist.

My skin prickled with tiny needles as I waited for the question that
would set me free from both this terrifying game of hearts and my
father's dominion. But Nick only pointed out the famed Poodle Dog
Restaurant with a laugh, and the moment dissipated in a fog of opium
smoke.

And thus, the game of hearts continued even as America disappeared behind us and we steamed toward the Far East.

My nerves about being in confined quarters with Nick eased somewhat after Chinatown—it helped that there were no other pretty
young women touring with us—and we settled into a comfortable

routine even as I reached an important decision. I loved Nick, that much was apparent, and couldn't imagine a life without him any more than I could imagine cutting off one of my own limbs. So I'd throw my lot in with him and hope for the best, if he'd have me.

Which still remained to be seen.

My mangled hands healed of their eczema and I began to eat again, filling out the plethora of white linen skirts that had been ordered for this trip. Still, I was aware of everyone's eyes on Nick and me while we played cards and took Spanish lessons in preparation for our time in the Philippines.

It took five long days of salty sea air and schools of flying fish to reach Honolulu. Once there, I nearly suffocated beneath the weight of the fragrant flower leis that the territorial governor in his wool suit and the natives in their grass skirts draped from my chin to my knees. I laughed uproariously when my outrigger canoe dumped me into the Pacific Ocean and managed to attempt both surf-riding (unsuccessfully) and dancing the hula (somewhat successfully). Afterward, Nick slung an arm around my shoulders, and the rest of the junket gathered around a bonfire on the beach to sing a quaint little ditty commemorating my dancing prowess . . .

Alice Roosevelt, she came to Honolulu
And she saw the Hula Hula Hula Hai . . .

Nick's voice was the loudest, his grin the brightest.

And I think before she reached the Filipinos,
She could dance the Hula Hula Hula Hai.

The next day, wearing only my itchy mohair bathing dress with its high neck and matching long black stockings, I missed our departure time and was almost left behind with Nick and my chaperones. We had to scrounge a disreputable-looking skiff to float us all out to the *Manchuria*.

"We could stay here forever, you know," Nick said before we clambered aboard, the Newlandses oblivious to our furtive whispers. "It wouldn't be so bad to be marooned forever on Hawaii."

I touched his nose with an irreverent laugh. "True, but it might be difficult for you to debate the latest tariffs from a stray hut on the beach. Especially if you took to wearing one of those grass skirts."

"Really?" He rubbed his chin. "I think I'd look rather dapper in a grass skirt."

I laughed, for he was probably right. To my eyes, Nick would always look the part of a dashing rounder.

Thinking back, perhaps things would have been better if Nick and I had stayed under the carefree Hawaiian sun, surrounded by the crash of ocean waves and the happy notes of ukuleles. But instead we steamed on toward Japan.

Banzai, banzai, banzai!

The Tokyo crowds quickly distracted me from my concerns over Nick, the Japanese people screaming my name and waving tiny American flags with their red and white stripes and forty-five stars. The women in their stunning silk kimonos bowed to me over and over until I worried they'd be dizzy.

"So, Miss Roosevelt," Taft shouted over the melee, "what do you think of Japan so far?"

I gripped his arm, rocking up and down on my toes to better see the crowd. "I love it!"

Most of all, I loved the attention. I carried myself straighter and spoke with more confidence, knowing that this was my chance to shine. Now I understood exactly how Father felt when a crowd went wild with rapturous applause for him, for I felt powerful enough to do anything with the masses chanting my name.

And that was just the beginning.

The next six days were a whirlwind of sumo matches, geisha dancing, fencing bouts, and jujitsu, most of which I watched while seated smack-dab next to Nick. My reality had shifted ever so slightly—with so many wonderful distractions, he was no longer the sole center of my world, yet there was no one else I'd rather have had at my side. Together we toured the Teahouse of a Hundred Steps—perched at the top of a flight of 102 steps, I counted—while admiring the view of Mount Fuji. And of course, we met the emperor, bowing to him three times and then joining his table at a luncheon in our honor. Although Taft had already held several secret meetings with the emperor, this was my first time in his royal presence, and I felt more than a little smug to be seated at his right hand. Over the course of the meal, I regaled him with stories of my father—the same father who would be negotiating the peace treaty between Japan and Russia after their recent hostilities.

"Father was a sickly child, so much that some days he could scarcely breathe from his asthma," I said to the interpreter as we sipped cups of green tea and smoked little pipes of Japanese tobacco. "In fact, the physicians told my grandfather not to expect him to survive his childhood."

The emperor leaned forward and I continued, basking in the attention. "But my father embraced a strenuous lifestyle, hiking, swimming, and boxing until he conquered his shortcomings. Now he could probably beat most Thoroughbreds in a footrace if he had to."

I sipped my tea and waited for the interpreter to finish, then reveled in the emperor's hearty laugh. He said something and the interpreter inclined his head toward me. "The emperor says that Mr. Roosevelt sounds like a most exceptional man, and he is pleased to make the acquaintance of his most impressive daughter."

How I wished my father were next to me to hear the praise! Instead I settled for Nick's wink from across the table and the warm flush of pleasure that stayed with me throughout the luncheon. Later, I strolled with Nick through the emperor's private garden, its cherry trees and wasabi plants never before seen by foreigners.

"Traveling suits you," he said, using the tip of his gold-tipped walking stick to poke a wasabi plant. Its green leaves looked deceptively like a sort of cabbage, but after tasting a spoonful at lunch, my still-burning tongue could attest to the fact that it was most certainly *not* cabbage.

"Traveling does suit me," I said with a mischievous grin. "As does my present company."

Nick didn't reply, only smiled distractedly. "This trip has made me realize how much I enjoy seeing the world. I believe I might like to be an ambassador one day."

"No more talk of being president? Or a congressman in a grass skirt?"

Nick scrubbed a hand over his face. "Maybe I'll settle for being Speaker of the House instead. With you at my side, anything is possible."

With you at my side.

It was a whisper of a promise, but I wanted more than that. I *needed* more than that. And at the same time, the cast-off little girl inside me worried whether my name and presidential father was the reason that Nick kept me so close.

I wrote constantly to Father, wishing I could confide my fears to him, but instead informing him in my letter from Tokyo that there would have been nothing left of him had he traveled with the delegation. I described the Japanese crowds cheering themselves hoarse and detailed the list of gifts I'd received, the fans and lacquered boxes, the gold cloth bordered with chrysanthemums, and even a fine embroidered screen, so many gifts that the delegation had started calling me Alice in Plunderland. I was filled with greedy delight at getting them, a frankly unashamed pig. Father responded with a picture letter on official White House stationery that made Nick laugh aloud.

"I didn't realize the president of the United States was also an artist," Nick said with a chuckle from the deck of the *Manchuria*, handing the paper back to me. For Father had sketched me my own cartouche with some sort of ax, an image of me smoking, and a strange-looking horse.

"One of his many talents. He's sent all of us children picture letters since we were little."

The letter somewhat healed my bruised ego over how my parents and I had parted, saying that I was remembered at home. "'*Her Excellencissima of the Middle West and Any Other Old Place,*'" I repeated Father's title for me, the briny breeze toying with my hair and the sun warm on my back. "I rather like the ring of that."

Nick shook a finger at me before reclining in his lounge chair and pulling his straw boater over his face. "Don't go getting any ideas, Alice Roosevelt."

I curled up on my own chair, intent on reading the letter at least ten more times. On the page Father and I could finally charm each other without danger of annoying the other with our shared over-exuberance. It seemed I'd finally made him proud, even if I'd had to travel to the opposite end of the world to do it.

How I wished the trip would go on forever!

After the excitement of Japan there was little to do back on board the *Manchuria* as we steamed toward Manila, the endless stretch of blue sky and bluer water making me want to climb the walls from boredom. The very air burned like a pepper thrown into a bonfire one morning as I sweltered in a high-necked, long-sleeved shirtwaist, trapped by the small scrap of shade provided by my parasol. Nick and my father's old friend Bourke Cockran sat with several other congressmen in the merciful shade around the canvas bathing pool, drinking chilled fruit juice while discussing Father's upcoming negotiations with Russia and Japan.

In direct violation of Mother's maxims of how a lady should comport herself on a fine summer day, I could already feel sweat dripping down the backs of my legs, which made it difficult to look cool and composed. Mrs. Newlands, my chaperone, was nowhere to be seen.

I snapped shut my parasol and gave my hat the heave-ho, then began unlacing my white boots.

"Gentlemen," I said, loud enough so everyone on deck might hear, "if you'll take a plunge into the swimming pool dressed as you are, I promise an encore."

Nick, dapper as always as he lounged in his white suit and hat, watched as I mounted the stairs. His eyes flicked to the other men, every one of them watching avidly to see what would happen. I thought Nick would join me, but he only leaned forward. Was he daring me?

"Cowards." I addressed all of them with my wicked grin, but in truth I spoke only to Nick as I tossed him my watch. "If you won't, I will."

Before any of them could protest, I jumped in fully dressed and feetfirst with a delicious splash of cool water and emerged with a merry laugh as I shoved my bedraggled hair from my eyes. I recalled for a moment the daily summer swims at Sagamore Hill, Father treading water like a spectacled sea monster while calling for me to dive until, trembling with fear, I splashed into the water with all the grace of a drowning duckling. The family used to claim that my tears after a diving lesson made a perceptible rise in the tide.

I hated to dive, but I could swim perfectly well.

Bourke Cockran and Nick now stood at the top of the steps as I back-floated toward them. "Don't you take a dare?" I taunted.

I was sure that Nick would take the plunge, but it was rusty-guts old Bourke who cannonballed in after me.

I shrieked with waterlogged laughter as Bourke's wave splashed me full in the face, yet I was disappointed it wasn't Nick who did the backstroke next to me rather than the man who'd once retrieved my first loose tooth from the sponge cake I'd lost it in. In fact, Nick stood frowning as I floated in the pool.

It's the public scandal that offends; to sin in secret is no sin at all.

Nick had proposed to two other girls, perhaps making him gun-shy of any further public scandals. Was that why he hadn't proposed, why he was striding away from me and back to his deck chair? Was I the sort of girl to have a lark with, but not the sort to marry?

Bourke's laugh demanded my attention as he shook water from his graying hair. "Alice, you could make a stuffed bird laugh," he said in his delightful Irish brogue. "I think you must give even your father a run for his money."

I forced a grin wider than Father's. "Every day."

We floated and splashed about until Bourke offered me a gallant hand so we could clamber out of the pool. To my chagrin, I discovered then that a wet linen dress is indeed different from a bathing suit, namely in that it weighs more than a suit of armor when drenched.

Bourke handed me off to Nick, who waited with a towel and looked for the first time as if he didn't know what to do with me. I gave a dripping curtsy to the politicians, letting my disheveled hair hide my flush.

"Was that really necessary?" Nick whispered so only I could hear as he led me away. He looked far from pleased, whether at my shenanigans or from my swimming with another man, I couldn't tell. What had been an amusing escapade now seemed tawdry, and I hated him for it.

"Yes," I answered with a glare. "And it was a fizzing good time too."

I shook him off, my embarrassed flush now an angry burn. Nellie Taft sniffed as I passed, one gloved hand on her husband's arm and an ugly sheen of sweat dampening her upper lip. "Alice, I swear you're just a wild animal put into good clothes. Don't you ever consider your poor mother before you commit such terrible scandals?"

"Of course, Mrs. Taft." I forced my cheekiest grin. "After all, it only would have been a scandal if I'd jumped in naked."

That left her sputtering, and sent me into a fresh gale of contrived laughter as I stomped away, leaving a trail of wet footsteps in my wake.

A few nights later, I opened our welcome ball in the Philippines. I was finally comfortable despite the heat in a breezy *baro't saya*, the national Filipino costume redolent with Spanish lace and colorful embroidery that the native women had taken three months to stitch for me. The Russian rear admiral who claimed my first waltz snapped his heels the moment the violins ended and marched toward Taft, ostensibly to discuss the matter of his detained ships floating in Manila's harbor after Russia's recent defeat at the hands of the Japanese. I saluted Taft, having done my patriotic duty for the evening, and happily offered the rest of my dances to Nick. We didn't discuss the pool incident, but Nick seemed to have forgiven me and was willing to break this particular rule of propriety.

Hang propriety.

"This place really does seem like Wonderland sometimes," Nick said as we floated effortlessly across the floor. The Filipino orchestra wasn't keen on ragtime, but belted out every waltz under both the sun and the moon on their bamboo violins and nose flutes. For once I didn't mind the staid music as it allowed Nick to be so near that I might have rested my head against his shoulder. In his arms that night I felt happy and loved, if not entirely secure.

"I'd stay here forever if I could," I murmured.

"Would you?" he asked. "I thought Alice eventually wearied of Wonderland."

"Not with all the splendid gifts and half the world falling at her feet. A girl can get used to that."

It didn't seem fair that men like my father and Nick basked in adulation all the time, while girls were supposed to be modest and retiring. Why shouldn't I love the attention? After all, I *was* my father's daughter.

Nick's hand guided me still closer, yet I didn't care that I could feel the stares of Nellie Taft and her ilk hot on my back. "We should return one day when we're old and gray to see how things have changed," Nick said. "I'd bet they'd still chant your name. Maybe mine, too, if I play my cards right."

And there it was: a whisper of a hint of an understanding.

We weren't married—at least not yet—but if we had been, the evening of the Filipino ball might have been the last night of our honeymoon.

From Manila we headed out to the more remote islands of the Philippines, where a group of the tougher travelers and I went ashore at the island of Sulu, tossed by swells so turbulent that even my steel-lined stomach lurched. At the end of the pier we were greeted by the Moro chieftains in their best costumes of vivid silk shirts and beaded jackets. The Muslim sultan of Sulu was a wry, savage-looking man, scarcely four feet tall, with a feral sort of bolo knife tucked into his striped silk sash.

"May I see it?" I gestured to the weapon after we were properly introduced. My fingers itched to touch the blade, for it reminded me of the one Maggie Cassini had once worn. "Your knife?"

"Of course, Miss Roose-e-velt." Each word a blend of Filipino accent and the British English he must have learned to deal with the merchants who plied his shores. The sultan presented the blade with a flourish to rival Barnum & Bailey's impresario, and studied my every move while I tested the heft of the blade. After that, he followed closer than my own shadow.

At the conclusion of the tour, he cleared his throat as he snapped the thread that fastened a huge pearl ring to his sash. "Miss Roos-e-velt," he said in halting English. "My people wish you to remain with us. It is with great honor that I make you my wife."

After all these years of the *Times* and other papers printing headlines about my fake engagements, I finally received my first *bona fide* proposal, but from absolutely the wrong man. I wanted to laugh, but a glance at Nick's stony face killed the impulse. "I am honored," I said to the sultan, with a polite little bow. "But I believe you're already married."

The man's smile revealed crooked white teeth with a missing back tooth. "I have been blessed with six wives already, but you, Miss Roos-e-velt, would be my sultana, my final—and most beautiful— wife."

"I'm afraid I must decline the kind invitation," I said. "You see, I have my heart set on marrying an American."

"Oh?" He rubbed his hands together; apparently sultans weren't immune to a good dose of gossip. "So you are already promised to another?"

"Indeed I am."

I wanted to take the words back the instant they were out of my mouth. All eyes swiveled toward Nick, who became suddenly engrossed in conversation with Mr. Newlands even as his neck flushed a violent crimson. I wished I could kick myself under my skirts; I should have giggled and made some girlish excuse, but instead I'd insinuated that Nick and I had some sort of clandestine arrangement.

And that wasn't the end of it.

"What was that?" Nick thundered under his breath as we boarded the ship. "Now the entire junket thinks we're secretly engaged."

"If *I* thought we were engaged, which I don't," I said, poker-red anger competing with a quavering fear that made my voice tremble, "then I'd have told them so in no uncertain terms."

Nick threw up his hands and stormed off, leaving me alone on the gangplank.

Perhaps I'd misunderstood Nick's intentions. It was quite possible that I was just a plaything, to be easily discarded as he'd done with Miriam Bloomer. I had no doubt that we loved each other, but was that enough?

Or would that love cause us more heartache than it was worth?

After that, it was as if Nick had disappeared from the junket, for he no longer sought me out, and he refused even to join my table at dinner. To distract myself, I settled for reading and rereading a faded atlas as if it were an adventure novel, refusing to think of Nick and thinking only one thing.

I'm here. I am actually here.

I was tracing our proposed route through China with my finger when Uncle Will announced himself.

"I heard you asking for books and newspaper articles about the countries we're visiting. You might enjoy this, if you haven't read it already," he said, handing me a well-worn copy of *The Travels of Marco Polo.* I opened the front cover and could just make out where his name had been penciled and recently erased. A gift then.

I beamed at him. "I do love a good book. Thank you."

"My pleasure. It's abominably hot, but I wondered if you'd humor an old man with a stroll around the deck." His mustache had been freshly trimmed and he looked rather natty in his white summer suit, despite his impressive girth. I didn't know how he endured the heat with his weight, but he never lost his good humor.

"With you, Uncle Will?" I exchanged the volume of Marco Polo for my parasol. "Always."

He smiled and gallantly offered me his arm. We chatted about the infernal heat and the troubles of downtrodden Korea at the hands of the Japanese. Taft finally stopped and mopped his brow with a well-pressed handkerchief. "You know that your father sent me here as your guardian, correct?"

"That and to negotiate with the Japanese," I said. "I'm not sure which was the more odious task."

Taft chuckled so that his mustache twitched. "You're a dear girl, Alice, and I like you very much."

"Thanks, Uncle Will. I like you too."

He cleared his throat. "You know that I'm also an old friend of the Longworth family."

I wasn't sure I liked where this conversation was heading. "I do."

"Do you love him, Alice?"

My stomach writhed as if I were facing my father just now. Or a firing squad.

"Who?" I asked.

"You know perfectly well who I mean. Nick Longworth."

"That old bald-headed man?" Taft gave me a pointed look and I sighed, scared of speaking the truth aloud. But I was weary of playing games, even if Nick hadn't spoken to me since the Philippines. "More or less, Mr. Secretary, more or less."

Taft scratched both his chins. "That's what I was afraid of. And I take it you two have an understanding?"

I didn't know precisely what Nick and I had, but I forced Taft to start walking again, mostly so I didn't have to look him in the eye. "An unofficial sort, yes."

"Love wisely, Alice. Nick is ambitious," he said. "He'll make a good politician, but a poor husband for a girl like you."

I bristled, but Taft cut me off. "You've got a solid head on your shoulders, so I'm just going to come out and say this. Nick Longworth's not the man for you. I don't think either of you is so much in love with the other as to guarantee the other's happiness."

And there it was: the same worry I'd had, finally given voice.

Yet this was so much bigger than when I'd left Washington. We received American newspapers every morning on the trip—albeit several days late—and I'd been utterly appalled when the Associated Press reported that it was Nick, and not Bourke Cochran, who had jumped into the *Manchuria*'s pool with me, no doubt part of their tropical romance angle. I was under no illusion that the entire country would expect wedding bells within six months of us stepping foot on American soil.

And I couldn't—wouldn't—go back to Father and Mother harping on me over my name appearing in the papers, how many Lucky Strikes I smoked, or how much I'd overspent my allowance.

So I laughed away Taft's concerns.

"Nick's a doll and I'm lucky to have him," I said. "After all, there are few men willing to take on the president's daughter, don't you think?"

"That's what I worry about," Taft said. "That Nick is more enamored with the prestige of having a Roosevelt on his arm than he is with you yourself. You deserve better, Alice."

If Taft was right, it was the same story I'd replayed over and over with everyone I'd met since McKinley's death had catapulted my father into the White House. But surely Nick was different. And even if he wasn't, with a little determination I knew I could find happiness with him. After all, he *did* make me happy.

Most of the time.

I stood on tiptoes to peck Taft's cheek. "Thank you for the warning, Uncle Will. I promise to guard my heart." I was about to go, but stopped and squeezed his forearm. "Please don't breathe a word of this to my parents. I want them to hear it from me first, all right?"

Although who knew if there would be anything to report to them when we returned to America. That was entirely up to Nick.

Taft's eyes softened and he nodded. "Of course," he said. "Remember that you can always break it off until you've sworn your vows. I won't believe that you two are permanently engaged until I see the wedding ring on your finger." Then he patted my hand and trundled back the way we'd come, reminding me of a kindly sort of hippo.

I was so lost in thought that I didn't notice when someone came to stand behind me.

"What was that all about?" Nick asked, making me jump. Damn it all to hell and back, but I loved the way his arm snaked around my waist, brazenly claiming me as if our fight had never happened.

I looked at him then, truly *looked*, and wondered if this was the man who was going to make me happy until death parted us. I took it as a good sign that his very smile made my stomach flutter and knees wobble like that newfangled Jell-O dessert. "Just some last words of advice before the secretary of war leaves," I said.

Love wisely, Alice.

As Nick pulled me into the ship's empty saloon, I knew that despite Taft's warning I would probably always love Nick Longworth. And as his lips forged a dizzying trail up my throat that left me gasping, a line from Thackeray's novel *Vanity Fair* echoed in my mind.

It is better to love wisely, no doubt: but to love foolishly is better than not to be able to love at all.

As Nick's lips teased mine apart and we melted into each other, I had only one thought.

Thackeray, you don't know what you're talking about. Why love wisely when you can love like this?

In China, my teeth clattered as rickshaws pulled us to the Temple of Heaven with its magnificent triple-gabled Hall of Prayer for Good Harvests. Red-eyed, I'd stayed up until dawn reading Taft's copy of *The Travels of Marco Polo* from cover to cover and recognized Polo's description of the shifting crowd of filthy beggars and overpowering street smells that might have been written only yesterday instead of six hundred years ago. I doubted this was the impression the Chinese wished us to have of their empire since we were soon whisked away to the Forbidden City's summer palace, where I fidgeted with impatience while attempting to meditate in a Buddhist temple.

There I determined that meditating was *not* for Roosevelts. I was quite sure Father would agree.

Afterward, I stuffed myself with rose wine, antique eggs, and some concoction creatively titled Snowflake Shark Fins, which tasted like rubbery chicken.

"No grasshoppers," I said to Nellie Taft, relishing her pinched lips. "But I'm sure we could ask the kitchens to make some if you'd like."

"You are insufferable, Alice Roosevelt," she hissed, to which I responded with a wink.

That night I tossed and turned, punching what might have been a wooden log masquerading as a pillow, and rose the next morning with a crick in my neck for the grand event: our morning audience with Empress Dowager Cixi, a woman who ranked among Catherine of Russia and Elizabeth of England, Hatshepsut and Cleopatra as one of the great leaders in history.

I'm *going to meet the empress dowager,* I thought to myself. *Not my father, but me.*

"She's a murderer," Mrs. Newlands whispered as she buttoned me into the bridesmaid dress I'd worn to Eleanor's wedding. "All the business with her son, you know."

I scrubbed my hands with a cake of ginger soap delivered alongside a copper basin of tepid water and a command that I purify myself before meeting the empress. "I'm willing to overlook the rumor that she had her son assassinated so she might maintain her hold on the throne," I said, wincing at the painful rash of eczema that had cropped up after my discussion with Uncle Will. "After all, plenty of untrue things have been whispered about me."

The empress dowager sat on her high dragon throne flanked by great pyramids of fruit, her diminutive form draped in a loose Chinese coat with strings of gleaming jade and lustrous pearls around her neck. On her feet were a pair of beaded horse-hoof shoes that looked impossible to walk in, and I strained to tell whether her feet were bound, although I supposed an empress never had to walk far. Cixi by no means looked her seventy years with her piercing black eyes and cruel, thin mouth.

The empress spoke then, but I understood not a single word. Instead, a man in a pristine suit bowed to me. "I am Dr. Wu," he said, and I recognized the name of the international scholar and foreign minister to the United States. "I will be your translator today. The empress inquires after your health, Miss Roosevelt."

I opened my mouth to answer and almost jumped out of my skin when the empress of the East and West interrupted to bark at the esteemed Dr. Wu in a terrible voice, made all the more savage since I had no idea what she was saying.

Suddenly, Dr. Wu scurried down on all fours and pressed his wide forehead to the ground. I had the feeling that Cixi might at any moment cry, "Off with his head!" and that would be the end of Wu. Alarmed, I waited for him to rise, but the empress dowager simply continued the audience as if nothing untoward had happened. To my shock, Cixi placed her feet in their beaded horse-hoof shoes on his back, as if this were a commonplace occurrence.

"The empress would like to present you with tokens of her esteem." Wu scarcely glanced my way from his place on the floor, although his face had turned the color of sour milk while his ears burned scarlet.

I hardly knew how to respond, but managed to give a stuttering nod.

To my shock, I was draped with bolts of Chinese silks until I could hardly move, and terrifying gold filigreed nail sheaths were slipped over each of my fingers. The gifts kept coming; I had to balance a portrait of Empress Cixi seated on her throne in full royal regalia in one hand and in the other a replica sterling silver *junk* complete with miniature sailors on deck, both gifts to my father. I tried to bow— worried that I'd end up like Dr. Wu if I didn't act appropriately—but was too weighed down to manage a proper sort of kowtow. Instead, I nudged the slippery silk back up my shoulders. "I'll need an entire battleship just to carry all these treasures to America!"

"There is one more gift," Wu announced from the floor.

A Chinese servant arrived with a smallish sort of bamboo basket, which he placed at my feet.

It moved. I shrieked.

I leaped back, tottering under the weight of all the silk while fearing an attack by cobra or scorpions. Instead, the lid popped off and a tiny black Pekingese poked out its stern face, its fluffy tail wagging frantically. I squealed and dumped the other gifts into the servant's surprised arms. "I shall call you Manchu," I declared as I scooped up the wriggling black ball of fur and let him plaster my face with tiny puppy kisses. I hadn't had a pet of my own since Emily Spinach's demise and had never had a dog of my own. "And I will spoil you rotten."

A new puppy, more gifts than I could ever use, and audiences with famous empresses . . .

I could stay lost in this Wonderland forever.

After the wonders of China, Korea seemed a dull place, its populace gray and dejected, sliding helplessly into Japan's grasp.

I returned to the American legation in Seoul, far ahead of the rest of the party despite my having ridden a particularly ill-behaved native pony. Nick had opted to stay behind for the afternoon, so the company had been lackluster with the exception of Willard Straight, the tall and rangy secretary to the American minister who had surprised me with his ability to discuss topics ranging from Edison's most recent silent movie to Japan's current military power. I'd laughed at his banter, but found myself comparing him to Nick and coming up short.

What do I expect? Every man comes up short when compared to Nick.

The country air had been exhilarating, and the craggy mountains stood sharper than carnivorous teeth against the darkening western sky. We reached the stables and I dismounted, pulling a face at the horse that had tried several times to buck me and receiving bared yellow incisors in response.

"I don't care for you either, dear." I patted its dusty flank as the rest of the riding party reined in. "But at least I know I won't one day end up as glue."

I turned away with a laugh, only to hear a girlish giggle in answer. I whipped around to a scene ripped from my worst nightmares.

Nick stood with Emma Kroebel, a pretty blonde from Berlin whom I'd mostly ignored after being introduced to her as the chief mistress of ceremonies for the Korean emperor. I had instant flashbacks of Nick with Maggie as he leaned toward the fräulein and lifted a perfect lock of curled blond hair from her shoulder, his thumb grazing her collarbone in a manner that almost bent me double with pain. Every warning I'd ever heard about Nick blared in my mind in that instant, for there was no denying that Emma Kroebel with her broad German cheekbones and matching dimples was far prettier than me.

I forced myself to walk toward them, each step more painful than if I were treading over hot coals.

"Nick, darling," I said, brazenly taking his hand. "How good of you to wait and meet me." I felt a twinge of satisfaction when Emma scurried away like a rat chased from a prime piece of cheese. "What were you discussing with Fräulein Kroebel?"

Nick removed his hand and shoved two fists into his pockets. "Nothing, really."

"It didn't look like nothing." The shrillness of my own voice made me cringe, but I couldn't turn a blind eye to this. "Those dimples of hers seemed to have you spellbound."

Nick and I were almost the same height, but he shot a baleful glare down the few inches that separated us. "Don't," he said.

I tilted my chin defiantly. "Don't what?"

"We're not married, Alice, and even if we were, you don't get to dictate whom I associate with."

He stalked away, leaving me to wonder if he'd hoped to goad me into causing a scene and thus giving him an excuse to set me aside.

The only other option—which was just as terrible—was that he really was a gal-sneaker who would one day break my heart. Only as I gaped after him did I recall the rest of the riding party, which had by now dismounted and was staring at me.

I knew in that moment how Dr. Wu had felt, debased and demeaned in public by someone he worshipped. "Miss Roosevelt," Willard Straight suddenly said as he handed off his gelding to a waiting groom. "I'm very interested to hear your stance on whether Korea has any hope of ever achieving independence from Japan."

My eyes stung, but I forced a smile. "It's a topic I've recently written about to my father."

Straight offered his arm and I took it, noting everyone's gazes fall away from me. We walked a few paces before I answered in a subdued voice. "You don't care much about Japan's intentions, do you?"

"Not as much as rescuing a lady who's been ill-treated."

A born diplomat, this one. Unlike Nick, who could rile every last one of the saints.

"Miss Roosevelt—" Willard started after he'd seen me back inside the American legation, to which I cut him off with a wave.

"My friends call me Alice," I said. "You remind me of my favorite brother Ted, so I insist you do the same."

His smile made his blue eyes twinkle. "All right. I daresay you are quite the thief, Alice."

"A thief? That's a serious charge, you know."

"Or perhaps a collector," he mused, then leaned forward conspiratorially. "From what I've read and seen, you stockpile men's attentions wherever you go."

Before I could be offended, he gave a pointed glance above my shoulder. I followed his gaze to see Nick staring at us from the second-floor balcony, daggers fairly shooting from his eyes.

Willard poured me a glass of banana milk from the legation's refreshment table. "I daresay half the married men in America would consider divorcing their wives for a chance with you."

Someone should have told that to Charly. And Nick.

Still, I recognized that whippet-thin Willard was flirting with me. I grinned into my glass of banana milk, especially as I could imagine the steam rising from Nick's head.

"And the unmarried men?" I asked Willard, raising my eyebrows.

"There's proof on the balcony that all you need to do is snap and we'll come running," he answered, nonplussed. "Thus, I take it upon myself to implore you to make sure you choose a good man. Otherwise, you'll break America's heart."

We'll come running. Did that mean I'd made an unwitting conquest of Willard, too?

His words were simple censure from an unexpected quarter; yet one more voice weighing in on Nick's suitability. So far the score was decidedly *not* in his favor.

I longed to pour out my heart to the pages of my diary that night, but instead found myself staring at a blank piece of American legation stationery in the sputtering light of an oil lamp. Buoyed by Willard's comments, I was heartsick and weary of playing games with Nick, of never knowing where I stood with him. That would all end tonight, for better or worse.

I paused, hesitating before I committed the words to paper. Once this was in Nick's hands, I stood a very good chance of returning to America in disgrace and without hope of ever marrying.

But things couldn't continue as they were.

I dipped my pen in the inkwell and scrawled the ultimatum in my awful, awful handwriting.

Nick,

You losing your temper and getting these uncontrollable dislikes for me has to stop. Indeed, I cannot help feeling hurt in what you are trying to bring about—something which will give you an excuse to get out in as gentlemanly a manner as possible of what you consider a most unpleasant hole.

*I shall not give you that excuse unless you consider this sufficient. But
your behavior has been ridiculous and most contemptible—I am
disappointed.*

—A

Now Nick would either have to commit himself fully to me or cut
his losses and run. Either way, we'd soon be steaming back toward
America, where the harsh glare of the press awaited.

The ball was in Nick's court.

Nick didn't respond that night. Or the next day. Or the next.

Much as I wanted to be a rotten misery-guts and stay in bed, I was
to be honored with a reception at the graveside of the Korean emper-
or's beloved empress. Somehow I didn't think I should arrive in my
bedclothes.

"This is the highest honor the emperor can bestow," Willard informed me as he led me through the intricate maze of corridors. I'd
dressed carefully in a scarlet gown and had rouged my lips in an effort
to bring some color into my face so Nick wouldn't think I'd been pining for him. I felt overdone next to Willard in his plain pressed linen
suit, carrying a heavy-looking camera apparatus under his arm. "I've
been charged with documenting the event for posterity."

"After so many official appearances," I said, "you can rest easy
knowing I've perfected my smile for the press. I'm starting to wonder
how my father manages it day after day."

"Well, you know what they say." Willard might have been thin as
a blade of grass, but he swung open with ease the ornately carved
garden doors enameled with leering dragons and raging demons.
"Practice makes perfect."

There was the usual cavalcade of well-dressed flunkies and dignitaries at the graveside, the party flanked by an impressive collection

of ancient Korean gods and marble statues of exotic monkeys and spotted leopards that would guard the royal graves for eternity.

I turned on my most effusive smile as that twit Emma Kroebel in her official role as chief mistress of ceremonies announced me in a nasal voice that grated on my last nerve. Over the course of the next hour, I shook hundreds of hands and bowed to the Koreans until I was dizzy. Yet Nick never once glanced my way.

Someone else, however, did.

"I have something for you." Willard's expression was somber as he gave a false yawn, his gaze flicking to where Nick strolled with Emma Kroebel beneath an arbor of juniper trees. I knew then that Willard's diplomat's eyes missed nothing. "But you have to promise not to laugh."

"You have my word."

He retrieved a paper from his pocket and unfolded it before handing it to me. It looked like a page from a children's nursery rhyme collection—that is, until I read the first lines.

"'*When Alice Came to Plunderland*.' You wrote me a poem?"

"And illustrated it." He gave a sheepish smile. "There's a fair bit of twiddling one's thumbs as secretary to the minister of a backwater country."

His poem reminded me of Father's picture letters, only more elaborate, especially the scene of me being carried in an oriental sedan with all manner of awed Koreans in the margins and the American eagle supreme at the bottom.

"'When Alice came to Plunderland,'" I read, "'the streets were strewn with yellow sand, the drains were filled with ink . . .'"

My raised eyebrow made Willard's cheeks redden. "I never said it was *good* poetry," he said, trying to snatch it out of my hand.

"You can't take back a gift." I clambered atop the back of a stone elephant, dangling the paper out of reach and squashing my burst of laughter as heads swiveled in our direction. My heart juddered painfully as I spied Nick still chatting with his German fräulein. "Take my picture?" I called to Willard, sounding for all the world as if I was having the time of my life and feeling a tiny moment of triumph when Nick glanced up. Our eyes met, but this time it was me who tipped my nose at him. I waited for the camera to go off, then hopped down the statue and looped my arm through Willard's, Nick's gaze hot on my back.

It was low of me, but two could play his little game. And I would win.

Later that night, after I'd finished undressing and preparing for bed on board the *Siberia*, Manchu yapped from his place at the foot of my narrow bed, heralding the knock I'd yearned so long to hear, three hard raps followed by three staccato taps.

Nick.

I slipped into the cool silk of a green crane robe—a gift from Empress Dowager Cixi—and peered through the cracked door to find Nick in his shirtsleeves, his dinner jacket discarded and his violin in position.

We Roosevelts have the stamina to ride a horse cross-country all day, the fortitude to debate public policy long into the night, and the gift of turning the attention of everyone in a crowded room solely onto ourselves. What we don't have is an ear for music.

Yet, as Nick began to play, I could hear the talent in the way each note trembled, the golden sound hovering in the air and reverberating down the corridor.

And while he might not have said the words, I knew this was his apology.

What I wanted was to pull him into my room, to rail against him and kiss him until we were both breathless, but the sound of other cabin doors opening and disheveled heads in nightcaps swiveling down the narrow hallway stopped me.

"Wait," I said, before shutting the door firmly in his face.

I redressed in a flurry and twisted my hair into a loose chignon before dropping a kiss on Manchu's head. "I knew he'd come around," I whispered with a wild grin to my little dog before stepping into the dark corridor. Wordlessly, Nick took my hand and together we hurried above deck, where a sweep of silent stars dangled overhead. I waited for him to begin his serenade afresh, but he only pulled me into his arms.

"I can scarcely recall the days before I knew you, Alice." He crushed me to him, the violin forgotten. The sweet smell of rosin lingered on his fingertips as they threaded their way into my chignon so my hairpins came loose. "We may fight like cats and dogs, but life is the bleakest shades of gray without you."

It was exactly how I felt about him, not that I'd admit it.

"I hope you've been miserable without me," I said, careful to make sure my voice was light. After these past turbulent days, it felt safer to keep myself remote rather than let him realize the power he held over me.

"Utterly," he said. "Especially tonight when you were with that Straight fellow."

I don't know who kissed whom, but soon we were devouring each other, the ship moving languidly under our feet as we clung to each other like two drowning souls.

I was the first to pull away. "Will you come with me to Sagamore Hill?" The question was fraught with meaning, for to have him visit my family would mean that he would ask Father for my hand. My heart ceased beating and time itself seemed to stop as I waited for his answer.

He tucked a stray tendril of hair behind my ear and tugged me closer, so I could feel his chest rise and fall with his breath. "I'd like nothing better," he said.

In that briefest of moments, I was the happiest girl in the world.

I expected a battalion of red-hot telegrams from Father the moment we docked in San Francisco. There was indeed a whole host of messages, but I breathed a sigh of relief to discover none were what I anticipated.

Dear Alice,

I find myself delighted at all the work that you and Secretary Taft have accomplished during your junket to the Far East. I have high hopes for a long-term peace between Japan and Russia.

In regards to your Plunderland gifts, I suggest you leave them in the customs house until we can determine how best to pay the colossal duties. Except Manchu, of course.

Yours
affectionately,
Father

This was accompanied by a picture letter with a sketch of me in my trademark hat, *hitting the pipe with a possible congenial friend in the empress dowager.* I laughed at that as I tucked the letter into my purse and Nick guided me down the gangplank, feeling the familiar flush of pleasure that now accompanied Father's letters.

My parents might have been silent about Nick, but the papers blared louder than the seven trumpets of the apocalypse. Reporters pummeled us about our trip once we stepped foot on San Francisco's dock. We didn't have to wait longer than two minutes for the big question.

"Alice, when are you going to become Mrs. Longworth?" a bespectacled newspaperman asked, camera in one hand, notepad in the other, and a stubby yellow pencil tucked behind his ear.

Nick and I had prepared for this and only laughed in unison. "I'm afraid we don't have time for questions," I said. "We have a train to New York to catch."

Yet the reporter had sunk his teeth in and refused to let go. "Anyone might guess the truth from the way Nick never leaves your side," he said, pencil now scribbling away.

"Then you'll have to keep guessing!" I called over my shoulder.

Nick grew more relaxed over a glass of chilled whiskey as our new speeding train neared New York, even as my stomach curdled and my skin itched with a vengeance. Black clouds chased us from the station into a waiting car, and rain pelted the windshield as my own worries gave me a fierce drubbing.

What if Taft spoke to them? Mother already dislikes Nick. What if Father doesn't approve, or worse, what if he forbids the wedding?

My thoughts tormented me until Nick guided the car out of the old oak forest and Sagamore Hill came into view with its wild, unmanicured sprawl of lawn. Not even the old brick-and-slate-toned house with its wraparound piazza remained unchanged since I'd last been home; Father's nearsightedness had turned to blindness in his left eye after a boxing match before I'd left, and led him to complain that the house looked small, so it now sported a vast northern addition. Archie's face appeared in one of the upstairs windows and soon my siblings, parents, and most of the servants streamed out onto the front stoop to greet us.

"We're so happy you're back!" Quentin wrapped his arms around me, the first in a torrent of hugs from my siblings. I laughed as my massive hat was knocked askew when I bent to retrieve Manchu from his carrying basket, whereupon my dog was promptly claimed by Ethel and Archie. Damp and somewhat bedraggled, Nick and I mounted the front steps, where I reintroduced him to Father and Mother, waiting with bated breath.

Would they call him a scoundrel and order him to hightail it back to Washington?

But Father only solemnly shook Nick's hand, then clapped him on the shoulder as if they were old friends. "Come inside, young man, and out of this rain. I want to hear all about the junket."

"Your father is so proud of your work in Asia," Mother said to me as she guided me inside, where tennis racquets were still stored helter-skelter in the front fireplace beneath a mounted Cape buffalo head. She rang the elephant tusk gong to signal for dinner. "He crows to anyone who will listen about the trip's success."

Heat flared in my cheeks at the rare praise. For once I was struck speechless.

We gathered in the dining room, and I sat on my hands to keep from scratching them while my siblings taught Manchu to beg and each asked Nick the three requisite questions that were required for all guests to Sagamore Hill. I was fairly twitching by the time we reached Quentin's final query. "Did you really eat rotten eggs in China?" he asked.

Nick looked at me and laughed. "Indeed we did. And you know what? They're not as bad as they sound."

Yet the question I dreaded never came, not even as plates of fried chicken and dandelion salad were served and cleared away, the kerosene lamps dutifully flickering to stave off autumn's darkness. My nerves were in rags by the time the stern-faced nanny shuffled my siblings off to bed and Father proposed we move the conversation to the cavernous North Room.

"You run along," Mother said with a yawn. "I'll fall asleep midsentence if I stay up much longer."

It took a moment for me to muster my courage and follow my stepmother instead of Father and Nick. Mother had already disappeared upstairs, but the door to the Red Bathroom was open, light from the new electric lamps spilling into the hallway. I knocked with an unsteady hand.

"Come in, Alice," she called.

Of course she's been expecting me. She probably knows exactly what I'm going to say too.

Mother had already taken down her graying hair and was squeezing a bit of peppermint Dentomyrh toothpaste onto a horn-handled brush. Water poured into the huge tub, long ago dubbed the Sarcophagus by us children for its tomblike feeling when we hid inside it during rounds of hide-and-seek. Somehow I felt just as small as I had then.

"It's good to be home." I found myself biting my lip and forced myself to stop.

"We're glad to have you home," she said. "I meant what I said before, about your father being proud of you. We both are."

Those words should have been a symphony to my ears, but I scarcely registered them before blurting out my news. "Nick and I are engaged."

Not even an announcement that the bathroom was afire would have ruffled Mother's composure, much less a proclamation of something as mundane as a wedding. I wanted to shake her as she finished brushing, spit delicately into the basin, then wiped her mouth on a towel before facing me.

"Your father and I suspected as much." I waited for a grim prognostication against Nick's suitability as a husband, but she only squeezed my shoulders. "Is he asking your father's permission now?"

I nodded. "I imagine so. Will Father give it?"

"Of course, if it's what you want. The entire country is waiting with bated breath for the news."

In that moment I didn't care what America wanted. I was four years old again, all knees and eyes, desperately seeking my parents' love and acceptance. "Do you approve? You had concerns about his age and his drinking—"

Mother cut me off with a raised hand. "Nick Longworth has a comfortable income and comes from an esteemed family. He's an intelligent man who will go far in politics. What more can your father and I ask for in a son-in-law?"

"That I love him?"

Mother actually smiled at that. "We supposed that much was obvious."

"He has grand aspirations." I said the words hesitantly, as if divulging a state secret. "Maybe ambassador or Speaker of the House. Perhaps even president one day."

"A man to follow in your father's footsteps." Mother pressed her forehead to mine. "I hope you'll be very happy together, Alice, just as your father and I have been." She pulled me into a rare embrace. "I'm off to bed now. You should go down and visit with your father."

"I will." I paused in the doorway. "Thank you, Mother."

I'd scarcely walked through the elephant tusks that framed the North Room's entrance—a gift from the emperor of Abyssinia—when Father swept me into a hug that took my breath away.

"Congratulations, Mousiekins," Father said, smelling of leather and soap as I hugged him back. "It seems you brought home not only a peace treaty, but a new son-in-law for me as well!"

Then Nick was pressing a glass of Madeira into my hands, and together we toasted the future, the blank eyes of Father's mounted bison and six-point elk staring down at the three of us. As we stood around the fireplace, I mused that perhaps Father and Eleanor had been right, that nothing in this life was worth having unless it meant pain, effort, and difficulty.

Chapter 8

DECEMBER 1905

Tucked away in the quiet of the White House's Blue Room, far removed from all the wedding hullabaloo, I used a letter opener to remove a clipping of a new ditty out of California from the first page of my wedding scrapbook.

Here's to Alice Roosevelt,
Who's won a home with Nick—
The lad who failed so many times,
But finally made it stick.

I crumpled the paper—its back still damp with rubber paste—and threw it into the wastebasket, opting to replace it with a headline from the society pages.

ALICE ROOSEVELT'S WEDDING: The Greatest Most Spectacular Social Event Probably in All of American History . . .

After all, no one needed a reminder of Nick's many prior relationships and failed proposals.

Instead, I pasted the new headline alongside souvenir photographs of Nick and me surrounded by pudgy cherubs. I could have sworn the imps' damnable smiles were mocking me.

Still, try as I might, the scrapbook didn't entirely distract me from the letter I'd received that morning, a painful reminder that my marriage's success was far from guaranteed.

Dearest Alice,

You'll have heard that I'm officially installed as Countess Gizycki now, but how I wish I might trade in my title for my old life! I realized my mistake the moment I arrived at Josef's dilapidated, freezing excuse for a castle in Narvosielica. Worse, my husband has since been revealed as a violent and inveterate gambler and womanizer. I wish I'd never met him, or that my parents had been more steadfast in their refusal to let me marry him.

Keep me in
your thoughts,
Cissy

PS Please don't mention my travails to Maggie. I can't bear to hear her laughter all the way in Poland.

PPS Congratulations on your upcoming marriage. If I couldn't have Nick Longworth, I suppose you may as well enjoy him.

I glanced around the Blue Room, its walls crammed to the chandelier with a vast assortment of flowers and presents. The gifts were really butter upon bacon, but Mother insisted I record them in the scrapbook. So I did, the pen scratching as I tried again to take my mind off Cissy's bleak news.

Eight bolts of Chinese silk embroidered with the shou sign of longevity from Empress Cixi.
A hideous inlaid mosaic table from the king of Italy.

American mousetraps and bales of hay, plus a hogshead of popcorn from a family in Iowa.

A linen centerpiece from the children of the Colored Industrial Evening School, in recognition of Father's attitude toward the Negroes, and a railway car of coal from the United Mine Workers of America in appreciation of Father's services during the 1902 strike. (Mother refused to house the latter in the Blue Room.)

Idly, I bit the end of my fountain pen. It was *my* wedding, yet Father somehow managed to overshadow me even during my own engagement.

"Hello, my darling girl." I startled to find Nick behind me, a small paper-wrapped parcel in hand. We'd scarcely had a moment to ourselves since we'd returned from the Far East, and my very bones ached for him.

"Another gift, this one from the Cuban government." He rubbed his freshly shaven jaw in a way that made me wonder if he felt as weary as he looked. "I told Mrs. Roosevelt that I'd bring this one to you before we go down to meet my mother for breakfast."

I suppressed a shudder at the mention of Nick's mother. Susan Longworth had moved to Washington when her son first became a congressman, and I'd met her only in passing. She was a formidable, straight-backed sort of widow who still wore her black weeds, but both of us obviously loved Nick so I knew that we'd get along. I reminded myself that I'd faced the dragon empress dowager of China; surely I could conquer one Cincinnati matron over eggs and bacon.

All while hoping and praying that she'll move back to Ohio before we return from our honeymoon.

"Would you like to open this one?" I asked Nick, midway through tugging loose the twine on the Cuban parcel.

He shook his head. "It's addressed to you."

As were virtually all of the gifts. There was no doubt who was the star of this match, but Nick bore his position as national bridegroom passably well, despite the way he'd snapped at the press the other day when they asked how many presents he'd received from foreign kings.

I freed the package of its wrapping to reveal a black Boucheron box. Nick gave a long whistle, for inside was the first wedding present I truly loved, a stunning pearl necklace that must have cost the Cuban government a small fortune.

Nick lifted the necklace from its velvet and fastened the clasp behind my neck. He pressed a chaste kiss to my temple. "These old pieces of sand look quite dashing on you."

"Why, that's very kind of you." I touched the lustrous pearls before turning to face him. My pulse picked up in the old familiar way as I leaned closer, but he barely brushed his lips to my forehead before he gestured to the open door.

"My mother awaits," he said.

I rose and wrapped my arms around his neck. "Surely she can wait a little longer."

But Nick was steadfast. "Somehow I doubt that's the impression either of us wishes to make."

"Fine." I pursed my lips in a mock pout and we trailed down the stairs in silence until Nick stopped me just outside the informal breakfast room. "Mother was a bit unprepared for our engagement," he confided. "Be kind to her."

"I'm no fool. Why make an enemy of your mother if I don't have to?" He frowned and I kissed his cheek. "Of course I'll be kind."

But it was as if Nick hadn't even heard me as he was announced, for he broke into a smile cheerier than the breakfast room's yellow brocade drapes. Mother was already milling about the Turkish coffee carafe with Susan Longworth, who hurried to embrace her son.

"Nicky, darling," she exclaimed. "How I've missed you, dearest!"

I stood awkwardly and waited for Nick to introduce me. Finally, the embrace subsided and Nick gestured me over. "Mother, I believe you know Alice."

"Indeed I do." Mrs. Longworth folded her hands in front of her in the perfect impression of a tight-lipped Victorian governess. A stream of little furs assaulted each other around her neck and down her front, but otherwise she was swathed from head to toe in the darkest shade of black. "Little did I know she'd soon be joining our family. In fact,

I was just telling Secretary Taft not two months ago that my Nicky was a thoroughly confirmed bachelor." She looked askance at me. "I see I was mistaken."

"My apologies for the suddenness of our announcement." I'd rather field questions from a hall of angry newspapermen than face Susan Longworth with her cold gray eyes that flicked over me with unmistakable disdain.

"No need to worry, dear." Her voice was decidedly brittle to my ears. "I kept abreast of your journey to the Far East via the papers."

"It was quite the expedition," Mother said, while the White House staff paraded in with silver platters of bacon, hard-boiled eggs, and Vienna rolls. "The president was impressed with all that both Alice and Nick accomplished among the various heads of state. In fact, Mr. Roosevelt will be here presently to join us."

"I look forward to meeting him." Susan Longworth infused her voice with false cheer as our seats were pushed in behind us. "Still, I can't help but reflect upon how times have changed since my days as a young woman. It used to be unseemly for a girl to have her name in the papers more than three times. Why, Alice, I'm sure your name has been in the headlines at least three hundred times since your father succeeded President McKinley!"

I swallowed my retort that surely Susan Longworth had never done anything worth mentioning more than three times. Instead I was held hostage by Nick's warning glance.

"Alice is wildly popular with the reporters." Mother unexpectedly rode to my rescue as she unfolded her monogrammed napkin and smoothed it over her lap. "She truly is America's darling."

I saved myself from gaping, but only just, considering how firmly Mother had been against my name appearing in the papers. What was happening here?

"So many daring escapades." Mrs. Longworth's eyebrows raised over the rim of her teacup while I made quick work of my first mug of coffee. This conversation had already obliterated any appetite I might have had. "But I suppose Nicky did always fret that he'd tire of a wife at the breakfast table." She shot him a look of sympathy. "I daresay you'll never find Alice dull, dear."

Mother didn't give Nick a chance to respond. "It's fortunate for Nick that Alice is so utterly charming. Indeed, she has such a sunny temperament and is so terribly thoughtful about others."

I almost choked. There was no doubt that I was in trouble if Mother was lying for me.

Thankfully, my father chose that moment to materialize and save us all from the ninth circle of hell.

"Welcome, welcome," he said, a toothy grin splitting his face in two. "Please forgive my tardiness, but I'm under strict orders to deliver this. The Ponca Indians addressed it to Shining Top." Father read the tag through his spectacles and then offered the massive package to Nick. "I assume that means you."

All heads swiveled in Nick's direction. I scarcely noticed his encroaching baldness these days, for, if anything, it only made him more ruggedly handsome and heightened the intensity of his eyes, which for me still possessed the power to make the whole world fade away until only we two remained. My future husband was all man, utterly unlike the inexperienced boys I'd once flirted with, what with their crooked smiles and mops of messy hair. Nick's kisses—and more—had attested to that on more than one occasion.

As always, Nick only gave his old puckish smile at the ribbing and swept a self-assured hand over his head. "It's becoming a bit of a fly rink, isn't it?"

"What on earth is going on?" Susan Longworth asked, suddenly peevish. "Who is this from, and why?"

"The Ponca Indians were marching down Pennsylvania Avenue, asking how I could be the boss of my own wigwam if all the horses, beads, and buffalo hides belong to my wife." Nick shrugged as he unwrapped the twine and brown paper, revealing a lustrous buffalo skin. "I suppose one could say it's an engagement gift."

I wouldn't have expected that Susan Longworth's expression could grow any sourer. I was wrong.

"I'm sure they meant well. And it wouldn't matter to me if you were bald, gray, and poor," I told Nick. "You're still *my* Shining Top."

For some reason, that made my future mother-in-law almost apoplectic.

"I just don't understand," she sputtered. "How dare they insult you—"

Mother interjected then to officially introduce Father to Mrs. Longworth, to which Father responded that he was *"dee-lighted!"* to meet her, while she was surely *"charmed."*

"How many bridesmaids shall you have, Alice?" Susan Longworth asked once Father had taken his place at the head of the table and loaded his plate with hard-boiled eggs and crusty rolls.

"None," I answered, both hands clinging to my steaming mug of coffee.

From the look on her face, I might have just admitted to planning to walk down the aisle naked. "None?" she parroted back.

"I'd have to have at least one hundred and fifty if I had any," I said, although that was only partly true. In fact, I had the double problem in that every girl in America wished to be my bridesmaid but all my friends—including Cissy Patterson and cousin Eleanor—were already married. Still, this was the first time I'd had anyone question my decision to walk to the altar unattended.

I persevered until the coffee grew cold and Nick's mother took her leave just before noon, but not before wringing promises from Nick that he'd be home before supper. Mother shot me a sympathetic look before she and Father rose to walk Susan Longworth out, distracting her by discussing the recent rumbles that Father was to receive a Nobel Peace Prize for his work on the Portsmouth treaty that reconciled Japan and Russia.

The very same treaty that I'd helped set the stage for by traveling to the Far East. Thus, perhaps I'd played a role—however small—in helping Father capture the prestigious Nobel Peace Prize. Not that any of that mattered to Susan Longworth.

"I hope you don't have any pressing desires to spend cozy family holidays together," I muttered to Nick as an usher shut the double doors behind them.

"Don't worry," he said. "She'll come around. She'll have to, if we're all to live together here in Washington."

"You can't be serious."

"I won't evict my mother from her home, Alice. She'd never survive such a slight."

I scoffed. Susan Longworth could have survived onslaughts by Hannibal and Napoleon. What fresh hell was I getting myself into?

"Perhaps she can live in Ohio while we have the town house here in Washington?" I asked. "We're about to be married, Nick. I don't want to share you with your mother."

He picked up the buffalo skin and gave it an emphatic shake, his shoulders set. "I'm marrying into your family, Alice, which means you're also marrying into mine. That requires sacrifices on both our parts."

I held up my hands in surrender. I'd set out to conquer Nick's mother today, but instead had made myself a new rival. I wasn't about to alienate Nick, too, even if it appeared I might end up living under the same roof with my latest foe.

What's done was done. We'd flaunted our engagement to the world, and neither of us could back out now even if we'd wished to. Nick loved me and I loved him, although I recalled Taft's grim warning.

I don't think either of you is so much in love with the other as to guarantee the other's happiness.

I wondered if he was right, whether we were indeed doomed for not loving each other enough. I shook off such dark thoughts, scratching idly at my eczema. However much Nick and I loved each other, it was enough.

It would have to be.

Chapter 9

"That's the last time I'll ever write Alice Lee Roosevelt," I said, signing the Alibi guest book with a flourish. Earlier in the day, Nick had been allowed to sit in the Speaker's chair to celebrate the looming end of his bachelorhood and cheered for a full minute by the entire House, which he'd crowed about on our way to the rehearsal in the East Room. That had gone off without a hitch, save the fact that Father couldn't be pulled away from state affairs for either the ceremony or the dinner that followed at the Alibi.

"I much prefer the ring of Alice Roosevelt Longworth." Nick pressed his lips against my hairline, which Mother pretended not to notice as she drew Susan Longworth into a sudden conversation regarding whether champagne should be served at the wedding brunch.

"Me too." I bumped my hip against his with false bravado. After all, I'd fooled my family—even the entire country—countless times by covering my anxieties with a display of exuberance. I wondered if that was what my father did, too, if his brash exterior concealed some unknown secret fear.

I almost laughed at the thought, for anyone who had met my father knew that he wasn't afraid of anything.

Still, I had my doubts about the wedding, our marriage, and the future, all of which only loomed larger as the night wore on.

Mother came to me just after I dressed for bed that evening, having left Nick to the debaucheries of his stag party. She pulled tight the coverlet at the foot of my bed, dark shadows beneath her eyes and shoulders slumped with exhaustion from the strain of the last few months of wedding preparations. "I've come to see if there's anything else you need for tomorrow."

"I have a white dress and flowers enough to choke a greenhouse." I gestured to where my gown hung on the back of the closet door, its eighteen-foot silver brocade train spread out to prevent the satin from wrinkling. "I think that's all I need."

"I suppose you're right." A small and slightly awkward silence followed, during which I might have apologized for being such a terror over the past few years, had I trusted myself to speak. Instead, Mother cleared her throat and fixed her gaze on the ceiling as if there were some erstwhile crack there.

"You know, before you were born, your mother needed a little something done in order to have you." She studiously avoided my gaze. I'd never seen Mother so discomfited and might have laughed aloud if I hadn't been so dumbstruck. I waited for her to elaborate, but she only turned off my bedside lamp as if she suddenly couldn't wait to get away. "I just thought you should know, in case you find yourself in similar straits in the future." She hesitated at the door. "Rest well, Alice. You have a big day ahead of you tomorrow."

I stared at my door, too dazed to chase after her and demand answers to my questions. Father and my mother had been married three years before I'd arrived, an abnormally long time to wait for a baby, but I'd never considered that she'd needed an operation to have me.

I lay in my narrow bed until well after midnight, alternately mulling over this new mystery and recalling Cissy's mortification the day of her wedding until I'd almost convinced myself that I should call the whole thing off.

But if I do, I can be sure the news will be splashed all over the papers. Something along the lines of Clock Strikes Midnight for Princess Alice: Jilted at the Altar by Debonair Congressman.

Finally, I kicked off the coverlet to reread Papa Lee's most recent letter, his small, meticulous handwriting illuminated by a stark shaft of moonlight. My grandparents wholeheartedly approved of Nick, and Papa Lee had drawn up a simple list of rules that we should follow as newlyweds. I read them over and over until I had them memorized.

Get up in the morning and breathe fresh air.

Make your breakfast of something besides lemon juice.

Leave off cigarettes, cigars, and cocktails.

When traveling, leave at home the dog and snakes.

Conduct yourself so as to be happy, and to make him happy too.

The last admonition would prove the most difficult, I mused as I paced the length of my room, but surely we could accomplish the first four with ease, even if I'd have to curtail my smoking.

Could Nick make me happy, or would we only make each other miserable?

Did every bride worry like this before walking down the aisle?

I might have paced the entire length of Washington as the clock ticked away my final hours of freedom. It was only after I heard Father tromp up the stairs from Nick's party (suitably early before the gathering became too convivial) that I collapsed into a fitful sleep.

I woke late the next morning to the warmth of a sunny springlike day such as one often gets in Washington during the winter. Sunlight streamed through the rose-pink curtains in a fashion that told me it was close to noon and the start of the wedding. I opened the door, expecting to see Mother waiting but finding Auntie Bye and Rose, my favorite White House maid, instead.

"It's about time," Bye said as she pushed past me. "If you weren't up in two minutes, I was going to break down that door of yours."

"Where's Mother?" I peered down the hall, expecting an uproar, only to find it strangely empty. "And Father?"

"The president is downstairs writing letters about election fraud

and the Naval Academy." Bye hummed while she inspected my pristine gown, her eyes narrowed as if she expected that I'd spent last
night playing dress-up in the moonlight. "Your mother has been up
since daybreak, knitting with your grandma Lee and asking if you
were up yet. We've only got one hour until you have to walk down
that aisle."

"Well, we'd better get to work then," I said. "I'll never hear the end
of it from Mother if I'm late to my own wedding."

On went my delicates and corset, then my American-made satin
gown trimmed with lace from my mother's own wedding dress and
embroidered with the Roosevelt crest of roses. Auntie Bye arranged
my Cuban pearls and a diamond necklace from Nick around my neck,
and pinned a gold brooch from Mother and Father to my dress.

"Hold still," Rose admonished as she struggled to fashion my elaborate pompadour with its froth of fragrant orange blossoms. I groaned
when she added the veil, for it felt as if I were wearing every one of the
crown jewels on my head.

Finally, with only minutes to spare, she and Bye declared me ready.

I stood in a hurry and gave a nervous giggle to find that my hair
could easily topple me.

"One false turn and I'll keel over headfirst," I said.

"Hopefully without a photographer nearby." Bye chuckled, but her
eyes shone with unshed tears. "Let's go find your parents."

We found them at the top of the stairs, Father in a charcoal frock
coat with a pearl-white tie and Mother in a rucked navy afternoon
dress. My brother Ted might have passed for a younger version of
Father in a dark suit and with his hair plastered flat as he waited to
walk Mother down the aisle.

"Promise me that you won't stop raising hell just because you're
about to become an old married matron," my brother said with a
wink as he handed me my bouquet of white orchids.

"You have my word," I said. The steady crush of voices from downstairs was making my stomach roil. "Is Nick here yet?"

Ted rolled his eyes. "Of course he's here, Sissy. Standing in the

East Room, waiting for the love of his life to make her grand entrance. Have you seen her?"

I gave a weak smile. "Maybe."

Mother ignored us to adjust my veil atop my pompadour—the cursed thing was going to give me a devil of a headache—before patting my cheek. "You make a beautiful bride," she said before motioning for Ted to take her arm. I could just make out the notes of Beethoven's *Moonlight Sonata* over the swell of a thousand voices, reminding me of Nick's moonlight serenade on board the *Siberia*.

Then Mother and Ted were gone, leaving me alone with Father.

I waited for him to say something, *anything*, but he only cleared his throat. After all these years, on the most momentous day of my life, my father still didn't know what to say to me.

I could feel rare tears boiling to the surface, but I refused to cry. I wished he could just cut me open and see the emotions inside, for I couldn't find words for them. "Well, now I'll finally be out of your hair, Father," I managed to croak out.

He replaced his pince-nez and clasped my gloved hands, squeezing them once. "Oh, Mousiekins," he said, his voice gruff. "How I wish Alice Lee could see you today."

It was the first and only time he'd ever mentioned my real mother to me. My chin wobbled and my face grew painfully hot, but just then the United States Marine Band picked up the tinny notes of the "Wedding March." Father cleared his throat and moved with decisive motion behind me.

The sight of my father—the president of the United States—stooping to straighten my colossal train reminded me of who I was. I willed steel into my spine as he stood. "Shall we?" he asked.

I looped my arm through his. "We shall."

I entered the East Room with my head held high, passing Supreme Court justices, senators and congressmen, and a whole slew of diplomats before sighting my grandparents, siblings, and the rest of my family, their faces alight with pride. It seemed that all of Washington had been crammed into the White House to see me married; even

Maggie Cassini inclined her head to me with a gorgeous ostrich feather hat that must have come straight from Doucet in Paris. I willed my face into a placid mask, despite the way the knot of my stomach pulled itself tighter.

Yet my heart froze to see one statuesque woman next to Nick's mother, stylish in a delicate butter-colored gown. I recognized Miriam Bloomer from Nick's early days in Washington, when they'd been engaged.

Why was *she* here? Had Nick's mother—or heaven forbid, *Nick*—invited her?

I had no choice save to banish those worries and keep walking toward the minister and the crush of American Beauty roses that Mother had insisted upon, a veritable field of pink blossoms to match the Roosevelt name. Yet I cared only for the man who waited for me with one pale rose pinned to his suit jacket.

Nick gave me a carefree wink, and almost all my worries disintegrated.

Everything will be fine. After all, neither of us can survive without the other, right?

We repeated our marriage vows while half of Washington looked on, Nick's hand squeezing mine in silent reassurance when my tongue hitched on the part where I promised to love, honor, and *obey* him for the rest of my days.

"I'll only hold you to that to the best of your ability," he whispered, to which I wrinkled my nose. Then his lips brushed mine in the most chaste kiss we'd ever shared. It was done.

"Ladies and gentlemen," the minister proclaimed. "May I now present to you Mr. and Mrs. Nicholas Longworth!"

And just like that, the wild hoyden Alice Roosevelt was replaced with a respectable congressman's wife. Funny, but I didn't feel any different.

Afterward, a crowd of congratulatory congressmen swallowed Nick while Mother shooed the other guests out so the official photographs could be taken. She'd already warned me that she'd forbidden the usual crush of reporters from the White House grounds, but Frances B. Johnston of my early Washington photographs had been invited back with her camera.

"Your place is in the middle, Mrs. Longworth," she said.

I glanced over my shoulder for Nick's mother, before realizing it was me she was speaking to. Frances directed me onto a carpeted platform while sending wild-haired little Quentin—the knees of his new suit were already scuffed—to round up my father. "Who's tall enough to adjust the bride's veil?" Frances called as she fluffed my train.

I struggled to right my confounded veil, gone askew again with the weight of my pompadour, but Mother and Auntie Bye were deep in discussion and oblivious to my travails. I spied Nick in the crowd, but who was that dark-haired girl he was talking to?

Her back turned to me, I caught a glimpse of pale yellow, the same shade as freshly churned butter. Miriam Bloomer?

"Eleanor sends her most fervent congratulations." Cousin Franklin popped up and blocked my view, standing on tiptoe to straighten the flowers and tulle atop my head. I tried to peer around him, but the crowd had shifted, obstructing my view of Nick. "She wishes she could be here."

"You're a terrible liar, Frank. You'll never make a competent politician." While I was glad that Eleanor wasn't here to compare to me, there was no denying that her conciliatory presence would have been a welcome balm even as my hands began to itch under their gloves.

"The bustle of the White House has always made Eleanor nervous." Feather Duster gave a genuine smile and gestured with his chin to the crush of people beyond the door, many breaking their necks for a peek inside. "Can you blame her?"

I chuckled. "Today would have made her positively overwrought. Yet another way Eleanor and I are such opposites."

Franklin stood back to admire his handiwork. "I don't know if you two really are so different," he said. "Not in the ways that count anyway."

I didn't care to ponder that now, so merely managed a smile. "Well, I promise to come visit after her confinement."

"Only three months left." Franklin beamed in the cheerful manner of all soon-to-be papas stretching back to time immemorial. His enthusiasm made me wish I had a likeness of his overeager face to send to Eleanor.

"Congratulations again, Alice," Frank said as both Nick and Father waded their way toward me. Frances positioned them at my sides, Nick to my left while Father leaned away from me with one hand stuffed in his pocket.

"Alice is your responsibility now," he said to Nick, looking straight ahead as Frances adjusted the lens. "You'll have to do your best to keep her from the worst sorts of trouble."

I bit my tongue. *Because apparently Alice can't take care of herself.*

"I'll try," Nick said. Without so much as holding my hand, he felt a million miles away. "But I make no promises."

It was with no small sense of relief that the camera flash went off in a blast of light and smoke, and Father jogged down the platform steps without another word. Guests were already filing into the State Dining Room, and suddenly I wished I could lose myself in the crowd instead of spending the remainder of the day under their scrutiny.

"You're my darling little girl no more," Nick murmured. "Now you're my darling little wife."

"Pah." I rubbed my temple with my free hand to chase away the ache gathering there. I wanted to ask him if it had been Miriam Bloomer he'd been speaking to, but swallowed the sour words. "I've never been anyone's darling little *anything.*"

"Well, you'll just have to get used to being my darling," Nick said. "And today you've made me the happiest of men."

Our private family brunch passed well enough, and despite the headache, I began to feel myself again with Nick laughing at my side. The only crisis came when the caterer's knife proved too small to cut the wedding cake with its jungle of sugar doves and orange blossoms. I glanced around to find the perfect solution.

"Pardon me," I said to one of the White House military aides. "But may I borrow your sword?"

"Of course, Mrs. Longworth," he said, presenting the polished blade to me handle-first.

The guests gasped in shock as I cut the cake, and I felt that same thrill as when I'd descended the stairs to my debut, as if my very skin were on fire.

It's not every girl who gets to be married in the White House or cut her cake with a saber. But I did.

Finally, Mother chased me upstairs to change into my traveling dress, an ugly beige thing that made me wonder whether I'd gone temporarily blind when I'd picked it out. From downstairs came the raucous sound of Nick being toasted by the Harvard Porcellian Club, to which Father had once belonged and had been glad to accompany singing the traditional club song. Of course, Father's voice was by far the loudest.

The door closed behind me and I tugged at the pins holding my pompadour together. "Help me escape from all this, will you?" I asked, expecting Mother.

But it wasn't Mother at all.

"You *should* escape, while you still have a chance," said a girlish voice, almost singsong in its timbre.

I turned to see Miriam Bloomer, her face unnaturally pale and gray eyes wide as if she'd dropped belladonna into them.

"What are you doing here?" I wished for something sharp to hold between us, but found only my bouquet handy. The devil only knew how Miriam had managed to sneak past the White House staff. Or how she'd been invited to the wedding in the first place.

Miriam's tiny hands fluttered delicately at her sides. She was taller than me, but gave the air of being infinitely fragile, like a fine-boned egret.

"I came to see you with my own eyes," she continued, those same eyes welling with tears. "To know for sure that I've lost him, once and for all."

"You shouldn't be here," I said, but she acted as if she hadn't heard me, only shook her head sadly.

"Guard yourself with him," she said. I exhaled with relief as she turned to go. "For Nick's in love with love, not you. No matter how he pretends otherwise."

The door closed behind her and I sat hard on the edge of my bed, heart pounding against my ribs and unsure whether to laugh or cry.

Nick did love me and we *would* be happy, Miriam Bloomer be damned.

With shaking hands, I'd finally torn loose my pompadour by the time Mother joined me, her eyes tight and drawn. I thought of all the countless weeks of planning that she had spent on the wedding, shouldering so many of the burdens that might otherwise have fallen to me. I dared not trouble her further by mentioning Miriam's distressing visit.

"Mother," I said as she wordlessly did my back buttons. "This was quite the nicest wedding I'll ever have. In fact, I've never had so much fun."

It was the closest I could come to saying thank you, for we Roosevelts weren't famous for expressing our feelings.

Mother leaned close to me, looking so tired that I worried she might faint. "I want you to know I'm glad to see you leave. You've never been anything but trouble."

Her voice was weary, but her wan smile told me she teased. Yet there was truth to her words, too, for I was sure I'd nearly driven Mother demented with all my escapades.

I smiled blithely despite the crushing pain in my chest, wondering how differently this scene might have played out were my real mother still alive. "That's all right, Mother," I said as I kissed her cheek. "I'll be back in a few weeks and you won't feel the same way."

I embraced her then, breathing in her scent of Pears' soap and heaving a sigh of relief when she hugged me back. I had dragged her through hell more times than Dante could count, and honestly, she'd earned a respite from me. But I meant what I said: I *would* be back.

After all, Washington was where Nick and I belonged.

The White House staff had outdone themselves spreading false rumors as to which exit Nick and I would use, the better to confuddle the press so we could escape and motor on to Friendship, the country estate where we'd spend the first few nights as newlyweds before our three-week honeymoon in Cuba and eight-week jaunt to Europe. Four cars arrived at the various gates of the White House to further confuse the crowd, but in the meantime, Nick and I laughingly climbed out the window of the Red Room and onto the south portico of the White House, where an electric runabout waited to whisk us away.

"Bon voyage!" Our families pelted us with the traditional shower of rice, although my rabble-rousing younger brothers used dried beans, probably because they'd deemed rice too small to make for proper munitions. We laughingly shielded our eyes and ducked into Nick's car, waving through the open windows as we pulled away.

Yet before the runabout pulled onto Pennsylvania Avenue and beyond that, into the vast unknown, I saw Maggie Cassini waving, and her voice reached my ears. "We'll miss you, Alice Roosevelt," she called. "Now that you've dropped down the line into plain Mrs. Longworth!"

I rolled up the window at that, but didn't have time to fret as Nick pulled me close and we kissed like old times, the feel of it searing into my bones and all the pieces of the world feeling mostly right again while the driver assiduously fixed his eyes on the road.

That kiss.

In that moment, it was all that mattered.

"Are you happy, Mrs. Longworth?" Nick finally asked when we were both breathless.

"Very," I answered, shaking the rice from my hair and snuggling against his chest for the long drive. It didn't take long before the noise of the car and the events of the day lulled Nick into a light sleep, leaving me alone with my thoughts.

I *was* happy. Yet I'd have been a liar not to admit that I was also nervous about the future that yawned before us.

Maggie's taunt still rang in my ears, burrowing deeper and deeper under my skin as I'm sure she meant it to. As a married woman I was no longer America's princess, but I *was* still my father's daughter. With Nick's ring on my finger and his name tacked onto mine, I was also a congressman's wife, yet I'd sooner die than turn into one of the stodgy congressional dames that I'd scorned on the Far East junket. I was too famous to fade into my husband's shadow. Instead I would stand beside Nick and give all these Washington politicians and their dreary wives a run for their money.

After all, I might be Mrs. Longworth now, but I was still Alice *Roosevelt* Longworth.

And I'd never let anyone forget it.

Part 2

THE CONGRESSMAN'S WIFE

I have a simple philosophy: Fill what's empty.
Empty what's full. Scratch where it itches.

—ALICE ROOSEVELT LONGWORTH

Chapter 10

A persistent robin chirping outside the window woke me on the sunny second morning of our honeymoon. I stretched, then reached out an arm to the other side of the biggest bed I'd ever slept in, frowning to find it cold and empty. Waking up in this suite with its canopied four-poster bed and antique mahogany furniture felt all so terribly grown-up, as if I were a child playacting at being an adult and about to be sent home any minute.

It took me a moment to realize someone was in the shower down the hall, singing in a deep voice some sentimental ballad. Groaning, I hugged a pillow over my face and ears, but it was no use.

"An early bird who sings too?" I hollered to Nick, loving the fact that there were no servants to hear us. "You might have told me that *before* I agreed to marry you!"

"Not all of us are night prowlers," he called over the splashing water. "How late were you up last night?"

"Oh, you know." I winced. "Late enough."

I padded from bed and slipped into yesterday's discarded shirt-waist and skirt, then nabbed Nick's gray wool jacket from the back of the rocking chair and turned the collar up so I could drink in the smell of tobacco and his spicy aftershave. "I'm going for a walk," I called.

"Don't be gone too long," he said, and I hesitated outside the washroom door, fingers on the handle before hurriedly shoving my hands deep into the pockets. I was down the stairs and almost to the door when my hand bumped a bottle on the hall table. It lurched and I barely caught the wobbly thing before it crashed to the floor.

Not just any bottle . . . a Gordon's sloe gin bottle. I winced, remembering the night before.

"To our future!" Nick had toasted after dinner, his tie undone and his feet kicked up on the leather ottoman. "And to the most wonderful wife a man could ask for."

"To our future," I'd echoed, but my enthusiasm waned as his toasts wore on and his words began to slur. I knew Nick enjoyed a tipple now and then, but by the tenth toast I was repulsed by the sloppy way he tripped over his own feet and splashed gin on the polished oak floors, all while singing off-key bawdy songs. I was repulsed and relieved when he finally passed out on the sitting room's leather sofa. I'd covered him with an eiderdown coverlet from our bed, cringing as he snored and reeked like a gin-soaked sponge.

We all make mistakes. Surely last night was a rarity that won't repeat itself.

Now I stepped outside into fresh air that smelled of green things just beginning to lift their heads. This was the same elegant estate where my father and mother had honeymooned, and I could easily imagine their happiness as they walked this same gravel path. Perhaps Nick and I might one day send our own children here.

I walked for an hour—three lovely miles that had me tempted to do another three—until I was positively red-cheeked and ravenous, yet I frowned to see a black mail carriage pull up the drive as I cracked the lid off a bottle of freshly delivered milk.

"Letters for the Friendship estate." The mail carrier jumped down from his truck, several unexpected envelopes in hand.

Few people knew we were here, but the mystery was solved when I recognized Mother's handwriting and saw that she'd forwarded the letters here to Friendship, leaving off my name to preserve our anonymity.

"Thank you," I said as the carrier tipped his hat at me, staring for a moment so I knew he recognized me despite my mussed hair and Nick's oversize jacket. I ducked inside before he could ask for a signed photograph.

The first few letters were congratulatory, including one from Eleanor that made me smile, but the last was written in an unfamiliar, slanting hand. I turned the envelope over, but there was no return address.

Dear Alice,

You are undoubtedly the happiest woman on earth today. I believe you to be all that is honest and pure; therefore, I do not believe that Nick told you before he led you to the altar that he is the father of a beautiful child, our *child.* My *child.*

My half-finished bottle of milk crashed to the tiles with a violent shatter of glass. Every word seemed to freeze me by degrees, so my teeth chattered and my fingers went numb.

Until three years ago he was content to remain away from everything pertaining to marriage, but ambition seized him, he met you, dear girl, and decided to win you at any cost. I have promised him not to reveal this for the love of him but think you should know the man you are to perhaps spend your young life with.

My breath came in searing gasps and my already off-center, kilterless world lurched off its axis. The letter was unsigned, but it might have been from Maggie Cassini or even Fräulein Kroebel from South Korea, or any number of Nick's jilted girls. Then I recalled Miriam Bloomer in my room on my wedding day, vulnerable and unhinged. Was this a cruel hoax she'd concocted to drive a wedge between Nick and me?

What if it wasn't a hoax? Or what if still another woman had sent it?

I crumpled the letter in my fist like a jagged stone, an animal moan building in the back of my throat. I swallowed it down, even as the world spun wildly around me.

Nick had chosen *me*. The letter was a lie. It had to be.

I repeated the words and twisted the gold ring on my left hand until I was steady. I'd march upstairs and demand the truth from him. After all, I was his wife; I *deserved* the truth.

Yet the angry words died on my lips the moment I flung open the bedroom door, the heat of my ire tempered by a sudden icy fear.

Nick was nestled in the eiderdown, his face smooth with sleep, one arm flung to my side of the bed as if he'd reached for me in a dream. I tried to imagine another woman in his arms and felt as if I might retch.

I could never face the world if Nick had had a child with another woman, even a cast-off one. The truth might well make me more miserable, for I'd made an irreparable decision in marrying Nick. Divorce simply wasn't done, no matter the atrocities committed by either spouse.

The somber grandfather clock downstairs chose that moment to toll the hour and scare me out of my skin. Nick's eyes fluttered open and a drowsy smile spread over his face.

A brutal miasma of emotions ripped through me, love tinged with a vicious hate I felt all the way to my bones.

He lifted the eiderdown in an invitation to join him. "I was just dreaming of you, my dear girl," he drawled sleepily. "We were in Cuba having the time of our lives."

"Is that so?" I turned my back to him and tucked the letter into the dog-eared pages of my diary. I was a wife now, no longer a hotheaded debutante who could throw a fit and hope that things would fall out right. Yet I would forever be a politician's daughter, and a politician wouldn't run headfirst into this problem without considering it from all angles. I would let this sit, and then decide how and when to confront Nick.

He yawned, oblivious to my inner turmoil. "Come back to bed and I'll tell you all about it."

Chin up. Back straight. No matter the truth, I would keep my dignity.

I climbed in next to him, shivering as if there were a thin layer of ice against my skin. He pulled me closer until my back was against his chest, a spot that had been pure bliss only yesterday but now had me lying stiff as a corpse.

"Right where you belong," he murmured, pressing a kiss against my hair.

I didn't speak, glad that he couldn't see my eyes as they welled with hot tears, blurring the vision of my diary and the terrible accusation it hid between its pages.

We knocked off two parties on our first night in Havana, one at the American Club and one at the palace. Nick hovered by my side the entire evening, his hand on the small of my back so I'd almost convinced myself halfway through the night that the letter must be a fraud.

Surely Nick couldn't have kept such a terrible secret from me all this time. Could he?

We were nibbling candied guava at the palace when Nick introduced me to a friend of his. "Alice, this is Warren Harding, the new lieutenant governor of Ohio. And this is his wife, Florence."

I offered my hand to a long-faced woman twenty years my senior. She squinted like a nearsighted horse, drawing attention to the red indentations on either side of the bridge of her nose. *Someone should have told her that it would take more than leaving off her spectacles to appear fashionable,* I thought, *especially in that terrible chartreuse gown. Is chartreuse even a color?*

"We're recuperating after Warren's electoral campaign." Florence spoke in a strident midwestern accent while our husbands commiserated on the state of the Ohio legislature. "And I suspect you're still recovering from the wedding of the century."

I smiled. "I'm not sure when I'll stop reeling."

"You're an Aquarius," she said. "The constant change of scenery on this trip will have you back to normal in no time."

"You dabble in astrology?" I'd read several books on the subject, but usually out of Father's sight as he deemed them silly and unscientific. It occurred to me that now I could read whatever I liked, without fear of censure.

"No political wife can afford to ignore the stars, unless she wishes to see her husband defeated at the polls," she said. "I even hired an occultist to determine the best days for Warren's campaign events."

That seemed a little extreme, but then I'd never been married to a campaigning politician. Perhaps I'd feel differently when Nick came up for reelection in a few months.

"You must call on us when you're next in Ohio," she continued. "I keep a little red book filled with the names of people who have slighted Warren and me, and will add your name to the front page if you don't drop in on us." Her smile was so enigmatic I couldn't tell if she spoke in earnest, but I found that I liked this Florence Harding. "I daresay we could fill an entire afternoon, if not several days, with absorbing conversation. You'll soon discover that's a rarity among Ohio's politicians."

Little red book or not, a visit with Florence Harding promised to be far more entertaining than enduring another lengthy diatribe on my shortcomings from Susan Longworth.

"I promise to look you up," I said as the Hardings excused themselves.

"Florence is a stoic to her very bones," Nick said. He jutted his chin to where Warren and Florence were already claiming their coats.

"What do you mean?" I asked.

"Old Warren is a notorious philanderer." Nick lit a cigarette and blew the smoke in their direction. "Just look at him now, right under her nose."

Sure enough, I watched in mute horror as Warren pinched the bottom of the pretty Cuban girl who'd retrieved his jacket. Florence simply shrugged her shawl over her square shoulders. It didn't escape my notice that Nick's gaze lingered on the girl's ample curves before he glanced my way and cleared his throat.

Harding caught my eye and winked as his wife disappeared into the night. I'd call on Florence the next time I was in Ohio, but Warren could drown on the way back to America for all I cared.

After Havana, Nick and I laughed our way through wind-torn automobile trips around the island before journeying by slow train to Santiago with the entire American diplomatic corps posted to the island. That would have been fine, had it not been for one unexpected surprise.

"Why, Willard Straight!" My cheeks flared with heat once we'd all sunk ourselves into the Pullman's plush green upholstery for our celebratory send-off. The last time I'd seen Willard was in Korea after the ghastly argument with Nick over Fräulein Kroebel, which I hoped we could all forget. "I wasn't expecting to see you here."

"I'm just off the boat myself," Willard said. "You're looking at the newest diplomatic attaché to Cuba."

I found myself suddenly flustered, wondering how I was going to maneuver a night, much less several days, on the same train with both Willard and Nick. As it turned out, I needn't have worried.

"If you'll excuse me." Nick didn't even acknowledge Willard. "Duty calls."

I stared after my husband, thunderstruck at his rudeness and that he was leaving me alone with Willard, as if he couldn't be bothered to recall that I'd once flirted mercilessly with this still-handsome man. A quick glance at the crowded bar solved the mystery, where a tuxedoed bartender poured rum and lime juice into double silver shakers. Up came the flush in my cheeks again, but this time it was from the heat of anger that Nick was drinking. Again.

"Pardon me," I said to Willard.

I fled into the open vestibule of the caboose, the warm breeze tugging at my coiffure while I glared at Cuba's sloping hills against the star-spangled sky. Hours might have passed before the tension in my shoulders eased and I forced myself to focus on the peaks my father had stormed during the Spanish-American War, remembering how he'd called the time he'd spent here his *"crowded hours."* As I listened to laughter spilling from the bar, I worried that I'd already left the most crowded hours of my life behind me.

"This is beautiful country, isn't it?"

I jumped as Willard retrieved two cigarettes from his coat pocket, lit them both, and offered me one. Too tempting to pass up, I took the shag in silence, drawing the sweet tobacco into my lungs before exhaling. "The hills are a bit disappointing. I always assumed from Father's description that San Juan Hill was on a par with Everest and Kilimanjaro. But I've sledded down bigger mounds as a girl."

Willard leaned against the vestibule, one knee bent so his foot rested against the wall. "Ah, yes, but was there was a regiment of angry Spanish at the top of the hill raining bullets at your toboggan?"

I laughed. "Only snowballs, thrown by my horde of heathen brothers. Although Father *did* bring back empty cartridges from Las Guasimas for us to play with."

"Of course he did. I assume it's second nature for Roosevelt children to play with ammunition instead of mundane fare like dolls and trains."

"Naturally." I shrugged. "We had rifles pressed into our tiny paws at a young age."

Willard pointed out San Juan Hill, the location of Father's greatest moment of glory. "Wasn't your father the only soldier on horseback that day?"

"He was, as he likes to remind everyone whenever he has the chance." I blew a line of perfect smoke rings for emphasis, but in truth I was inordinately proud of my father.

"I suppose he's happier than a cat in cream that you've finally settled down."

"It means I'm some other man's responsibility, which he fully approves of." I flicked the end of the cigarette off the train, watching the ember disappear into darkness as the train chugged steadily away. The dull roar of the wheels over the track was suddenly punctuated by a shout of raucous laughter from the bar carriage. Willard's eyes darted in that direction. Even in the dark I could read tension in the way his fingers drummed against the metal.

"And are you happy? As Mrs. Nicholas Longworth, I mean."

The question caught me off guard. I couldn't remember anyone ever asking if I was happy, for everyone always assumed that I was, given my family's position. I knew I *should* be happy, but right now my husband was well on his way toward drinking himself half-rats and I had in my possession a letter claiming he'd sired an illegitimate child. Marriage was proving itself the opposite of the soothing tonic I'd envisioned.

"I suppose I am."

"You don't suppose at happiness." Willard held my gaze even in the darkness. "You either are happy . . . or you aren't."

"Are you happy, Willard Straight?" I asked, mostly to deflect the question.

"I was," Willard mused. "Until I encountered a hotheaded thief who could teach queens how to sit a horse while debating politics like her famous father. I didn't know it in Korea, but she stole something rather critical to my happiness, and I fear she'll never give it back."

Thief . . .

I cleared my throat and took an abrupt step back to put more space between us. Only a year ago, Willard's flirtation would have set me to fluttering my eyelashes, but I was a married woman now. "I'm sorry to hear that, Mr. Straight, and I do hope the critical item is returned to you with great haste. However, I can report that I am most certainly happy in my new situation."

Willard raised his eyebrows; I wasn't fooling him. "I'm pleased to hear it."

I made some excuse and beat a hasty retreat back into the train, blinking at the sudden light and surprised to find Nick absent from the party that was still going strong at the bar. I suddenly worried that the men had overheard my conversation with Willard, yet there was nothing I should feel guilty about. After all, we were only sharing a conversation.

A conversation I'd enjoyed, if I was under oath.

Willard was only a friend. I might be married now, but I was still allowed to have friends, even if they were of the handsome, brilliant variety. It didn't matter that I had a husband who matched that same description, or that he wasn't quite the man I'd thought him to be.

I smiled to the remaining members of the party and slid open the groaning door to our dark Pullman car, only to be hit in the face with a wall of noxious rum fumes. My eyes struggled to adjust to the dim interior, and I almost hit the wall as I stumbled over something solid.

Nick was passed out on the floor, an overturned glass that had spilled daiquiri into the carpet at his elbow.

"Alice?" he groaned. "That you?"

I wanted to scream or to kick him senseless, but instead I only stood with clenched fists, stewing in my anger while Willard's question pummeled me over and over.

Are you happy?

Was I? Or I had I made the blunder of my life in marrying Nick? I *would* make this work. And I *would* be happy, even if it killed me.

"Go to sleep," I growled as I shed my dress and climbed into my cold and lonely bed.

This time I kept the bed's coverlet for myself. Let Nick shiver the night away on the hard floor and learn a lesson.

By the time Nick woke the next morning, I was already dressed in a lighthearted yellow day dress with a natty hat that belied my foul mood. A glance at the platform outside revealed a crush of newspapermen alongside a row of whiskered Cuban generals who had fought with my father, one with an armful of lavish butterfly jasmine that I presumed was for me.

"Pull yourself together," I said, looking down where Nick struggled to his feet. "This is not how I imagined my husband would ever act."

He gave a pained scowl and scrubbed a hand over his puffy eyes. "Then perhaps you'd best adjust your expectations."

I stood there for a moment, silently chanting Papa Lee's admonitions for a happy marriage even as I waved away the porter with his tray of pastries and coffee.

Conduct yourself so as to be happy, and to make him happy too.

Yet Nick and I were no ordinary couple, meant to follow ordinary rules. I was a political wife and Nick needed my family for his career.

A career I wasn't about to let him squander at the bottom of a bottle.

"You disgust me," I said to Nick, throwing the windows open to let in the coal fumes, just to torture him a little. Turning a blind eye to his overindulgence hadn't gotten me anywhere, so it was time to try a new tack. "We're expected for photographs at the Peace Tree in half an hour. Gargle with rose water so you don't reek like ethyl alcohol."

I turned and slammed the door behind me. It wasn't in my nature to simper and praise a man when he was acting like a stupid moonbrain. Where was the debonair congressman who had dared me to find out about Lieutenant Luckerman's wig and courted me with molasses taffy?

I received my answer after I spent five minutes regaling the press about our plans when we returned to America, including the fact that Susan Longworth planned to live with us. (I had a hunch on how to resolve that cataclysm, but we'd see how it played out.) Nick joined us in a white fedora that shielded his eyes from the worst of the sun, laughing adroitly with the uniformed Cubans and tilting his hat at their gathered wives and daughters. I watched him with a tinge of awe, for no one else seemed to notice his bloodshot eyes or the way his lips tightened whenever the sun broke from the clouds. It was easy to see how he'd been elected to Congress and broken so many hearts when he was at his most charming.

Yet that charm evaporated the moment we stood beneath the Peace Tree, where the Spanish forces had surrendered to America almost ten years ago.

"I'm pleased to see you're able to stand upright," I said from between gritted teeth, smiling as the press photographers set up their equipment.

"Spare me the sermon." Nick stared straight ahead, stone-faced. "I enjoy a little fun now and then, which, if I recall, was something you used to appreciate."

"My idea of fun doesn't involve finding my husband collapsed in a stupor on the floor. Life isn't all fun and games."

He looked down his nose at me, disdain chilling his reddened eyes. "It certainly hasn't been lately."

I gaped, icy-hot blood roaring in my veins as I shouted at him, "Maybe you should have thought of that before you married me!"

Suddenly, the air exploded with a legion of camera exposures. I flushed in mortification, for rather than a placid picture of the smiling Longworth newlyweds, we'd instead broadcast our first row as a married couple for the entire world, with the ridiculous Peace Tree in the background.

Willard Straight hurried over to us, gesturing with exaggerated movements as he expertly blocked us from view of the cameras. "I believe the reporters would like a shot with each of you on either side of the trunk here," he said as he positioned us, avoiding both our eyes.

But despite Straight's ministrations, the damage had been done.

Nick might conduct himself like a buffoon in private—or perhaps worse, considering the honeymoon letter that was still hidden in my diary—but I'd just committed the grievous sin of erring in public.

"I'm sorry," I gritted out as I took my place alongside the tree, humbling myself in an attempt to restore peace. I wasn't sure who I was supposed to be in this marriage, but I consoled myself with the fact that I'd held my own during the argument and had been successfully obnoxious about his drinking, to the point where perhaps Nick might think twice before getting boiled as an owl.

"I'm sorry too," Nick said, although his face told a different story. Still, I'd take the olive branch.

In the future, it might be wise to restrain my temper toward my husband, at least when newspapermen were present. I'd guarantee nothing beyond that.

Once again, the press assaulted us as soon as we set foot in New York, this time eager for details about our honeymoon. "How was Cuba?" one reporter asked. "You lovebirds looked none too pleased with each other at the Peace Tree. Have you two patched everything up or are there squalls ahead?"

That answers the question of whether that infernal Peace Tree photo made it back to America. Ugh, and double ugh.

"We surely don't know what you mean." I gave a sugary smile, using the broad rim of my hat to keep my face partially hidden.

Nick turned the full wattage of his smile onto the reporter and even wrapped an arm around my waist. "Our honeymoon was an endless delight."

I declined any further comment.

We continued mostly in silence by train and then car to Nick's Washington house on Eighteenth Street. I expected Susan Longworth to greet us at the door, a specter of black with a bun so severe it pulled tight the corners of her eyes. Instead, I found the house empty as the sound of the butler setting down my bags echoed down the hall.

"Mother returned to Rookwood," Nick said as he came in behind me. "Did you know she received almost a hundred letters from Americans who wished for you to be able to set up a proper house? She said she had no choice but to bow to public sentiment."

So my comments in Cuba had flown home like little birds as I'd hoped, and solved my problem for me. I'd never loved the American people so much as I did in that moment.

I didn't have a chance to respond, only shrieked with glee and dropped my valise as a barking black cannonball barreled its way down the hallway toward us.

"There's my good boy!" I gave a yip of laughter and gathered Manchu in my arms, submitting to a flurry of wet kisses. "Aren't you glad we're home?"

Home.

This town house, with its masculine gray curtains and framed maps of Ohio, didn't feel like home, although I could see that Mother had already sent my things over. There was my half-finished wedding scrapbook on the parlor desk and, in the study, the oriental silk screen Empress Cixi had given me. Yet it all felt out of place. *I* felt out of place.

"I suppose you'll want to rest up and go calling," Nick said as he hung his hat on the mahogany rack and dropped his gold-topped walking stick in the umbrella stand. I'd never given much thought to Nick's housekeeping, but the front rooms were fastidiously kept. Everything neat and trim, just like the man himself.

"Calling?"

"Isn't that what wives do?" he asked. "Pay social calls so you can nibble on stale tea biscuits and swap useless gossip?"

I wandered from doorway to doorway with Manchu, taking in the striped wallpaper and expensive furnishings. "Does that really sound like something I'd care to do?"

Nick's lips quirked upward as I glanced back at him, the first true smile I'd had since Cuba. "Not unless you plan to surprise everyone with your sudden domestication."

"I wouldn't last a day." I set down Manchu as the butler discreetly disappeared. "I'd shock everyone by turning down the wrong corner of my calling card or mistaking a sealed return envelope as an invitation for tea instead of an abject refusal."

Nick was suddenly behind me, his arm around my waist as his lips traveled excruciatingly up my jaw. "You'd devastate the entire Washington social scene."

I gasped, tilting my head back. "The sole purpose of social calls is to climb the social ladder. In case you haven't noticed, I'm already at the pinnacle of said ladder. Anyone who's anyone can find their way to *me*."

To which Nick only laughed, the warm rumble of sound against my throat making my toes curl. "Suit yourself. We're leaving for Europe soon anyway. And after that, Cincinnati."

Cincinnati meant Rookwood, and Rookwood meant Susan Longworth.

The nicest thing I could say about that entire city was that the Cincinnati zoo had recently named its baby elephant Alice in my honor.

Yet Cincinnati seemed far, far away as Nick swept me off my feet and mounted the stairs, carrying me over the threshold to our new bedroom and kicking the door shut behind us.

We left on the *St. Louis* a few weeks later, a ship chosen less for its comforts and more for the patriotic fact that it was a sturdy American vessel. I'd never been to Europe, and imagined the entire continent as scenes straight from Charles Dickens's and Sir Walter Scott's novels, sooty skies and labyrinthine streets filled with kidney-pie vendors and dust-streaked chimney sweeps in fustian dress. Our trip would be only eight weeks, but I wished that it might last forever. I'd always been aware of how I should comport myself as a politician's daughter (although I made no claims that I always upheld those responsibilities), but now I was doubly aware of my roles as both the president's daughter *and* a congressman's wife.

My first test saw me dressed once again in my wedding gown, this time with the prescribed three ostrich feathers in my hair for my formal presentation to heavy-shouldered King Edward, whose coronation I had once hoped to attend. The packed anteroom where we waited smelled of sweat and mothballs as I eyed Nick's ensemble, his jacket black as freshly spilled ink. "You should wear knee breeches more often," I whispered when our names were called and we walked behind the lord chamberlain to where the king and queen waited. "Maybe the next time you make a speech to the House."

"Some speech that would be," Nick said, even as the lord chamberlain shushed us. "No one would be able to hear me over the chamber's laughter."

I thought the breeches made Nick look rather dashing, but then he might have looked dashing in farmers' overalls and a straw hat.

"Mrs. Longworth," Queen Alexandra said after I'd kissed her hand and risen from making my prettiest curtsy. It was easy to see that she'd been beautiful once, but time and her notorious philanderer of a husband had aged her prematurely. "Are you enjoying yourself here in London?"

"Very much."

I thought that would be the end of my interview, but Alexandra's lively eyes skipped over me. "What has been your favorite part?"

I thought for a moment. "I enjoyed the debates in the House of Lords and House of Commons. All the shouting and name-calling, why, I thought it would turn into quite a brawler!"

"Truly?" That obviously wasn't the answer she'd been expecting.

"It's beyond dreary to read about a bill in the papers, but another thing altogether to witness its birth or death firsthand."

"Yet, you must see such activities at home in Washington all the time."

"I've actually never attended debates in Congress," I admitted. "But I intend to rectify that upon my return."

"Good girl," Queen Alexandra said. "In the meantime, I insist you join me for tea tomorrow."

"It would be my honor," I said.

"And you," the queen said, as if suddenly remembering Nick. "Mrs. Longworth's husband. How are you finding things in London? Are you weary of your wife receiving all our attentions?"

Part of me enjoyed watching Nick navigate from my shadow, further proof that my husband needed me by his side. "I'm quite content to allow Alice the limelight," he said. "She's a natural at it."

To which the queen only nodded. "A fair assessment, young man."

After that, we bowed to the king and chummed along like true newlyweds on our way to France.

As it turned out, Nick's sister Clara was visiting Paris with her husband, so we were pressed to sojourn at their apartment with its view of the Champs-Élysées. I'd met Clara only at our wedding and had scarcely said more than two words to her—although she'd managed to point out that she was related via marriage to the famed French Lafayette family—so I looked forward to getting to know her better. On one memorable afternoon we enjoyed a casual summer lunch of sparkling mimosas, fresh peaches, and croissants with cherry preserves. It was there that I learned how medieval the entire Longworth clan truly was.

I was surprised when Clara's maid delivered a letter to me on the sunny veranda, but there was no return address. Acrid bile rose in my throat.

Surely this wasn't another letter with fantastical claims of Nick's cast-off child, an accusation I still hadn't mustered the courage to ask him about.

"Who's it from, dear?" Clara asked, so there was no escape for me. Clara, her husband, and Nick watched as if I were some sort of exotic creature trapped between the glass slides of one of those new light microscopes.

"I'm not sure."

"Alice receives all sorts of strange mail from back home," Nick said. "One of the most recent was from a midwestern housewife, with instructions on how best to starch my shirts."

Strange mail. My already panicked brain wondered if perhaps Nick had found the honeymoon letter, but I'd checked that it was still hidden beneath the cover of my diary before we left.

I opened this new envelope with shaking hands, unable to hear the conversation over the dull roar in my ears.

Dear Alice,

It's been several months since you departed Cuba's shores, and I'm pulling out of the station soon myself. Your father has helped transfer me to Manchuria for what he claims will be a larger field for my talents. I was hoping you might meet me in New York as I otherwise fear it will be a long time before I see you again. I'd happily meet you upon your return, bearing liquor, lacquer, and lunacy, but it would be a hopeless thing to try to break the cordon of secret police that I imagine surrounds you day and night. I might simply want to offer you a nosegay and I'd be arrested as an anarchist with a little bunch of greenhouse bombs.

Yours truly,
Willard S.

I sagged with relief, swallowing down the nervous laughter that threatened to bubble loose from my throat. Yet I knew that Nick wouldn't take kindly to Willard's invitation, not coming as it did from the man who had witnessed our crackling row under the Peace Tree.

"We're in utter suspense over here," Clara said, her croissant forgotten on its plate. "And you've gone positively white, Alice. Who's the letter from?"

"An old friend," I said. "Willard Straight."

Nick set down his mimosa. "What does Straight want with you?"

I might be willing to flaunt every social convention in America, but I'd never lie to Nick. "He asks to meet with me when we're in New York."

Clara and her husband fell silent, and I swear every couple strolling the Champs-Élysées below strained to hear Nick's response.

"Of course you won't meet with him." Nick smeared a stain of cherry preserves across a croissant, although it seemed as if he might pulverize the unfortunate pastry. "As if the president's daughter would rearrange her schedule just because a petty diplomat asked her to."

Yet we both knew that Straight was no mere diplomat, especially as my father had gone out of his way to promote him (which was done at my urging, although I'd never tell Nick that). I frowned. Nick was my husband and I'd married him to escape my father's control, not replace it.

"I don't see the harm in meeting with him." I pushed away my plate. "Straight is an amusing fellow."

I knew it was the wrong thing to say before Nick's nostrils flared, but I didn't care. This was a test of sorts, to discover where the boundaries were drawn. Nick could eye pretty girls with all the world watching—and possibly even have an illicit child—but far be it from me to meet in a public place with one of my father's diplomats.

But Nick didn't have to say anything, not with Clara across the table, her thin lips pinched just like her mother's. "Perhaps in your family it's acceptable to do as you please with no thought for others," Clara said, "but I can't fathom a wife meeting with a man after her husband expressly forbade it. A wife's sole job is to obey her husband. And, of course, to provide him with a nursery of children."

I ignored the latter comment, for my monthly courses had been entirely predictable since my marriage, despite Nick's dedication in the bedroom. Already I recalled Mother's conversation the night before my wedding and worried that perhaps I, too, might need some sort of procedure if I was ever to have a child.

The very thought made me shudder. I was no stranger to pain, not after surviving both polio and a near-fatal abscess in my jaw, but I loathed the idea of going under the knife.

"Nick would never expressly deny me anything," I said, my voice sweeter than honey. "He knows to forbid something is the surest way to drive me to it."

"Dearest," Clara's husband said to her, pushing back both their chairs. "Perhaps we'd best let Nick and Alice discuss this on their own."

"Of course." Clara followed her husband in a perfect picture of obedience, except when she stopped at the doorway and shot me a look filled with venom. I knew then that I'd never find an ally among any of the Longworth women.

"There's nothing to discuss," Nick said as soon as the terrace was empty. His voice was cold and calculating, the sound of a politician negotiating in a smoke-filled room. "For we won't be stopping in New York City."

"You're a fool," I said. "There's nothing you could do to stop me if I wanted to go to New York and have a dozen clandestine meetings with Willard Straight."

"I could divorce you, Alice Roosevelt, and send you back to your father in disgrace. My reputation would recover, but yours never would. And neither would your father's."

I gaped at him then, for he was right. This was his ace in the hole, and one I'd never seen coming.

With that, he turned and walked calmly back into the house, leaving me suddenly freezing despite the July heat.

We boarded the *St. Paul* at Cherbourg two days later, and didn't speak to one another until we were back in the United States.

We did not go to New York.

Chapter 11

I stared up at Rookwood's foreboding brick exterior with a sinking heart. Not even a monkey with cataracts could have thought the Longworth manse pretty; a four-story tower I could well imagine throwing myself from connected two squat brick boxes, all painted a dreary gray and covered with fingers of creeping ivy. Yet we'd moved to Ohio for the campaign season and taken up residence at Rookwood, which meant that this was my temporary home. It also meant I could no longer avoid Susan Longworth.

I drew a steadying breath and slipped silently into the walnut-paneled entryway even as I cringed at the sound of my mother-in-law's voice down the hall.

Being a jelly-regular, well-bred widow meant Nick's mother was an unapologetic wag when it came to gossip. I'd believed I was her only whipping post, and was somewhat relieved to discover she found everyone worthy of a good tongue-lashing.

Except Nick. Susan Longworth's one redeeming quality was her absolute dedication to her only son. Heaven help the rest of us who had been so unfortunate as to emerge from the wombs of other women.

"Did you hear about poor Miriam Bloomer?" she asked today's representative of the Bitter Old Biddies Club, probably some well-to-do banker's wife. I paused unseen outside the Music Room's door, frozen by the mention of Nick's former fiancée.

"I heard she had a spell."

"A spell?" Nick's mother scoffed as teacups clinked against Wedgwood china. "More like a breakdown. Her family is sending her to New York to recuperate."

"To recuperate?" the other old cat asked. "Or to an asylum?"

So Miriam *was* unhinged, which meant she may well have sent the false letter about Nick's imaginary son. The relief I felt was cruel, but I still worried over that letter, my concern over it waxing and waning in direct correlation to how often Nick and I quarreled. Perhaps now I could put my fears to rest.

I could hear Susan Longworth's shrug. "To think that she might have been my daughter-in-law," she finally said. "Instead . . ."

The censure in her voice was so clear that I could well imagine her disapproving glower. It should be noted that Susan Longworth had only three expressions: her disapproving glower, her angry glower, and her euphoric Nick-is-home smile that was never, *ever* pointed in my direction.

"Instead you have the country's most sensational daughter-in-law," her fellow gossip-jockey supplied.

"That I do." Bromide sounded as resigned as if she'd been sentenced to a life of hard labor in a Boer work camp. "I daresay poor Nicky doesn't quite know what he's gotten himself into. I fear it will be too late when he finally figures it out."

White-knuckled, I backed away from the parlor. If I didn't return to Washington, my name might end up in the headlines for committing a most heinous crime against my mother-in-law.

I broached the subject with Nick that night.

"I won't leave Rookwood," Nick said as he closed the door to our bedroom. "It's my home."

"Well, I won't stay." I removed my wedding pearls from Cuba and set them in my velvet-lined jewelry box. "Not with Brom—I mean, your mother—here."

Oy vey, but I'd be in hot water if Nick ever found out I'd taken to calling his mother Bromide, even if I was rather proud of the nickname. My mother-in-law's splendidly dull conversation was more effective than a tranquilizing dose of bromide salts, and living in the same house with her was akin to having to swallow a foul-tasting medicine. Every damned day.

"I need you here." Nick's admission made my heart leap. "Your presence alone will swell the crowds when I campaign for the midterms this fall."

Off came my gloves, so roughly I almost ripped the stitching. "I didn't realize I was trapped in the backwaters of Ohio just so you could have your famous wife at your side."

"Cincinnati is hardly a backwater," Nick said, already in bed and turning off the lamp.

To which I only frowned. "That's what you think."

In the end Nick was reelected, a sweet victory as it meant all the rallies I'd attended and hands I had shaken were for a good cause. Nick and I spent the morning after the election in our robes and slippers, perusing the Ohio papers and the election results from across the country.

"William Borah won the Idaho senate seat in an upset over the Democratic incumbent," Nick mused as he sipped his coffee.

I cared little about Idaho, but indulged Nick since the sound of my things being packed for Washington put me in a cheerful mood. "Another Republican on Capitol Hill is an extra boon for the Grand Old Party," I said. "Don't they call him the Lion of Idaho?"

That had stuck in my mind when I'd heard it, for the only other politician I'd ever heard called a lion was my father. Borah had best pack a wallop if he thought to share the title.

"They do indeed. From what I hear, he reveres your father as a god. That can only be a good thing, eh?"

I shrugged. I'd always thought of Father as a sort of omnipotent being, so why shouldn't everyone else? In fact, for me the true laurels of winning the election came in the form of an unexpected telegraph from my father that same morning.

Dear Alice,

Let me congratulate you and Nick with all my heart upon the successful way in which both of you have run your campaign. I tell you I felt mighty pleased with my daughter and her husband.

—Your loving
father

My marriage hadn't fulfilled all my hopes and expectations—far from it—but at least it had cast me in a happy light in my father's eyes. That alone almost made up for Nick's drinking and our quarrels. Politics was our common language and one I was determined to use to my advantage.

So it was that when the House of Representatives opened for its new session, I stood alongside Mother at the annual diplomatic reception in the East Room. I'd hoped Nick would shepherd me through the introductions of the unfamiliar faces so I might later recognize them from the House gallery, but instead he pulled a Houdini and disappeared into a crowd of good old boys, but not before I caught his act of making two martinis disappear too.

I felt my cheer evaporating with each passing moment. Apparently, my usefulness had ended the minute the election results had been reported.

"You should speak to your father on your way out," Mother said after most of the guests had left, leaving only discarded plates and a stale fug of cigarette smoke in the air. Nick had yet to reappear, and I had a mind to make him walk home. "He has some questions about public policy he'd like to discuss with you."

"With me?"

Mother squeezed my shoulder. "He thinks you might possess a feel for the pulse of the people, considering how much of the world you've seen and all your time back and forth between Ohio and Washington."

So I did as I was told for once and stopped by the Executive Office—without bothering to tell Nick—and spent the remainder of the evening discussing with Father the rampant whispers of his third-term run over a platter of butterscotch sandies.

"Mother claims I tied with my tongue a knot I cannot undo with my teeth when I swore this would be my last term," my father said as he paced the newly remodeled office. His latest pet, a small black bear named Jonathan Edwards, gave up watching him and nosed around the office's new mahogany desk. "I think she may be right, yet I gave my word and I won't go back on it."

"You may need to inform the country of that, clearly and force-fully," I said. "Most expect you to run again."

"America is sick of my grin and they are tired of hearing what you had for breakfast." He repeated the retort he'd used with the press half-heartedly, although anyone with eyes could see it killed him to think of leaving his beloved White House. If he gave the signal, I'd have braved all manner of spotlights and sweaty palms to stump for him at every rally across America, but he only tossed a cookie to Jonathan Edwards to distract the beast from gnawing through a chair leg. It seemed to work, and the little bear made short work of the scattering of crumbs with his pink tongue before settling down for bed on the rug. "I believe Secretary Taft will make an adequate replacement."

There was no denying that Uncle Will, my surrogate father and chaperone during the Far East junket, had a good heart. Unfortunately, that might not translate to possessing the necessary backbone to be president of the United States.

I *tsked* at Father and brushed cookie crumbs from my lap, which prompted Jonathan Edwards to abandon his nap in pursuit of more treats. "What you mean is that Taft will do as you suggest, while never being quite so beloved as you."

Father stopped pacing long enough to twirl the massive globe in the corner, the same one he'd recently posed in front of for his own presidential portrait. "I think he'll do well enough." His finger landed on Central America and then hopscotched to the Far East. "Sadly, not every president can dig the Panama Canal or settle a war with Russia and Japan."

I laughed, then stood on tiptoe to peck him good night on the cheek. I expected the same awkward woodenness I'd always received whenever I'd dared to show him affection, but this time he only beamed at me, whether from his own accolades or my attentions I couldn't tell.

"Take care of yourself, Sissy," he said. "And that husband of yours too."

"Of course, Father," I said.

And I would take care of both of us, if not for Father, then for myself. Somehow, I'd convince myself that marrying Nick had *not* been a mistake.

The reminder of Uncle Will brought back memories of the Far East junket, and I longed to recapture the magic of its early weeks with Nick, of sneaking into Chinatown and dancing the hula together in Honolulu. There was no doubt I was playing with fire considering how things had gone in Korea, Cuba, and France, but surely there had to be some convenient paradise we hadn't yet spoiled with our arguing. Nick was never one to turn down an adventure, and together we sat in front of the fireplace, mulling over a whole world of maps and atlases.

I tossed aside the latest travel brochures with their lures of snow-covered Alps and Bavarian castles. "What about Alaska? Not even Father's been there yet."

"Somewhere warmer," Nick said. "Perhaps Hawaii?"

We'd fallen deeper in love on our first trip there; with a little luck we might recapture that magic. I could already smell the plumeria and feel the sand between my toes. "Maybe we can detour along the way, stop and see Yellowstone?"

Nick leaned forward and kissed me on the nose. "Anything for you, Bubbie."

And just like that, we were off again. I was no wilting violet who shrieked at the sight of Yellowstone's brown bears or wrinkled her nose at Old Faithful's sulfuric aroma. I tromped gleefully through the mud to get a close-up of the geysers just as I imagined Father might have done. I was living the strenuous life Father had always trumpeted about, inhaling the pine-tinged air while the sun warmed my hair and squirrels cursed us from high up in the trees. I saw, smelled, felt, and heard the call of America's rugged wilderness. And then I tasted it too.

"Nick!" I hollered, pointing to the sky and not paying the least attention to where I was stepping. "Is that an osprey?"

Damn it all if bird-gawking meant I didn't step wrong and fall facefirst into the red oozing muck of Yellowstone.

Trying to right myself only flopped me over so my backside matched my muddy front, prompting Nick to double over in a most provoking laugh. So much for my gallant husband coming to my rescue.

"Doesn't this beat all?" I said, happily mired in mud. "Now I suppose I have to go back to the hotel to change."

"I dunno." My darling husband leaned against a tree, then framed me with his hands as if he were a member of the press. "If we get a photograph of you, by tomorrow girls all over America will be covering themselves in mud and calling it Alice Red."

In retaliation, I aimed a fistful of the delicious mud at his snowy linen suit. And missed.

I pulled a face at him. "That first shot went wide, but there's no guarantee I'll miss the second. Or the tenth. I'm a very determined girl when I put my mind to something."

"You wouldn't dare." He whistled a careless tune and turned to inspect a sleeping geyser.

Which meant that he didn't notice I'd crept up behind him until I planted both my filthy hands on either side of his face and reached around to give him a wet and muddy kiss. And more.

Merry hell, but how we laughed when we tromped back into the hotel, both of us disheveled and covered in muck!

We continued our tour of Yellowstone like two moon-eyed newly-weds and then steamed to Waikiki, which was just as exotic and pic-turesque as I'd remembered it. Nick and I feasted on mahi-mahi until I feared the Pacific had been emptied of their fish, and not even my dour swimming suit—or our skinny-dipping—could scare away the rainbow-hued parrotfish or whiskered goatfish. "This is the life." Nick kicked his feet up on a wooden lounger outside our hut, his eyes sur-veying Maui's palm groves that were only a stone's throw from the ocean. "Pass me more of that roasted pig, will you?"

I did, wiping the juice from a slice of barbecued pineapple off my chin. Unbeknownst to Nick, fruit was about the only thing I could keep down these days, for I'd come down with a dour case of the mul-ligrubs. I hadn't mentioned it, for I was determined not to miss a mo-ment in paradise if I could avoid it. Especially as I suspected I might be pregnant.

Yet that didn't keep me from riding on horseback up the Haleakalā Crater at midnight, feeling like a vigorous lotus-eater straight out of Tennyson's poem. We spent the next two days leisurely ambling down the side of the volcano, unencumbered by our families or reporters, and whiled away hours in companionable silence with only the coos of zebra doves for conversation. Sometimes we rode side by side, our fingers entwined while the horses grazed.

"I love you, Alice Roosevelt Longworth," Nick said. "Always and forever."

"And I love you," I said.

For once in my life, I was perfectly content.

If there was such a place as heaven on earth, Hawaii was it, and had it not been for our political obligations, I'd have happily lived on that beach for the rest of my life. Instead, I found myself longing for the thatched roof and gecko sentinels of our ramshackle little cottage before our steamer even pulled away and we returned to dreary Ohio.

Back to reality. And politics.

Everything seemed to be going so well, and then came the day that I couldn't rise from bed.

"I'll fetch a doctor," Father said after he'd been summoned to my hotel room. Still sun-kissed and relaxed, I'd met him in Canton during his whistle-stop tour in Ohio to stump for Taft, and had opted to stay in a hotel so as to spend as little time at Rookwood with Bromide as was humanly possible. Now Father looked decidedly uncomfortable as I writhed in pain, but then he'd never been in his element around those who were weak or ill. "Don't worry, Sissy," he said from the doorway. "Perhaps it's good news; Mother was so exhausted the last time she was in a family way that she couldn't leave her bed. And we've waited a long time for our first grandchild, you know."

I didn't have a chance to respond, for my stomach was a seething mass of white-hot pokers jabbing me simultaneously in my kidneys, liver, and intestines.

Surely this wasn't what pregnancy was supposed to feel like.

"Appendicitis," said Dr. Nordhoff in her German accent after she'd finally examined me. "I'll get you moved to Cincinnati for the surgery right away. You're lucky that we caught it in time."

Lucky? Her verdict obliterated my hope of a pregnancy, and I was supposed to feel *lucky*?

Instead I could only gasp and curl deeper into myself, wrapping my battered body around this fresh pain. And fear.

Because, damn it, I was *afraid* of surgery.

"Alice will not be going to Cincinnati." Father's presidential voice surprised me so I cracked an eyelid open to see him glaring at the doctor. "She'll be moved to the White House instead," he declared. "The rooms there are more comfortable than any godforsaken hospital, and she might recover without the eternal glare of the press," he added when Dr. Nordhoff opened her mouth to protest.

So I was tucked onto the first train to Washington, groggy with pain but somehow content that my father had dropped the rest of his campaign schedule to see me home. He even carried me up the stairs at the White House himself, while Nick and Mother trailed behind.

"You'll be fine, Alice," Father said from the makeshift hospital that had been set up in the Rose Bedroom. "We're all rallying for you."

I managed a smile. "I've already beat polio and an abscess in my jaw," I said weakly. "I'll survive this, too, and rabble-rouse until I'm a bent-backed crone."

Still, my heart thudded wildly as Dr. Nordhoff placed the chloroform towel over my nose. The last thing I saw was Nick, with Mother and Father hovering in the background. Father held Manchu and lifted his furry black paw to make him wave at me.

"I'll be here when you wake up, Bubbie," Nick murmured, and gave my hand a final squeeze.

Suddenly there was so much I wanted to say, how much I loved him and how sorry I was that I wasn't pregnant, but the anesthetic rendered me mute just before it tiptoed away with the rest of my consciousness.

When I finally woke, only Mother sat at my bedside, her knitting needles clacking like old friends and a half-finished blanket draped over her lap.

"Welcome back," she said, setting down the needles as I groaned awake. "Dr. Nordhoff said the procedure went as smooth as butter. She'll be back to change your dressing in the morning."

I felt with a heavy hand the bandages on the right side of my abdomen, anticipating a stab of pain there. However, it was entirely numb, a sensation I was thankful for.

I survived, I thought triumphantly. *It'll take more than a little appendicitis to take me down.*

But I sobered quickly. I wasn't pregnant as I'd hoped—and we'd been married two years already—so perhaps another surgery loomed in my future. Yet, my mother had died after she'd had me, so perhaps I shouldn't be in such a rush.

One thing at a time, Alice . . .

"Where's Nick?" I grimaced at the desert in my mouth and throat.

Like a magician, Mother produced a porcelain mug of water and helped me take delicate sips.

"They've been sitting in the library since the operation started. Dr. Nordhoff noticed Nick looking a little green about the gills and suggested he vacate the premises before she ended up with two patients instead of one. Your father soon followed. They've been nearly hand in hand each time I go in to give them a report."

"Probably swapping stories to see who's survived the worst of my hijinks over the years." I wondered idly who would win, yet couldn't decide on an answer through the lingering chloroform.

"Actually," Mother said, "I've never seen your father sit still for so long, and he shooed away all the political couriers. You have both your father and your husband's undivided attentions, my dear."

I smiled as the medication lulled me toward sleep, but then frowned. Apparently, I'd had to undergo life-threatening surgery in order to capture the simultaneous attention of both men in my life.

Surely there had to be another way.

Chapter 12

Having my appendix plundered and my recovering in the White House brought one unexpected benefit: I could sit with Father much of the day to convalesce while he ran the nation. It wasn't just the current state of the country that had him pacing his office more than usual, but also its future once he was no longer at the helm. Taft, fresh off a steamer from the Philippines, was due to give the party's pivotal speech in just a few days at the Republican convention.

"Taft needs his hand held," Father said with a harrumph. It was high spring and he wore a spray of lemon verbena and rose geranium—his two favorite flowers—in his buttonhole. "If left to his own devices, he might well lose the election."

"Then hold his hand until he crosses the finish line," I said, gesturing with my spoon from my sickbed. Father had surprised me by bringing me a tray of steaming beef broth, and I was determined to drink every last drop, just because he'd cared enough to bring it to me. "This speech must galvanize the delegates to rally them to Uncle Will. It's imperative that Republicans continue to occupy the White House even after our family has vacated it."

Father cringed; apparently the new reality of an America without him as president was finally setting in. "Am I correct in assuming you think we shouldn't trust Taft to make a decent speech without hearing it first?"

I drained a spoonful of soup, choosing my words carefully. "Uncle Will's a bang-up secretary of war, but you can't deny he'll put the entire convention to sleep."

"He's not much of a speaker," Father admitted. "Good suggestion, Mousiekins."

Yes, I was a grown woman, but I still preened worse than a peacock to hear my father's praise.

I felt almost guilty for criticizing Taft when he lumbered into the room the next day, beaming like a well-fed Cheshire cat when he saw me. "It's been too long since I laid eyes on you, Alice," he said after he greeted Father. "And you went and got married in the interim."

"Indeed I have." I recalled Uncle Will's warnings against Nick, but only smiled and let him clasp my hand from where I sat on a striped davenport, under strict orders from my doctor not to move suddenly or laugh too hard lest I pop my stitches.

"I wish you only the best, Alice," Taft said, the leather wing chair beneath him groaning in protest. "Both you and Nick."

We proceeded with some social niceties over a plate of cinnamon tarts, Father dominating the conversation while Taft seemed to shrink in his chair. Finally, I turned the full wattage of my smile onto him.

"So, Uncle Will," I said. "What do you plan for the topic of your convention speech?"

He wrung his big hands, as if I were a teacher and he a pupil without his homework. I knew then that he hadn't planned his speech, just as I knew that Uncle Will wasn't the sort who could pluck a speech from the air behind a podium as Father sometimes did.

"Well," Taft said, fiddling with a cinnamon tart instead of devouring a whole dozen as he usually did. He looked at us with wide puppy eyes. "I thought I would talk about the Philippines."

There was a brief moment of silence, and then Father broke out in a deafening roar of laughter. Despite Taft's red face, I couldn't help myself and I joined in, clutching my sides and hooting at the very thought of Taft onstage discussing Manila or the lingering influence of the Spanish—none of which any American cared a whit about—and effectively alienating the entire Republican audience.

I laughed, that is, until there was a sudden pop on my abdomen that made spangled motes of pain dance before my eyes. I didn't have to look to know that I'd split my stitches.

"Are you all right, Alice?" Taft asked, even as I felt the blood drain from my face.

Father was already halfway to the door. "I'll get the nurse."

"You are an expert on the Philippines," I managed to gasp to Taft. "But perhaps Americans might wish to hear about topics pertinent to America? Like the tariff bill?"

"That's a sound suggestion," Taft said from where he now knelt at my side. "Why didn't I think of that?"

I winced as Father returned with the nurse. "I don't know, Uncle Will."

Not for the first time, I found myself wishing that Father hadn't promised not to run for a third term.

One look at his expression before the nurse shooed them both away told me he was thinking the same thing.

Despite his mediocre speech at the Republican convention, Taft was officially nominated.

It didn't escape my notice that the mere mention of my father's name at the primary convention set off a fifty-minute cheer that shook the dust from the rafters, whereas Uncle Will's nomination only garnered twenty-five minutes of indifferent applause. Taft's name would head the Republican ticket this year, but I was crossing my fingers—and all other pertinent appendages—that in another four or eight years, the name Roosevelt would be plastered on posters instead.

And after that, perhaps Longworth.

Nick and I were apart at least half of that summer, but he sent me flowers every day, including one fabulous arrangement of two dozen white roses delivered to Sagamore Hill. After that, I decided to surprise him with a weekend visit to Rookwood.

"Nicky needs his space today," Susan Longworth warned me before the butler had closed the door behind me. "You'll have to join me on a visit to Florence Harding for the afternoon."

While I didn't mind dishing with Florence about the importance of Mercury in retrograde or picking up campaign tips, the idea of spending the day with my mother-in-law made me want to catch the first train back to Washington. Or try my hand at hitchhiking.

"I haven't seen Nick in weeks." I removed my massive hat, this one black silk with an explosive spray of curling feathers. "He can have all the space he wants after I return home in a few days."

Home. Because try as I might, Ohio would never be home, no matter all that rot about a woman's home being at her husband's side.

I expected to sashay past Susan, but she grabbed my wrist in a vise. "We *will* have tea with Florence. Nick will have recovered from his upset by the time we return and then—and only then—can you see him."

I shook off old Bromide. Lord above, but the woman was a mastiff when it came to her son. My eyes narrowed. "What do you mean, his upset?"

Susan gave a delicate sniff, but I had the distinct impression that she was secretly giddy, chewing a choice piece of gossip like a cow with its cud. "Miriam Bloomer is dead."

I couldn't help myself—I gasped in shock. Wraithlike Miriam Bloomer, who had tried to warn me off Nick, who I still suspected as the author of the terrible letter I'd received on our honeymoon, was *dead*?

"How?" I asked, a wave of shame following my sudden relief. I clutched the back of a divan hard enough to rip the fabric as Susan continued blithely on.

"The poor dear was . . . fragile . . . after her split with Nick." Was it my imagination, or did Susan glance my way with blame in her eyes? "She had a terrible accident when you were in Cuba. Her face and much of her body was burned with acid, although no one's exactly sure how it happened."

I wondered for a moment how I hadn't heard of it, but Nick and I had been busy tearing into each other at that time. The sun might have exploded and I wouldn't have noticed.

"One of the Bloomers' maids left out a glass of cyanide to clean the tarnish off a belt buckle. They claim Miriam choked on a cracker and drank from the glass of cyanide, thinking it was water." Susan paused to dab her dry eyes. "The poor, poor dear."

I gave myself a moment to let the story sink in, jagged arrows of guilt pressing hard at my temples. Miriam was burned with acid two months after our wedding, and now she'd drunk cyanide? I recalled the broken woman who'd confronted me at my own wedding. It wasn't a far jump to imagine that she'd known full well what it was she was drinking.

No wonder Nick was experiencing an upset. I felt like I needed to lie down.

Instead, I replaced my hat, slowly securing its dagger-length hatpin. "After a story like that," I said, "I think I would enjoy tea with Florence Harding."

I tried not to let my mind wander during the visit, especially as Warren was out and Bromide was mostly silent for once, but I only had to nod occasionally as Florence gabbed about her husband's planned gambit for the Ohio governor's mansion. In the back of my mind I could only think that my actions—and Nick's—might have induced a woman to swallow cyanide. With Miriam's death, I'd no longer have to worry about her showing up on our doorstep with a son bearing Nick's jaunty smile. I didn't know whether to repent or celebrate.

That night, despite Bromide's suggestion that perhaps I should wait until tomorrow to speak to my own husband, I let myself into Nick's study, to find him sprawled in an armchair, his tie askew and a half-full tumbler of whiskey in his hand. I knelt before him and laid my head in his lap, the heat from the fire in the grate warm on my back.

"I'm sorry," I said. And I was. Miriam and I had no quarrel, and some part of me understood that losing Nick would have unhinged me too.

"Don't be." Nick ran a shaky hand over my head. "I'd have made Miriam miserable if we'd stayed together. I'm not sure which is worse."

"She made her choices and you made yours," I said.

And I made mine.

The words echoed loud in my head, for there was no denying that my husband had a special knack for making women miserable. Yet I'd *married* Nick—he couldn't shake me so easily.

I kept my head on his lap, my heart pounding everywhere I had a pulse. "Did you have a child with her?"

"Alice!" Nick sputtered so, I forced myself to look at him. His shock was genuine, and so was the pain in his eyes. "What sort of wretch do you think I am?"

"I received a letter on our honeymoon," I blurted out. I'd kept this secret for too long, and suddenly I felt as if I couldn't keep it another day longer, even if this was so tragically the wrong time to bring it up. I scrambled to my feet and retrieved my diary from my luggage, removing the letter from inside the cover before handing it to him. "From an anonymous woman claiming to be the mother of your child." A vein on Nick's jaw ticked so that I immediately wished I'd kept my mouth shut. "I'm sorry," I said. "I shouldn't have said anything."

"That's her handwriting." Nick read the letter, then looked up at me with empty eyes. "Why did you wait until now to ask me?"

"I convinced myself it was a hoax."

Nick stared at me a long moment, silent save the sounds of our breathing. "So you've had this rattling around in the back of your mind since then? Yes, there were other women before you, Alice, but I'm not the sort of scoundrel to hide an illegitimate child from you."

"I know," I said, feeling a tremendous rush of relief all the same. "It's just that my mother couldn't have me until she had some sort of procedure. It could be my fault that we don't yet have children."

Merry hell, but I was like a bottle of champagne come uncorked, all my worries erupting to the surface.

Nick stood and placed heavy hands on my shoulders, then pressed his warm forehead to mine. "Or it's very likely that it's my fault. But does it really matter, Alice?"

"Everyone expects us to have children. My father—"

"I don't care what your father wants. What do *you* want?"

I stopped at that. "I don't know. I think I'd enjoy a child, but I don't want to undergo another operation."

"Then no operation. We'll just try harder to have one." His eyes danced with mischief; I could tell Nick would very much revel in that particular challenge. Then again, so would I. "But for the record, I don't need a child to be happy."

"You don't?"

"I just need you."

I melted then, all the anguish and angst released from my shoulders as if it had never been. I threw my arms around him and clutched him tight.

"I love you, Nicholas Longworth," I said.

"And I love you, cantankerous, obstinate, and difficult though you may be." He released me so he could look me in the eye. "We have decades still before us, Bubbie, and we can have anything we want: a menagerie of ill-behaved children, a ministerial appointment to China . . ." He chucked me under the chin with a crooked finger. "Maybe even a big house on Pennsylvania Avenue one day."

"Perhaps a white one with pillars?" I suggested as I wrapped my arms around his solid chest, feeling warm and safe and comforted.

"Definitely pillars," he said. "And a fountain in front."

I kissed him long and hard then. "I've always liked the way you think."

"That's because I'm brilliant, you know."

Nick was right; we had each other and the whole world still before us.

He quirked an eyebrow at me, holding the honeymoon letter between us. "Do you want to keep this?"

I almost tossed it into the fire, then changed my mind. "I'll keep it as a reminder," I said, tucking it back into my diary. "That I need to trust you more."

As Nick pulled me back into his arms, I said a silent prayer for Miriam Bloomer. I only hoped she'd found peace now. As I hoped I finally had.

Nick and I were inseparable for the remainder of the summer, a happy little family of two, plus Manchu, whom we spoiled mercilessly as we traveled back and forth between Washington and Ohio. So we were hand in hand one sunny afternoon when the Secret Service ushered us into Father's presidential study.

"Are you still leaving on Inauguration Day?" I asked after I'd kissed his cheek. Something had happened after my appendix surgery; some age-old rule between us that forbade showing affection had relaxed so it was now acceptable upon greeting and departing, if no other time.

"As soon as Taft's sworn his oath." He thumbed through a stack of yellowing maps of Africa pulled from the Library of Congress in preparation for his upcoming safari. "Then no one in America can claim that I'm a puppet master lurking behind the scenery, pulling his strings."

Nick absently picked up a golden rabbit's foot that was holding down the corner of a map. "I've suggested to several congressmen the possibility of you returning after Taft's eight years." He inspected the good-luck token, a gift to Father from heavyweight champion John Sullivan that would accompany him on the hunting expedition. "The idea has garnered a fairly positive response."

I suspected the rest of Nick's plan, that after Father's second set of terms, my husband would run for his own term in the White House. Sixteen years was a long time to wait to be First Lady, but I supposed I could cultivate patience if it meant winning such a prize.

Father only harrumphed and gestured to a travelogue in front of me. "Hand me that, will you?"

I did, but held it hostage for a brief moment. "Father?"

His mustache twitched as he clasped the book. "Let's get Taft elected and then see what happens, shall we?"

I knew then that Nick's plan was no revelation at all. Father was only leaving the White House because he viewed it as a temporary situation that would be rectified in the future.

If Father could swallow this bitter medicine, so could I.

Taft *did* win the White House. And immediately thereafter, we Roosevelts launched ourselves into a series of lasts. The last Christmas at the White House, the last presidential New Year's toast, and even the last Roosevelt debut ball. My debut had ushered in the beginning of my father's administration and now Ethel's debut—a little rushed so she could come out from 1600 Pennsylvania Avenue—would close it. It was unlike my ball, with its distinct lack of cotillions and decent dance floor, but I tried to ignore the old familiar sting of envy as four hundred guests chattered away while drinking expensive Californian wine and dancing on the East Room's newly installed floor. As the tottering ancient older sister, it would have been easy for me to be a lemon-face that night, but Ethel really was beautiful, and I winced to realize how much would be slipping through our family's fingers come Taft's inauguration day.

"We'll be back here all the time, you know," Nick said as he guided me around the dance floor, full of dash-fire tonight in his starched tuxedo. The man always did have a knack for reading my thoughts. "No one knows what the future may hold."

"You're right." I rested my head against his shoulder. "It all just feels so final."

Sometime around midnight I persuaded Ethel to rest a moment. "Trust me," I said, handing her a glass of water. "You can't caper the night away in new shoes unless you pace yourself."

She barely stifled a yawn. "Honestly, I wouldn't mind going to bed right now." She glanced around. "Did Franklin and Eleanor come?"

"I'm sure they're busy with the babies." I hoped my face hadn't turned a hideous shade of puce, for unlike Nick and me, Frank and Eleo had two healthy little moppets and another on the way. "But you'll likely see them next month at the diplomatic reception."

Ethel looked crestfallen, for like our father, she adored Eleanor. Both my cousin and sister were cut from the same unassuming, obedient cloth. The very thought made me shudder. Yet Ethel perked up—whether from honest cheer or because she'd learned to emulate our mother's public face—when a geriatric congressman asked her for the next dance.

We did see Franklin and Eleanor the following month at the diplomatic reception. Father had recently taken to keeping guests at dinners until well past one in the morning—I think to savor his final days of entertaining—and while I usually enjoyed such events, that night I had a miserable cold. I considered begging off in exchange for a good night's sleep, but mustered the will to endure a few hours. After all, I could sleep when I was dead.

A dusting of powder disguised the worst of my red nose, and then Nick and I were off, two young swells about the town. I immediately wished I'd stayed home once we arrived and the buzz of conversation set off a veritable racket in my head.

"We don't have to stay, Bubbie," Nick said the moment we'd checked our coats, but I only waved him off.

"You go on," I said. "I'll just sit and listen."

He kissed my cheek. "I'll check on you later."

I stood against the wall, nursing a cup of hot tea from a sympathetic waiter and watching Ethel as she navigated the crowd.

"She reminds me of her mother," someone said, and I turned to see Franklin's grin, Eleanor matching him for height at his side. She wouldn't go into confinement for a few more months, but no style of dress could have disguised the telltale swell of her belly.

Hello, envy, my green-eyed friend . . .

"Cousin darling. Cousin dearest." I mustered a smile. "It seems like forever since we saw you last."

"Too long," Eleanor answered. She seemed more awkward than usual as her eyes strayed to the floor. Not for the first time, I hoped that Feather Duster didn't have high political aspirations. If so, he'd be on his own with a wife like Eleanor, no matter how much my father lauded her as the pinnacle of womanhood.

"We heard Ethel's debut was a success," Franklin said, stepping in for his wife. "It seems only yesterday she was in pigtails."

"Time flies." I tried to avoid sniffing too much. "How are your own little bald Pygmies?"

"Wonderful." Franklin's eyes lit up like only a father's could. I quelled a fresh pang of jealousy as I dabbed my nose with a handkerchief. "James just turned one and careens about the house like a drunken little man."

"A terror after my own heart." I laughed, although the sound came out mangled. "And your daughter?"

Eleanor gave a tight smile. "Anna is very protective of James."

I smiled as Franklin's attention was snagged by a whiskered diplomat. "They sound divine," I said to Eleanor. "You must enjoy being a mother."

"I find it more trying than anything." Eleanor's murmured admission surprised me when she finally dared to look up. "Their behavior bewilders me, and they obey the servants more than me. Just yesterday I was telling James to stop monkeying around in Franklin's chair. He yelled, 'I won't!' and then promptly fell and hit his head."

I laughed, even as I mused that Eleanor's parents—an alcoholic father and a society blue blood who'd endured her own children—had likely done little to teach Eleanor about being a mother. "You should bring them to Sagamore Hill this summer for a visit. Father would take to them like ducks to water."

The very thought of Father cavorting with Eleanor's children turned the words to ash in my mouth. I was no saint; if she accepted the offer, I'd have to make myself scarce at Sagamore, lest I be devoured by a ravenous flock of green-eyed demons.

Yet Eleanor only waved away my suggestion. "Oh, no. They'd bother your mother and Uncle Theodore far too much."

"Have you met my father?" My snort was made all the more indelicate by my cold. "He's a six-year-old trapped in a grown man's body. They'll get along just fine."

Eleanor didn't say much more, only excused herself to make the social rounds while I coughed my way through subsequent conversations with Nick's colleagues. I was searching for Nick to call for the car when I overheard Eleanor talking to the wife of the Canadian ambassador.

"Dear cousin Ethel really is a doll," she said, admiring my sister where she sat demurely with a cluster of diplomats' daughters. "She doesn't appear spoiled by her foray into adulthood the way Alice was. But then, Ethel really was never along Alice's lines at all."

I stiffened. The heavens themselves must be cracking if drab little Eleanor, who could barely speak two coherent sentences in public, thought to insult me.

Had I not been only half able to breathe with an entire orchestra of drums pounding inside my skull, I might have sauntered up to Eleanor with a catty remark to put her in her place. Instead, I only glowered unseen at her ramrod-straight back and stormed away.

That was only the first of many insults I endured in the final days of my father's presidency.

A few days before the inauguration, I received a ticket from Nellie Taft to allow me into the White House inaugural luncheon.

Allow. *Me.*

Alice *Roosevelt* Longworth.

I threw the ticket down in front of Nick. "We're not even out of the

White House, and Nellie has the gall to *allow* me back for lunch? I've happily wandered in and out of the White House for eight years, and that old schoolmarm dares to look down her nose at *me*?"

Nick scarcely glanced up from his papers, probably more work on the recent tariff bill that had been keeping him up late most nights. "You really only lived there for a couple of years, Bubbie. Not even your father has occupied the mansion for a full eight years."

"Seven and a half rounds up," I muttered, grabbing back the ticket. "I should salt the grounds of the new rose garden Mother installed, or rig the showers to spray Nellie with mud. That would teach her to tangle with me."

Nick was only half listening. "I'm sure you'll think of something, dear."

And I did.

On the final day of my father's term, after taking a final tour of the house that I adored so much, I found myself on my knees in the dirt of the colonial rose garden Mother had ordered to replace the old horse stables, although without the salt I'd threatened. Instead, I'd recalled a thing or two from my visit to New Orleans.

"Do your patriotic duty," I whispered as I buried the lumpy doll that resembled a tight-lipped schoolteacher. For verisimilitude, just that morning I'd added the oversize mushroom of gray hair and stitched its wide mouth into a frown with red yarn. I didn't want to hurt Nellie Taft, just inconvenience her as she'd inconvenienced me.

It didn't take long for my black magic to start working, for Taft's inauguration day dawned gray and bleak, with thick drifts of snow and bone-chilling winds. The sun came out long enough only to create a loathsome slush, and the air was so cold that the mouthpieces of the brass band froze and their reeds split. I rolled my eyes at the window as Taft's most ardent supporters braved the miserable weather for naught. Whereas Father would have ventured out into the storm of the century to see his people, our portly new president planned to repeat the oath of office in the warmth and comfort of the Senate chambers.

I'd stayed in the White House the night before as a sort of last hur-rah and contemplated whether I should make a show of watching Taft's swearing in, but Mother changed my mind.

"Shall we go have lunch?" she'd asked. I knew she was looking forward to retiring to the quiet life of a civilian, especially since keep-ing up Father's spirits these past weeks had been a Herculean task. Still, the atmosphere was heavy with an obscuring fog of melancholy. Already the White House staff had packed up all of our belongings, and the Tafts' crates of household goods waited expectantly to be opened by an entirely new staff, as Nellie had dismissed most of our existing servants in a fit of pique. We were to be out before noon, come hell or high water.

"Lunch sounds divine," I said. "I'll telephone Nick and have him whip up some Toothsome Terrapin at the Alibi. The press will hound us anywhere else."

"Perfect." Mother's rare hug told me she wasn't immune to today's import either. "I'll tell the others."

My throat felt tight, so I lingered only long enough to bid good-bye to the army of White House staff, dressed for the final time in their blue and white Roosevelt livery.

"We sure will miss you, Mrs. Longworth," said one of the ushers. Ike's prominent nose was still the most memorable feature on his oth-erwise congenial face. "You and your siblings made this drafty old place fun. I doubt whether Mrs. Taft will be sliding down the stairs on tin trays tonight."

I laughed at the memory, remembering how Ike had helped me find lunch trays to take my siblings stair-sledding seven short years ago. "If it were up to me, I'd have a ninety-nine-year lease on the White House," I said. "Luckily, I'll be back tonight for Uncle Will's first dinner, although I expect it to be a rather dour affair."

It felt as if I were being expelled from the Garden of Eden when Ike shut the front doors behind me. I could only imagine how Father felt.

Lunch with Mother at the Alibi was somber, and Nick sent me with a jar of Toothsome Terrapin for Father's lunch when I went to say good-bye to the family at the train station. This was the last time I'd see them before Father and Kermit boarded the steamer that would carry them to Africa. I'd never given much thought to my middle brother, but now I found myself inordinately jealous of Kermit. How I'd have loved to go on safari with Father, to spend the days in the red dust tracking down lions and the nights laughing around the heat of a roaring campfire.

"We've had a good run, Sissy," Father said as he embraced me. He'd eschewed the tradition of returning to the White House in the new president's carriage, claiming it an absurd custom, but I suspected he simply didn't want to see the old house if he was no longer its resident.

"We have indeed," I reassured him. "And it's not over yet."

Nick and I returned that night for Taft's first White House dinner, no longer the president's daughter, merely a *guest*. What a mundane sort of word!

"I'm afraid I lost my ticket," I joked blithely as I breezed past Ike with a wink. "There needs to be a standing rule: Alice Roosevelt Longworth needs no ticket."

Uncle Will—President Taft now—patted my hand. "I'll make it my first executive order, my dear."

As Nick spoke to Uncle Will and Nellie ignored me, I realized that the real reason I'd been invited was because of Nick's support of Taft, whereas until now it was *my* name that had opened doors for Nick.

I didn't relish being the plus-one. I much preferred it the other way around.

I maneuvered my way past Nellie and the carnivorous orchid corsage she'd pinned to her bust, although I did pause to ask how she was feeling, and gave a knowing smirk when she claimed to have a sore throat following the day's dreary weather.

Well done, my little voodoo imp.

"Poor dear," I said to Nellie. "But then it's not surprising that your throat is raw after all that griping you did about the servants. Isn't it poor form to dismiss so dedicated a staff, especially considering all their long years of service?"

I moved on before she could respond, but not before her eyes crackled with lightning. I almost told her about the trinket I'd left in her backyard, but then she'd have been really put out.

"Alice, darling," Nick said, steering me toward a handsome man dressed in his evening togs, flanked by one of the most plain-faced women I'd ever seen, cousin Eleanor excepted. "This is Senator William Borah of Idaho and his wife, Mary. Bill was sworn in this morning."

At first glance Borah appeared a man who might be equally as comfortable in a library or a wrestling ring. He was an imposing figure only a few years younger than my father, square and solid with soulful eyes and a thick shock of dark hair like a black-maned lion.

"Congratulations." I took Borah's hand before it was offered and gave it a firm shake. "Welcome to the den of snakes."

"It's a pleasure to make your acquaintance, Mrs. Longworth," he said in a deep rumble of a voice. He exuded a sort of stillness, like the calm before a storm. "Especially after so many years of reading about your escapades in the papers."

"I wish I could say they were all exaggerated," I said with a waggle of my eyebrows. "But I'd be lying."

He laughed and I found I liked the rich, honest sound. "That is something I suspect you rarely do, given your penchant for telling people exactly what you think."

"Billy," Mary Borah said, her soft voice a reprimand. But I only answered his laugh.

"My reputation precedes me," I said as the dinner gong sounded. "Shall we?"

I switched my place card so I might sit across from Taft—thoroughly enjoying Nellie's scathing glare at the scandalous breach of etiquette—and quickly had her husband chortling at my caustic observations of his new cabinet members. Really, it was too easy to poke fun at them, considering that he'd assembled the dullest band of white-haired yes-men to be found this side of the Mississippi.

"I declare I'll have my hands full with settling in," Nellie suddenly said to no one in particular, speaking more loudly than was necessary. "I was dismayed today to find the White House in very bad condition."

That was utter rubbish, considering that Mother had been up most of the night ensuring that the transition went smoothly, not to mention our full army of White House staff who had been working nonstop for days to pack up one presidential family while preparing for another.

It was Mary Borah who shot me a sympathetic glance while I bit the insides of my cheeks. Yet it was her husband who distracted me from committing a felony.

"So, Alice, I assume your father's read up on all the dangers in Africa for his upcoming safari?" Borah asked.

"You assume correctly."

"You know, J. P. Morgan was quoted the other day as saying he hopes every lion does his duty while your father is in the bush."

I laughed at that. "Well, Morgan has been bitter with Father since he broke up the Northern Securities Company. That little brouhaha cost old J. P. millions."

I spent the rest of the evening ignoring the Tafts entirely and chatting up Bill and Mary Borah, both of whom I found I enjoyed, even if Mary rarely spoke. She was the sort that could never be the butt of my jokes, for it wasn't fair to take aim at innocent sheep. As Nick and I said our good-byes that evening, I mused that I might just enjoy my time on Washington's sidelines. After all, there was more to life than just politics.

I'd have been hard-pressed at that moment to tell just exactly what else. But this new Alice was going to find out.

Chapter 13

The following summer often found me curled on a settee in the early morning sunshine, a pile of books at my elbow and at least one open on my lap. I'd made it my goal to match Father's pace of finishing at least one book a day, so aside from my love of poetry, I'd recently devoured Mendel's and Darwin's works, and penned several letters to Father in Africa to ask his opinion on their evolutionary theories. The rest of my mornings were split among astronomy and botany, and consulting my new copy of *The Oxford Book of English Verse*. Since our European honeymoon I'd found that no matter how deep American patriotism ran in my veins, there was a hidden Anglophile streak in me, too, so much so that I'd planted the seed in Mother's mind that perhaps next spring we might meet Father in England after his African safari, for I was already feeling restless for another international trip.

I read every book I could get my hands on, that is until the release of a new little German volume.

Emma Kroebel—she of the blond curls and cavernous dimples—had written a memoir about her time in Korea. Well, to call it a book was perhaps too generous. In fact, the German fräulein who had enchanted my husband had written a gossip rag unfit for lining bird-cages.

"This is beyond scandalous, even for you, Alice." Nick glanced up from the day's issue of the *New York Times*. "I do wish I'd been there to see it all."

"You were." I grabbed the paper and resisted the urge to crumple it into nothingness. Instead, I forced myself to reread the terrible article. "Except for the portion where it didn't happen like this at all."

With the entire wretched book to choose from, the *Times* had decided to translate a particularly damning—and flagrantly untrue—passage about me.

I drummed my nails across the table. "I think I'd remember 'bursting onto the scene of the empress's tomb at the front of a cavalcade of equestrians, wearing scarlet riding breeches and glittering boots while brandishing a whip and smoking a cigar.'" I actually enjoyed the image, except for the part where it was a bold-faced lie. "She should have at least said Lucky Strikes instead of a cigar if she was going for authenticity."

"True, you've never been one for cigars." Nick kicked his feet up onto the leather ottoman. At least one of us was nonchalant about this obloquy dragging my name through the mud. I'd done plenty of outrageous things in my life, but it was uncomfortable to have blatant untruths published about me. Nick took a sip of his coffee, and not for the first time I was thankful that his alcoholic binges seemed to be waning. "I do remember the bit about you riding an elephant statue. Kroebel claims you called out to me to take your picture, but I distinctly recall Willard Straight doing the honor."

I colored at that, for I still had the photograph that Willard had later sent me, and could only hope that my old friend wouldn't expose the truth now that all this had gone public. "I only did it to get your attention, you ninny. If you recall, you'd been mooning over Fräulein Kroebel and her pretty dimples since our first night in Korea. I might have ridden naked to the empress's tomb and you wouldn't have noticed."

Nick waggled his eyebrows at me. "Trust me, *that* I'd have noticed."

I rolled up the paper and swatted his chest with it. "Be serious. What am I going to do?"

"You, my dear, are going to do nothing."

"You can't possibly suggest that I allow some blathering blonde to publish utter lies about me? Not only that, but she's probably going to sell more copies now that the *Times* has printed this worthless drivel." I tossed the newspaper into the rubbish bin and started to pace, but Nick rose in one fluid motion and barred my path.

"As I said, Bubbie, *you* will do nothing." He put his hands on my shoulders. "This drivel, as you put it, is beneath your notice. Instead, you shall allow your white knight to come to your rescue."

I cocked my head, unsure whether I liked the sound of this. "Go on."

"I was in Korea, wasn't I?"

"You were," I said slowly.

"So I'll speak with the people at the *Times* and set them straight. Who do you think America's going to believe? The congressman husband of their favorite First Daughter or some money-grubbing German tart?"

I might have argued that I was accustomed to taking care of myself, but perhaps it wouldn't hurt to let Nick restore my honor. "That's very kind of you, husband of mine," I said, leaning over to kiss his cheek. He turned so I caught his lips instead.

"Well, I'm all ears if you can think of a reward for my chivalry," he said.

I gave him a real kiss then, my fingers playing at the back of his neck in the manner I knew he enjoyed. "I'm fairly certain I can think of something, if you come upstairs."

"After you, Mrs. Longworth," Nick said. "I'm at your beck and call."

"Precisely the way I like it." I laughed as he chased me up the stairs.

Merry hell, but I loved that man far too much sometimes.

Nick's valiant justification of me seemed to do the trick. He went on record claiming he had never heard of the Berlin authoress, but complimented Kroebel's imagination and claimed that her story had been a great source of amusement to us. Fräulein Kroebel lashed back in the *Times* that she was neither a lunatic nor a liar, but the damage to her story was done.

America loved me. My husband loved me.

All was right in the world, now that the gadfly had been swatted. Unfortunately, another rose to take her place.

"I must say, Mrs. Longworth, you're awfully spry on your feet." Nick's frenetic footwork matched mine as we danced the frisky new Turkey Trot at the president's diplomatic reception that January. "Do you think they'll let us dance like this when I'm the new ambassador to China?"

My chest heaved as the final notes exploded and we clapped for the ragtime band. I paused to waggle my fingers at Nellie Taft, who had been glowering at me all night. "I think we can teach the Chinese a thing or two about dancing during your ambassadorship."

"Congratulations on your new position." Bill Borah—who, along with his wife, had passed us on the dance floor several times—overheard and shook Nick's hand. His slow smile belied his deep voice. "I suspect the next time we see you both you'll be ordering grilled sparrows on a stick and drinking snake wine."

"I much prefer antique eggs," I quipped. "At least a hundred years old or they're not worth eating. Speaking of snake wine, I'm downright parched."

"That's my cue," Nick said to Bill.

"A lemonade, right?" I asked Nick. He pulled a face, but gave me an obedient salute as he and Bill moved off in search of drinks. It had been a while since Nick last got owled, but he'd agreed that it wouldn't be seemly for the freshly minted minister to China to be too deep in his cups tonight.

I glanced around, looking for someone interesting to chat with as Mary Borah was drawn into conversation elsewhere, and spied the wife of the new Russian ambassador. Maggie Cassini's father had been recalled to the Motherland a while back, which didn't hurt my heart a single bit as he'd taken his daughter with him. The Russian matron pulled out her cigarette holder and began to smoke, immediately garnering Nellie Taft's dagger-wrought stare. It still wasn't considered proper for women to puff in public, and I knew the First Lady would have kittens if I joined in.

Naturally, I retrieved my own red holder and case of Lucky Strikes from my purse. Why did I never seem to have a lighter handy?

"Allow me."

I grinned to see the president himself present me with a lighted match. "Thanks, Uncle Will."

"Anytime," Taft said. Unfortunately, his wife was at his side in an instant, pulling him away from me as if I'd suddenly come down with a contagion.

"Your mother would be appalled to see you right now," she whispered before she steered him away. "You look like a steam engine on a crimped track."

I shrugged. "Mother has seen me smoke plenty." I looked out over the assemblage of Washington's finest diplomats and laughed, gesturing with my cigarette. "I do wonder what she'd say to see all of them smoking though."

Nellie's face twisted in a paroxysm of horror as she saw what I meant. Following my lead, virtually every woman had pulled out their own cigarettes, and a noxious haze was filling the ballroom. I smirked and Nellie snarled at me, whispering furiously in Taft's ear just as Nick meandered up with two drinks.

"What was that all about?" he asked. "Nellie looked ready to spit at you."

"Nothing," I said. "She's just determined to hate me."

I thought I'd won a victory against Nellie Taft that night, but she bested me. When it came time to announce the new minister to China, it wasn't Nick's name that Uncle Will read as everyone expected, but some panderer whom I knew Nellie had favored.

"So much for China," Nick said, now knocking back his second shot of single-malt whiskey.

"At least you've still got your work in the House," I said, but he didn't respond.

I told myself that Nick would adjust quickly, even as I glared at where Nellie Taft simpered from her place next to her whale of a husband. I wanted to be angry at Uncle Will, but it was difficult to be mad at someone so jovial, even if he didn't have the backbone he was born with.

There was no doubt in my mind that this little sleight of hand was Nellie's retribution against me. Poor Nick had only been caught in the crossfire.

As I watched him pour a third shot, I told myself I'd repay him somehow. I just wasn't sure how.

There were few diversions on the steamer that carried me away from Nick to meet Father and Mother in London after the African safari. I made excuses to avoid the nightly black-and-white dinners, and pretended not to notice the calling cards from passengers eager to take a turn with me around the deck. I was further dismayed to find that newspaper tycoon William Randolph Hearst was on board after all the false engagements he'd reported before my marriage to Nick. I contented myself by making the sign of the evil eye whenever I passed his cabin.

Mother and Kermit both waved to me from beneath England's leaden-gray skies when we finally docked, not a scrap of color anywhere with the black mourning crepe that draped all of Southampton in honor of the late King Edward. I flung myself into their arms, exclaiming at my brother's deep tan from the African wilderness. "You're as brown and rangy as a hyena!" I said, hugging him close and swallowing a surge of jealousy. "Where's Father?"

Mother gestured for my brother to take my bag while the porters transferred the remainder of my luggage—including a hatbox version of the Leaning Tower of Pisa—to a waiting car. "There could be ten of your father here and it still wouldn't be enough. First he had to attend King Edward's funeral at President Taft's behest, and he's been giving so many lectures at Oxford, not to mention writing his book about the African expedition," she said. "He sends his apologies and promises to stay up all night talking politics with you and your brother."

My disappointment must have shown, because Kermit poked me in the ribs with his free hand. "You'll have to wait to see Father, but someone else asked if he could help fetch you." He waved to someone on the other side of the crowd. "Over here, Willard!"

Taller than most everyone on the dock and virtually unchanged since I'd seen him last, Willard Straight jogged toward us in his bowler hat and gave a grin that would have made a tougher girl than me weak in the knees.

"Aren't you a sight for sore eyes, Mrs. L." He surprised me with his semiformal address. "I'm here with the consul general and when I heard you were coming, I'm afraid I strong-armed your family into allowing me to drive. I assume you'd like to go straight to the hotel to see the colonel?"

I cringed to hear my father demoted to his rank from the Spanish-American War, even if it was the moniker he preferred now that he was no longer president. Fortunately, there were still plenty of opportunities to amend that in the years to come.

"You always seem to know exactly what I want before I've thought it myself," I said.

"Follow me," Willard said. He guided my mother through the crowd while Kermit fell into step beside me.

"How are things back home?" my brother asked. "Father is on a rampage, claiming Taft is undoing all his good work."

"Taft does what he's told, including whatever the Republican bosses command of him." I'd been wrong thinking that Willard hadn't changed at all; he'd let his hair grow out a little in the back. "So far he's rolled back Father's conservation programs, fired his chief forester, and waffled on tariff issues, including the one that's causing Nick so much grief."

"Then don't plan on getting any sleep tonight," Kermit said as we approached the car. To my surprise, he handed me onto the front bench next to Willard. "They drive on the wrong side of the road here, Sissy," he said. "I'll take the back if it means you'll let Willard drive. He's got the knack of it."

So I sat next to Willard, all the while aware of his sidelong glances.

"Alice, dear," Mother said from the back seat. "How fares Nick these days?"

"He's sore over losing the post to China." I shifted in my seat at a fresh pang of guilt. "But I daresay he'll recover. He's so successful at everything he touches in the House. I told him the other day that he'd likely be Speaker before the decade is out."

Babbling *and* boasting? What was wrong with me?

I felt my cheeks go pink under Willard's gaze as the three of them discussed trifles until we arrived at the hotel. Mother and Kermit bustled ahead to tell Father of my arrival just as the second car arrived with my luggage. Alone with Willard, my heart thudded at ramming speed.

"It's dreadfully good to see you again, Alice." He dispensed with the formalities now that there was no one to overhear. "You look well. Too well, in fact."

"Too well?" Surely that trill of a giggle wasn't mine. "Would you prefer I come down with a touch of fever? Or a bout of measles?"

"Nothing so vile," he said. "I only dared hope that the Alice I greeted might be as lovelorn as the last time I saw her."

"That seems a dreadfully wicked thing to hope for a friend."

"Not at all." He shrugged. "You'll have to forgive my forwardness, but I won't let you slip through my fingers again, not if there's anything I can do to help it."

Rarely did anyone render me speechless, but Willard had earned that distinction. I gaped at him a moment, wondering if this was how Nick had felt when on the make with a pretty girl, the exhilaration of knowing you were doing something clandestine and enjoying it despite yourself. At the height of Nick's drinking, Willard's declaration would have made me doubt my own honor and fidelity.

But now?

Although Willard had helped me weather more than one storm at Nick's hand, it was Nick whom I loved, Nick whom I'd married.

"I'm afraid you never quite saw the best side of my relationship with Nick," I said, avoiding Willard's gaze as I removed my gloves. "Everything is capital between us now. I love him from the top of my head to the tips of my toes."

I dared look at Willard, shocked at the raw grief I saw on his face before he schooled his features back into a diplomat's mask. I recalled the way it felt to have my own heart broken and dared reach up to touch his face. He cupped his hand over mine and leaned into it for a moment.

"I'm glad for you," he said. "Not glad for me, but all the same, I do enjoy the thought of your happiness."

I leaned over to kiss Willard's cheek. "Not long ago I'd have jumped at your offer," I said. "But I'm afraid it's no good now."

"A victim of my own timing." Willard offered a wistful smile, one that I suspected hid some dark depth of disappointment this time. "Then may Nick always endeavor to deserve you."

"He does," I said.

Willard leaned back and cleared his throat. "We'd best get inside. Your father isn't a man to be kept waiting."

True to form, my father chose that moment to burst from the hotel. "Alice!" he exclaimed, flinging his arms open. His grin was wider than normal, and this time it was all for me. "Come here, my dear girl!"

I might have been physically exhausted from crossing the Atlantic and emotionally battered from Willard's unexpected proclamation, but all that fell away when my father enveloped me in an embrace that threatened to knock my oversize straw boater off my head. "Come inside," he said as I straightened my hat. "I need a good dose of common American politics; I've spent so much time with royalty this trip that if I meet another king I should bite him!"

He exchanged brief pleasantries with Willard, then hustled me toward the entrance. I turned and gave Willard a stiff nod that reeked of farewell.

"Au revoir, Mrs. L," he called with a wave.

"Good-bye, Willard," I said.

I'd have watched my old friend until he'd disappeared, but Father interrupted my sad reverie. "Alice?" he called, and I saw he was holding the door open for me. "Are you coming?"

"Of course, Father."

Still, I spared a moment's glance in Willard's direction, wondering if I'd ever see him again.

I knew then—perhaps had known for years—that my father was the sun that I orbited. I'd married Nick, but even still, he was only a distant star in comparison, and a man like Willard . . .

Well, poor Willard never stood a chance.

I stayed up all that night talking politics with Father and Kermit, bemoaning Taft's reactionary policies when it came to national parks and dealing with the Republican bosses.

"Every American deserves a square deal." Father ran a hand over his thinning hair. He'd trimmed down during his African safari and had boasted earlier in the evening of the animals he and my brother had killed, enough rhinos, elephants, and giraffes to fill every museum in America. But now he looked deadly serious. "I'm mightily disappointed in Taft," he said. "My friend has been a miserable president, despite being a promising first lieutenant. I plan to give him a few choice words upon my return."

"You know, I'd bet my roadster that you're at least tenfold more popular than Taft."

"Based on what I've heard, Sissy, that doesn't mean much," Father said.

"It would," I said, testing the same waters from the past election when I'd thought Father might push for a third term. "If you wanted to run against him in the 1912 election."

"I heartily regret making that two-term promise," my father admitted. "I'd cut off my right hand if I could take it back." He stood before the fireplace, one arm on the mantel and a fist on his hip. "It would be a mistake to go head-to-head against Taft in the next election. Unless the people demanded it, of course."

My eyes met his and I recognized the spark there. "Of course," I said, nodding slowly. "That would change everything."

"Indeed." Father caught my gaze.

I knew what our strategy would be then, to fan the flames of my father's popularity back home until he had no choice but to run for president again.

It was only later that night as I lay in my narrow hotel bed and drifted toward sleep that I recalled Nick's ardent political support of Taft and Taft's lifelong friendship with the entire Longworth clan.

If my father *did* run against Taft, that would leave my husband wedged sharply between a rock and a very hard place.

I pushed the thought from my mind. We could cross that bridge when—if ever—we came to it. For there was no doubt that I'd leave Taft high and dry to support my father. And as my husband, Nick would do the same.

Mother was right that Father was in high demand throughout London, so much so that one evening I'd had to send him out on our balcony at midnight just so the cheering crowd below would disperse. I loved the British capital just as much as I had on my honeymoon, perhaps more so considering my staggering win at the recent London Derby. I managed to win enough to pay for my entire trip, including a three-day jaunt to Paris for a whirlwind tour of plays, restaurants, and races.

However, upon my return to London I found an unexpected letter waiting for me.

"When was this delivered?" I asked Mother. I was weary from the day's trek across the Channel, but the familiar handwriting made me feel as though I'd downed a bucket of coffee.

"A few days ago, I think," Mother said. "Perhaps the day you left?"

"I'll be back in a couple of hours," I said, already heading for the door. "Don't hold dinner on my account."

It wasn't long before I stood outside a weathered brownstone that had long since seen better days. I expected a butler or at least a lady's maid to usher me inside, but instead a plain-faced woman with unkempt hair flung open the door.

"Alice!" she cried. "I've been watching the streets for you for days. How dare you keep me on pins and needles for so long."

"Cissy!" I was shocked at her wild hair and stained housedress. Despite her tangled mop of greasy hair, she wore a bold slash of coral lipstick that made her look positively garish. "I didn't know you were in town. I assumed you were still in Poland with your count."

Her face darkened and she yanked me inside, slamming the door and latching it with not one but four different locks. Had I taken a wrong turn and fallen into Bedlam? My nose twitched at the dust, and suddenly I wished I'd sent a card rather than coming myself.

Except I didn't keep calling cards. Perhaps I'd start after this.

"If only you knew all I've been through," Cissy said. She pulled me deeper into the dank house. "These past years have been such a trial."

I recalled Cissy's penchant for dramatics and resisted the urge to roll my eyes. "Whatever do you mean?"

"I left Gizycki," she said. "He doesn't know I'm here. I have only the clothes on my back."

"You've separated?" I sat down on a dusty settee and willed myself not to breathe lest I succumb to a sneezing fit. "Why?"

"He's a terrible brute. I learned to overlook his dalliances with everything female under the age of fifty, and even the time or two he knocked me against a wall. But when he turned against Felicia . . ."

"Felicia?"

"My daughter," Cissy answered.

It took a moment to recognize the pang of emotion I felt not as shock or sympathy, but something far more primal.

I was *jealous.*

Across from me sat a friend who had left her entire world, and I was envious because she had a child and I didn't.

Sometimes I still worried that there was no hope for me.

"I took Felicia and left him, but he found us. He kidnapped Felicia and has been holding her in a convent in Austria." A sudden torrent of tears flooded down Cissy's cheeks. "He's demanded that I pay a million dollars for her return."

Then came the sympathy, followed by a wave of helplessness.

"I'm so, so sorry," I said to Cissy, not knowing what other platitudes to offer. Was there ever anything to say when a woman's life came crashing down around her head?

"I have nightmares of what he'll do to her." Cissy hiccupped through her sobs. "I've petitioned both President Taft and Czar Nicholas to help bring her back. And I've filed for divorce."

"Oh, Cissy." I handed her a handkerchief from my purse. Separations between husbands and wives were scandalous, and it was a miracle Cissy's story hadn't made it into the papers yet. A divorce would ruin my old friend socially, and her daughter too. But perhaps that was a price worth paying for freedom. "How utterly awful for you. I'm sure everything will work out." I flailed in vain for the right words— *any* words—but I was more useless than a trapdoor on a lifeboat when it came to soothing bruised feelings. "It always does."

We sat in silence until Cissy cleared her throat so the sound echoed off the empty walls. "Let's not talk about Gizycki anymore. How's that Nick of yours?"

I kept my face blank, disoriented at the sudden change in subject. "He's dreadfully busy back home in Congress."

Cissy only sniffed, like a dog scenting the air. "I sometimes wonder what my life would be like if I'd ended up with him instead of Gizycki. I don't suppose I'll ever forgive you for stealing him from me."

I thought she spoke in jest until her lips went taut as a rope. "I seem to recall that he proposed to Maggie before he was engaged to me." My words tasted bitter. "And you were already married by then."

"Yes, but only because I couldn't have Nick. I *did* hate you when I read of your marriage, you know."

I had no response, only wondered if my husband was a magnet for deranged women. First Miriam Bloomer, then Cissy, and Maggie.

Oy vey. What did that say about me?

Perhaps I *had* taken a wrong turn into Bedlam after all. I managed to sit through the remainder of the awkward visit, but was relieved when I could finally beg off without seeming as if I was running away.

"I do hope everything gets resolved between you and the count," I said before I slipped out the front door. "You must look me up when you come back to Washington."

"I will." Cissy patted her hair as if she were a coy debutante instead of a disheveled woman fleeing a failed marriage. "Neither you nor Nick shall be able to escape me when I'm a free woman."

My heart truly did ache for her terrible situation as I walked down her steps, but I found myself wishing that it would be a long time before I had to endure five minutes in the same room with Cissy Patterson again.

Little did I know she was soon to become an albatross hung around my neck.

The exuberant welcome Father received in New York's harbor was enough to assuage all doubts regarding the upcoming Republican nomination; I'd have guessed at least one million people turned out to witness the return of their beloved colonel.

"Only conquering heroes the likes of Alexander and Caesar have been feted with this much pomp and circumstance," I said to Father as the cutter *Androscoggin* docked at the Battery. The shout that went up filled the park and the nearby streets, possibly all of New York itself. "And you're only returning from a hunting expedition."

Father smiled at that as we stepped ashore. "Poor Taft won't stand a chance when it comes time for the Republican primaries."

Rainbow confetti clung to my hat, and my ears threatened to ring for days as Nick hugged me close. He'd come aboard at quarantine and taken my breath away in his dapper white linen suit before he'd swung me around and crushed me to him, making me realize how lucky I was to have him instead of a husband like Count Gizycki. Now we trailed after Father, who was grinning his trademark grin as hundreds of reporters, policemen, and citizens pressed close to grasp his hand. "Happy belated birthday, Bubbie," Nick said. "There's a present for you in the car. It's a good one, if I say so myself."

"Seeing you is enough for me," I said, meaning every word.

"Then I should just return the gift?"

"Well, far be it from me to turn away a present."

With Father already lost in the crowd, I hugged Mother one last time and promised to see them in two days for Ted's wedding, then ducked into the car with Nick.

"Happy birthday." He handed me an awkward sort of package tied together in muslin and cinched with a cheerful red bow.

I opened the gift and laughed aloud. "Roller skates!" I clapped my hands in glee. "It's been ages since I've zipped around on skates."

"It's the latest craze," Nick said. "I've a pair at home. We'll put them on and go door to door to all of our friends and see who wants to join us before supper."

"Perfect!" I planted a sloppy kiss on his cheek. "I love you, Nick Longworth. Promise me we'll never be apart this long again."

"Not this long," Nick agreed. "But I have to head to Cincinnati soon."

I did my best not to grimace as if he'd just shoveled mushy peas into my mouth, but didn't quite succeed.

Cincin-*nasty.*

"Don't worry." Nick must have read my mind. "You can stay with your family in New York. It seems like you had a hanging good time together in London." He glanced at me, his expression suddenly hooded as he navigated through the packed side streets. "I heard Willard Straight came to visit you as well."

"He did indeed. In fact, he even proposed, but I told him you'd beat him to the punch and I was already married."

Nick made some horrible choking sound, swiveling to look at me so fast that the car swerved and almost hit an electric light pole.

"I kid!" I cried as Nick righted the car. I thought to hide the truth in plain sight by mocking what had really happened, but I hadn't planned on killing us in a fiery automobile crash. "Willard met me at the dock, but that was all I saw of him," I said. "I suspect he's already off to a new diplomatic posting in some exotic locale."

"Good." Nick's smile seemed forced. "For a while there I thought he was going to try to turn your eye. Not that it would work, you being married to me and all."

He winked and I laughed. "As I reminded him."

We left it at that. Yet it seemed Nick had more on his mind.

"I take it from all this hullabaloo that your father is considering a run against Taft next year?" he asked.

"Only if America asks it of him." In truth, Father was champing at the bit to declare himself, but everything would have to be perfectly orchestrated if he was to lure the Republican nomination away from Taft.

"For my sake, I hope he doesn't," Nick said.

"Because of Taft."

Nick nodded. "Our friendship is more solid than ever. Did you know he celebrated his birthday by lunching alone with just me?"

I bit my lip, musing silently. Certainly no one would expect Taft to bow out of the race gracefully, so Nick would have to sacrifice his longstanding friendship with Uncle Will, even if he didn't realize that yet.

But surely a return to the White House would be worth a few sacrifices?

I placed the new roller skates on the floor so I could lean my head against Nick's shoulder. "Promise me that no matter what happens with Father and Taft, it won't come between us." I felt a pang at turning my back on Taft, but he was ill suited to running the country, whereas my father had been born for the role. Perhaps Uncle Will could be placated with some other lofty appointment, maybe on the Supreme Court bench or a diplomatic position back in his beloved Philippines?

"This could get ugly for me," Nick mused. "Taft is from my district in Ohio, and my constituents will expect my loyalty."

Hmmm . . . I hadn't thought of that.

"But family comes first," I said. "And we *are* family."

Nick only drew me closer with one hand while he expertly maneuvered the road with the other. "For now, let's just worry about whether I'm going to humiliate myself on those skates tonight."

I felt his lips against my hair and was reminded of another drive, Nick's arm around me as we headed to the Friendship estate and our honeymoon. A storm had been brewing on our shared horizon then, but we'd weathered it. We'd ride out this one, too, and escape with no more than bumps and bruises.

Chapter 14

FEBRUARY 1912

Father declared that his hat was officially in the presidential ring mere months after his return from Africa and Europe. I found Nick in the study the night after the announcement, his head in his hands and a half-empty bottle of gin on the side table.

My heart crawled into my throat as I wavered at the door. I'd anticipated some fallout from Father's campaign, but it had been ages since Nick had repeated the alcoholic debauches from the early days of our marriage, which I hoped to never revisit.

"Nick, darling," I said, coming to kneel before him. "Whatever is the matter?"

On occasion, it was my wifely duty to ask ridiculous questions I knew the answers to, especially when my husband looked downright despondent.

Nick blinked bloodshot eyes, as if he hadn't noticed me until that moment. "You're my wife and your father is running for president, yet I can't show my face in Cincinnati if I don't support Taft. Your father tells me that of course I must support Taft," he said dismally. His gin-soaked breath might have bowled me over. "He even said he'd sock it to any Roosevelt creature who dares worry me in Cincinnati."

Not for the first time I found myself loathing Nick's home city. But now probably wasn't the best time to bring up Cincin-nasty's lesser points.

"Taft says I should do what I please," Nick continued, "but of course, he never says much of anything else."

Because jovial and well-intentioned Uncle Will was content to agree with whomever he last spoke with. Politicians had to be made of sterner stuff, which was why we were in this pickle to begin with.

"No matter what I do, it will be a tragedy," Nick continued with a sigh. "I support Taft and keep his standpatters happy while looking like a traitor to you. Or I support your father and turn my back on everyone who sent me to Congress."

"It won't be a tragedy if you keep your head down," I said, revising my earlier plan that Nick would have to declare for Father. "Keep a low profile and this will all blow over."

"Not until November. You forget that I'm up for reelection too."

I balked at that, for in the hullabaloo over Father's nomination I *had* forgotten that Nick's seat was up for grabs. If both Father and Nick lost the election, then there would be no reason for me to live in Washington. I'd be consigned to live in Cincin-nasty.

I'd rather die a thousand deaths. And not just any ordinary deaths, more the flaying and disemboweling sort.

"You'll win handily," I said quickly, "just as you have the last five times."

Nick shook his head and reached for the gin bottle. "I think perhaps I shouldn't run again. I can't wobble between Taft and your father. I stand for what your father believes, but I've been friends with Taft for too long." He gave a ragged sigh. "I'm damned if I do and damned if I don't. This won't end well, Alice, no matter what you may believe."

"Then I'll have to believe it for the both of us." I infused my voice with false cheer as I took the gin bottle from him. "You'll feel better about everything after a good night's sleep. Let's get you up to bed."

Nick followed me like a lamb, albeit an inebriated one. He was snoring soon after I tucked him in so I crept downstairs, gathered up all the alcohol in the house, and poured every last bottle down the kitchen sink.

I'd told Nick all would be well, but that didn't stop a dark shadow of desperation from chasing me into my dreams that night.

If Nick or I had hoped for any wisdom from the Longworth tribe, those notions were disabused when we returned to Cincinnati. We'd scarcely taken off our coats at Rookwood when two tragedies occurred. First, the butler informed us that Nick's sister Clara was in town and had been lambasting my father to the papers for days. Second, Bromide opened her mouth.

"Nick, when do you plan to declare for Taft?" Susan Longworth asked, lips pursed in her disapproving glare. "There must be no question that the entire Longworth clan stands with our old friend." Her meaning was clear as she gave a haughty sniff in my direction: either I was a Roosevelt or a Longworth.

"Lovely to see you, too, Susan," I said.

"Let Alice at least take her hat off before opening the floor for debate." Nick kissed his mother's cheek, but Bromide glowered at me.

"Clara's in the dining room," she said. "We've been waiting to discuss this over lunch."

"I feel a bout of indigestion coming on," I muttered under my breath as we followed Bromide. To which Nick only groaned, "Play nice, Alice."

"Your father would fashion himself a crown if America would let him," Nick's sister Clara sneered as I stared down at my plate of greasy roast beef and wilted salad greens. My stomach was knotted from all my bottled savagery, yet Clara was a simpleton if she thought I was going to let her insult slide.

"My father is entering the race on principle." I clutched my fork so tightly I feared it might snap. "If your good friend Taft had proven himself capable of running this country, then my father wouldn't be in this mess to begin with. Instead Uncle Will has been a laughingstock of a president. Honestly, his greatest accomplishment has been installing a new bathtub in the White House after he got stuck in the first one."

"Ladies—" Nick began, but Clara cut him off.

"Your father is a megalomaniac who suffers from overweening personal ambition." Her voice rose with every word until she was shrieking like a cat in heat. "If he becomes president, we can anticipate him minting coins of his own face and commissioning statues of himself on Pennsylvania Avenue. A good man like Taft doesn't stand a chance in the face of your father's machine!"

My father's *machine*?

"How dare you!" I stood so fast my chair toppled behind me. "My father is the only man who doesn't play machine politics in this country, and you're too much of a simpleminded idiot not to see it!"

"And you're too much of a daddy's girl not to realize what a tyrant your father is!" Clara shrieked.

"Shut up!" Nick stood at the head of the table. "Both of you! I refuse to listen to another moment of this."

I gaped at Nick, his words fanning my anger into a full-blown conflagration. "You dare tell me to shut up?" I leaned on the table, the bullets of my next words aimed at all of the Longworths. "I'm in this fight for all I'm worth," I said. "And you mark my words, we Roosevelts *will* win."

I turned on my heel and stormed out the door, bound for the first train to New York.

Hell is empty and all the devils are here.

Apparently, Shakespeare had Cincinnati and my in-laws in mind when he'd penned that line.

Let the whole lot of Longworths rot for all I cared. I'd expected Bromide to put up a fight over Taft, yet as the car drove me to the station, only one thought echoed in my mind.

I'd never expected my own husband to betray me.

． ． ．

Nick and I reached a cease-fire via stilted late-night telephone conversations between Ohio and New York, but there was no permanent fix for the fissures that streaked through the bedrock of our relationship.

"I think it would be best for you to stay away from Cincinnati for a while," Nick said one night. We were sitting in our Washington drawing room after a satisfying meal of salmon cutlets and Bermuda potatoes (strangely, I seemed to recover my appetite when away from his family), and Nick was tuning his violin. He'd only had a glass of chardonnay with dinner before picking up the violin and discovering that the G string was out of tune. "The feeling back home is unbelievably bitter."

"You mean your family is bitter," I muttered.

"You know what I mean." His tone brooked a warning, which meant I should turn on the charm.

"I'll stay away from the entire blasted state if it will make you happy." I expected Nick to growl at me again, but he only lifted his violin to his shoulder, the bow poised to plunge back into Mozart.

"That includes going to hear your father at the Republican primary in Ohio," he said. "It won't go over well with my constituents if that gets into the papers."

I frowned. Father had already won several primaries, including the recent one in California, and I was eager to watch him win over Taft in his own home state. It would appear entirely normal for me to support my father, but it would also scream to the entire nation that I was at odds with my husband if I attended the primary rallies in Father's favor.

Rock and a hard place, indeed.

I shrugged, feigning nonchalance. "If that's what you wish."

"It is."

Nick resumed playing, each note a jagged black point digging deep into my temples. "I'm going to bed," I said the instant he finished. "I'm off to Sagamore Hill early in the morning."

Nick frowned, the disappointment writ clear in his features. "I thought we'd both be here until the end of the week."

"Change of plans," I said blithely. "I forgot to mention it earlier."

"Then I'll come to bed too." Nick set down the violin. "I miss you, Bubbie."

I held my hand out to him and he tucked it into his waistcoat pocket before turning out the lights.

Ah, Nick, my darling little lamb. I loved him with all my heart, but I idolized my father with every fiber of my being.

How am I going to choose between them?

Politics had always been the daily dish at Sagamore Hill, and now it was the only item on the menu.

"Of course you must do as Nick suggests," my father said the very next day. Oyster Bay was awash in the green of summer leaves, and birds chirped happily overhead as we walked side by side down to the Eel Creek boardwalk. This was no cozy meander or point-to-point walk resurrected from my childhood, but a brisk trot the likes of which had exhausted many of my father's aides during his years in the White House. I, however, kept up just fine, and thought I might continue these sorts of walks on my own as a daily habit to clear my mind, especially during this political mess. "Your husband is an astute politician. He'll win his primary handily."

Despite Nick's worries, it was easy to see that he would trump the no-namer running against him. What I really cared about was my father's race. "The party stalwarts are all Taft's men," I said. "What if you win the primaries, but they still deliver the nomination to Taft?"

"The archaic rules of the Republican Party only stipulate how the delegates *should* vote," Father said. "Not how they have to vote. It's possible, too, that Taft might purchase delegate votes for the Republican convention, especially from the southern states."

"So despite all your positive primaries so far, this is still anyone's election."

Rather than answer, my father stopped abruptly and motioned with a finger over his lips for my quiet. I squinted at where he gestured and saw a little olive-plumaged bird with a shocking red crest flitting from branch to branch.

"A ruby-crowned kinglet," my father said with a broad grin once the bird had darted out of sight. "I studied them while writing my first book on birds."

I stared at him a moment, struck by the fact that he was poised in the midst of the political battle of his life, yet he was perfectly content to stop to spy on birds. However, unlike inept and doddering old Taft, my father immediately returned to the business at hand.

"Well, Mousiekins," he said, resuming his brisk pace. "If the Republican Party proves so corrupt, then I'll just create a third party and beat them at their own game."

"Really?" The wheels in my mind churned double time at this new twist. Moves and countermoves, that's what politics was all about. "If anyone could do it," I mused slowly, "it's you."

"I've never been one for half measures." Father pounded his fist into his open palm for emphasis as the forest fell away to reveal the boardwalk and beach leading to Cold Spring Harbor. "I'm prepared to go all the way, but it may not end well if I have to run as a third party and the Democrats elect a progressive like that Wilson fellow out of New Jersey."

"My money says that they'll nominate someone who leans right," I said. "Then the country would have to choose between you and two stodgy conservatives."

Father's lip quirked in a half smile. "I can recall a time not too long ago when you felt I was too conservative, what with all my tyrannical rules."

"I've always been a very liberal daughter."

He laughed at that, mustache twitching as slipper shells crunched in the sand underfoot. "You've turned out quite all right, Mousiekins. I do hope that husband of yours knows what good advice you give."

I colored at the compliment and stooped to inspect the remains of a dead horseshoe crab that had washed ashore, so he couldn't see my blush. "Well, I hope to give you plenty more advice, preferably once you have a view of Pennsylvania Avenue. I'll be with you every step of the way, even if it does mean you have to run as a third party."

"Let's hope it doesn't come to that," Father said. "Regardless, this won't be pleasant for Taft."

I cleared my throat and did my best impression of Father, which was quite polished after years of practice. "'*Don't hit at all if it's honorably possible to avoid hitting.*'" I lowered my voice and shook a stern finger. "'*But never hit soft.*'"

Father gave an honest guffaw of laughter. "A wise man must have taught you that."

I squeezed his shoulder as, together, we inspected the view of the beach where I'd spent so many happy afternoons as a child. "The very wisest."

So it was that I found myself in Chicago on the eve of the Republican convention. I'd dutifully followed Nick's suggestion that I not attend Ohio's Republican primary, but he'd said nothing about my attendance at the culminating Republican convention. One look at the set of his shoulders as I stepped out of the hired car behind Father and I could see he was not pleased at my sleight of hand.

"They're everywhere." Nick jutted his chin at the horde of newspapermen waiting outside the Blackstone Hotel. His eyes were rimmed with ugly circles as he cast a splenetic glare in my direction. "And they all want to know one thing: who I'm voting for in November."

The reporters might have turned into Viking berserkers the moment they caught sight of my father and me. They yelled and flashlamps went off like exploding stars.

"Mr. Roosevelt, do you expect to win the nomination?"

"Mrs. Longworth, look this way! Spare us a smile!"

Normally I'd have been in my element in the zoo of cameras, but Nick was irritated and my head pounded from subsisting on only several cups of coffee the entire day. I turned so that my signature broad-brimmed hat hid us from the reporters. "I'm going to my room," I said to my father.

But Father was already working the crowd, grinning and pumping hands so several well-wishers would have sore fingers for days to come.

"Come with me?" I asked Nick, relieved when he nodded.

"This has been a nightmare through and through," he said when we were finally upstairs. Due to our conflicting schedules, Nick had booked us separate suites, and I'd swallowed my argument that our timelines would align if Nick would declare himself for my father. Yet even as he sat across from me, I felt as though my husband were on the other side of the globe.

Of course, I couldn't say as much. Instead I unrolled my stockings and dropped them to the floor. Every bit of me ached as if I'd fought a heavyweight champion on the way here. The best time to consult with Father was over breakfast while we both gulped down tubs of black coffee, which meant that my habit of sleeping until noon was suspended until he won this election. I was running on almost no sleep and starting to feel it.

"I need to ask your father to look at my speech, make sure it hits the right balance between him and Taft." Nick sighed, his expression worthy of a man sentenced to life in prison. I wanted nothing more than to fall asleep right then and there, but this election was dragging Nick through hell; surely I could ease his mind for a little bit.

"I'll help you with the speech."

"Really?"

"Of course. Father has me look at all his speeches now."

So, sitting side by side, I helped Nick mark what he might cut on his convention address. It was a good speech, just a little rough around the edges and made all the better for our working on it together.

"I'm off to meet with Warren Harding," Nick said as he folded away the papers an hour later. "I'll be back in time for dinner."

Yet his place remained empty even as the dessert plates were cleared away, and I had to make his excuses to Mother and Father.

Nick still hadn't returned when I finally climbed into my empty bed in my lonely suite. I reminded myself that this was why we'd booked separate rooms; Nick must have forgotten a late-night meeting with Harding or the Rules Committee or even the Republican bosses.

Heaven only knew when he made his way back, but the next day he was short-tempered and nursing a devil of a headache. I didn't ask questions, as I didn't care to know the answers.

"They're going to nominate Taft," he said after he'd waved away my suggestion of aspirin. "And there's no way for your father to get around it."

"Are you sure?"

"The Rules Committee plans to refuse him his rightful share of the contested votes." Nick wouldn't even meet my eyes as he said it. "The official announcement won't come until the final night of the convention a few days from now."

I looked to where Father was posing for a photograph with a well-dressed herd of constituents, my heart folding in on itself. "We'll be forced to put on brave smiles until then."

"I'm afraid so."

"Well, it isn't over until my father says so."

I soon learned the conservative Republicans weren't done plotting. Nick and I stood together in the crowd at the Chicago Coliseum later that night when Warren Harding sidled up behind us with Florence looking imperious and slightly annoyed with her husband.

"Nick!" Harding exclaimed, clapping my husband hard on the back and acting for all the world like they were dear friends. I wished he would disappear, but I inhaled a steadying breath on my cigarette and pasted on a false smile. I'd dressed carefully tonight in Nick's favorite shade of blue, and wanted nothing more than to leave this crowd and spend an evening alone with my husband. Instead I had to pretend I was enjoying myself.

Unfortunately, Florence saw right through my act.

"I fear Warren has been a bad influence on your Nick," she said consolingly, her chest spangled with buttons of Taft's face and the

GOP elephant with the slogan *It Is Nothing but Fair to Keep Taft in the Chair.* I was so irritated at her blatant support of my father's political enemy that I could scarcely hear her next words. "I try to keep Warren on a tight leash at these public events, but I hope you're not too upset at him for keeping Nick out carousing last night."

"Carousing?" Suddenly my cigarette burned too hot. I stubbed it out beneath the toe of my new black heels, turning my attention to Florence.

"It's inevitable, I suppose. It's easiest to turn a blind eye to their flirtations, so long as they keep their other women out of the public eye and the newspapers. Warren said that Nick was very discreet—a room at the Hotel Sherman under a false name and all that, which I suppose is all we wives can ask, don't you think? After all, boys will be boys."

Flirtations? Other girls? A hotel room under a false name?

The humiliation hit me like a fist, a hundred fists, a thousand.

While I'd waited up, thinking Nick was schmoozing with the Rules Committee, he was instead breaking his vows to me? Yet Florence spoke as if we were discussing recalcitrant boys instead of philandering husbands.

It wasn't possible. Whatever Nick had done before our marriage and no matter the trials of this election, he *was* faithful to me. My mind couldn't conceive of any other reality.

"Perhaps Warren engages in flirtations with other women," I said, as if it were only the two of us in the entire Coliseum. "My husband does *not*."

Florence's visage hardened. "Of course, my dear," she said almost kindly, but I detected a note of condescension. "I must have been mistaken. My sincerest apologies."

I turned my attention to our husbands, although it took a full minute until I could shake the buzzing in my ears to hear what they were saying.

"I was just speaking to some of the boys from Columbus," Harding said, draining the last of his brandy. "We agree that your hands are tied as a mere congressman, and believe you'd do a bang-up job as governor of our fine state. What do you say? You support Taft and I clear the way to the governor's mansion for you?"

It was obtuse and raw of Harding to make such an offer, much less in my presence while we attended the convention where my father was fighting for his political life. I didn't give Nick a chance to open his mouth. "Nick and I would never accept anything from you," I said, my loathing of Warren finally bursting free from its dam. "One cannot accept favors from crooks."

Harding's face flared an unbecoming shade of crimson, and his bushy brows knit fiercely together. Florence pursed her thin lips and I knew she'd be writing my name in her little red book of nasties before the night was over.

"Alice doesn't mean that," Nick said quickly, but I only glowered.

"Of course I do," I said. "I always say what I mean, unlike you politicians."

I turned on a heel to leave, but Nick stopped me with a hand on my arm. "You must apologize, Alice," he berated me.

"I'll do no such thing." I flung his hand off, tempted to spit in his face. "Although while we're at it, perhaps *you* should consider apologizing to *me*."

"What are you talking about?"

"I just had to defend you to Florence regarding your whereabouts the other night." Nick tried to hush me as heads swiveled in our direction, but I was beyond caring. "Would you disabuse her of the notion that you took a room at the Hotel Sherman with another woman?"

To his credit, Nick paled a shade—or three—before steering me away from the Hardings. "I did let a room that night," he whispered. "But it didn't mean anything, I swear it."

There were no lies, no attempts at concealment, just the terrible, brutal truth. With his words, my heart shattered into a million jagged pieces. Florence had been right.

And I'd *defended* him.

Suddenly all the doubts I'd ever harbored about Nick came crashing down a thousandfold, so I wasn't even sure whether he'd ever truly loved me.

"How many nights like that have there been since we were married?" I asked. "I'm not such a simpleton to assume this was the first."

"I don't know, Bubbie."

He didn't know. He didn't *know*?

I started walking, wishing I could run. Run away from the crowd, the Hardings, Nick, and never look back. "Don't you dare call me that."

"It was a handful of times," he said as he maneuvered in front of me, his palms in the air. "Sometimes I just get so overwhelmed and then I have a few drinks . . ."

Further proof that Nick and alcohol should never mix.

"And there were women?"

"Yes, there were women. I'm sorry, Alice—"

"I don't want to see you during the rest of this convention, do you understand?" I said. "In fact, I never want to see you again."

"Alice," Nick began, but I shoved past him, hard. I wanted to scream and throw things and go for a dangerously fast car ride, but instead I squared my shoulders and maintained a steady pace, biting the insides of my cheeks to maintain my impassive mask.

I clung to that mask as if my life depended on it until I was back in my hotel room with the door safely shut behind me. Then, with a mangled sob, I threw a vase, a bedside lamp, my wedding ring, and God only knew what else at the wall, shrieking and raging incoherently all the while.

Me, who never cried, and now I couldn't stop the scalding tears as they streamed down my cheeks and I screamed my rage to the world.

Goddamn it, but how did I let this happen? How did I let myself be betrayed?

Nick was celebrating Taft's nomination with the Ohio delegation the following night when my father took the stage at the Orchestra Hall and officially declared that he would run on the platform of the newly created Bull Moose Party. I sang myself hoarse alongside Mother, Ethel, Kermit, and Archie to the new tune of "We Want Teddy" while Father's supporters cheered for their beloved colonel, all of us flat-footed in support of the man who deserved to be our next president.

"Where's Nick, Alice?" the newspapermen asked, but I only grinned from ear to ear, wondering why no one could see me bleeding inside.

"Did you hear my father?" I asked. "Don't you think that was his best speech yet?"

The *New York Times* the next day trumpeted the headline *Longworth in Trouble*, but they didn't know the half of it.

"Alice." Mother had followed me to my hotel room that morning, the *Times* in hand. "What is going on with you? And don't tell me nothing, because I can tell something is wrong."

"You're right; something is very wrong," I said as I threw things into my traveling trunk. "I'm going to divorce Nick." The very words made me want to vomit; I'd thought them over and over since that terrible night at the Coliseum, but this was the first time I'd said them out loud. They sounded final, like a blow I might never recover from.

"Divorce, Alice?" Mother reared back as if I'd said I was going to saw off my own foot. "Why on earth would you even say such a thing?"

"Because I'm deadly serious." I breathed defiance as I threw rumpled stockings into the trunk, yet I couldn't bring myself to tell her of his betrayal. "Nick isn't what he seems. He does whatever he wants, regardless of the harm it causes his political career, or me."

"Divorce would ruin you, and Nick."

"I don't care."

"Have you spoken to your father about this?"

"No. I won't trouble him. Not right now, at least."

I continued to lob things into the trunk while Mother stared at me. At least I had the satisfaction of knowing I'd stunned her into silence, which no one had ever managed to do. A knock at the door made me pause, a pair of shoes lifted mid-throw. I expected—and even hoped for—an apologetic Nick, but instead my father appeared as if somehow silently summoned by my mother. I'd often wondered if they shared some sort of magical bond, and had hoped for something similar in my marriage to Nick, but those hopes were now shattered beyond repair.

"Good morning, Mousiekins," Father said. "I came to say goodbye and thank you for all your help before your train leaves. I expect we'll see you at Sagamore Hill in the next few weeks?"

"I'll be there soon." I shot Mother a warning look. "I have loose ends to tie up in Washington."

Like packing up my life and leaving Nick.

Mother was suddenly at my side, her hands on mine stilling my haphazard attempts to pack.

"Alice just told me she plans to divorce Nick," she said to Father.

The oppressive silence that ensued might have filled a month of Sundays. Once again I felt like a little girl in a bustling train station, desperate for her father's approval.

"I see," Father said, coming to sit on the bed next to me. "That just won't do."

"It's *my* marriage. I can dissolve it if I want to." I tried to keep my voice level even as I felt my control slipping away. "Don't worry; I'll wait until after November so I don't ruin your election. I won't be the Liability Child."

"Liability Child?"

I waved a hand. "When we were little, I overheard you call Ethel the Asset Child and me the Liability Child." Father winced, but I was too far gone to worry about his feelings. "I swear I won't cost you the election."

"That's not at all what I'm troubled about," Father said. "My chief concern is for your happiness."

"Well, I'm not happy right now, that's for damn sure."

Mother hugged me with one arm and pressed her temple to mine. I knew this was serious when she didn't bother to correct my swearing. "Marriage doesn't guarantee your everyday happiness," she said. "And sometimes it feels like the heaviest of burdens."

I looked from one parent to the other. "That's not how you two act."

Mother actually laughed then. "Of course it's not. We keep our squabbles behind closed doors, where they belong. But I promise, we *do* squabble."

"And Mother usually wins," Father said. "Because she's invariably right."

This would have been sweet had our situations not been so abysmally different. Nick and I had surpassed the bickering stage before we'd even been engaged. "Well, I'm glad you can pass off a facade of perpetual bliss, but I can't. And I'm sick of trying."

"What brought this about?" Father asked. "What has Nick done that's so unforgivable?"

"He publicly supports Taft—" I said, but Father cut me off with a raised hand.

"Which I told him he must. No, Alice, this goes deeper than that."

I wanted to bottle up the truth and bury it where no one would ever find it, but suddenly the weight of all my hurt and dejection was too much to bear. "He's drinking again." I paused before I lobbed the final grenade at them. "And there are other women."

Goddamn it, but those words hurt to say. Like a hundred thousand needles cutting at me, until I had to look at my hands, my arms, just to make sure I wasn't bleeding everywhere.

Mother and Father just stared at me, and I knew with utter certainty that Nick's vices were more foreign to them than chopsticks. What kind of failure was I that I'd chosen such a degenerate as my husband?

"Nick loves you," Mother finally said. Emphatically. "Of that I have no doubt. He's personable and affable by nature, but I can't imagine he'd be unfaithful to you."

"Tell that to Nick," I said with a hollow laugh. Everything was hollow, as if the very words rattled and echoed where my heart should have been. "He admitted to letting a hotel room with other women on this very trip."

That drained some of the color from both their faces. Father was the first to recover.

"This election has been a heavy burden for Nick—and you—to bear, but it will be over in a few months," he said slowly. "This decision will impact the rest of your life; it isn't one to make at the height of your anger."

I picked up the rumpled blue shirtwaist I'd worn when Florence had told me of Nick, remembering how carefully I'd dressed for him before throwing it into the cold fireplace where the hotel maid could burn it later. Mother's brows knit in consternation and I could well imagine her thoughts: *Divorced* and *deranged. Whatever shall we do with Alice now?* I gave a wild laugh, my hands fluttering. "I don't think a few months' time is going to change my position on whether I should keep a philanderer as a husband."

Father frowned and clasped my hands to still them. "What you really have to decide is this: Do you think you'll be happier in a year's time with or without Nick?"

I thought of living alone, of never hearing Nick's violin serenades or downing a bowl of his Toothsome Terrapin, of never laughing as we danced the Turkey Trot or roller-skated down Pennsylvania Avenue. Of having to read about his life in the papers and never receiving another love note from him.

I sat down, suddenly deflated. "I don't know."

"Marriage is difficult," Mother said. "I don't agree with everything your father says or does, but we'll always be friends. Throwing away five years together isn't a decision to take lightly."

Nick *was* my best friend, but I'd lost friends before and lived to tell the tale. However, divorcing him would leave a far deeper scar than my split with Maggie Cassini. *If* I could even recover from such a heartache.

Father must have seen the doubt in my expression, for he squeezed my hands. "When you're at the end of your rope, Sissy, tie a knot and hold on. Think on it awhile. Go home to Washington and then meet us in Sagamore Hill. Perhaps a bit of breathing room would benefit both you and Nick."

Nick and I did sometimes get along better when there were several states' distance between us. Perhaps that would give me time to cool down, but I worried it might also give Nick the opportunity to sink deeper into trouble with his girls and gin.

I'd always been a gambler. I'd let the cards fall where they may, and hope life didn't deal me a flop hand.

If it did, I could always cut my losses and fold.

I told myself not to think of Nick on the train—I hadn't even stopped by his room at the Blackstone Hotel to say good-bye—so that meant having to occupy myself during the interminable hours on the ride home. Fortunately, half of Washington was on this particular train returning from the nomination, and lucky for me, it was the Republican half. I could kill two birds by whiling away the hours in the pursuit of a few senators and congressmen willing to join my father's side.

I meandered my way through the luxurious Pullman, ensuring my purple and gold Bull Moose campaign pin was on straight while I made gracious conversation beneath swaying crystal chandeliers. Until . . .

"So, Alice, when will Nick be returning to Washington?" asked one of his House colleagues. "I'd have thought he'd be here with you today."

My heart heaved into my throat and I stood paralyzed, dumbstruck by the seemingly innocuous question.

Be brave, like Father. Deflect and keep smiling.

"Oh, you know," I said brightly. "Planning his campaign while I work with my father. Speaking of which, how do you feel about his proposal for an eight-hour workday and a minimum-wage law for women?"

Head held high, I worked my way through the more progressive Republicans before turning my attention to the easiest of pickings.

"Tell me, Mr. Borah." The dining car hummed with idle conversations as I claimed the open table across the aisle and allowed the Negro porter to place a linen napkin in my lap. "Did you earn your nickname from that wild mane of hair, or is it a consequence of your renegade habit of voting based on your conscience and ideals?"

He grinned that slow grin of his, leonine eyes sparkling. "You know, Mrs. Longworth, I think it's both. I'm just thankful it's better than the other nickname my Idaho constituents saddled me with."

"Oh? And what might that be?"

He glanced about to make sure no one else was listening before leaning across the aisle to whisper. "The Big Potato."

I made a decidedly inelegant noise. "I suggest you stick with the Lion of Idaho."

"Agreed."

Now that the small talk was out of the way . . .

"I must say, Mr. Borah, that I'm mightily displeased with your party after that debacle in Chicago."

Bill took a menu from the porter, but didn't even pretend to peruse it. "It's a crime what the Rules Committee did to your father," he said.

"Music to my ears." I shook my head as the porter offered a bottle of chilled white wine. I needed all my wits about me just now. "I take it that means you'll support my father's new Bull Moose Party?"

Borah closed his menu. "You don't beat around the bush, do you, Mrs. Longworth?"

"Being direct saves time. Life is too short to waste a single minute."

"Then I, too, shall be direct. Regrettably, I'm unable to support your father."

I scowled. "You've been outspoken about your support of him in the past."

"True, but now he's running as a third party."

"You supported William Jennings Bryan for his presidential bid in 1896. He ran on the Populist ticket."

Borah's eyebrows grazed his hairline. "How do you know that? You were only a girl at the time."

I shrugged. "I've studied the entire coterie of Washington's Republicans, the better to estimate who might be persuaded to my father's side."

Thus, I knew which men were ruled by party lines and which were more flexible in their voting habits, and Bill Borah of Idaho was the front-runner in the latter group. I was taken aback that it was requiring even this much persuasion to make him turn his coat.

"You're a quick study, Mrs. Longworth," Borah said. "But the episode with Bryan persuaded me of the futility of third parties. Much as I'd like to see your father in the White House again, I'm afraid he hasn't a hope of winning."

"Then you'll support Taft, the lesser man?"

"I'm afraid so."

I suddenly felt as if all the other conversations on the car had ceased and everyone was listening to me lose this debate. I sipped my water so I might gather my thoughts. "I'm sorry you feel that way, Mr. Borah. I shall be sure to send my condolences when my father wins the election."

Borah laughed, a rich and pleasant sound had it not been for the fact that he'd just rebuffed me. "I don't doubt that you will, Mrs. Longworth. In fact, I look forward to it."

I spent the rest of the meal pushing bites of prime rib around my plate and smiling too gaily at everyone. Several times I felt Borah watching me, as if he might restart our conversation, but I assiduously avoided him, opting instead to stare at the golden blurs of wheat fields that streaked by outside.

If a man like Bill Borah, who honestly revered my father, wasn't planning to vote for him, what chance did he have of winning? And if Father had no hope, why in merry hell had I jeopardized my marriage to help him win?

The next few months were a trial that made me want to pack my bags and book passage on the first steamship out of New York. In the weeks after the convention I'd come down with a chronic cold, plus what I deemed a marked case of schizophrenia as I tried to juggle both my father's campaign and my disintegrating marriage. I imagined an escape via a well-appointed cabin to Egypt or India or China or the great West or South America or the South Seas. Anywhere except where I was.

An opportunity to blow off some steam came in the form of an invitation to Grace Vanderbilt's oriental costume ball in Newport. Somehow, word of my plans to attend made it back to Nick, who broke his vow of silence to call me.

"Don't go, Alice," he said, his voice crackling on the other end of the line. I could hear him pouring a drink in the background, and almost hung up the phone that same instant. "For my sake, and your father's."

"It would be ridiculous to avoid a party for political purposes." Why had I even taken this call? Because I was an idiot and thought he might apologize? "It's not as if a gala thrown by the Vanderbilts will be a scandalous natty-narker."

That was a dig at Nick's recent behavior, but it didn't get his hackles up as I'd hoped. "Grace Vanderbilt has publicly contributed to your father's campaign," he said. "You know your attendance will wind up in the papers."

"You care too much what people say."

There was a long stretch of silence. "Things are going badly for me, Alice."

For once, politics seemed to be a topic in safer waters than our own relationship, which neither of us dared mention.

"You make things out to be worse than they are."

"Really? The other day in Cincinnati I ran into two friends who've supported my past campaigns. The first won't vote for me now because my father-in-law is the head of the Progressive Party and he's not a progressive. The second said, 'Sorry, Nicky, but I can't vote for you because you're for Taft and I'm a Roosevelt man.'"

I rolled my eyes, feeling entirely unsympathetic. "We knew this election would be difficult."

"Do not go to the Vanderbilt ball and make things worse than you already have."

"Worse than I already have?" I might have reached through the telephone to throttle him. "It's difficult to tell which of us has made things worse. I'll do as I damn well please," I seethed. "And don't you forget it!"

Nick's voice was cold, even coming from four hundred miles away. "As if you could ever let me."

The party wasn't the most extravagant I'd ever attended or even the most enjoyable, but anyone watching would have thought I was having more fun than a drunken debutante. Grace and I scarcely knew each other, but I became the star of her ball, costumed in a sapphire sash and trousers with a gold coat and turban made from the Chinese brocade that Empress Cixi had given me years ago. I lost track of each quadrille's unique theme of Russians, Gypsies, and the seasons as I whirled faster than a dervish down by the beach as the stars came out and then faded away. My toes went numb long before dawn, but I kept dancing even as tuxedoed servants laid out a breakfast of Yarmouth bloaters and soda scones under a well-established sun. I finally collapsed onto a pile of satin pillows next to Grace and her friends, my hair long since gone loose and half a beach of sand in my silk slippers.

"Did you hear that Cissy Patterson's gone and left her Austrian count for good, now that President Taft interceded to help her get her daughter back?" Grace asked the cluster of weary partygoers, all in various states of dishevelment. She still wore an enormous stomacher of blinding diamonds pouring down her front like the waters coming down at Lahore, with a matching diamond tiara crammed into her hair. Her news banished my yawns and drooping eyelids. "Worse still, she's gone and filed for divorce."

"What a scandal." One woman gave a disdainful sniff. "No one worth their salt will have anything to do with her—or her family—when she returns to America."

Grace laughed. "Well, I certainly won't."

Normally I'd have spoken up in Cissy's defense, but my troubles with Nick crimped my tongue. Cissy's husband had carried on countless affairs, beaten her, and kidnapped their daughter; yet society still condemned her. What would they say about me when I left Nick because of his dalliances and drinking?

"Excuse me," I said, picking my way around all the people whose names I'd already forgotten. "But I think I've finally worn myself out."

I slept most of the afternoon and finally emerged the next morning to find that the ball had made the headlines of all the society pages, with photos of me next to Grace front and center.

"Don't we look fabulous?" Grace asked. She'd shed her diamonds in favor of a silk day wrapper, her normally tight curls loose around her face. She suddenly snapped at a waiting maid. "I almost forgot. This came for you."

The maid offered me a silver tray, upon which rested a Western Union telegram addressed from Ohio. I didn't need to guess who it was from. Neither did Grace.

"Tell Nick I'll never forgive him for missing all the fun," she said, but I only offered an empty laugh, feeling her studying me.

"He told me before I left to have enough fun for the both of us," I trilled. "And I told him to keep me informed on how the labor vote looks."

"Good woman." Grace squeezed my arm. "Our menfolk do like to feel important, don't they?"

"They do indeed."

And while I promised myself that Nick would never get under my skin again, I felt like a child about to be reprimanded for damaging something precious.

Still, I'd have gone to Grace's party ten times over, no matter what Nick said. I might be his wife, but he'd never controlled me. And he never would.

I smiled to Grace and wended my way to the beach to open the telegram. "Damn you, Nick," I said after reading it, crumpling the paper in my hands. "Damn you to hell and back."

SAW YOU IN THE PAPERS. NO DOUBT FOR AMERICA WHO
YOU SUPPORT NOW. IN ILESBORO TO GOLF. SPENDING
TIME WITH BETTY HIG.

I read the words at least ten times before tearing the damned thing to shreds and hurling them into the salty breeze, watching until they finally drowned in the choppy waves. We'd hit a new and terrible low if Nick thought to crow about his time spent with other women. Our marriage was the epicenter of an active battlefield, and we were both aiming every gun and cannon we had at its dying heart.

I'd once thought that love was like a war. Why had no one warned me that falling *out* of love was a far bloodier battle?

Nick's silence since Grace's party had been stony, reminding me of the treatment he'd given me on our Far East junket so many years ago. Unfortunately, I couldn't avoid Ohio and the Longworths forever.

Two nights after Father's speech, I was at Rookwood, suffering through a solitary—and silent—dinner with Nick's mother. My husband was out doing who knows what with who knows who, leaving me alone to suffer through Susan Longworth's imperious sniffs. I wondered if she knew about her son's recent villainies, even as I knew she'd surely make excuses for his behavior.

Nicky never expected to settle down.

Nicky can't help that he's so charming; the women just flock to him.

If only you'd been a better wife to Nicky . . .

The phone in the hall rang, making both of us jump over our tepid lamb with mint sauce and tasteless orange lumps I assumed were creamed carrots.

"It's the *Philadelphia Inquirer* on the telephone for you, Mrs. Longworth," the maid said. "I told them you were dining, but they said it was urgent. Something about Mr. Roosevelt."

I might have kissed both her plump cheeks for the disruption. By now I was accustomed to speaking to the press on my father's behalf; I considered it my privilege to help his campaign at something I was so good at.

And it was a double boon to do it under Susan Longworth's roof, especially while a box of envelopes that Bromide had stuffed for Taft sat in plain sight on the sideboard, which I was choosing to ignore lest we ruin the Turkish carpet in a bloodbath.

"Thank you." I dabbed my mouth with the linen napkin. "I'll take it."

"I recall a day," Bromide nattered under her breath, "when a family might have finished an entire meal without being interrupted by a ringing device."

"Yes," I muttered as I picked up the phone in the hall, "but a rescue by telephone is far better than one by a noose." I picked up the receiver. "This is Mrs. Longworth," I said. "How can I help you?"

"Hello," came a crackly male voice on the other line. "This is Bill Starr with the *Philadelphia Inquirer*. We were wondering if you had any comments about tonight's assassination attempt on your father."

The world ceased spinning, vertigo sucking the oxygen from my lungs as I reached out blindly for something to keep me upright.

"Assassination attempt?" I choked on the black words. "What do you mean?"

"Don't you know?" The reporter's voice seemed as if lost down a long, dark tunnel. "Your father was shot in Milwaukee tonight."

All the air was sucked from my lungs, and I clutched the phone receiver as if it were the edge of a cliff. *This can't be happening . . .*

"Mr. Roosevelt is one helluva man," the reporter continued from far away. "The fanatic shot him from point-blank range. Everyone wanted him to go to the hospital, but he gave an hour-long speech before they persuaded him to see a doctor."

It was several long moments before I could make my mouth work. "He's alive?" I finally made myself ask, dreading the answer. "My father's still alive?"

"Of course, or at least he was an hour ago. In fact, I was calling to see if you had any comments on how this will affect his campaign. Will he continue to run, or will this put him out of the race entirely?"

I stifled a sob of relief. "I'm sorry," I said. "I have no comments at this time."

I was only dimly aware of the reporter's voice squawking at me from hundreds of miles away as I hung up the phone. I stood staring at the damask wallpaper, trying to sort out my swirling thoughts into some semblance of a plan, and almost jumped out of my skin when the receiver jangled in its holder. I scrambled to answer it.

"Hello?" I asked.

It was Ruth Hanna McCormick on the other end, the wife of one of my father's most ardent supporters in the Senate and also one of his campaign organizers. "Your father is being treated in the hospital," she said in her fairy-tale drawl when I demanded to know how he was doing. "He's more than fine. He went onstage after it happened and asked everyone for quiet, then announced, 'Some of you may have heard that I've just been shot. But it takes more than that to kill a Bull Moose!'"

I laughed, but the sound came out strangled. "Of course he did." I felt so damn helpless trapped in the cage that was Cincinnati. Ruth seemed to read my thoughts.

"Everything is fine, Alice, really. He's being given an antitoxin to protect against blood poisoning and is being transferred to Chicago tomorrow for surgery. I'll tell everyone you'll be there before the rooster crows."

I sat down after she hung up, suddenly able to breathe again, until I realized that Susan Longworth hovered at the dining room doorway, arms crossed tight in irritation. "Enough of this secrecy, Alice. I insist that you tell me what is going on."

"My father was shot."

Her hand fluttered to her heart. "Dear heavens. Shall I send someone to find Nicky for you?"

"No," I said. "I'll leave on the first train in the morning. Nick probably won't be home by then, and if he is, he'll still be drunk."

It was mean and petty, but I didn't care. The truth was, Nick should have been wrapping his arms around me and assuring me everything was going to be all right. Instead, Bromide just tipped her nose into the air. "I understand that you're fragile right now, so I'll forgive your unkind remarks about my son," she said coolly before retreating into the dining room.

I'm not fragile, you sour-faced nitwit. I've never been fragile a day in my life and I'm not about to start now.

I took the stairs two at a time to my bedroom, willing the hours before dawn to disappear, all the while racked with worry for my father. I ached for Nick, but as I'd guessed, he still wasn't home when I vaulted down Rookwood's front steps to the car that would drive me to the station.

To this day, I have no idea what I saw on the train ride, or whether anyone spoke to me. All I cared about was that I got to my father as fast as possible.

Arriving at Mercy Hospital, I was reminded of the time I visited Father after the trolley accident at the beginning of his presidency. Yet, this time my heart stopped at the sight of Mother in her traveling clothes and hugging Ted outside Father's hospital room, both of them pallid while my other siblings sat huddled together on wooden chairs.

Terrible thoughts assailed me then—that Father had taken a turn for the worse or had died in the night or during his surgery—but my brother looked up at just that moment.

"Father's fine," Ted reassured me with a wan smile. "The lion will live to roar another day."

I sat down hard, the sleepless night and all my worries pig piling on top of me all at once.

"We've all been in to see him since they tried to take the bullet out," my sister Ethel said. She might have been Mother's twin, not a hair out of place despite the fact that our father had gone knocking on death's door last night.

"He said you needn't have bothered coming," Mother added. "But I told him you'd fly to his side for a paper cut."

"When can I see him?" I asked.

"After they finish changing his bandages. They attempted to remove the bullet during surgery, but it's too close to his heart to risk." Mother broke off her embrace with Ted to come hug me. "I'm glad you're here, and Father is too. You know how he always likes to be the center of attention."

I sat in silence for those next few minutes, listening to my siblings chatter among themselves, mostly about next month's election and Ethel's upcoming marriage to a wealthy surgeon. Yet I couldn't focus on more than a few words at a time as Ethel described the *point d'esprit* on her wedding gown. Mother must have noticed, for she sat next to me and squeezed my hand.

"There's nothing you could have done. You can't always be glued to your father's side, Alice, much as you might wish it."

I leaped to my feet when a doctor finally emerged from Father's room. "He's ready for visitors." I pushed past the poor man, barely hearing Mother tell the rest of the family to give me a moment alone with Father.

Flowers and stacks of telegrams filled every surface that would hold them, yet this was nothing like the trolley accident, for the man who lay in the hospital bed this time was a decade older and paler than January from blood loss. But as Ted had claimed, our father was still a lion, albeit one who looked like every animal in the jungle had taken a swing at him.

"You seem cross, Sissy," he said by way of greeting.

"I'm allowed to be cross," I whispered, for my voice wouldn't work. I'd spent most of my life scrambling for Father's love, and now that I had it, I'd almost lost him. "You could have died."

"Pah!" He shifted in his seat to reach a mug of water. "I don't care a rap for being shot. It's a trade risk which every prominent public man ought to accept as a matter of course."

But not every prominent public man is my father, I wanted to say.

Instead, I only handed the cup to him, but his lips curled as he peered inside. "I'm not sure what it takes to get a cup of coffee around here." He relented when he saw my teary eyes. "I was never in any mortal danger, Mousiekins."

"Oh? Now you're a doctor too?"

"I checked my lips as soon as I realized I'd been shot. They were clean."

I waited, but the punch line wasn't forthcoming. "And?"

Father looked disappointed. "Any hunter worth his salt knows a wounded creature is doomed once it starts bleeding at the mouth." He gestured toward a side table where a maroon leather case and a folded manuscript rested, both damaged and spattered with blood. "My spectacles case and speech slowed the bullet so it didn't hit my heart."

I had to sit down at that.

"And then you decided to give an hour-long speech?"

"Ninety minutes, actually. It would have been longer, but it was a damnable inconvenience to have a bullet in me. Still, the crowd loved it when I opened my vest so they could see I'd been shot."

I pressed hard at the bridge of my nose, simultaneously awed and exasperated. I liked to believe I was adept at manipulating the press and public opinion, but there was no doubt that I was in the presence of a master. Or a masochist. "Don't go getting any ideas about garnering more votes with similar circus tricks."

Father tipped an imaginary hat at me. "Wouldn't dream of it. While I'm always willing to try anything once—and being shot *was* an interesting experience—carrying one bullet in my chest is enough. I don't need to compete with Andrew Jackson."

"Who rattled when he walked after all the duels he'd fought," I said, completing one of the bedtime stories Father had told us children when we were young. I was aware of my siblings filing into the room, and just like that, my moment alone with Father was over. I hardly listened to all their conversations until Ethel suddenly asked me, "Where's Nick?"

I colored, although I knew Ethel hadn't meant anything by the inquiry, that Mother and Father would have kept quiet our marital troubles. "He might make the train tonight," I lied, for truthfully I had no idea when I might next see my husband. "He's giving campaign speeches every day."

Thus, it was a surprise when Nick showed up at the hospital around dinnertime, rumpled and looking slightly worse for wear. My joy at seeing him was soon quashed by the way he slurred his greeting.

"I came as soon as I could," he said. I was aware of my family watching us intently. Their gazes skittered away at my sharp glance.

"Thank you," I said tightly. I gave Nick a few minutes with Father and then ushered him to a drab little restaurant across the street. We hardly spoke as we ordered boiled salmon; I didn't trust myself to utter a single word as I watched him down almost a full bottle of chardonnay by himself. As soon as our plates were cleared I ordered a car and gave the driver instructions to return my husband to the station.

"I'll stay," Nick started, but I shook my head.

"Go home," I said, my tone sharper than usual. "You've done enough already."

"I'm sorry, Alice. Truly I am, for everything."

I knew what he meant, but I didn't have it in me to forgive Nick, not now and possibly not ever. So I only shrugged. "Sometimes sorry isn't enough."

Nick seemed about to say something more but then ducked into the car and shut the door with a dull thud.

I watched the car disappear, all the while hugging myself and choking back tears. If Father almost dying couldn't mend the rift between us, I doubted whether anything could.

We'd danced ourselves to the end of our love. And I still had no idea what to do about it.

"Congratulations on your eighty-eight electoral votes," I said glumly to Father as I set down the morning's papers. Bare-armed trees shivered in the wind outside Sagamore Hill's windows, a portent of the dark winter to come. "Taft only won a measly eight, so that's something to cheer, right?"

My father had been defeated, so I doubted whether there would ever again be anything to cheer.

"If you say so, Sissy." Father stared at the fire burning in the library's hearth, the portraits of his heroes—Lincoln, Grant, and my own grandfather—silently commiserating with us from their frames. The silence stretched until I could hear both our hearts breaking over the election results, which crowed that Woodrow Wilson had claimed the White House. "How did Nick fare?"

It seemed a complete afterthought to check whether Nick had won his congressional seat. I thumbed through the election results. They weren't in yet.

I refused to call. Let him come to me.

Yet the call didn't come, even as the hours ticked by and Father received word that things looked bad for Nick.

He patted me on the back. "Tell Nick it's hard to fail, but worse never to have tried to succeed."

Oy vey. I doubted that tidbit of wisdom would go over well, even coming from my father, who had just experienced the worst failure of his life.

"I've been bruised and betrayed," Nick said when he finally rang after everyone else had gone to bed. His words were garbled and I could well imagine the bottle in his hand, his shirtsleeves rolled up and his collar undone. "Do you know how many votes I lost by? Ninety-seven," he supplied without waiting for me to respond. "Ninety-seven measly votes that *you* cost me. All those appearances you made for your father, not for me. You were supposed to be my rock, Alice, but you betrayed me."

I'd dreaded the snapping point of our relationship, but now that it was finally here, I was already so battered that I felt merely bruised by the false hopes that were shattered by his words. False hopes that we'd survive this campaign, that our marriage would recover, that we'd love each other again.

"*I* betrayed *you*?" I could scarcely spit out the words. "I think you need to check your facts."

I slammed down the receiver, quivering with anger. Only then did I clap my hands over my mouth as the fuller magnitude of this disaster hit me.

For the first time in eleven years I had no reason to live in Washington, no father or husband in office.

"Oh, God have mercy," I moaned before I sank down on my bed. "Not Cincin-nasty . . ."

Home of the wretched Longworth den of harpies and Nick's harem of female paramours. I'd rather writhe in the fleas of a thousand camels for all eternity.

Of course, there was a single solution that would free me from all my torments.

Yet I knew I was too pigeon-livered to face the ensuing firestorm that would target me and my family if I demanded a divorce. I'd always been the press's darling, but they'd turn on me like a pack of rabid wolves if I left my husband.

Yet I heard Father's earlier advice ringing in my ears, telling me that somehow, I'd survive this too.

When you're at the end of your rope, Sissy, tie a knot and hang on.

I'd clutch at my rope awhile longer. It remained to be seen how long I could hang on.

Chapter 15

Cincinnati wasn't *so* awful.

In fact, if one subtracted Rookwood, Bromide, and Nick from the city, it might have been altogether palatable. Instead, every day was akin to a root canal.

A botched one, at that.

One afternoon I went walking up the hill that overlooked the Ohio River, where Nick and I had once picnicked together, for I'd started walking six miles a day to help clear my mind. Butterflies frolicked in the dappled sunshine, and I was enjoying the view of the shaggy country around me while I planned the menu for tonight's dinner party. I was halfway between deciding which consommé cousin Eleanor would prefer when I came upon Nick seated on a park bench, a freckled woman five years my junior fitted around him as if they were jigsaw pieces.

I should have kept walking. *Why* didn't I keep walking?

The girl looked up and I expected her to push away from Nick, for one or both of them to stutter that this wasn't what it seemed. Instead, she only laid a possessive hand across Nick's chest.

"Hullo, Mrs. Longworth," she said, fluttering her fingers in a wave.

Dumbstruck, I waited for Nick to speak, but my darling husband said nothing, although the crimson flush creeping up from his collar told me he wasn't as composed as he wished to appear. "Alice—"

I forced myself to walk past as if I didn't care one bit that my husband was curled around another woman. I felt dumber than snake mittens that Nick was flaunting his women in public now, while I was powerless to stop it. So this was to be his revenge for my defection to my father: my complete and utter humiliation.

Act the opposite of how you feel, I thought, *and perhaps you'll fool them all.*

"Don't trouble yourself," I called to him over my shoulder. "I'm glad to see you putting your free time to such good use."

I continued walking, ignoring the handful of passersby who called out greetings. I wanted only to find a quiet corner somewhere and hit something. Why was it that men had all manner of acceptable outlets to let off steam—singlestick, boxing, or even football—while women were expected to simper and pour tea, regardless of their own inner turmoil? I refused to go home and wallow, marching in the opposite direction of the park until dusk threatened. Then I remembered the dinner party, suddenly imagining all the guests whispering about my marital troubles while standing in my house, drinking my champagne, and talking afterward to the reporters I'd trained.

I considered walking to the railway station and never looking back—press and political careers be damned—but in the end I returned to Rookwood and changed into what might have been an appropriate evening ensemble, or could have been my mohair bathing suit for all I noticed. To my dismay, Eleanor arrived first. "I'm afraid Franklin had to return to Washington," she said, handing me an indifferent bottle of wine as the butler closed the door behind her. "So you're stuck with just me tonight."

"What a disappointment," I said dumbly. "Frank's such great fun to tease."

"Do you know, but I brought your father's most recent letter to Frank." Eleanor dug into her skirt pocket. "He's full of advice now that Franklin's assumed his new position as assistant secretary of the navy. Following in Uncle Ted's footsteps again."

"I'm sure." Yet I stopped listening when the door knocker sounded and more boisterous guests arrived. I wanted to die when Manchu yapped at the door and I saw Nick, somehow already dressed in his evening togs.

And holding the door open for the freckled chit from the park.

"Eleanor," Nick said warmly, stopping to shake my cousin's hand. "So good of you to come. This is Virgie Newcastle."

If Eleanor thought that Nick would further explain this young woman's position, she was sadly mistaken, for he only steered Virgie into the dining room.

I died a thousand silent deaths when Nick laughed too loudly at her jokes, all the while ignoring me as stoically as I avoided him. Instead, I held tight to Manchu while Nick mixed Virgie a martini from our twelve-bottle bar. Then I watched while the freckled interloper downed two glasses of whiskey and smoked at least fifteen cigarettes, all before ten o'clock. (She might have been a girl after my own heart, had she not been after my husband instead.) I wanted to shove one of Virgie's shags down that pretty throat of hers, but that probably wasn't proper hostess behavior endorsed by *Godey's Lady's Book*.

I wondered if *Godey's* had a chapter on what to do with philandering husbands. At this rate I'd be able to write ten volumes on the topic.

Unless I wanted to draw undue attention to Nick's infidelity— which I most certainly did *not*—there was nothing I could do except laugh and cover my horror with more bombast than usual.

"Are you all right, Alice?" Eleanor asked when she finally hugged me good-bye. "You look flushed." My cousin grimaced in response to Virgie lighting still another cigarette. Merry hell, but I wanted to confide in Eleo then, to spill the whole sordid story and have her pat me on the back and tell me everything would be all right. Virgie's high trill of a giggle stopped me, some zinger of a joke she'd told that had everyone laughing. I, of course, joined in, making sure my throaty chortle was the loudest of all.

Distract them so they can't see the obvious. For surely no self-respecting wife would tolerate her husband's mistress right under her nose.

Unless she had no choice, that is.

"Just worn out," I said to Eleanor, playing it off. "A good party is so much work."

"You're a gifted hostess." My cousin shoved her arms into a fur stole as if she couldn't wait to get away. If only she could take me with her. "I envy it."

"Don't envy me," I said, grinning brightly to take away the sting in my eyes even as Manchu licked at my chin. "Really."

I almost hoped then that empathetic Eleanor would realize something was amiss. But if she did, she chose not to comment.

With a hollow heart I watched her go. After that, the rest of our guests departed in a timely manner, including simpering little Virgie Newcastle.

Enough was enough.

I caught the totty little muck-snipe's arm at the door and gave her an effusive smile. "I suggest you restrict your interludes with my husband to the park," I said through my teeth. "I've spent plenty of time boxing with my father. There's no telling what will happen to your pretty face if I catch you in my home again."

Naturally, my hand happened to twist the soft flesh under her arm just then, resulting in an unladylike yip of pain from the stroppy tosspot. Virgie blanched an unbecoming shade of white and dashed away without so much as a farewell to Nick.

I'd spent today writhing in the hottest fires of hell, yet I still had to deal with my husband.

The coward tried to sneak off to bed, but I blocked his way on the stairwell, setting down Manchu, who wisely scampered off.

"You crossed the line today," I snarled, impressed with my own sangfroid. *Never let him see how much you're hurting.* "Not just crossed it, but leapfrogged the damned thing and kept running. If you're determined to squander your life, so be it, but you will not humiliate me in the process. I am a president's daughter and a congressman's wife, and you will treat me as such."

Nick looked me up and down as if he'd never seen me before, yet I couldn't decipher the expression on his face. Disgust? Anger? Self-reproach?

He sighed. "And I'm just the second-rate clodpoll you happen to have the misfortune to be married to," he said. "Don't think I don't realize that you measure me against him with every move I make—"

What on earth was he talking about? Did Nick think *I'd* been unfaithful?

"Him?" I asked, interrupting. "Do you honestly believe *I'm* cheating on *you*? Is that why you're so determined to flaunt all these women in my face?"

"Your father, Alice."

"What?"

Nick shoved his fists into his pockets. "I can never cast half the shadow Theodore Roosevelt can, and because of it I'll always be an eternal disappointment to you."

I opened my mouth to argue, but all the words evaporated.

Nick was right; he could never measure up to my father, no matter how hard he tried. Perhaps he'd stood a chance once, but his drinking and carousing had forever blackened my love and, worse, my respect for him. His words doused my anger just as suddenly as it had flared to life, for perhaps Nick wasn't solely to blame for destroying our relationship.

I couldn't love him as he needed and he couldn't love me as I needed either. Uncle Will's prophecy had finally come true.

"I'll give you a divorce," Nick said, scrubbing a hand over his jaw, lined with stubble. "If that's what you want."

"I don't know what I want." I sank down onto the stair, holding my head. I felt Nick sit next to me, and found myself desperately wishing that I could love him again, trust him. Those days were long gone, yet perhaps we could still salvage something from the ruins of our marriage.

"I won't leave you," I said. "Not unless you want me to."

"I'd never want that, Bubbie. Not in a million years."

My shoulders sagged with relief. To hear him ask for a divorce would have been more than I could take.

"We can't keep on as we have been," I said. "I need time away from you, from all of this. I'm going to spend the winter at Sagamore Hill." I spoke slowly, pulling the painful words from somewhere deep inside me. "You can do as you please here in Ohio, if you can be . . ." I searched for the word even as part of me died inside. ". . . discreet. You owe me that much."

"Of course, Bubbie," Nick said. He gave me a look stolen from a whipped puppy, but I refused to let myself be moved. "I don't want to lose you."

There was no doubt in my mind that the passion Nick and I had shared in our early days was spent, and I had no idea if it could ever be replaced with something else. Only time would tell.

I rose and turned to walk up the creaking stairs, but he clutched my hand. "I'm sorry," he said.

"I know," I answered. "So am I."

In fact, I was more than sorry.

I was shattered, defeated, and exhausted. But I was still hanging on, which I supposed was something.

Snow swirled outside the windows as Ethel awkwardly lowered herself into the seat beside me, but I could barely bring myself to look at her or her rounded belly. The head of the table was almost worse, what with Father's empty chair while he and Kermit were gallivanting about South America on a fresh grand male adventure mapping the River of Doubt. My family was accomplishing great things, everyone save me, that was.

"You're coming to the Straights' New Year's party, aren't you?" Ethel asked as the glazed ham was brought in, her round face aglow with happiness. After only seven months of being married, she and her husband were expecting their first child in April, whereas I'd been married almost eight years and had nothing save an estranged husband to show for it.

A child might have bound Nick closer to me, and kept his eyes—and more—from wandering. Too late now.

Instead, all my family and friends were blissfully and inconveniently happy, even Willard Straight, who'd recently married some obscure diplomat's daughter. Misery might love company, but not when all the company was so blasted cheerful.

"I think I'll stay here—" I started, but Ethel didn't let me finish as she handed me a platter of mashed potatoes.

"A party will be just the thing to bring the sparkle back to your smile. You should go." She folded her hands atop her stomach. "Unless Nick would object."

"Nick couldn't care less what I do." I dared not say more and ruin the holiday, and instead forced false gaiety into my voice even as I fed Manchu pieces of ham from under the table.

Ethel was too damn smart and saw through my ruse. "Every couple has their spats, Sissy. The whole family is rooting for you and Nick, all the way down to the dogs and the guinea pigs."

So they'd guessed my troubles, but still loved me anyway. I rose and hugged her then, a rarity between us that might have shocked her into early labor.

"I love you, Ethel."

"I love you too, silly goose. Always have and always will."

"Fine," I said. "I'll go to the party. But just for a bit."

I did go to Willard's little soiree on New Year's, mostly because I was sick of my own morose company. I'd learn to dance in the rain, even if it killed me.

"It's a lovely party," I said to Willard's wife, Dorothy, over the din of firecrackers at the stroke of midnight. It was a large gathering full of all their friends and family, and children careened about the dark lawn, banging pots and pans together in a devilish symphony. "Thank you for inviting me."

"We're very glad you're here," Dorothy said. She was plain-faced, but kind, the sort of woman who might have made any man mostly happy. "Any friend of Willard's is a friend of mine."

"I've never seen him so content." I watched as Willard looked up at his wife and twin smiles bloomed on their faces.

Hello again, my green-eyed friend.

Yet I managed a smile. "It's about time someone made an honest man out of him."

Dorothy chuckled. "I do what I can." She surprised me by touching my forearm. "Happy New Year, Alice."

I sat alone on the porch's old chair swing as the last of the rockets and Roman candles burned themselves out. Dorothy wandered about the lawn amid the party's off-key rendition of "Auld Lang Syne," picking up bits of singed paper from the firecrackers until Willard pulled her into his arms and kissed her full on the mouth. I forced deep the sudden pangs of jealousy at the simple joy of their love. Finally, Willard mounted the porch steps to stand next to me.

"That's a somber face for such a celebration, Mrs. L," he said. "Surely the New Year is worth a smile or two?"

"I suppose leaving this year behind is worth a firecracker." As always, I didn't feel the need to discern with Willard. I could be my caustic old self and he wouldn't mind. "Although I'm not sure the next year promises to be much better."

"It could be a very trying year, especially if Europe has anything to say about it. The problems in the Balkans are a veritable tinderbox ready to explode."

Father's campaign and then my problems with Nick had overshadowed most everything else in the world, but I'd found it difficult to ignore the troubling news coming out of Europe, their twisted morass of alliances and military buildups.

"Do you think America will be drawn into the conflict?"

"I think it will be difficult to avoid."

I sighed. "It's times like this when I wonder why I didn't pack myself off to China or Hawaii when I had the chance. Perhaps I still might."

"That which doesn't kill us makes us stronger. And you're one of the strongest people I know." He squeezed my shoulder, his hand lingering before dropping to his side. He looked away, but not before I caught the flush that marred his normally nonplussed expression.

There it was again, that spark between us. I supposed it would never disappear entirely, but there was nothing to be done about it.

Willard turned as Dorothy mounted the steps, her pockets full of singed paper. He offered her his arm and me a jaunty smile. "Happy New Year, Mrs. L."

"Happy New Year, Willard. You, too, Dorothy."

I was overwhelmed by a wind of conflicting emotions as I watched them clasp each other's hands beneath the sky's dazzling display of fireworks. I was truly glad that Willard had someone to share his life with, while also painfully jealous that such domestic tranquility had escaped my grasp.

I was under no illusion that I would ever possess such simple bliss. I would never have the perfect husband or find myself surrounded by a gaggle of dimpled children on the porch of a picturesque house. I wasn't sure what the future held, yet I wanted more than I had now, and I was no longer willing to wait for life to give it to me. Instead, I'd seize it with my own two hands.

Little did I know that the assassination of an Austrian archduke all the way across the Atlantic would soon give me the purpose I craved. On that cold and clear New Year's night a great and terrible war loomed that would soon envelop us all.

For us, the Roosevelts, the First World War was our Great War. All our lives before and after were just bookends for that heroic, tragic volume.

Chapter 16

"The war is so terrible I can think of little else," Mother said. We were sitting in the still-warm autumn sun in the apple orchard at Sagamore Hill, Mother dandling Ethel's baby on her knee. My sister and her husband had volunteered to assist ambulance hospitals on the European battlefields almost the same instant as Archduke Franz Ferdinand's assassination even though it meant leaving behind their son, but we were all proud that she was doing her bit to better this great world tragedy. "All of Europe seems to have turned to barbarism," Mother said with a frown.

"Father says that wars are to be avoided, but some are better than certain kinds of peace." I stood and helped myself to a green apple from a tree my siblings and I climbed when we were young. "Kaiser Wilhelm must be stopped. To think I actually christened that man's boat."

"Yes, well, your father believes we'll beat the Huns if America finally declares against the Triple Alliance. I'm just thankful he's too old to lead the charge against the kaiser himself."

"Too old," I said, taking a bite of the apple. "And too ill."

Mother frowned, and I knew she still worried about him. I'd been horrified when Father had returned half-starved from his South American expedition on the River of Doubt, brown as the saddle that made up part of his luggage, his skeletal body racked with malaria and suffering further from a festering leg wound. Three other men had died on the treacherous journey: one drowned, one murdered, and the other abandoned as a murderer, but Kermit had managed to bring our father home, still mostly in one piece.

Yet when we were alone, my brother had confided that Father had begged to be left to die in the Amazonian rain forest after he'd injured his leg, had even planned to take a lethal dose of morphine to keep from being a burden on the rest of the party. I hadn't wanted to believe Kermit; I couldn't envision my larger-than-life father pleading to end his life. Worse still, I couldn't fathom the idea of a world without him.

I stretched my legs, causing Mother to wrinkle her nose in disdain. "I'm not sure I'll ever get used to seeing you in slacks," she said as she fed Ethel's son tiny slivers of peeled grapes from our arbor.

"It's for the war effort." I turned my toes this way and that, admiring my ankle-length silk pants. "They're comfortable, economical, and save cloth."

Mother scoffed. "I think you just like them because they're scandalous. If you truly wanted to help the war effort, you could always take up knitting sweaters for the soldiers like your cousin Eleanor."

Now it was my turn to wrinkle my nose. America had yet to enter the war, but no patriotic woman moved without her knitting these days. I'd tried my hand at a scarf and ended up hurling the entire skein across the room, swearing never to take up needles again, not even in defense of my country. "Bah," I said to Mother. "I may as well send the men tangled balls of yarn for all the good it would do."

Mother rocked Ethel's son until his eyes drooped, thumb jammed in his mouth. We all spoiled him rotten with sweets and toys, as if that might lessen how much we missed his mother. Yet it wasn't just Ethel who already had a foot in the war. "I'm putting together a package for Quentin to send off later this week," Mother whispered. "I do worry for him."

"I still can't believe he memorized the card for the vision test," I said, for Quentin's eyesight was so poor he'd have failed otherwise. "Father won't stop crowing about it."

"Quentin has an itch to fly all over France." Mother bit her lip. "He's just a baby."

"He's nearly eighteen, Mother, and probably learning to fly loop-de-loops in that plane of his." I recalled the way he'd rocked on his heels with excitement—my overgrown puppy of a brother who loved anything mechanical—when I'd hugged him good-bye at the train station. Yet my words only made Mother wince. "I'll write to tell him to stay out of trouble."

I'd do no such thing, but instead urge Quentin to have the time of his life. Yet Mother seemed somewhat reassured by my piecrust promise. "I'm glad Nick was finally reelected," she said. "Perhaps he can make some difference in Congress, although if the sinking of the *Lusitania* didn't persuade Wilson to call for war, I doubt anything will."

For Wilson, who had defeated my father, was a mollycoddle pacifist.

"Wilson has the backbone of a chocolate éclair," I said. "Did you know I haven't received a single invitation to the White House since that man was elected? I'm hosting a salon next week, and I only invited people I know will enjoy lambasting both him and his political poltroonery."

"Yes, I hear from your father that you've become quite the combination of Poe's raven and Cassandra."

"With a dash of malevolent political observer," I added, tossing the apple core to one of our pigs who was rooting about for elderly apples. "I have high hopes of seeing the white-livered coward impeached before the next election."

Mother frowned. "I had to watch your father ride off to war almost twenty years ago, Alice, and it almost killed me. I don't think I could stand to watch all my sons go, too."

I dropped a kiss onto her forehead. "We Roosevelts are lions, Mother. It will take more than a little war to take us down."

She only sighed. "I hope you're right, Sissy. I hope you're right."

There would be no Roosevelts in the White House in 1916.

Wilson was reelected on the platform that he'd kept us out of war. Then, on April 2, 1917, the coward finally asked Congress for that selfsame war.

Better late than never, I suppose. Yet for all my hawkish statements before the declaration, I quickly found myself wishing that Wilson had kept America's head buried in the sand.

The sun was setting over Sagamore Hill in a glorious eruption of red and orange as Father and I rode our horses back to the stables. Spring was unfolding the season's first flowers, and soon the green dance of summer would be upon us; one would hardly guess the war to end all wars was playing out on the other side of the globe. "I had an interesting conversation with the publisher of the *Washington Post* today," I said to Father. "He claimed my prognostications about the war have been on the nose, and asked me to write a regular column."

"That's excellent, Sissy," Father said. "Will you accept?"

"I doubt it," I said. "I prefer chatting one-on-one to writing down my predictions. There's something about looking a man in the eye that's lacking in reading a dry newspaper column." I looked askance at my father. "The publisher mentioned that you had a meeting with Wilson the other day. He asked what it was about, but I told him I had no idea."

"I asked the president to let me resurrect the Rough Riders and lead a regiment in France," Father informed me as we passed the little pet cemetery with its stone plaques marking where several of our horses and family dogs had been laid to rest. "Congress has already approved the plan, and I can have them trained and in the trenches before the draft army will be ready."

"That's not funny," I said to him, but his teeth gleamed whitely as he grinned, looking in better spirits than I'd seen since his return from the Amazon. He'd regained some weight, but still had recurring bouts of malarial fevers that Mother and I both fussed about.

"It's no joke. I worried that I might have to recruit the division in Canada and march under a British flag—I planned to have a Bull Moose sewn into the corner—but now that Wilson has declared war . . ."

It felt as if someone were standing on my lungs. "What does Mother say?" I managed to ask.

"She thinks me too old, but I'm not even fifty-nine. Think of me as a reserve fleet that can still take out a few Krauts or two."

I imagined my father slogging through the never-ending mud at Verdun or Marseilles, charging through the barbed wire hell that was No Man's Land, or being gassed by the Germans—and drew a breath so sharp it made my horse sidestep anxiously.

"Wilson will never let you go."

"He will if I promise to get myself killed." Father's massive grin collapsed when he saw my face. "Don't fret, Sissy. I survived one war; I'll survive this too."

"You've already done your service." I could scarcely pay attention to my mare as she picked her way down the darkening road. "Your efforts would be best spent here at home, persuading America to vote for anyone other than Wilson."

"Wilson is a little runt and his cowardice is an unpardonable sin," Father said. "But my mind's made up. I'm going, Sissy, as soon as that Byzantine logothete in the White House signs the paperwork."

It wouldn't do to argue further, so my mind zigzagged ahead, trying to ferret out what favors Nick or I might call in to keep Father from being granted his own regiment. Yet I couldn't let Father know that.

So I tried a different tack.

"Surely Mother can't spare you with all of my brothers—and Ethel—already off fighting."

With the declaration of war my four brothers had enlisted so that only I remained out of uniform. I'd seen it as my duty to help Father recover and guide the election back home, yet now even that was slipping through my fingers.

Father sobered at the mention of my siblings. "I can't let my children fight this war for us, not while I'm still able-bodied. I worry for them," he said. "Quentin especially. Those airplanes are death traps—I know because I've ridden in one—regardless of what the Wright brothers and the military claim."

"Quentin will be fine," I said with more assurance than I felt, for this was the first I'd heard of Father's concerns. "And so will Ted and Archie and Kermit."

"They're doing their duty and soon so will I." Father straightened in his saddle as we finally arrived at the stables. "You just wait and see, Sissy."

Fear's cold fingers curled around my heart as he spurred his stallion forward and trotted into the yellow light spilling from the stable.

Sorry, Father. Not if I have anything to say about it.

I spent the next few weeks surreptitiously entreating all manner of cabinet members and congressmen to block my father's application, even the one I'd hoped never to ask favors from again.

"Please, Nick," I said to my husband one day as he was headed out to Capitol Hill. It was the most I'd spoken to him in a month, but I'd have danced the Cakewalk Strut with the devil if it meant keeping my father safe. "Do whatever you can. My father *cannot* go to France."

"I'll see what I can do," he said. "But it's not as if I hold much sway with the current president."

Although I loathed Woodrow Wilson with every fiber of my being, I'd have kissed the preposterous little schoolmaster on the mouth when he refused my father's request to resurrect the Rough Riders. Rumor was that the president favored the idea of sending Father to war, but his advisors played up the fear that Father would repeat his heroic return from the Spanish-American War and seize the White House in the next election.

I'd never been so thankful to have a coward in the Oval Office.

"Of all the insufferable, miserable, mediocre men!" Father stormed in his library at Sagamore Hill, shaking the official telegram that had just arrived. "Wilson is a politician of monumental littleness! Why, I'd like to take him by the lapels and give him a shake he'd not soon forget—"

Mother and I exchanged bemused looks and went out onto the piazza together to hang the banner Father had purchased with grim elation that same day. A bold red flag with four blue stars for my four brothers: Ted, Archie, Kermit, and Quentin. "The stout lion's whelps are scattered abroad," I said quietly, doing my best not to poke my thumb with a pin.

"Ethel's coming home, but I'm terrified for your brothers," Mother admitted without meeting my gaze. "I suppose you can't bring up boys to be eagles and then expect them to be sparrows." She clasped my hand and squeezed it so hard I worried she might break a few bones. "Thank you, Alice, for keeping your father home."

"I don't know what you mean."

"I know you wrote letters and begged favors from everyone you could think of in Washington. Nick called and told me. He even put in a word at your request."

I glanced up at the open window of Father's study. "I did no such thing."

"Don't worry; I won't tell him," she said, standing back to admire our handiwork with shining eyes. "Pray for them; pray that they all come home."

I'd never been one to pray, but I accelerated my own wartime contributions, posing for publicity photographs while buying liberty bonds from Girl Scouts and staffing a Red Cross canteen alongside cousin Eleanor. My cousin didn't even bother to hide her surprise when I showed up at the tin-roofed canteen near Union Station two days in a row.

"I always thought it a pity that all your energy should go to waste," she finally said once she'd picked up her jaw from the floor. "I promise I'll find you enough to keep you occupied until the kaiser surrenders."

I had no doubt Eleo would keep her word. The mere thought made me want to take a nap.

"I don't know how you do it," I said as I tied my apron. "Coming here and then going home to Frank and the children."

Six children, in fact, the same number that Father had. Yet, I suspected not all was well on the home front, for I'd recently seen Franklin driving twenty miles deep in the country, sans Eleanor, who I knew was in upstate New York at the time. Frank hadn't seen me; his hands were on the wheel but his eyes were on the lovely girl—who I later found out was his secretary—next to him. I'd made my peace with the fact that it was common during Washington summers for politicians to bundle their families up to the mountains so the paterfamilias could acquire something attractive. Yet I wondered if Eleanor knew what her husband was up to. Was it my responsibility to tell her?

If she did know, she didn't show it. "Don't tell anyone," she whispered to me, "but I come here to escape the children. I've spent the last decade having a baby or getting ready to have one, and some days I swear I'll go mad if I have to dress them in one more smock or plan one more dinner of boiled hot dogs. It doesn't come naturally to me to enjoy the little chicks, or understand them."

So cousin Eleanor wasn't entirely perfect. I wallowed like a pig in summer mud at this new knowledge. "Children *can* be petty dictators. I certainly was."

Eleanor gave a weak smile. "It doesn't help that Franklin's mother is determined to contradict me at every turn."

Now *here* was a topic I could really bite into. We spent the next few minutes bemoaning the tyrannical mothers-in-law that our husbands had saddled us with. Perhaps gossip wasn't an entirely worthless hobby; I hadn't felt as close to Eleanor since we were girls running an obstacle course against the boys in Sagamore's old barn as I did in those few minutes.

"Perhaps you can help me with something," I said, knowing that a new project was the best way to improve Eleanor's mood, especially if that project involved helping others. "I've been asked to serve on a committee to provide housing to government employees in the District of Columbia. It's a bear of task, what with all the staff changes for the war."

In truth, it was a beastly bore of an undertaking, which was why I hoped to off-load it onto Eleanor's capable lap. My cousin smiled as she emptied a tin of something that resembled baked beans. "I'd be happy to help."

I'd leave the good deeds to Eleanor. After all, not everyone could be a saint.

I planned to spend much of the summer in Oyster Bay with Mother and Father, but our celebration of July Fourth was marred by news that both Ted and Archie had been gassed and wounded. Thankfully, they were recovering and would be sent stateside as soon as they were well enough to travel. Then came Bastille Day only ten days later, and with it renewed hope for France's freedom and the end of the war.

And then came the first telegram.

I glanced up from the pages of Osborn's *The Origin and Evolution of Life* at the sound of the front door closing. Mother and I were sitting together in the floral blue drawing room, but she was too engrossed in untangling a skein of yarn that had rolled onto the mountain lion rug to notice Father usher the local Associated Press correspondent into the library across the hall. Yet his brows furrowed with worry when our gazes met, then he shut the door behind them. I waited only a few moments before setting down my book and following to listen at the keyhole. I thought perhaps it was a reporter interested in Father's stance against Wilson's newly proposed League of Nations, but I couldn't have been more wrong.

"We intercepted it, but it's censored to be almost unintelligible," the visitor said from the other side of the door. "My apologies, Colonel, but I thought you'd like to see it anyway."

"I appreciate your concern," Father murmured. "I'd ask you not to mention this to anyone, especially Mrs. Roosevelt."

"Of course, sir."

"Ted and Archie are in hospitals." Father's footsteps echoed as he paced. "Kermit is on his way from Mesopotamia to France. So it must be Quentin."

My veins filled with ice water, and I longed to see the telegram. Surely this wasn't what it seemed . . .

"I'm terribly sorry, sir. You have my deepest condolences."

"Nothing is decided until I receive official word," Father said gruffly. "I'll knock down any man who claims otherwise."

I barely straightened and pretended to arrange the tennis rackets in the hall fireplace before the correspondent walked out. He hesitated as he saw me, but then continued wordlessly to the front door.

Mother glanced up from her knitting as I resumed my place in the parlor, mountain lion fur crunching underfoot and gooseflesh rippling up my arms. "Is everything all right, Sissy?" she asked me.

I nodded, heart pounding. "Yes, of course."

But nothing was all right, and it might never be right again.

I longed to go to Father and ask a hundred questions, but waited until he'd gone upstairs before I snuck into the library to read the cable. It only took me a moment to find it in the top drawer of his desk, the glass eyes of his mounted hunting trophies surveilling me from the walls.

WATCH SAGAMORE HILL—

The censors had blotted out the rest.

Surely Father was wrong; it wasn't possible that Quentin was in trouble on the other side of the globe. I shook away the very idea, for my brother was only twenty, far too young for anything to happen to him.

But if not Quentin, which of my brothers? Had Ted or Archie taken a turn for the worse? Had Kermit fallen in combat?

I felt sick as panic clawed its way up my throat.

Father remained secluded in his Gun Room upstairs and I scarcely slept that night, tossing and turning, terrified at what the dawn would bring.

I was just finishing my daily six-mile walk the next morning, my feet leaden and my heart heavy, when I rounded the corner and saw the same Associated Press reporter's car in the drive. I wanted to unsee it, to turn around and delay the inevitable. Instead, I forced myself to keep walking even as my hands began to shake. The ashen-faced correspondent in a pressed suit and spit-shined shoes—clothes fit for a funeral—passed me on his way out.

"Who?" I asked, clutching at him. "Who was it?"

"I really can't say. The unofficial report—"

"Whoever it was, I'm his sister," I said. "Tell me."

He could scarcely meet my eyes. "It's Quentin."

Quentin, the one of us who had lived the least. Quentin, who had brought his calico pony up the White House elevator to cheer up Archie when he was only five. Quentin, who had carved a baseball diamond into the White House lawn and thrown snowballs at Secret Service agents from the roof. Quentin, who had been the first to volunteer for this Great War to do the thing he loved most.

Fly.

A boy should never die doing the thing he loved. He should die warm in an old man's bed, fondly recalling all those wild adventures.

"You have my condolences, Mrs. Longworth," the correspondent said. Then he backed away and retreated down the stairs to the safety of his waiting car.

Numb as I was, I expected—perhaps even needed—the house to be filled with the sounds of grief, but it was eerily silent, as if holding its breath. My father's retired White House valet, Amos, who had joined the Sagamore Hill staff, stood in the hall clutching a family picture taken on the grounds of the White House. The photograph gleamed behind its glass, all of us looking somber with little Quentin on the end leaning against our father. It was the same photograph my youngest brother had covered in spitballs when we lived in the White House, along with portraits of Jefferson and Jackson.

"Where's Father, Amos?" I asked in a trembling voice.

Amos's beautiful dark eyes were filled with tears. "In the North Room, ma'am."

I ran. I found Father staring down at the unofficial yellow telegram through his spectacles, the paper fluttering in his shaking hands. He glanced up and for a moment I wondered whether he was truly seeing me. Then he spoke in a bewildered voice. "My dear boy is gone. My Quenikins. How can that be?"

He handed me the paper, but I only skimmed a few words before my eyes welled with tears, the numbness banished in a flood of grief.

Killed in aerial combat.

Northeast of Paris, between Château-Thierry and Reims.

. . . Two bullet holes to the head.

My poor, poor brother, mowed down before he even had the chance to live.

Father cleared his throat and drew a ragged breath as he took back the telegram with unsteady hands. "Go up to Mother. She went to her room as soon as she heard."

I didn't move, save for the tears that cut hot swaths down my cheeks.

"Go, Sissy," he growled, but the sound was anguished as he dropped the cursed telegram into the elephant foot wastebasket and collapsed into a carved wooden chair that suddenly seemed too small for him, shoulders heaving and head cradled in his hands.

I stood immobile, frozen by my own shock. I'd never seen Father cry, never known him to be less than stoic in the face of any tragedy. Yet, when his mother and my mother died on the same day two days after my birth, my father had been alone in the world and teetered on the brink of a bleak madness. This time he wasn't alone.

I knelt at his feet, astonished as the tears ran down his weathered cheeks. "I'm here, Father. And I'm not going anywhere."

"It should have been me." He choked on the words, his eyes wild as I'd never seen them.

"Don't say that—" I started, but he cut me off.

"I'd never have expected to come home alive if Wilson had let me raise a regiment. It should have been *me*." He broke then, the dam of grief proving too powerful to hold back. I was terrified at the force of it, of seeing my formidable father crushed beneath its weight. And so I did all I could, holding him even as tears for him and myself and Quentin and all our family poured in torrents down my cheeks. At some point Mother came in and the three of us held each other, rocking and aching with a pain that bore all the way to our marrow.

Finally, we grew quiet, leaving a roaring silence in the wake of our grief.

We never again mentioned Quentin, not because we didn't love him or remember him every day, but simply because the pain ran too deep, especially for Father. In the days that followed, I dug the report of Quentin's death out of the elephant foot wastebasket and kept every clipping in the papers that mentioned my youngest brother, including the announcement that the nearby airfield would be commissioned as the Quentin Roosevelt Airfield, and a French *Le Temps* article that sent condolences to Colonel Roosevelt and reminded us that the fallen would live in memory throughout the centuries.

For, after all, that was all we truly had in the end.

Memories.

And yet, sometimes memories simply weren't enough.

Armistice Day, and thus the end of the war, dawned a few months after Quentin's death.

A few months, made of mere weeks, each composed of a handful of days. Had Quentin survived those months, weeks, days, he'd have come home to us.

Instead, my brother was buried in a French cemetery, his grave marked with the broken blades of his propeller and two basswood saplings bound with a wire from his Nieuport plane, so far away that my parents couldn't perform the simple act of leaving flowers on their son's final resting place. I learned from Ted that the Germans had made a postcard depicting my dead brother and his downed plane for propaganda, but it had backfired and outraged the German people, who still thought highly of my father.

And now the Germans had been defeated. Goddamn them to hell and back.

I went to bed late the night before the cease-fire, but was jolted awake by a cacophony of whistles that started blowing as if the world were about to end.

Despite the cold and the early hour, I shrugged into a scratchy wool overcoat and thrust my feet into a pair of Father's oversize boots before tromping outside, my hair loose and still matted from sleep. All of the houses were so dark I might have been entirely alone in a city doused in black for a funeral, but every whistle in the city was on full blast. I clamped my hands over my ears to block out the noise; one whistle would catch a wailing melody and turn to a crescendo of harsh harmonies. It was as if the morning stars were singing together and the sons of God were shouting for joy that peace reigned again.

But I was too jaded to believe in lasting joy. Happiness was illusory, always jerked from my grasp when I least expected it.

Still, I supposed the armistice was a moment to remember, a moment when the world saved itself from falling over the edge of an endless abyss. There were countless victory celebrations in Oyster Bay in the days that followed, but I stayed home with the windows shut tight, refusing to join the clamorous mobs that stirred noise for the sake of hearing themselves.

That's where I was when Amos delivered Dorothy's letter. And I, thinking it was just another letter of condolence, tossed it aside unread until after dinner, when the family was all gathered together in the study for our nightly reading and poetry recitations. I couldn't concentrate on Archie's delivery of Rudyard Kipling's "If—" as I was too distracted by the still-foreign sight of my brother leaning on a cane from the shrapnel that had shattered his knee, and picked up my stack of mail instead, Dorothy's letter on top.

Dear Alice,

From the hope of peace comes more death . . .

I read the rest of the letter and returned to that line until the ink ran from my tears. I was sitting holding the ruined paper when Archie stopped his recital.

"Alice, whatever is the matter?"

I held out the paper, then stifled a sob. "Willard Straight is dead."

A hush fell over the room and Mother came to sit beside me. "But how can that be? The war's over."

"He was arranging the American delegation's arrival at the Paris Peace Conference when he fell ill with influenza." I looked up at my father, my vision ablur. "They buried him in France, just like Quentin."

After that, Mother and Archie had to help me upstairs to lie down. My last glimpse of Father was of him standing before the fireplace holding Quentin's picture, his face whiter than snow and every muscle in his body tensed as if he expected a fresh assault at any moment.

This war had turned our loved ones into ghosts. Ghosts who would haunt us forever.

Death made me ache for times long past and carefree summer days, to see Quentin laughing as he ran his hands over a fuselage and to flirt with Willard again. Instead, I had only the cold consolation of yellowing letters and photographs, which I took out so often that they threatened to crumble to dust in my hands.

Father had written after my mother's death that "*blackbirds rarely sit behind the shoulder of one whose pace is fast enough.*" I wondered if this was why he'd crammed so much into one life, for fear that some old grief would come and tear him to pieces with its jagged teeth. Now he had this new pain to ensnare him, and my father was no longer a young buckskin who could escape to the Badlands or run for lofty political offices as a distraction.

I worried that Quentin's death would break him, but Father surprised me by throwing himself into his work, just as he'd done when my own mother had died.

I decided to follow suit.

Father and a group called the Irreconcilables began a crusade to keep America free from the web of Europe's entangling alliances, regardless of what flimsy promises Wilson might make while in Paris. But Father was almost sixty, and the schedule of speeches and meetings wore him down until I feared he'd make himself ill.

"You should rest," I said one day as we sat in my drawing room, so cozy on these winter evenings when the curtains were closed and the lamps all switched on. My new home on Embassy Row had become the focal point for the Irreconcilables whenever Father was in town; the other day I'd peered over the banister and counted thirty-three newspaper correspondents stacked shoulder to shoulder in the small hall.

"Bah." Father's eyesight was so deteriorated that he sat hunched over his speech; he only glanced up long enough to scowl at my concerns about his health. "I've never rested a day in my life, and I don't intend to start now."

So I helped him revise the two-hour-long address he went on to deliver at Carnegie Hall regarding Wilson's new fourteen-point plan for peace, but the following night he was troubled with a painfully swollen ankle.

"Perhaps I should shorten my speeches," he joked, but Mother and I insisted he go to the hospital when the ankle grew worse. There the doctors found a detached blood clot, which might have killed him had it gone untreated, and he was forced to stay in the hospital indefinitely for fear of a second such attack.

The doctors might as well have sentenced him to prison.

I was at his side when they informed him that the combination of rheumatism, vertigo, anemia, and lumbago meant he might soon be consigned to a wheelchair. To which Father responded, "All right. I can work and live that way too."

Yet I couldn't imagine the lion who paced and roared and never sat still confined in such a manner.

I visited him as often as I could and worked hard enough for both of us as the days turned to weeks, taking up his banner against the League of Nations and stepping in for him at various luncheons. My fear of speaking in public meant that Ted took Father's place onstage, but we did our best between us to fill Father's shoes.

"I doubt you ever sat still so long in your life," I said to him on Christmas Day after he was finally allowed to come home. (My father would have sooner climbed out the window on a rope of bedsheets than spend Christmas in a hospital.) I'd held on to Mother when Amos opened the car door and Father emerged, his suit hanging looser than I'd ever seen but his face still wearing a toothy grin as he leaned on a cane, the other arm in a sling from a newly inflamed wrist. Yet his face was colorless, like paper laid over bone. "The old lion is home!" he cried as he flung open his free arm.

Ethel's children bounded down the steps to launch themselves at him. "Come inside, Grandpa," they squealed, oblivious to his weakened state. "See what Santa brought!"

Once he was settled by the fire with his bearskin slippers on his feet, Father exclaimed happily over their dolls and train sets and then retreated to the leather chair in his Gun Room on the third floor, a half-finished editorial for the *Kansas City Star* in front of him and a mug of coffee—the same that Ted had always described as a tub—cooling next to his typewriter. The room was named for the brace of inlaid dueling pistols and the ivory-butted six-shooters and modern hunting rifles that hung on the walls, but in truth Father had often used this room as a sanctuary from us children. I felt like I was breaking a cardinal rule just being here, but Father didn't seem to mind.

"Aren't you supposed to be resting?" I asked as he scowled at the editorial. He'd insisted on climbing both flights of stairs—just to prove he could—and I could tell from the gray hue of his face what the effort had cost him.

"Sissy, I almost went mad from boredom in that blasted hospital. I don't care what the doctors claim; my health is bully and I'll never set foot inside another hospital so long as I live." Despite the boast, his voice trembled, and an arsenic bottle sat on the desk, awaiting his next injection to lessen the agony of his inflamed wrist. He might have been full of Christmas cheer, but he seemed weaker even than after his return from South America, as if the body that he'd built up all his life was finally wearing out.

But I knew it was more than that.

Quentin's death had snapped something deep inside him, something I feared could never be mended. What he needed—and what we needed for him—was a task to throw himself into heart and soul, to heal him and take his mind off his grief.

Luckily, I had just the thing.

"The Republicans are already hailing you as the next president of the United States." I ran a hand over his collection of rifles and pistols. "In a couple of years we could be celebrating in the White House, just like old times."

I expected him to perk up with excitement, but he only stared blankly out the window, his eyes endless dark tunnels. "That would be something, wouldn't it?" He blinked, then made a great show of inspecting his hippopotamus foot inkwell. "Perhaps with all this talk of women's suffrage, you might one day run for office yourself."

I snorted. "The very thought of giving campaign speeches makes my mouth go dry." My voice was louder than usual, as if I had to fill the conversation with enough bluster for both of us. "I suppose it would be fulfilling to vote for the next president, especially if that president happened to be you, but I'll leave running for office to you and Nick."

"How is that husband of yours?" Father set down the inkwell. "It's been some time since I've seen him."

Nick and I saw each other fleetingly for events in Washington and maintained a civil decorum, but I winced at the fresh remembrance of coming upon my husband the last time I'd visited Washington, *in flagrante delicto* on the floor of my bathroom with his latest conquest.

My old friend Cissy Patterson.

"Sorry, Alice," Cissy had said when she was finally decent. My now-former friend was finally divorced from her Polish count and reunited with her daughter. Few dared even speak to Cissy in public, but apparently Nick had no such qualms about a disgraced divorcée. I thought Cissy was actually apologizing until she had paused to apply a fresh coat of coral lipstick and gave me a wink. "But I did warn you that I had my eye on Nicky."

I'd always known Cissy was high-strung and volatile, but now I knew she was a husband-stealing quiff too. I should have been furious, but could only summon an ember of anger. Cissy had wanted Nick fifteen years ago, and now she had him, although she was a fool to believe he wouldn't lose interest in a month or so.

"Nick's fine, I think," I said to my father. "I've had several letters from him. He's enjoying being back in the House."

There were volumes to be said in all I couldn't—*wouldn't*—say, but Father seemed to guess them. "You've done the best you could with what you had, Sissy." He gave a wan smile. "My only regret is that you didn't have at least half a dozen children to bring a sparkle to your eye. I've accomplished much in my life, but you and your brothers and sister are among my finest achievements."

I felt a mixture of pride and melancholy at his words, for I'd long since reconciled myself to the fact that I'd never have children. But my life was full and I still had family.

Most of all, I had my father.

After years of striving for his love and approval, I'd finally earned both. And I liked to think he'd come to rely on me, at least a little bit.

His eyes grew heavy, so he seemed ready to drop to sleep at any moment. I could never remember him doing something so mundane as napping, but I stooped and dared press a kiss on his forehead. He surprised me by patting my hand. "I enjoy talking politics with you," he murmured, his eyes still closed. "Your dauntless spirit has been a real help to me over the years."

"We'll talk about your campaign once you've rested," I said. "Merry Christmas, Father."

He pressed the back of my hand to his dry lips. "Merry Christmas to you too, Mousiekins."

Two weeks later, Father had improved enough that I was at home in Washington, enjoying a rare moment of peace and quiet. Dawn already streaked the horizon, but I hadn't yet gone to bed. Instead, I sat with my bare feet nestled in the fur of the library's tiger rug—a gift from Father's African safari—idly smoking a cigarette in front of a dying fire while fully absorbed in Robert Louis Stevenson's novel *Prince Otto*. I particularly liked the character Seraphina, a philosophizing politician who runs her country in the absence of her milksop husband. *That* was something I could certainly empathize with.

"Alice?"

Speaking of milksop husbands . . .

"This just came for you," Nick said. "I met the courier on the walkway." His rumpled clothes made it clear that he'd just come in from a late night. At least this time there was none of Cissy's flagrant coral lipstick on his collar.

I waved him away. "I'll read it later."

"It's from Archie, at Oyster Bay. It's marked urgent."

Puzzled, I opened the telegram. I stared at the stark black letters of the message, trying to make sense of them. Then *Prince Otto* crashed to the floor.

Only five words. Five terrible, horrible, life-changing words.

THE OLD LION IS DEAD.

The letters swirled on the paper, pounding over and over in my head until I collapsed from their weight. I curled into myself on the cold floorboards, as if that might somehow protect me from this mortal wound, leaving me unable to rise or move. Every heartbeat thudded out a mournful litany.

Dead, dead, dead.

"No!" I gasped the word over and over as if that might somehow make this all disappear, until that single word elongated into an unending scream of loss, of having everything that mattered—the sun, the sky, my own *father*—ripped away forever. Nick was frantically pulling me up from the floor, and I could see him shouting my name even though I couldn't hear him over my scream. He pried the telegram from my grip, then crushed me to him.

"Tell me he's not gone," I sobbed. "Tell me!"

Nick held me until I calmed, an unearthly, terrible quiet roaring in my ears.

"I'll call Sagamore Hill," he whispered.

All I could do was lay unseeing on the ground while he was in the next room for what seemed an eternity. It was as if I'd been shot in the heart and merely waited for heaven or hell to claim me. My husband's footsteps on the parlor floor wrenched me back to the land of the living.

"It was another blood clot, this time in his lungs," he said gently. "Your father went peacefully, Alice, in his sleep."

My hands flew to my mouth in a vain attempt to stifle the torrent of sobs that burst from my chest. I couldn't stop, couldn't breathe as grief's terrible fists pummeled me.

My father was gone, yet I couldn't fathom this world without him.

I howled then, gutted by a pain and loss so deep that I thought it would kill me. I *wished* it would kill me. I cried and keened on the floor of the parlor until I was hollowed out, scraped empty of tears and dead to everything.

"I'll make arrangements for you to travel on the first train to Sagamore Hill," Nick finally said while he stroked my head. He'd been there the entire time, though I'd hardly noticed. "Ethel and your brothers are on their way as well."

I nodded mutely, numb to everything except the crushing pain in my chest. When I finally rose, I had to clutch the door frame to catch my breath, screw my eyes shut to keep from falling to the floor again and into some deeper abyss.

I felt Nick at my side before I felt him pick me up. "You'll get through this, Alice." He cradled me tight, a feeling that was oddly comforting even after so many years living as strangers. "You're a survivor. It may not feel like it right now, but you'll survive this as well."

Maybe he was right, but in that moment, survival seemed an impossible feat.

I stood in the North Room of Sagamore Hill the day after Father's death, reading and rereading his last dictations and the rough draft of an article for *Metropolitan Magazine* still stacked on his desk by his downstairs rhino foot inkwell. Next to it was a half-finished letter for Ted, which I'd save for my brother when he arrived from France. Outside, Oyster Bay's flags fluttered at half-mast and black crepe swathed the brick firehouse and the Masonic lodge.

I'd arrived at Sagamore Hill the day before, my heart swollen with grief as if it might choke me, and had walked about ever since as if caged in some horrible nightmare. For Mother's sake, I refused to break down again. I'd had my cry and would henceforth do as Father would have wished: soldier on with a stiff upper lip. Yet I scarcely knew how I'd manage. Father was already laid out in the drawing room and I'd stared at him a long while, trying to convince myself that those were his lifeless hands that had never stopped moving, his pale and bloodless face that would never again break into his trademark grin.

No.

He would be buried in Oyster Bay's cemetery a few days hence. Then he'd be gone forever, which I could hardly contemplate.

I startled as Mother came to stand behind me. Neither of us dared sit, for this room was a shrine to the man we'd both loved. His hunting trophies—mounted bison he'd taken as a young rancher in the Dakota Territory and an African lion rug—waited for his return, and his favorite leather-bound books were piled to near bursting on the alcove's shelves. These were only a small fraction of the eight thousand books kept in the house—for Father had believed that books were ammunition for the battle of life—and he'd read them all, some more than once. Mother ran a hand along the mantel and paused to pick up Father's Nobel Peace Prize medal, then set it down reverently.

"Your father was gone so often, always chasing one dream or another." She took down his Rough Rider hat—the one he'd had extra spectacles sewn into so he'd never be blinded during battle—from where it hung on the antlers of a mounted elk, then crushed it to her chest. Poor Mother had aged ten years since I'd last seen her. "Yet, this time there's no steamer waiting to reunite us, no crowd of well-wishers eager to shower him with confetti on a dock somewhere."

There was nothing to say to that. If I spoke of how much I missed him, I'd shatter into a thousand pieces.

"He led a good life," I managed to eke out. "Strenuously lived and vigorously loved."

"I wish we'd all had a chance to say good-bye." Mother's chin wobbled for a moment, so brief I thought I might have imagined it before she replaced the Rough Rider hat and regained her composure. "I should have called the physician when he made up a bed in the Gate Room to keep from disturbing me, or insisted that he sleep in our bed so I might have heard—"

I closed the space between us to clasp her tight to me, breaching a wall that had been erected between us since my childhood. "You did nothing wrong. Death had to take him sleeping; if he'd been awake, there'd have been a fight."

And my money would have been on Father. It always had been, for everything.

"How are we supposed to say good-bye?" she whispered, her eyes darting from one wall of the study to the other.

"I don't know. I honestly don't know."

Yet we had no choice. The dead have it easy; it's the living who truly suffer as life continues its relentless forward march.

The funeral dawned rainy and overcast, filling Youngs Memorial Cemetery with the scent of wet grass and damp earth. Father's plot was tucked into a quiet corner surrounded by old trees and mossy steps. I knew he would have appreciated the seclusion and the spread of green, scarcely more than a mile away from his beloved Sagamore Hill.

He was everywhere that gray day, in the tapping of the red-bellied woodpecker he'd cataloged as a boy, in the books on evolution he'd stacked in his study that I thumbed through after a dinner I didn't eat, and in the way Ethel's children roughhoused in the parlor after a dessert of Sagamore Hill cinnamon sandies. I even sensed his presence as Nick stayed by my side throughout the entire day, his unusual steadiness a ballast to my torrent of grief.

I could scarcely move without wanting to break down and sob every moment of that day and the weeks to come. Yet Father's voice echoed in my head, reminding me to never give up in the face of adversity, even though what I really wished was to turn my face to the wall and cry until my eyes ran dry.

Instead I did the only thing I knew to do: threw myself into finishing the work that Father left behind, beginning with his stance against Wilson's League of Nations and its entangling alliances with war-torn Europe.

I would take up Father's torch. I wouldn't stop carrying it until the day I died.

Part 3

THE *OTHER* WASHINGTON MONUMENT

*If you can't say something good about
someone sit right here by me.*

—ALICE ROOSEVELT LONGWORTH

Chapter 17

JANUARY 1920

"We do not support any sort of league at all, especially one that gives our great country a single vote to every six of Great Britain's." Bill Borah shook his Senate desk with an emphatic pounding of his fist that served to accentuate his deeply resonant voice. "If isolationism was good enough for George Washington, it's good enough for us!"

In direct violation of the Senate rules, the floor and galleries around me erupted into a mixed cacophony of cheers and pounding feet at Borah's triumphant speech, yet I remained riveted to my customary bench in the gallery. I came to the windowless Senate chambers more and more as the debates over Wilson's pitiful League of Nations grew heated, especially as Borah had taken my father's Irreconcilables under his capable wing. Father had been gone only two weeks, but I knew he would have approved of his cause being taken up by someone so accomplished and charismatic.

"Bill Borah *is* magnificent, isn't he?" Cissy Patterson gave me a sly smile as she lit the end of her shag. Everyone else had given her a wide berth—the stench of divorce still clung to her—so somehow she'd ended up seated next to me. "I wonder if his stamina outside the Senate matches his passion for giving speeches." She waggled her eyebrows in a crude sort of way. "If you know what I mean."

I most certainly did. Worse, I was appalled that I had once called this woman my friend.

"He's married, Cissy," I said, loosing the daggers from my eyes. "To a very kind woman, in fact. Stay away from him."

She raised an eyebrow. "A wedding ring's never stopped me before."

There was no mistaking her potent glance at the circle of gold on my left hand. Until now, I'd tolerated Cissy with Nick simply because the other option was to care, and I'd made up my mind not to do that. But now, so close on the heels of Father's death, I was heartily sick of enduring her callous insults, of enduring what life had thrown at me.

So I stood and looked down my nose at her. "You're a bitch, Cissy, you know that?"

I expected her to take offense as I moved to distance myself from her, but she only grinned when I glanced back, although the expression didn't meet her eyes. "That's me," she said. "The shanty-Irish bitch."

I gave a disdainful sniff that would have made cousin Eleanor proud, and turned my full attention back to the Senate floor.

Forget Cissy. Think of Father and focus on the matter at hand.

I'd consider the failure of the League of Nations my final gift to Father. To that end, I was willing to commit high treason if necessary.

Nick's eyes widened when I found him lurking in Cissy's otherwise empty roadster after the House session ended, a light dusting of snow starting to fall. It wasn't my imagination that he tried to make himself smaller when he saw me approach. "Alice," he said as he rolled down the window. "I thought you'd still be listening to the Senate."

"Hello, darling," I said, wanting to make this quick before Cissy made an appearance. Not for the first time I wished that Nick had better taste than Cissy Patterson, yet I supposed it wouldn't do for me to lecture him on his choice in mistresses. "Anything productive today?"

"I think we have enough votes to pass the women's suffrage movement. And the dreaded Volstead act." His visage darkened and he surprised me by climbing out of Cissy's car and slamming the door behind him. "I can't believe I'm going to see the banning of alcohol during my tenure as congressman."

I thought Prohibition a foolhardy experiment, but privately hoped it might curtail the worst of Nick's excesses. "I marvel that anyone thinks it possible to legislate a human appetite out of existence."

"Not *my* appetite," Nick said as he straightened his tie, his attention catching on something—or someone—on the steps behind me. "In fact, I have plans to brew bootleg gin in our kitchen sink. Warren Harding gave me the know-how."

Desperate times called for desperate measures, I supposed. So much for curbing excesses.

"Well, I just wanted to say hello before I head home," I said to him. "I invited a few senators and their wives for a little tête-à-tête tonight."

Progressive senators who, like me, loathed the idea of the League of Nations. There was sabotage afoot, and I doubted whether Nick had the stomach for it.

"What time?" Nick asked.

"We'll start around eight. But you don't have to—"

"I'll be there." He surprised me by kissing my cheek, then jogged back up the Capitol's steps. The mystery was soon solved as I watched him draw up alongside a slim woman of *raffinée* beauty a few years older than me: music aficionado Alice Dows. I'd seen her at the opera once or twice, always dressed in chiffon and squired by a man not her husband, as Tracy Dows conveniently avoided Washington in favor of a family estate on the Hudson River.

It seemed Cissy's days were numbered. Thank heaven for small blessings.

Yet luck wasn't on my side that night, for not only did Nick show up with his moderate Republican opinions, but Cissy Patterson darkened our doorstep as well.

"What a lovely little soiree," Cissy opined as soon as the butler opened the door. Loyal and arthritic Manchu—his snout fully white with age—made such a show of voicing his displeasure at her appearance that I had to shut him in a room upstairs, even though it was

Cissy I really wanted to lock away. Now Cissy made a great show of adjusting the gaudy art deco bracelet on her wrist, a flashy aquamarine belt of gems with a ruby buckle. Apparently, divorcing an evil Polish count had *some* benefits, even if people still turned up their noses at the sight of a divorced countess. Unfortunately, the hideous bracelet matched a choker around her neck, which she fingered in a blatant attempt to draw attention to it and its obvious price tag. "With all these stalwart Republicans here, do I sense a *coup d'état*?"

If she did, she was far more intelligent than I gave her credit for.

"Nothing to concern an old shanty-Irish bitch such as yourself." I leaned close. "Especially not when Nick's so attentive to Alice Dows. It seems you're now truly the other—and forgotten—woman."

It was cruel—the best insults always are—but I reveled in the way her face fell as she followed my gaze to where Nick was seated at the piano with Alice Dows, her playing an impressive rendition of Chopin while he accompanied her on the violin. A steady stream of senators coming into the hall ushered Cissy on her way, leaving me free to greet Father's old advisors, cadaverous Medill McCormick and his wife, Ruth, who had called me after my father was shot in Milwaukee. After all, I hadn't arranged this little gathering to spend it with the likes of mealymouthed Cissy Patterson.

"I hear the House resolution for the Susan Anthony amendment is gaining traction," I said to Ruth, who was a huge proponent of women's political rights. "I keep pressing Nick for his outlook on the vote."

Ruth's face lit up brighter than a Christmas tree. "The Senate appears promising too. Hopefully by this time next year you and I will be planning our votes for the presidential election."

I still felt blasé about the entire suffrage idea; one vote in a ballot box seemed a molehill compared to the mountain of political power I wielded in my dining room. But I was glad for other women to have a say for the first time, and I was happy to support Ruth.

"I certainly won't vote for Wilson," I said as a car door closed outside, heralding the last of the guests. "I'd sooner vote for Lucifer than our current commander in chief."

Ruth and Medill exchanged twin smiles. "Agreed," they said in unison, and for a moment I was struck by how pleasant and reassuring it must be to live in such harmony with one's spouse. Yet, as they moved inside and I caught a glimpse of Nick pouring drinks for both Cissy and Alice Dows, I knew that was an impossible dream.

"Go mingle," I told Ruth and her husband. "See what damage you can concoct for Wilson's plan before the soup is served."

They hadn't even left the hall before the doors opened to admit the final guest: Bill Borah. The Lion of Idaho looked as if he were fresh from a cattle ranch as he shrugged off his coat with easy grace, releasing a sprinkling of melting snow from his shoulders.

"What's this about damaging Wilson's plans?" he asked as he hung his jacket on the waiting rack. "Whatever it is, I'm all in."

I gestured him into the dining room with its warm smells of crab soup and roast beef. "That, Senator Borah, is why you're here: to determine the best way to kill this League of Nations once and for all."

I half expected him to protest, for he'd rebuffed me once before when I tried to draw him to my father's side before the 1912 election, but this time Borah only dropped his voice in a downright conspiratorial manner. "I'd condone open political warfare if it would keep America out of the internationalism that menaces our very foundations."

"I'm glad to hear it," I quipped. "In fact, I'd expect nothing less."

I offered to pour him a drink, but he demurred, gesturing toward my own cup of cider. "Nothing stronger for you, either, Mrs. Longworth?"

I wrinkled my nose. "Intoxicated people bore me."

He chuckled. "Me too."

Thus began the first meeting of what would become known as the Battalion of Death. Nick was the lone politician present with only lukewarm feelings regarding the League of Nations, although I breathed a sigh of relief when, like a good Republican, he fell on our side of the line just to spite Wilson.

"And you shall be the battalion's colonel," Ruth said to me as everyone raised their glasses in agreement. My eyes teared up over the reference to my father's title, but I quashed those feelings as maids brought out silver bowls of snowball custard. It was better and more productive that I complete Father's mission to destroy the League of Nations than to indulge in frivolous emotions.

The battalion spent the night concocting a plan for a senatorial round robin to gather votes against the League of Nations, and I was considering treating myself to a rare glass of victory champagne as the guests began to trickle out the door. Only then did I notice that Nick was gone.

"Mr. Longworth left to meet Mr. Harding for drinks," our butler informed me. "Mrs. Dows accompanied him."

I smiled my thanks; Nick and Alice Dows had behaved themselves throughout the night and Cissy steamed to watch them together, which as far as I was concerned meant high marks for the other Alice. Yet my smile faltered after I'd retrieved Manchu from his stint in solitary confinement and heard Cissy Patterson's high trill coming from the library.

Oy vey, but I loved that woman like the devil loves holy water.

I almost dropped poor Manchu when I entered to find Cissy not reading (as one might expect in a room full of books), but instead tangled together with Bill Borah. Fortunately, unlike the time I'd found her in the bathroom with Nick, this time she had her clothes on, including that eye-numbing necklace and bracelet. Still, I felt a deep stab of dismay. Why was it that my husband and a man I admired were the only two people in the country who didn't scorn Cissy?

I cleared my throat, at which point both parties adjusted themselves in a hurry. "I have a knack for finding you in odd rooms in my home, Cissy," I said. "Nick is off with Alice Dows for the evening, so I took the liberty of retrieving your coat."

Cissy used her thumb to wipe the corner of her mouth. "And here I thought we were friends, Alice," she said.

"There you go thinking again. Careful or you might injure yourself one of these days," I said in a falsetto as she flounced past me with a scowl, Borah all but forgotten. "Have a good night, and send my regards to hell."

"Mrs. Longworth." Borah ran a hand through his thick mane of hair. "Please forgive me—"

I held up a hand even as Manchu wriggled to be put down. "Far be it from me to critique your choice of mistresses." I spied several of Cissy's hairpins on the floor, picked them up, and curled my fingers around them so tightly that I might have snapped them. "But I must admit I'm disappointed."

Far more than disappointed, in fact.

I crossed my arms in front of me, my scowl deepening as Manchu sidled up next to Bill, his tail pumping furiously. *Traitor.* "You could do far better than Cissy Patterson."

For surely there was a curly-tailed sow wallowing in the mud somewhere that would make a better companion than Cissy I'll-Sleep-With-Any-Man-That-Moves Patterson.

Borah reddened all the way to the tips of his ears even as he bent to rub Manchu's chin. "That woman is *not* my mistress," he said so vehemently that I found myself wanting to believe him. "She asked me after dinner if I'd ever read *The Sorrows of Young Werther.* When I admitted that German Romanticism isn't my taste, she insisted I come in here to read a passage. Unfortunately, I realized too late she didn't have reading in mind at all. She was rather, er . . . persistent."

I smiled at that, for Borah really was naive if he'd believed Cissy's ruse. "Perhaps you should bring Mrs. Borah to all our future functions as a sort of shield," I said. "We missed her tonight."

Borah frowned, and I noted then that although smile lines had carved themselves onto either side of his mouth, his forehead was relatively free of scowl lines. A happy man then. And one that had a way with dogs, if Manchu's half-closed eyes and lolling tongue were any indication. "That's very kind of you, but Mary prefers to sit out these events so she doesn't have to hear me nattering on about treaties and the like." He sighed. "You have my word that I shall take care not to fall into any further literary traps at the hands of Ms. Patterson."

I laughed. "For the record, *The Sorrows of Young Werther* isn't worth the time it takes to read. I much prefer Hawthorne for a bleak read, or Dickens for something dark and dreary about the human condition." I pulled the well-worn volumes from their shelf and handed them to him.

"Two of my favorites." He thumbed through them reverently. "I noticed them before Ms. Patterson, er . . ."

"Took up your full view?"

"Yes." He grimaced. "They're in good company alongside some rather impressive Americans."

I looked to where several of Father's volumes by the Founding Fathers now stood. Books were piled everywhere in this, my favorite room: on the floor, chairs, and even the oversize wine velvet sofa where I liked to while away the early morning hours before going to bed. "I've always fancied a dinner with Hamilton and Jefferson. Throw in Washington and Madison, and it would be an affair to remember."

"Do send an invitation my way if you ever manage it." Borah replaced the volumes. He looked askance at me, giving me a chance to notice the gold flecks deep in his eyes.

Which meant I was noticing his eyes. Which meant I needed to stop.

"As it was, I enjoyed this particular dinner immensely," he continued. "Ms. Patterson's company excluded."

"Then I'll be sure to invite you to all future events hosted by the Battalion of Death," I said. "So long as you do your part getting that round robin signed."

"Aye, Colonel." Borah gave a loose salute, then paused at the door to the hall. "Your father would be proud of you, Mrs. Longworth," he said. "You truly are made in his image."

I felt tears threaten again and blamed the few sips of champagne I'd managed. I'd compared love to a battle, but I'd learned now that grief was an ambush, lying in wait to attack when least expected. Would my poor beleaguered heart ever stop aching?

"Thank you, Senator," I managed to say as I followed him to the front door.

"After you came to my rescue tonight, I insist that you call me Bill," he said as he shrugged into his long wool jacket and replaced his hat.

"All right, Bill," I said. "Then you must call me Alice."

He tipped his hat to me and walked out into the night, powerful and sure of himself.

Manchu gave a sad little yap after the door closed, then pushed his furry head against my leg. "I know," I said, bending down to scoop him up. "I like him too."

In fact, I liked Bill Borah more than I should.

I saw little of Cissy Patterson in the months that followed, although I did send her a nasty note with the hairpins I'd found in the library. With her usual verve, Cissy wrote back.

Dear Alice,

Thank you for the return of my hairpins. Please look in your chandelier as I think you will find my garter there.

—Cissy

Whether she meant from her failed interlude with Bill or her numerous encounters with my husband, I didn't know, nor did I care to find out. I was just relieved that Nick stopped bringing her around.

In the meantime, I was constantly on Capitol Hill for work for the Battalion of Death, so much so that Senate guidelines for the family gallery were relaxed to include immediate members of ex-presidents' families, a rule that Bill Borah introduced on my behalf.

"The Senate bows to your every whim, Mrs. Longworth," a New

Hampshire senator groused when I arrived that day. "Would you like the Constitution changed too?"

To which I only shrugged. "Perhaps. I'll let you know."

Honestly, if I couldn't be on the floor of Congress, I at least deserved the best seats in the place.

Which meant I was constantly running into Bill.

The man was sometimes stern and taciturn, but never boring, as comfortable in a library as he was prowling the Senate floor, peppering his speeches with clever remarks and quotes from all my literary and historical heroes. Borah was a progressive and a maverick in Congress, unbeholden to any man or party as he championed an eight-hour workday, anti-child-labor legislation, and workers' unions. He might have been nineteen years older than me, but he'd been dubbed an Apollo in his youth, and time had done little to dim his looks. My attraction to him grew with every well-informed word he uttered, even as my heart grew more alarmed.

Bill was married and so was I, facts I couldn't forget. Yet I couldn't fathom why Mary Borah never came to watch her husband; I'd have listened to him read a telephone directory. I reminded myself of Mary often, and the fact that I'd enjoyed her company on occasion. Still, I wasn't the only one who noticed Borah's charms, or their effect on me.

"I think I'd like to run for Congress one day," Ruth said from her seat next to me in the gallery. "Either for the House or the Senate; I'm not picky. Maybe even president too."

I nodded distractedly as I leaned over the balcony rail. "Of course."

"And then I'd introduce legislation to mandate ice cream socials on Sundays and bobsledding in summer."

"That will be nice."

Ruth's snort properly knocked me out of my reverie. "Alice Longworth, you haven't heard a word I've said. Instead you look like you want to devour that man."

"What?" The blood rushed to my face and I drew back from the balcony, losing my view of Borah. "I don't know what you're talking about."

"Don't play coy with me." Ruth waggled an indignant finger at me. Several audience members glanced our way, and I motioned for Ruth to keep her voice down. "You and Bill Borah are kindred spirits, happiest with your noses shoved into century-old books."

"He *is* well-read," I admitted, although that was as far as I planned to budge on the subject. Ruth arched an elegant eyebrow at me.

"You've had little enough happiness, Alice. Lord knows Nick's a decent friend, but a husband?" She pursed her lips together. "I've watched for months the way Borah lights up when you enter the room, how you both come alive during the battalion meetings. He's your intellectual twin."

I couldn't resist smiling at that, for my discussions with Borah *were* rather spectacular. That man could turn any subject on its head and force me to look at it from an entirely unique angle. And he was perhaps the only person on this earth—aside from Father—who'd read more than me.

"I'm not averse to a sort of intellectual affair with Borah," I whispered. "But that's as far as I'm willing to go."

Ruth gave me a knowing smile. "Of course."

But I meant it. After all, I was no Cissy Patterson.

Still, at that moment, Bill glanced up at me in the gallery and held my gaze, as if he read me like a beloved book, lost and recently found. I shook myself loose and pretended to search for something in my purse, as if I wasn't straining to hear each word the man uttered. I felt eighteen again, smitten and wanting to gush to my diary about his every word. A glutton for punishment, I sought him out after the session. "Give me a task," I said.

"A task?" He waved to a passing senator, but his eyes never left me.

"Something to help the battalion. Anything, before I go mad from inaction."

Bill scratched his chin. "You know, you might be the perfect person to target the mild reservationists in the Senate. Get them alone, persuade them into supporting us . . ."

"Twist their arms if I have to."

Bill's laugh was like the low purr of a saxophone. "Exactly."

After that we talked and talked—about the League, Darwin's theory of evolution, whether Tolstoy or Dostoyevsky was the pinnacle of dismal Russian literature—until only the Negro cleaners remained as the Senate lights flickered off.

But all we did was talk.

I reminded myself as Bill waited with me for my car that I was not some lovesick girl. Yet it had never been my nature to curb my impulses and emotions.

I needed a distraction.

So I did as Bill suggested and took one of the mild reservationists with me to Wilson's bland homecoming at the conclusion of the Paris peace talks. It was a hot summer night, and the sparse crowd pleased me to no end as we waited at Union Station for the president's train to arrive. I climbed onto the running board of my car when Wilson finally passed by. I crossed my fingers and made the sign of the evil eye.

"A murrain on him, a murrain on him!" I chanted over and over, cursing Wilson and his plan to destroy America, just as I'd once cursed Nellie Taft. My senator companion hushed me and cast terrified looks at the Secret Service, but I only scoffed. "Who are you afraid for? Me or Wilson?"

The bearded little gnome of a senator couldn't answer that, only hurriedly ducked back into the car before the Secret Service could escort us away. I was fairly certain he'd support us out of fear that I'd hex him next.

Not long after, I read the newspaper headline and wondered at my own power of magicks.

President Wilson Suffers Stroke, Unable to Campaign for League Ratification.

I felt remorseful for Wilson the man, but didn't suffer a moment's regret for Wilson the politician.

All this came just in time for Bill Borah to deliver the final speech against the League of Nations before the Senate began the tedious process of voting whether to ratify the agreement. I sat transfixed above, listening to him invoke Washington, Jefferson, Monroe, Lincoln, and Frederick the Great as he argued that this supposed peace was a disastrous alliance that would cause democracy to lose its soul. Speaking before the massive crowd tonight would have made me break out in hives, but Bill's eloquent tone might have rivaled Seneca or Socrates as he gestured emphatically at all the important points, just as Father had done during his own speeches.

"He's surpassed himself," whispered a disgruntled Democrat as a ragbag of frowsy senators milled outside the chambers before the vote began. It was almost midnight and no one noticed that I lurked about the dark periphery of the hall.

"Borah could sell sand to a desert," another muttered, and I thrilled at their next words. "We don't have a hope."

I held my breath until I almost fainted as the votes were cast. The final vote was forty-one to fifty-one against the treaty. "We've done it, Father," I whispered, while the Republicans burst into cheers on the floor. "The League of Nations has been defeated."

And I had Bill Borah to thank for it.

I embraced all the grinning battalion senators as they exited, all of us crowing with victory as they shook my hand and we congratulated each other.

Borah stood apart from the pack, rolling a small piece of silver between his thumb and forefinger. At first I thought it was a coin, but then he held it up with a lopsided smile. A tuft of hair flopped over his forehead that I longed to brush back.

"The apostle Paul," he said of the token. "My father gave it to me before he died, a reminder to keep my strength of character in the face of difficult odds. It's sentimental, but I carry it with me for my most important debates."

"Not sentimental at all," I said. "And it seems to have done the trick tonight."

Bill replaced the token in his pocket. "It took more than a lucky talisman to win this fight. America has you to thank for this victory."

Pleased, I brushed away his compliment. "We're having dinner at Dupont Circle." I'd already sent a congressional telegraph to rouse our cook for an impromptu celebration. "As the champion of the hour, don't dare claim you have other plans."

"I wouldn't dream of it." The smile he gave me was all in the crinkles around his eyes, and it made me warmer than if I'd downed a bottle of wine. "I daresay this is how Caesar felt after crossing the Rubicon. Tonight will go down in history as one of our finest achievements."

Our achievements.

I knew not whether he meant our party, our country, or just *us*, but his words made me bold.

"Don't bother calling your car," I said. "You can ride with me."

I didn't wait for an answer, just sauntered away. My heart beat a violent tattoo as I waited to see if he would follow.

He did.

We walked in silence in the dark November night, our breath wafting up into the star-spangled sky until we reached the car. Borah closed the door behind him, filling the small space with the scent of tobacco and the outdoors, like winter's cold in a silent pine forest. I didn't think, just let myself feel and indulge in a carefree moment of victory.

Then I kissed him.

It was a kiss that had been pent up for weeks, maybe years, twisting and burning until it was the only thing that mattered in this world. I'd been half-alive for so long, and this single kiss made me feel suddenly and gloriously alive. Yet Bill was married and so was I, which made it so terribly wrong, perhaps the worst wrong I'd ever committed.

Except it felt *so* right.

I barely managed to pull away before I lost myself entirely.

"I'm sorry." I turned the key in the kick switch, the chill of the hand lever seeping through my thin gloves, and dared to glance at Borah, unable to decipher his expression. "I was swept away in all the excitement—"

I expected him to slam the door and leave, Borah with his high ideals and lone-wolf persona. Instead, his warm hand was at the back of my neck, thumb caressing my cheek. "This is more than just excitement, Alice. Far more."

There was no denying the desire in his eyes, so raw and unfettered it drove my pulse to a frenzy. The second kiss was hungry and unyielding, tasting of paradise. I kissed him like my life depended on it.

Perhaps it did.

"The dinner," I murmured against his lips. "Everyone will be waiting."

He growled deep in his throat. "Let them wait."

And we did.

It was Borah who finally broke off the kiss with a ragged sigh. I wondered what he thought as he flexed and unflexed his hands, as if struggling to regain his famous aloofness. "Alice," he said. "We're both married."

"I know." And his was a real marriage, unlike the sham I maintained with Nick. The hollowness in my chest expanded with a vengeance, leaving me even emptier than before I'd kissed him. I'd taken a chance, placed a bet, and now I would lose all.

How I wanted him to argue that we'd find a way. Yet I knew that was a castle in the air.

I started the car and we drove in silence, the windows slightly fogged. We separated the instant we walked through my doors, and celebrated with the rest of the battalion like nothing monumental had just shifted between us. Still, I was intimately aware of the sound of his laugh and the timbre of his voice as we sat toadstool-style with the rest of the group around a hastily concocted dinner of scrambled eggs and champagne, enjoying what now felt like a hollow victory.

My disappointment was crushing when he was the first to excuse himself, as if our interlude in the car had never happened. Morose, I imagined him going home to Mary, even as I envisioned Nick in some club, a whiskey in one hand and this week's girl in the other. The servants had locked the front door and left for the night, so it was just Manchu and me when I heard the lightest of knocks from the front porch. Five taps—not three—so quiet at first I thought I'd imagined it. Manchu sniffed at the door, gave a chuff of happiness, and cocked his head at me as if to say, *What are you waiting for?*

I glanced out the window, my entire body going warm and tingly at the sight I most wanted to see. Bill leaned against the alcove, his pale gray coat melded to his form. The lights were all off, and dawn was just a cold haze on the horizon. Yet something dangerous flared deep inside me: hope.

"I know it's not respectable for me to be standing on your front porch alone and uninvited," Bill said when I opened the door.

It was almost impossible to speak over the lump in my throat, and my voice came out low and breathy. "Strangle what's respectable."

He ran a hand through his thick hair. "I tried to stay away, to go home to Mary, but I couldn't." Desire and duty fought for control of his expression as he opened his arms in a gesture of surrender. "I've never felt for anyone what I feel for you. I've tried to fight it, but I can't anymore. Say the word, though, and I'll go . . ."

"Don't you dare."

My words banished his uncertainty and he stepped toward me, hands cupping my face, his eyes reflecting the need I felt burning deep inside.

"I knew you were trouble on the train after the convention, when you tried to work your charms on me for your father's benefit," he said between kisses. "I just wasn't sure what brand of trouble."

"The best kind," I said as I tugged him inside and kicked the door closed behind us. The emptiness inside me filled, and the ache of desire propelled me forward until I was kissing him again. This was a man I could go on kissing until the end of my days. "As you're about to find out."

So very much trouble, indeed.

Chapter 18

I believed in a simple philosophy: to fill what was empty, empty what was full, and scratch where it itched.

My heart was empty and Bill filled it. It was as easy as that.

I'd flouted virtually every social nicety since my youth, but never had my behavior given cause for wags to whisper about my faithfulness to Nick. Now, each morning I scanned the headlines and gossip columns for rumors linking Bill and me. And I breathed a sigh of relief each day as I realized that America's attention was fully focused on the upcoming election. Bill and I were playing with fire, but I seized with two scalded hands all the sanctioned opportunities to meet that our shared Republican agenda allowed us.

Because, try as we might, neither Bill nor I could keep away from the other.

I assured myself that seizing a little happiness couldn't possibly be the worst mistake I'd make in this life. Could it?

I hurried to meet Bill one idyllic summer afternoon for a brief stroll in Rock Creek Park, the trees dressed in every shade of green and the squirrels chattering happily overhead. Nick had come home that day reeking of a stew of women's perfumes, which effectively took the edge off my guilt. Yet I no longer cared about all that with the sun on my face and Bill at my side. Starved as I was for love and touch, greedy for intellectual conversations like those I'd had with my father, Bill was everything I needed. That sun-drenched afternoon our discussion veered drunkenly from themes of *Hamlet* to the virtues of an anti-lynching bill until finally settling on the upcoming election.

"You know they're bandying about your name for the ballot," I suddenly said, daring to entwine my fingers with his as we entered a secluded copse of trees. My head fairly spun; if Bill won, I'd be wife to the majority leader and mistress to the vice president.

Mistress. Pishposh. It seemed ridiculous that I could be anything so scandalous as a man's mistress while nearing forty years old and married myself.

Bill's thumb stroked the back of my hand in a manner that sent warm shivers up my spine. "I don't put any stock in it. Everyone in the party gets mentioned at least once for the nomination."

"That isn't true and you know it. You could be president one day." With Father gone and Nick squandering himself in an alcoholic haze, Bill was my best hope for putting someone of my choosing in the White House. Ted might follow, but my brother needed a few years' more experience, perhaps as governor of New York, a position that could springboard him into the Oval Office.

I leaned my head against Bill's shoulder. "Would you accept if you *were* nominated?"

"Perhaps, but I won't get my hopes up." Bill pressed a stealthy kiss onto my temple. "I'm too much my own man to ever be chosen."

Part of me wished that he'd confide his burning desire to take the presidential oath of office, but another piece of me heard echoes of my father. He'd been too much his own man for the country's Republican bosses, so they'd tried to bury him in the casket of the vice presidency.

Their plan had backfired. Spectacularly.

"Nick is headed to Ohio tonight to plan Warren Harding's campaign," I said derisively. The Hardings were still more bitter to swallow than a dose of cod-liver oil, and I found it laughable—and entirely unrealistic—that Nick was fully in favor of putting the snollygoster on the Republican ticket this year. "If you'd care to join me for dinner."

Bill frowned. "I promised I'd accompany Mary to the symphony this evening."

Guilt hit me like a bucket of cold water. I refused to show my disappointment, for while I'd reconciled my qualms about cuckolding Nick—turnabout being fair play and all that—an uncomfortable miasma of remorse and envy threatened whenever I thought of Mary Borah, who remained blissfully unaware of my relationship with her husband. I affected my sunniest of smiles. "Then you'll have to tell me whether you preferred their rendition of Bach or Handel."

"Perhaps we can meet tomorrow?" Bill asked after we'd released each other's hands when a governess leading a gaggle of children approached from the opposite direction. "After I meet with your brother?"

"I'll be counting down the hours."

"You know, I think Ted has a real shot at a bona fide political career. He tells me he has hopes of following in your father's footsteps and being appointed assistant secretary of the navy if the Republicans recapture the White House."

I smiled at that, for I was pleased that Ted and Bill had taken to each other. "Well, with you as a mentor, I have no doubt he'll reach great heights."

We approached the Capitol, the bronze statue of Freedom atop its dome piercing the brilliant blue sky. "This is me," Bill said. "So I'll just say hello."

Hello. In a relationship fraught with secrecy, it had quickly become our code for three words we could never say aloud.

"Hello," I said back, a smile on my lips.

In that moment, I felt greedy for every happiness life had to offer, including grasping each stolen interlude with Bill and seeing all the men in my life achieve political greatness.

After so many recent tragedies, surely life owed me that much.

. . . .

"Harding?" I dropped the newspaper, my jaw crashing to my toes as my brother and I waited to meet with a group of Father's old Rough Riders to urge them to stick with the Republican Party. "They can't be serious. Warren Harding for *president?*"

Ted nodded. "And cousin Franklin as vice president for the Democratic ticket alongside some nobody named James Cox."

Franklin! I couldn't imagine Feather Duster one heart attack or assassin's bullet away from the Oval Office—now *that* was the stuff of nightmares!

"Harding is a decaying Roman emperor," I told Ted. My favorite brother had been campaigning hard for the Republicans in the hopes of garnering their support for his bid at a major office in the near future. "The times don't call for top-shelf politicians. The country is handing him the election."

"You don't think Cox and Franklin have a chance?"

I scoffed. "Only if America continues to confuse Frank as one of our siblings. Which so far he's been happy to allow." I sighed. "I suppose we'll have to play nice with Warren, although he leaves a foul taste in my mouth."

And play nice we did, until that afternoon when an aging Rough Rider asked about Franklin's political platform and his defection from my father's party.

"Our cousin Frank is a maverick," Ted claimed in no uncertain terms. "He does *not* have the brand of our family."

They were harsh words, but I agreed with the sentiment. The way I saw it, the entire Roosevelt clan should be closing ranks around Ted to catapult him to the White House, not turning their coats to support the enemy.

Franklin had deserted the party and played Benedict Arnold, so he deserved whatever he got. Unfortunately, not everyone agreed.

"How could you, Alice?"

I sighed, glancing at the clock on the mantel as it chimed ten o'clock. The fact that Eleanor was out this late was a testament to the ferocity of her anger. On any other night I'd have sat back and enjoyed the fireworks, but Bill was due to arrive any minute, and I couldn't endure Eleanor's censure or questions about a man who was not my husband showing up on my doorstep at so indecent an hour, especially when my husband was out of town. "How could I what?"

"Let your brother make such terrible comments about Franklin. To make matters worse, you supported Warren Harding. *Harding*, Alice." Eleanor threw her hands up in a way that reminded me of Mother. (Although Mother would never have dared leave the house in such a dowdy dress and tattered hat. Was that some sort of cat fur sewn to Eleanor's collar and cuff?) "I ask you!"

I shrugged. "I can't stop Nick from supporting his friend, even if that friend happens to be rotten to the core." I waved a hand at the radio, which was still droning on about the election results, before turning it off. "Harding didn't need to kiss babies or give the same tired speech for the umpty-umpth time in order for America to hand him the election."

"Yes, but Frank lost," Eleanor said. "I wouldn't care so much about that, had our own flesh and blood not turned on us. You're family, Alice, and you betrayed us."

I stared after her as she stormed out, wondering who this harridan was that had replaced my mouse of a cousin. I rather liked her, but needless to say, I didn't speak much to Frank or Eleanor after that.

Out with the old, in with the new.

In August of 1923, Warren Harding finally did America a favor and died after eating a plate of bad shellfish. I considered the brevity of his tenure in office a mercy to him and the country, even when dull Calvin Coolidge assumed his place as president.

The bad news was that just before Harding's death, our decaying emperor had been embroiled in the scandal of the century—the ridiculously named Teapot Dome scandal—after his cabinet appointees leased navy oil reserves without competitive bidding. Normally I'd have been ringside to cheer as Harding's legacy went down in flames, but unfortunately, with their own holdings in the Sinclair Consolidated Oil Corporation, my brothers were splashed with mud from the Teapot Dome too.

"This is a three-ring circus for the press," Bill said from the edge of my bed as he loosened his tie. "The Senate hearings for your brothers today were grueling."

I sat behind him dressed only in my slip, rubbing the knots from his shoulders as I recalled the endless hours of testimony I'd listened to from the gallery. My wrinkled black dress was flung along the back of a chair, as if I'd attended a funeral rather than a hearing. "What's the sentiment amongst the rest of the senators?"

"They agree that Archie exonerated himself by quitting his position at the Sinclair company once he suspected that the outfit was dirty. But Ted . . ."

I groaned. "Not Ted."

Bill heaved his wide shoulders into a shrug. "It's one thing that he worked for the companies who received the oil leases and oversaw the transfer of those leases as the assistant secretary of the navy. It's another thing entirely that his wife held a thousand lucrative shares of Sinclair stock. Congressman Stevenson is calling for Ted's resignation from the navy department."

My temples throbbed, and Bill turned, weaving his fingers through my hair in the most delicious way. "Stevenson's resorted to haranguing Ted's wife to the press," I said, closing my eyes. "Ted told me he plans to challenge the old man to a fight."

Bill gave a sharp inhale, and his fingers fell away. "With his eyes on the New York governor's mansion? Alice, that would be catastrophic."

"You think I don't know that? It's a blessing this isn't the 1700s with a pair of dueling pistols handy, or Stevenson would already be bleeding out on the plains of Weehawken." I sighed. "Maybe it's time for me to put in my two cents."

"Talk some sense into him. Beat it into him if you have to."

I coiled the telephone cord around my finger only a few minutes later. "I hear you're going to pound Stevenson," I said to Ted by way of greeting.

"I am," Ted responded over the crackling line. "And I plan to hit hard."

"There's no denying he deserves it," I said even as Bill motioned to me to go further. "Stevenson's a rat. However, he's also elderly and wears glasses. Remember to ask him to take them off before your first punch."

A long pause over the line. "So you think I shouldn't fight him."

"Quite the opposite. I'm confident your constituents will line up in droves to vote for a brawler who pummels grandfathers."

"Sometimes I wish you weren't so damn insightful."

"I know, darling. Me too."

Ted didn't fight Stevenson. In fact, the matter was dropped when it was discovered that Ted's wife had sold her shares of Sinclair stock before the scandal, and at a loss. Still, I cringed that the Roosevelt family name had been smeared with mud for the first time ever, which was something neither we—nor our enemies—could ever forget.

Unfortunately, I jumped straight from that fire into a boiling inferno. For just after my fortieth birthday and mere months before the November elections, I discovered I was pregnant.

Father once said that if you could kick the person in the pants most responsible for your trouble, you wouldn't sit for a month. For me, a month seemed a bargain.

My sentence was closer to nine months. Or a lifetime, depending on how you viewed it.

Then again, I hadn't gotten into this trouble on my own.

"Are you sure?" Bill stared at me white-faced from across the mahogany partner desk in his office, the massive granite fireplace cold on this late summer afternoon and the entire suite empty after I'd hinted for Bill to dismiss his clerk and stenographer. Moments ago he'd been happily surprised to see me, for I rarely darkened his doorstep, but he didn't look quite so happy now. More like astonished, with a side dish of gobsmacked.

Which was precisely how I felt.

"Beyond a reasonable doubt," I said. "I came straight from the physician."

"I don't know what to say." Bill rose, and sat heavily in the round-armed chair beside me. This was the first time I'd known him at a loss for words, which didn't bode well.

"It's no cause for celebration," I said. "Heaven only knows how I'm going to explain this to Nick. Immaculate conception doesn't seem a viable option."

"So there's no chance . . . ?"

The question hung in the air. I wondered then if Bill wished I *had* been sleeping with my husband. But I only shook my head. "None at all."

"I still don't know how this happened. I assumed, since you and Nick were childless . . ." His face flared crimson. "I assumed too much."

"Oh, Bill." In truth, I'd almost laughed in the physician's face when I realized that it was Nick who was sterile all these years. Now I stood and paced, needing to move to clear my mind even as my hands fluttered uselessly. "I assumed the same, given that you and Mary never had children . . ."

Bill looked at me, stricken. "Oh, Alice. Mary and I *did* have a child."

I jolted at that, for I'd never heard a whisper of a child between them. Bill removed something from his pocket and fiddled with it absent-mindedly: the silver token of the apostle Paul flashed in the light.

"We were young and in love, and I was a brainless cad, doing all my thinking below my beltline. I'd have married her regardless of the fact that she carried my child." He sighed, a sound so fraught with painful remembrances that it bruised my heart. "But her father insisted she *take care of it.* The math wouldn't have added up, you see, and as Idaho's governor, he couldn't countenance the scandal to the family name."

I sat across from him and took his hand, so big and strong even as he looked at me with vulnerable eyes. "Mary did as she was told," he continued. "Only it was done badly. She's been unable to have children ever since."

"You couldn't have known it would happen that way," I said, but it was as if he hadn't heard me.

"It was all my fault, and I couldn't even help her afterward. I slipped into a dark shadowland and almost did myself real harm." He shuddered, his expression raw. "I would have, had it not been for Mary. It took a long time to forgive myself."

This was a new, frightening side to Bill I'd never known before. But we were in this together, for better or for worse.

"There's nothing to forgive this time," I said. "Do you understand?"

Bill tucked the silver medallion back into his pocket and ran a hand through that thick hair I loved so much. "Then where do we go from here, Alice?"

We. That single word made all the difference in the world.

"I've thought through the options, but there are only two choices." I picked up a fountain pen, tapped it frenetically against the desk. "Either I have the child, or I don't."

The last words left a terrible taste on my tongue. Abortions were illegal, but a woman like me could arrange for such an operation. Yet my father's voice echoed in my mind.

My only regret is that you didn't have at least half a dozen children to bring a sparkle to your eye.

I'd finally gotten around to fulfilling his wish, but as always, I'd had to do things the hard way. Damn it, but I cringed to think of what he would have said if he were still alive to the news that I was carrying a child that didn't belong to my husband.

"I'd never make that decision for you." Bill laid his hands over mine, stopping the pen's tapping. "But I can't bear to think of you following in Mary's footsteps. I don't know what I'd do if something happened to you."

I felt the love and protection in those hands covering mine. Ten heartbeats passed, then twenty.

"Then I'll let it happen," I finally said.

"Let what happen?"

"*It*. The pregnancy. The child."

He looked at me with shining eyes. "Really?"

"Really. If it's what we want."

"It *is*. Oh, Alice, it is." He hesitated.

"But . . . ?"

"I'm old enough to be a grandfather, you know."

I laughed at that, so much tension suddenly released that my shoulders sagged with relief. Surely this situation had been replayed countless times throughout the course of history, a mistress finding out she was pregnant with her lover's child, yet rarely was the cast so laughably old. At forty, I'd long since put to rest any ideas of having children, and Bill was sixty. But Bill and I weren't the only players in this story.

"What about Mary and Nick?"

Bill winced and rubbed the bridge of his nose. "Mary is a softhearted soul; this will devastate her. Am I an utter cad to want to keep the truth from her?"

I thought of gentle, kindly Mary, and was reminded of fragile Miriam Bloomer. I wouldn't wish the same horrific fate on another woman. I shook my head. "It's for the best."

Although who knew how long we could keep the truth hidden?

"What will you tell Nick?"

Because, unlike Bill, I didn't have the option of not telling my spouse. In a matter of months, the entire country would know that I was pregnant. And my husband would know the child wasn't his.

It was anyone's guess as to how Nick would react. He'd be within his rights to divorce me, although that would be political suicide. There was always the chance he'd shrug it off, just as he'd done with our own inability to have children. Or he could proclaim me a Jezebel to the world and hope the press took his side.

What a fine kettle of fish this was.

"I don't know," I said. "I'll just have to punt from here."

Borah's jaw clenched, but he bit back whatever he wanted to say.

"Bill," I said. "If the truth gets out . . ."

When *the truth gets out* . . .

"My career will be ruined," Bill said. "It's a risk I'd be willing to take if it was just me taking the fall. Somehow, we'll make this work, Alice. We've accomplished harder things."

"Really? Name them."

Bill passed a hand over his eyes, then gave a lopsided grin. "Well, I can't think of any off the top of my head."

I chuckled. "Who knew having a child would be more difficult than defeating the League of Nations?"

Bill pulled me from my chair and pressed my forehead to his. "You're the love of my life, Alice. Never forget that, all right?"

Warm in his arms, I realized with a heavy heart that by necessity, Bill's support in all this would be silent, especially as he campaigned in Idaho and I navigated this morass with Nick. For the next eight months while this child grew within me, I would be on my own.

And after that?

Panic threatened as I realized that I'd be raising this baby into a child, a teenager, an adult. Possibly alone.

A child is forever.

One of Eleanor's favorite sayings surfaced in my mind then.

A woman is like a tea bag. You never know how strong she is until she gets in hot water.

There was no doubt I was being boiled right now. How strong I was remained to be seen.

I wrote Nick a letter that night, short and stark, revealing to him the outright truth about the baby I now carried. I wrote the words because I feared I lacked the courage to look him in the eye and claim the same moral failings I'd condemned him for all these years.

Then I sat in the parlor and waited for him to come home.

The clock chimed eleven o'clock. Eleven thirty. It was well past midnight when he finally traipsed home, grinning from ear to ear and swaying on his feet like a palm tree caught in a tropical storm. And reeking of bootleg gin, as I'd come to expect.

"Alice, Bubbie, darling!" He aimed his umbrella for the stand, but missed so it clattered to the floor. "You'll never guess the news I heard today."

My heart lodged firmly in my throat and I clutched hard at the letter I'd written. Surely Nick hadn't caught wind of my condition, not so soon . . .

He sauntered over and gave me a sloppy kiss on the cheek. "I'm being considered for the Republican keynote at the Chicago convention. Can you believe it?"

"Is that a fact?" I said even as I rocked with relief. He stumbled, so I had to help prop him up. "Let's get you to bed, shall we?"

He chortled. "I remember when I wanted nothing more than to hear Alice Roosevelt say those words to me." He closed his eyes as I guided him up the stairs. "I loved you so much, Bubbie. Still do."

"Hush," was all I managed to say, for my tongue had suddenly become a useless piece of gristle in my mouth, weighed down by guilt. Nick had almost passed out when I laid him on the bed and undressed him as best I could. He was already snoring before I tugged his silk socks off.

My skin went cold as I tucked the letter into my skirt pocket. I'd told Bill I was going to punt, and now a golden opportunity presented itself.

I wasn't that sort of woman. Or was I?

I tucked a blanket around Nick and lingered for a moment in the doorway. Then I sighed, shed most of my clothes, and climbed in next to him, wishing I could relax into the heat of his body. This simple action—one I'd repeated a thousand times a thousand years ago—

was underhanded and I knew it. Yet I didn't want to kick myself a few months down the road because I'd let this opportunity pass me by.

I'd decide later if I wanted—or needed—to use it.

It was good that Nick was gone in the following weeks, for my stomach flopped like a fish on land at the merest whiff of nothing, so there were days I lived in bed with only books to keep me company. Bill had left Washington for Idaho, and although he wrote frequently, his letters served only to make me ache for someone of flesh and blood that I could confide in.

Mother and Ethel were out of the question, for both were too perfect to understand what a mess I'd gotten myself into. Thankfully, Bromide had passed a few years ago, so I didn't have to worry about her ever finding out that I'd betrayed her precious Nicky. God forbid I should even think of telling beatific Eleanor, whom I hadn't spoken to since Feather Duster ran for vice president and who had sought to distance herself from our side of the family since the Teapot Dome scandal.

I despaired of ever feeling normal again, or speaking to another human of my woes, when an angel appeared on my doorstep.

"Alice Roosevelt Longworth, you are a fiend," Ruth McCormick said when she showed up unannounced. She'd marched straight up to my room laden with a vacuum flask of chicken soup and a hot water bottle, took one look at me and the bucket by my bed, and declared she wasn't leaving until I was recovered. "I knew there was something wrong when you didn't return my calls. How long have you been like this?"

"Weeks," I said. "But it feels like forever."

Ruth felt my forehead, and I was reminded of a good witch from some fairy tale. "You don't have a fever, but you look like death itself. We need to get you a doctor."

"No, really." I tried to think of some excuse, but failed. "I don't want to bother anyone."

"It's no trouble. I'll ring our physician and he'll be here in two shakes of a lamb's tail."

"I've already been to the doctor, Ruth," I said, which finally stopped her.

"Oh?" She stared down at me, hands on her hips. "What did he say?"

There was no point in lying; soon the world would know that I was on the nest. "That this will all clear up in about nine months. Well, more like seven now."

Ruth clapped her hands together. "That's wonderful news!" Yet her eyes quickly narrowed. "You don't seem excited. Did the doctor give you a diatribe about your age? Don't worry, I had the same lecture three years ago when I had Bazy and it's utter hooey; there are plenty of women who've given birth into their fifties even."

"No, it's not that. It's just . . ."

Ruth and I were friends, yet that was no guarantee that I could trust her. But I needed someone who I could be entirely honest with.

Whether she liked it or not, Ruth was that person.

"Close the door," I said.

She lifted an eyebrow, but did as I asked.

"You should sit down," I said.

She didn't sit. "Spill it, Alice."

So I did, the entire sordid story. Ruth proved that she was made of sterner stuff than I'd imagined, for she never gasped or shrieked or pursed her lips in disapproval, just sat and listened. When I was done she opened the vacuum flask and handed it to me with a spoon. "Eat. I know it's the last thing you want, but you need sustenance. Otherwise I *will* call that doctor."

I managed a few bites while waiting for her to speak, but she only stared out the window, lost in thought.

"What do I do?" For perhaps the first time in my life, I wanted someone to point me in the right direction and give me marching orders.

"First, you tell Nick you're pregnant."

"With his child? Or Bill's?"

"I can't answer that." So much for being told what to do. "You have to do what you think best for the child, right? And Nick is bound to find out sooner rather than later. You don't want him hearing it from the papers."

Just the thought of the newspapers crawling over this story like ravening ants made me want to retch. I'd traded spanks and spits with reporters for years, but who knew if I'd be able to fool them this time or whether one of the press-hounds would snuffle out the truth?

"I don't want to announce the pregnancy." I pushed the soup away, my gorge rising. "Not until after the elections in November."

"Then don't. Plenty of women keep the fact hidden until they absolutely can't hide it anymore. I swear no one will hear the news from my lips. All you have to do is lie low."

I grimaced. "That's something I've never been very good at."

"Then it can be the first item on a long list of new talents you'll acquire with motherhood, along with how to survive without sleep and how to get chewing gum out of hair." She screwed the lid back onto the flask. "And as soon as you feel up to it, you're coming to Chicago."

"Why?"

"So you have a neutral location to see Bill away from Washington's all-seeing eyes and also so you can meet my obstetrician. He's the best in the field of special cases and delivered all my babies."

"I'm sure someone in Washington will suffice. And I don't deserve to see Bill right now."

"Alice, don't punish yourself—or the baby—just because you feel guilty. Jump into this headfirst, with all the gumption and gusto we've grown accustomed to from the one and only Alice Roosevelt Longworth."

"You really are a benevolent despot; you know that?"

"One of my finest traits." She grinned. "By the way, peanut butter is the answer."

"What?"

She waved a hand. "For how to get chewing gum out of hair."

"I'll remember that."

She stood, all business again. "Everything is going to be all right, Alice. I swear it."

"Thank you, Ruth," I said. "For everything."

She only smiled. "Of course. That's what friends are for."

Friends. I hadn't had a true friend in ages, perhaps in forever, considering how Maggie Cassini had betrayed me and Cissy Patterson had snapped up my husband the first chance she got. But as Ruth left I felt as if she had taken some of my burden with her. Then my stomach lurched as I remembered that I still had to tell Nick.

Thankfully, my bucket was close at hand.

"Sit," I said to Nick when I saw him a few weeks later, freshly triumphant from his convention speech in Chicago. There was no doubt that my husband's star was on the rise, *if* he could keep the drinking under control and *if* word didn't leak that his wife was carrying another man's child. I'd been sure to catch Nick in the afternoon, before he started tinkering with his homemade still. All the same, my stomach churned like I'd swallowed some sort of demon.

Which I supposed wasn't too far from the truth.

"Are you all right?" Nick actually looked concerned as he sat next to me in the library. "I know you were sick. You look thinner."

"I'm not sick." I folded my hands in my lap to keep them still. "I'm pregnant."

I let the silence hang, to hang myself with it. Nick stared at me. "You're . . ."

"Pregnant."

In a moment the pieces would fall together, and I'd endure the condemnation, the yelling, and the demands for a divorce. I'd rehearsed this scene in my head so many times I was prepared for every possible outcome, yet my heart thudded in my chest so hard I thought my ribs might shatter.

But Nick only blinked. "After all this time?"

"Apparently so," I said, steeling myself for the onslaught.

"Then that means . . ." He ran both hands over his shining scalp, the last hair there having fled long ago. Yet, even after eighteen years of marriage, my husband still possessed the rare power to surprise me. "Was it the night they told me about the convention speech? I woke up next to you . . . I assumed . . ."

The night I'd climbed into bed after him.

Now was my chance to come clean about all of it, but Nick stared at me with the one expression I hadn't anticipated—complete and utter naked hope—that a whole rosy future unfolded before me, one with a little family of three who celebrated Christmas together and went for tea at the White House. I could scarcely swallow around the lump in my throat.

I *was* a coward.

I crossed my ankles and shrugged. "I suppose. Even a blind squirrel finds a nut once in a while."

I held my breath, waiting for him to brand me a liar or worse, but he only leaped from his chair and whooped, drawing me up into his arms to spin me around. "I'm going to be a father!" he cried. "You're going to be a mother! This calls for celebration!"

He released me to rummage a bottle of bootleg gin from its secret spot behind our encyclopedias. Then he set it down. "You know, I've changed my mind," he said as he slowly replaced the bottle as if in a daze. "I'd like a lemonade instead. Will you join me?"

Now it was my turn to stare, my mouth not quite closed. I nodded. "I'd be happy to."

Nothing I'd ever done had persuaded Nick to quit drinking—and God knew I'd tried—but this child had accomplished the feat with its very existence. Perhaps it *was* a miracle.

As I followed my husband to the kitchen, all I could think was that we may as well have been on the far side of the moon: me expecting another man's child, Nick thrilled to be the father *and* abstaining from getting tom-tiddly over the news.

As we clinked our glasses of lemonade together in a celebratory toast, a sick feeling twisted my gut. Was this a sort of second opportunity for Nick and me to mend our fences, for me to set Bill aside so we might build a family together, and live happily ever after?

Was such a life even possible if it was built on a lie?

More importantly, was that life even what I wanted?

In that moment, I had no idea.

I waited for the bubble to burst, for Nick to ferret out the truth, but he only insisted that I put my feet up in the afternoon and cut back my daily walks to three miles instead of six. He was adorably attentive, and while he didn't entirely stop drinking, he avoided the worst of his usual excesses, which I considered a true triumph.

I wondered if everyone would feel the same way.

I confided in a coded letter to Bill about Nick's elation over the news, but received only vague responses in return. His brief letters made me worry that he might have fallen into his shadowland again or, worse, that he, too, had envisioned my possible life of domestic tranquility with Nick and was pulling away. Or perhaps he'd harbored secret—and now ruined—hopes that Nick *would* divorce me, that somehow the pieces would magically land so that Bill could be a proper father to our child. I couldn't blame him if he had, for I'd had similar daydreams before speaking to Nick. My world had turned upside down so many times over the last few weeks that I was positively nauseous from the constant tailspin.

Or from morning sickness. It was hard to tell for sure.

In response, my letters became terser. I tried to tell myself that it was for the best, that if Bill sought to distance himself, so should I. Yet setting him aside felt like carving out my heart with a dull spoon, and after so many months apart, I leaped at the opportunity to see him when our travel itineraries crossed.

So, not long after I felt the child move for the first time—like the popping of effervescent champagne bubbles—we met at a corner table in an ill-lit restaurant that smelled of stale cigar smoke. The official story, had anyone cared to ask, was that the famous wife of the future Speaker of the House was here to discuss campaign planks for the upcoming election with a powerful member of the Senate Judiciary and Foreign Relations Committees.

I wondered if we'd ever be as carefree as we were the night of the League of Nations defeat. The flutter deep in my belly told me likely not.

"Hello, hello, hello," Bill said after he pulled out my chair for me, his hand lingering on mine as I took my seat while his eyes burned with a thousand unsaid words. If I hadn't felt like a burgeoning hippopotamus, I'd have floated out of my chair with the realization that he hadn't set me aside, that he still loved and wanted me and the child I carried. The knowledge made something warm unfurl in my chest, some piece of my heart that I'd walled away when his letters had become more reserved.

I should have known better. Even after all these years, I'd never learned to trust in love.

Perhaps having a child would change all that.

"Hello, Mr. Future Vice President," I said. It was common knowledge that Bill was Coolidge's first choice for a running mate for the upcoming election. I expected a triumphant grin in response, but instead a dark cloud passed over his eyes.

"I won't be on the ticket." He looked at the menu, the ceiling, the salt shakers, anywhere but me. "I'm going to refuse the nomination."

"What? Why?"

He gave a pointed look at my waist, its telltale swell hidden beneath the generous cut of my dress. "Oh," I said, dejected once again. Not long ago, I'd had high hopes for Nick's and Bill's and even Ted's political futures. How had things broken apart so quickly? And so completely?

"Think of the scandal if word got out. You, me, Nick, Mary, your family . . ."

"Ted is running for governor of New York," I said slowly. "His first step toward the White House."

"This is bigger than just us, Alice. There's the child's future to think of as well." The menu came up again, hiding half his face. "I take it from your letters that Nick believes he's the father?"

"He does."

Another downturn of his eyes. Another door closing somewhere. "That's probably for the best."

And there it was. I knew then that we'd both entertained wild dreams about us raising this child together. Dreams that could never be.

Unlike all my other scrapes, my affair with Bill was possibly the worst—and best—mistake of my life. We had made a child together, but in doing so, had irrevocably lost each other. Because now I could never afford to give up the subterfuge of being Nick's faithful wife. If not for me or Bill, Nick or Mary, then for the very child I carried, who would forever bear the dark stain of scandal if the truth got out.

I sipped my water, needing something to clear my throat. "I'm sorry, Bill. I wish things could be different somehow . . ."

He only mustered a smile and squeezed my hand. "Don't apologize. You're giving me an extraordinary gift, one that I'd long ago given up hoping for."

The rest of the meal was a somber affair, for we both knew it would be another painfully lonely stretch before we saw each other again. There was even a reporter outside the restaurant waiting to take my picture when we left, a reminder that it would be reckless and irresponsible for Bill to come up when he dropped me at the Drake Hotel.

I'd been reckless and irresponsible my entire life, but at forty and pregnant, I supposed it was time I started acting the part of an adult. That didn't mean I couldn't indulge in a lingering kiss from the passenger's seat when Bill stopped at one of the newly installed traffic lights, the last fiery rays of the summer sunset reflected on the surface of Lake Michigan.

"Hello," I said, a little breathless when I finally released his lapels.

"Hello." He cupped my cheek in his rough hand and I leaned into it. "Always hello. For you and little Alice."

Bill's earlier dour mood had dissipated into one of deep contemplation, as if he'd decided to savor every moment tonight. Now he left a trail of feathery kisses down my bare neck that made me wish the traffic light would never turn green.

I tilted my chin, giving him more to work with. "Are you so sure it's a girl?" I managed to murmur.

"I hope it is." He pressed a kiss to my temple as the light's buzzer sounded, heralding the last five seconds before it was our turn. "Nick may claim her," he said, his voice raw. "But I want to see her grow up. Please."

"You never have to ask." I might have gotten lost in the pools of his gray eyes. "You're her father, Bill."

Green light. The car started to move, giving Bill an excuse to keep those gray eyes on the road, my hotel looming one block ahead. "Do you think you'll ever tell her? About me, I mean?"

"When she's older," I said, which was the truth.

"Of course." He offered a meager smile as we approached the Drake Hotel.

"However, there *is* one thing I know, William Edgar Borah."

"And what is that, Alice Lee Roosevelt Longworth?"

"That this little girl—or boy—is lucky to have you as its father. Its *true* father."

We sat a moment in silence, content to be in each other's company. Then I let myself out, already starting to feel a bit like the waddling old badger my father had once kept in the White House, if not quite as mean. Not for the first time, I shuddered to think what Father would have said if he knew I'd carried on an illicit affair and had an illegitimate child; it didn't bear thinking on.

Sometimes we disappointed our parents. Unfortunately, as I looked back at Bill, I wondered if by her very conception I was one day destined to disappoint my child too.

I decided the best way to distract myself from reality was to jump headlong into Ted's campaign for governor. Fortunately, the new fashion of flapper dresses meant that loose waistlines were in vogue even for elderly matrons such as myself, so no one—not even Mother—was the wiser regarding my condition when I showed up that autumn at Sagamore Hill.

"I really think I have a shot at this," Ted told me while we sat in Father's library, Mother and the rest of my siblings out on the lawn enjoying the twilight. It was a sedate sort of evening, the kind that normally would have set me to throwing an impromptu dinner party or striking out for an evening walk. Yet I found I enjoyed the calm and Ted's steady company after all the recent excitement in my own life. "I only hope people don't automatically think of the Teapot Dome scandal when they see me."

"No one remembers Teapot," I fibbed, since the hearings had been less than a year ago. Still, voters *did* have a short memory and this was Ted's shot, Ted, who had always been nervous about trying to live up to Father's memory and was now preparing to follow in his overly large footsteps. "You're Theodore Roosevelt's eldest son, you're brilliant, and you've already won the primary. You're a natural for the governor's mansion. I'd say even for the White House in a few years."

Ted's grin was almost as wide as Father's had once been. "That's my hope."

I gave a nonchalant shrug. "Then we'll make it happen."

"I'm mighty sorry that Bill Borah declined the nomination for vice president. You were right about that." Ted had called while I was still in Chicago to tell me that the party had officially chosen Bill to run alongside Coolidge. I'd warned him that Bill would reject the nomination.

Between my husband, lover, and brother, I hoped one of them would find their way to the Oval Office. Yet I'd destroyed Bill's chances with more force than an anarchist's bomb.

To be fair, we ruined his chances together, and had fun doing it too. Still, it was impossible to shake the heavy yoke of guilt that had settled on my shoulders since Bill had told me he wouldn't run.

"I have something for you," I said to my brother. "Let me get it."

I hurried up to the room that had been mine as a girl—no longer wallpapered in a rousing shade of pink since each of my brothers had claimed it when they came of age—and knelt on the tiger rug to retrieve a velvet jewelry box from beneath the narrow bed. To my surprise, Ted was waiting in the hall when I emerged, and studying me with a rather contemplative expression.

"Here," I said.

"Alice," he said without taking the box. "Is everything all right? You seem pensive tonight."

"I'm fine." The baby fluttered in my belly, as if demanding the truth with a pounding of tiny fists. I could have confided in Ted as I had Ruth, but I didn't want a shadow to darken such an idyllic evening, or his campaign for governor. "Take it."

Ted opened it to reveal a girl's simple golden locket. He looked at me questioningly. "I'm not one for fashion, but don't you think this will clash with my tie?"

"Don't be daft," I said. "Open it, but carefully."

He did, unveiling a lock of brown hair interspersed with strands of gray. Realization dawned on his face. "Is this . . . ?"

"A bit of Father for good luck and guidance while you campaign."

A clipping of hair I'd snipped just before Father's funeral, desperately needing to hold on to some part of him. From Ted's shining eyes, I guessed that he understood.

"I wonder if we might scrounge up his golden rabbit foot for me too," he said. "The one he always took hunting."

I laughed. "You're not hunting constituents, only persuading them to vote for you. And they'll do it in droves. How could they not?"

Ted tucked the locket into his palm. "Thank you. I'll make sure it gets back to you."

I might have told him to keep it, but it was my last bit of Father. So I only nodded.

"We should probably join the others," I said. "Otherwise they'll wonder what we're plotting."

I should have been paying more attention, not thinking of how much I missed Father or what the coming months would bring or Ted's chances at the governor's mansion. But I was thinking all those things and I *wasn't* paying attention when my foot missed the first stair.

I careened forward, fast at first and then in slow motion, twisting sideways until I crashed with full force into the sharp edges of the stairs before tumbling helter-skelter down the flight, trying in vain to curl into myself to protect the baby until I rolled to a stop on the crimson-carpeted landing two thirds of the way down.

Pain. So much pain, and it was everywhere, all at once.

"Alice!" Ted's footsteps pounded behind me and then he was at my side. "Are you all right?"

Amid the noise of his question, silence fell in my head as I stared up at the stained glass skylight. My body felt as if every bone had been hollowed out and filled with jagged shards of panic and agitation. I'd be bruised worse than a brawler tomorrow, but it wasn't me I worried about. I pressed frantically on my stomach, hoping to prod the baby into moving to let me know it was safe.

"What's wrong?" Ted hovered nearby. "Is it your ribs?"

"No." I continued to push gently, my panic cresting when there was no response. I hadn't wanted to burden my brother, but now I dared glance at him crouched beside me. "I'm pregnant."

Ted blanched, but recovered quickly. "I'll ring for the doctor."

But I only clutched his wrist in a death grip, for at that moment I felt the familiar sensation of the baby's movement, as if my tumble had jolted it awake.

"It's fine," I said, brightening and laughing with relief.

"I'll ring for the doctor anyway."

"No." I shook my head, suddenly sober. "Then I'd have to explain to everyone why I called him out for a simple tumble down the stairs." Another flutter in my belly. "The baby's fine."

Ted stared down at me, then blinked hard and helped hitch me to my feet. "So, when can we expect the happy event?"

"February," I said, although that was a tidbit I'd neglected to share with Nick in order to keep up our happy charade. Hopefully, he'd just assume the baby had come a few weeks early. "Sometime around my birthday."

Which was also frighteningly close to the day my mother had died, two days after giving birth to me. I didn't care to think about that right now. Or ever, for that matter.

"Mother will be thrilled," Ted said. "In fact, the whole dang country will be beside itself."

I hadn't given much thought to what America would think, but I had only myself to blame for the country's continued interest in the minutiae of my life. I'd refused to fade into the background after I'd married Nick, and now my child might well grow up trailed by a line of reporters all eager for stories about Theodore Roosevelt's grandchild. My parents' reticence at my name appearing in the papers after Father became president was all too clear.

"And Nick?" Ted asked. "Is he thrilled?"

"Over the moon." I was suddenly exhausted—not to mention bruised from my tumble down the stairs—and the thought of the country's reaction to the news I'd soon have to break left me even more drained. I kissed Ted's cheek. "I'm going to bed," I said. "Tell everyone I said good night."

I felt Ted's gaze on me as I gingerly climbed back up the stairs. "I'm fine, really," I called over my shoulder, careful to hold the handrail this time. Of all my brothers, Ted loved me best, but I hoped that his campaign for governor would prove more interesting than his pregnant sister. For perhaps the first time in my life, I wanted nothing more than to hide from the limelight.

Unfortunately, we don't always get what we want.

Only a few days later I received a letter from Bill. I hadn't mentioned my fall down the stairs to either him or Nick, as there was no need to worry either of them, especially as the baby appeared to have taken up acrobatics over the last few days.

Dear Alice,

I hardly know how to write. I am so uneasy and anxious lest your terrible accident cause you illness. Such falls sometimes injure internally. About the only message I can send is, Hello, Hello, always and ever Hello.

—Bill

I found Ted in the Gun Room on the third floor, where, as a boy, he'd once kept a china closet museum of insects and butterflies that required guarding lest Archie pilfer them. Now, as a man, my brother sat in Father's ornate cattle horn chair typing yet another speech for his gauntlet of campaign events. He startled when I slapped Bill's letter on the desk in front of him. "Did you tell Bill that I fell down the stairs?"

Ted stopped typing, squinted as if trying to remember. "I might have mentioned it in a postscript the other day when I offered to go west to help him with his reelection campaign."

"Why?"

"Why did I offer to help him campaign? Well, I've always admired Borah and I'd hate to see him lose his seat."

"Bill's seat is secure." I waved the letter. "Why did you tell him I'd fallen?"

"Do you really want me to answer that?"

I glared at him, arms akimbo even as I became suddenly unsure whether I should have broached the subject. "Yes."

Ted rose and shut the door behind him. "I put myself in his place, Alice," he said quietly. "If the woman I loved was carrying my child and fell down the stairs, I'd want to know."

I let myself collapse into an old chair, feeling as if an enormous burden had been lifted from my shoulders only to be replaced by another equally as heavy. "Oh, Ted. How long have you known?"

"Alice, I've watched you with Bill for years. Anyone who cares to look can see that you love each other. And it's no secret within the family that you and Nick are a political match."

"*Years?* You've known for *years* and never said anything?"

Ted shrugged. "It wasn't my place."

I sighed. "You're too damn smart for your own good."

"Tell that to my constituents." Ted flicked the half-finished speech in his typewriter. Just like that, absolution and acceptance from my brother. If only the rest of my family would prove so easy when the time came. For if Ted had figured it out, so too would the others.

"You'll knock them dead tomorrow, I promise," I said, glad for the change of subject. "And I'll be there to cheer you on. Provided there's no more gossip between you and Bill about me."

"Deal. One more thing, Alice."

I quirked an eyebrow.

"Be careful. There's some in Washington who suspect you and Bill of being more than just good friends. There's a few who even call you Aurora Borah Alice when they think no one is listening."

That *was* witty, and had I not been balanced on a knife's edge, I'd have probably laughed out loud. "So I suppose I shouldn't name the baby De*borah* if it's a girl?"

Ted only readjusted his speech in the typewriter tray. "You need to distract them, redirect their attention somehow."

I waved away his concern, mostly because I didn't know what else to do. I could scarcely imagine the hell I'd be plunged into if the country learned the truth while I was pregnant. Worse still, if *Nick* gleaned the truth now that I'd tried to dupe him. "We'll deal with that later. *After* we get you elected."

For when life became difficult, politics was always there to provide a shiny distraction.

And more problems.

"You have your speech?"

Ted waved his papers at me while I adjusted his tie. "Yes, Alice, I have my speech. I remembered to put pants on, too, in case you hadn't noticed."

I tweaked his nose like I had when we were little. "Good boy."

But Ted was looking past me. "What in the Sam Hill is *that*?"

I shielded my eyes from the autumn sun. We were in Buffalo and had just been prepping for the biggest speech of Ted's campaign, but now a low rumble had started among the crowd and grown to the volume of a dozen angry beehives.

"A Buick." Ted answered his own question before his entire face twisted into a grimace. "What is that on its roof?"

"Is that Eleanor?" I asked, equally confused as we watched our horse-faced cousin emerge and give us a little wave. "*Oy vey.* What the hell is she doing?"

Our confusion didn't last long, for Eleanor had outfitted a blue Buick with a giant canvas teapot that belched steam, and painted slogans on the sides that read *For Honesty and Efficiency Vote for John W. Davis and Alfred E. Smith.* They were, of course, the Democratic candidates for governor.

"A teapot for the Teapot Dome scandal," I whispered. "This is retribution for your comment about Frank being a maverick and him losing the vice presidency."

Ted groaned. "She's retaliating in grand style."

Our conversation at the wartime canteen came back to me, Eleanor longing to do something more than play the part of a housewife and mother. I wondered if Franklin had sent her out or whether she'd volunteered, considering that he rarely went out in public after a recent bout of polio had left him crippled. It seemed Eleo may have found her calling in political sabotage.

Ted went out and gave his speech, but the reception was lukewarm at best, and afterward people flocked to Eleanor and her gaudy teapot rather than to meet my brother. I picked up one of a hundred discarded flyers from the car lot afterward, each word damning my brother and the entire Republican Party.

Things went downhill from there. Fast.

The Singing Teapot—as it came to be known—showed up at Ted's next campaign event. And the whistle-stop speech after that. And the town hall meeting after that. It dogged my poor brother everywhere from Buffalo to Manhattan in the weeks leading up to the general election, 218 stops in all.

"I didn't know she had it in her," I growled to Ted at another pathetic attempt at a rally, the Singing Teapot already having done its damage the day before. A few people in the tiny crowd had waved pennants for my brother, but many others had shouted obscenities at him during his speech. "I'd be almost proud of her for growing a spine if it wasn't you she was targeting."

"She's ruined me." Ted ran a hand through his hair. "This was my shot, Alice. If I blow it, I may as well kiss good-bye to politics, much less the White House."

"Eleanor is rabble-rousing so Franklin will have a clear shot at the ticket himself in coming years." It was a solid tactic, not that I'd admit that out loud. There was no denying that the Hyde Park Roosevelts had one-upped our Oyster Bay clan. "Feather Duster has only ever ridden on Father's coattails and our good name; he doesn't deserve to set foot in the New York sanitation department, much less the governor's mansion."

"Tell that to them." Ted jutted his chin toward the restless crowd. "The name Ted Roosevelt has become synonymous with the biggest scandal in American history, all thanks to Eleanor."

"That doesn't mean we're going to go down without a fight," I said. "And if we do lose, like the Republican elephants we are, we'll never forget."

I'd certainly never forget Eleanor's mudslinging a month later when news came that Ted lost the election by 100,000 votes and his political career evaporated overnight.

I swore then that one day I'd return the favor by making Eleanor's life a living hell.

One thing at a time. First I had to deal with my own self-made hell.

Chapter 19

"Excuse me, Mrs. Longworth," the reporter from the *Chicago Daily Tribune* asked on the other end of the line. Ruth's family owned the paper and she'd set up this interview to let the cat out of the bag, but I could hear the man's papers trembling in fear of my biting his head clean off. "I apologize for asking, but America's dying to know." Another terrified pause. "Are you pregnant?"

None of your damned business, you nosy bastard.

Ted had suggested that I distract the press, redirect their attention. So that's exactly what I was doing, commandeering the spotlight from the baby and Nick and Bill, and placing it firmly back where it belonged.

On *me*.

Even if this was the one time in my life where I wanted nothing more than to fade into obscurity. Unfortunately, I couldn't afford that luxury.

So I'd rehearsed my lines until I was reciting them in my sleep.

"Hell yes!" I said. "I'm always willing to try anything once!"

They were Father's words, borrowed from after he'd been shot. I answered a few more questions before hanging up: Due in a few months. Nursery renovations well under way. Absolutely *dee-lighted* (in my best impression of Father). Don't care if it's a boy or a girl.

Yet, not long after the *Tribune* article, the newspapers seemed to shake loose the truth. My cheeks burned with a rush of blood as I read headlines of *Mrs. Longworth Expecting the Stork*, instead of *The Longworths*, and stories that mentioned me as Borah's *most intimate friend*.

I picked at my hands after I shredded the papers. I'd always reveled in the press coverage of my public exploits, but this had turned my love for Bill into something sordid. Nick usually scanned the major headlines, but perhaps he was too distracted with his plans to become Speaker of the House to read the back-page society columns that I so diligently hid from him.

Still, when Congress opened I resumed my long-vacated position in the House's family gallery, so I could be closer to Nick instead of filling my normal seat in the Senate to watch Bill. And I was honestly proud when I sat alongside Grace Coolidge to witness my husband assume his role as the Speaker of the House.

Perhaps, with a little luck, everything was going to turn out all right.

Bill and I continued to exchange coded letters as my due date approached and I settled into a lonely room in Chicago's Drake Hotel to be closer to Ruth's obstetrician while Nick remained in Washington.

Dearest Alice,

I am wondering how you are getting by. I'm afraid you will be lonesome, but you're so very wonderful. I wish I could be with you, but, Alice, these next weeks are going to be the most wonderful of your crowded life. Marvel of marvels—be careful and listen to the doctor, won't you? As always, hello, hello, hello.

Hello again,
Bill

My life *had* been crowded up to this point, but now I worried that I would be alone for the delivery or, worse, that the child would come on my birthday or two days later, both black days considering the history of my own birth. February 12 went by with relatively little fanfare, save a special chocolate cake Ruth brought by along with a command that I must celebrate my forty-first year. Then on February 14, the same day my own mother had died, I went into labor.

Ruth was once again my guardian angel—or my benevolent despot, whichever came first—as she rushed me to the hospital, and I almost sobbed with relief when Mother arrived at my bedside.

"Having a baby is like trying to push a grand piano through a transom," I said after it was all over. I'd delivered a six-pound baby girl who resembled my father with her fierce expression, at least to my awestruck eyes. The little howling bundle of pink flesh had broken the Valentine's Day curse of my own birth, and I loved her all the more for it. I'd once wondered if this child would allow me to truly trust in love, and as I gazed at her, I suddenly believed it was possible.

Mother telephoned Nick as soon as the nurse had placed her in my arms, and I swear I could hear the standing ovation he received in the House before he hopped the first train to Chicago. But Bill . . .

I dared not call the father of my child from the hospital with its solitary phone located at the nurses' station. After all, what reason could I, Alice Roosevelt *Longworth*, have for leaving my bed to personally inform one of ninety-six senators of news of my delivery?

Bill. I longed for him—*ached* for him—but instead, Nick appeared at the hospital the very next day. I was woolgathering, my mind wandering as I stared at my daughter in her bassinet, and didn't hear him until he was standing at my bedside.

"Damn it, Alice," he whispered. "I've never been so jealous in all my life."

"Jealous?" I held my breath until my lungs threatened to burst, watching as Nick reverently touched my daughter's downy head. Surely he'd seen the papers by now, drawn what was the only conclusion.

Instead, he blew me away with a smile that threatened to cleave his face in two, transporting me back to bygone days when he'd wooed me over steaming pots of Toothsome Terrapin at the Alibi. "Because our daughter looks much more like a Roosevelt than a Longworth."

Because she *was* a Roosevelt and not a Longworth. I could be mean at times, sometimes even cruel, but I couldn't—wouldn't—continue this deception any longer. It was too much, even for me.

"Nick—"

"But she's young yet," he finished, his eyes bright with tears. "I'm so in love, Alice. I didn't know how much I wanted a child until this moment, but now I can't imagine I didn't know what I was missing."

Nick was smart, brilliant even, but his wish for a child had blinded him to the obvious. Would it be crueler of me to crush him with the truth?

The very idea should have made me giddy with relief, but instead a savage twist of guilt turned my stomach as I thought of poor Bill.

Oh, the tangled webs we weave . . .

"What will we name her?" Nick asked.

I gestured for him to pick up the pink-wrapped bundle. "Paulina," I said. "After my favorite apostle."

Nick raised an eyebrow at that, since I remained an avowed and aggressive atheist. My daughter's name was a secret gift to Bill, for I'd named our child after his favorite apostle. Nick—and the world—would never guess that little secret.

"Hello, Paulina," Nick whispered.

Hello, hello, hello.

Maybe it was the leftover emotions from giving birth, but I couldn't stop the tears from welling at that moment. Me, who prided myself on never crying.

I cried still more to hear that Bill learned of our daughter's birth through the papers, just before Ted finally thought to phone him with the news.

Dear Alice,

Hello more than ever, hello. There are to be two Alice Longworths—did not believe such a wonder possible! All the evening papers had an account of the coming of the baby. The first I knew of it was when I glanced down and saw your picture. I tremblingly reached for it—fearing that you might be very ill—but when I read the wonderful news I put that old paper in my desk as a memento.

Hello, hello, yes hello.

Nick returned to Washington and Bill kept up a steady stream of letters—at least one each day—while I remained in Chicago with Ruth to adjust to motherhood. It was a long month before the obstetrician deemed us well enough to travel home, and thus, Bill didn't meet his daughter until she was almost five weeks old.

He cradled Paulina in her frilly pink-and-white dress, which was a gift from Ruth. My pale daughter rarely cried, and looked even more tiny and delicate cupped in her father's broad hands, which were freshly calloused from his recent trip to Idaho's ranches. A bell rang in the hallway outside his office, calling all senators to a pending vote, but Bill ignored it.

"I don't know if I've ever been so happy," he murmured. A shaft of afternoon sunlight fell from the windows as he moved Paulina so her head rested on his shoulder. Both of them gave such contented sighs that I thought my heart might fracture from such bittersweet joy. When he glanced up, he looked like a much younger man, his brown eyes alight with sheer rapture.

"Thank you, Alice." His voice was thick with emotion. "For my little Paulina, and for her name."

"You're welcome." I glanced at the clock, feeling the merciless march of each passing minute. Ted had accompanied me on a pretense so I had an excuse to visit Bill, and had stepped out to give us a moment alone, but he'd return any moment to collect Paulina and me.

Bill kissed Paulina on the back of her neck and our daughter cooed happily, chubby arms flailing. "Kiss this spot every evening for me," he whispered. "A special good night from her proud papa."

"I will."

His eyes locked with mine. "She's perfect, Alice. Truly."

Much as I might have wished to stay in the moment forever, Bill visibly winced as Ted appeared at the doorway while congressional aides bustled about their errands in the corridor beyond. Every visit between us, every meeting from here on would have to be guarded. Bill reluctantly handed Paulina back to me even as Ted studiously avoided looking at us.

"Mary wants to meet her," Bill murmured as I stood. "She's insistent, in fact."

Paulina started to fuss, probably sensing my shock. I'd scarcely seen Mary since Bill and I had begun our affair, had skirted her so I could ignore my own guilt. "Why would she want to do that?"

"I think she may have guessed the truth." He ran a hand over his face, erasing the illusion of youth so he looked every bit his sixty years. "I can never tell if Mary really is a featherweight, or if it's all an act to hide a deeper mind."

My daughter heavy in my arms, there was only one thing I cared about in regard to Mary Borah. The latest tidbit from the gossip columns echoed in my mind. *What do a new parquet floor and the Longworth baby have in common? There's not a bit of "nick" in either of them.*

"Will she expose us?" I asked.

"I don't know." Bill watched, the love apparent in his eyes as I rocked Paulina. "You don't have to do it if you don't want to."

"Perhaps meeting with Mary will put the gossip to rest," I said, thinking out loud. "Or maybe she'll curse me to hell and back."

"Ha." Bill kissed my forehead. "Mary doesn't have a malignant bone in her body."

Perhaps, but Mary had never faced rumors—or the truth staring her in the face—that her husband had fathered a child with another woman. I sighed. What did I have to lose except my dignity? "I'll telephone her."

So I did, that very same day, even though my hands had taken to itching worse than they had during the Far East junket. Best to get this over with before I flayed off my very skin.

"Hello?" Mary's voice was higher trilled than a robin in spring. Had it not been for this request of hers, I'd have continued to believe her to be an empty-headed sort of wife, the kind that kept the silver polished but never formulated an original thought. Perhaps I'd underestimated her as I had Eleanor.

I'd never make that mistake again.

"Hello, Mary," I said. "It's Alice Longworth."

My blood drummed loud in my ears while I waited for her response. Would she shriek like a wounded harpy or hang up on me?

Instead she acted as she always had. "Hello, Alice!"

Hello . . . A fresh fist of guilt pummeled me as I heard Bill's voice in my mind.

Mary continued, "I'm so happy to hear from you."

Was she truly happy? Or secretly plotting my downfall? I'd have had better luck nailing currant jelly to a wall than deciphering her tone on the other end of the line.

I infused a smile into my voice. "Listen, Paulina would love for you to come over and have lunch with her one day soon."

It was silly, but somehow couching the invitation as coming from an innocent infant seemed safer. There was no doubt now that I had less spine than a worm.

There was a fraught silence, and I could well imagine Mary twining the cord around her fingers, choosing her words carefully. "I'd love to meet her," she finally said. "I'm free tomorrow."

"Perfect," I said brightly, happy to keep the conversation short. "I'll see you around noon."

Needless to say, I didn't sleep that night, only clawed at my hands and imagined a million and one painful ways Mary could denounce me to the world. I was a wreck by the time the butler announced Mary the next afternoon. Bill's wife was dressed in a shapeless white jacket with an ill-fitting fur collar, not at all looking like a villain bent on revenge.

"She's beautiful," Mary enthused when she bent over the bassinet where Paulina was napping. "All babies are lovely, but this one of yours is especially precious. You must make sure she receives the best of everything, especially her education."

I'd prepared to do battle for Paulina and was ready to bribe, co-erce, or cajole to keep Mary from going public if necessary. I hadn't prepared for compliments and kindness. Or perhaps I simply hadn't read from the same rule book as everyone else, given how many peo-ple I'd misjudged in my life.

"Pond's Cold Cream offered me five thousand dollars to pose for one of their ads," I said hesitantly. "I thought it would make a good start for Paulina's college tuition."

"An excellent nest egg," Mary said, straightening. "You know, it's my greatest regret in life that Billy and I never had any children. You must bring Paulina to visit us often, Alice."

"I couldn't bother you," I said with a careless wave of my hand, finally beginning to relax. "Babies make such a fuss and all."

"I insist. And you must bring her when Billy is home. I mean it, Alice."

She knew.

Looking into those wide doe eyes with their feathery creases at the corners, I had no doubt that Mary Borah knew my secret.

"Why?" I whispered, feeling suddenly small.

Mary only cleared her throat and clasped her hands before her. "I suppose Billy has told you that we—I—made decisions in the early years of our marriage that resulted in our lack of children." Her eyes dropped briefly when she spoke, and I knew she was referring to her abortion. "This daughter of yours is a gift from God, Alice. For all of us."

I searched her face for any trace of trickery or malice, but found only an earnest sort of hope. Somehow, for some inexplicable reason, Mary had forgiven me, or had at least chosen to ignore my transgres-sion with her husband.

To see my daughter as a *gift*.

If cousin Eleanor was a saint, then Mary Borah was downright godly.

Standing in front of this simply dressed, dumpy woman, I wanted only to bolt. Yet I recalled Bill's expression of wonder when he'd first laid eyes on Paulina, and knew I couldn't deny him—or even Mary—this chance to watch his daughter grow up.

I cleared my throat. "I don't know what to say."

"Don't say anything. I'll make sure a place is set for you every Sunday for tea." Her command gave me a glimpse of a backbone I suspected Bill didn't even realize existed.

"Every Sunday for tea," I repeated, still dumbstruck. "We wouldn't miss it."

"Good." Mary's smile was utterly genuine, although I thought I detected a glimpse of sadness lurking behind her eyes. Paulina chose that moment to wake, gurgling softly and shaking indignant fists to let us know we'd neglected her long enough.

"Would you like to hold her?" I asked Mary.

Her fingers fluttered and she looked at Paulina with awe. "I'd like nothing more."

So Mary held Paulina, who quieted immediately, and we entered some sort of fragile truce.

I only hoped it would last.

All seemed well, that is, until Cissy Patterson surfaced again. It was impossible to count all the ways I loathed that woman.

I'd enjoyed not seeing much of Cissy in the year prior to Paulina's birth. After losing Nick's affections, she'd married a New York lawyer and taken to writing droll columns for the *New York Daily News* and William Randolph Hearst's papers. I steered clear of her poison pen, for after all, my former friend had already made me want to bleach my eyes on more than one occasion. No need to torture myself further.

I should have known something was amiss when Cissy mailed me a freshly printed blue hardcover novel titled *Glass Houses*, along with a note containing only a single handwritten line.

From the vindictive old shanty-Irish bitch.

The book was written under a pseudonym, but I gasped as I turned each page until finally I was cursing out loud. "That villainous half-faced piranha!"

Her characters were transparent facades easily identified as Cissy, Bill, and me, with the women fighting for the sordid affections of the powerful senator. Nick was mysteriously absent—I suspected because Cissy still cared for him—but she had taken the interlude in my library and expanded it into a full-blown, salacious novel. There was no doubt that this hateful book would rekindle all the gossip of my affair with Bill, which I supposed was Cissy's plan. Several times I hurled the book across the room before I finally refused to read any further. I cared not a snap of my fingers what anyone thought of me, but I *did* care what they thought of Paulina and Bill, nor did I want Nick finally putting two and two together.

This was echoes of Fräulein Kroebel, only I didn't need a white knight to come to my rescue this time, even if I had one willing to do the job.

"I'll confront her," Bill said as he slammed the book shut so hard that the sound reverberated off the tunnel's underground walls. Thankfully, we were the sole occupants in the wood-paneled trolley that hustled harried senators from their offices in the Russell building to the Capitol. "I never thought I'd be a proponent of burning books, but I'll make an exception for this one. Cissy too. She's a bona fide witch."

I was glad that we were alone in the trolley, as I didn't want Mary, or anyone else, to catch wind of our meeting or the novel. Fortunately, Bill's wife wasn't much of a reader, so there was a good chance she might not notice the brewing scandal, for a while at least. I was only thankful there were no character sketches of her between the pages, as I'd come to genuinely admire Mary Borah. "This is scurrilous gossip." Bill hit the heel of his palm against the cursed book with more force than was necessary. "What in God's name was she thinking?"

"That she'd get attention? That this will make Nick leave me and crawl back to her? Cissy's mind has always been murky at best." I held up my hands as the trolley came to a stop. "Don't worry though; I have a plan."

"A plan?"

I nodded as Bill handed me out of the trolley car. "Cissy lost both you *and* Nick. Now I'm going to do my best to make sure she leaves us the hell alone."

"For the record, Cissy never had me." Bill waggled a stern finger at me and I laughed, feeling for the briefest of moments like this was old times. "What, pray tell, is this plan of yours?"

"You'll see," I said. "Just trust me."

I courted the papers more than ever in the weeks that followed, so my name far overshadowed the release of Cissy's scandal rag. Yet this time I made sure it wasn't my evening gowns that the reporters cared about, or my latest escapades.

Instead, I scheduled a flurry of press interviews that presented to the country a new, more politically minded Alice, one who wielded power over the Speaker of the House in the hopes that the reporters would see me as being cut from the same political cloth as my father instead of just a convenient topic for gossip columns.

I was on the cover of *Time* in February of 1927 shortly before Paulina turned two, and the *New Yorker* couldn't stop singing my praises.

As one of Washington's most influential women, a night at Mrs. Longworth's dinner table is more sought after than an invitation to the White House. She is the smartest Roosevelt still alive, and just like her father.

I took out a lifetime subscription to the *New Yorker* after that.

I'd expected the scandal over Cissy's tell-all to fade away, but instead, her poison pen only became more vitriolic, insinuating via her newspaper columns that I'd use my charms to influence a certain powerful chair of the Senate Foreign Relations Committee. I worried more and more that Nick would question me about Bill, although my friendship with Mary and our continued Sunday dinners provided a sturdy smokescreen to hide behind.

In the midst of all that, I almost laughed aloud to find that my name was being bandied about as a contender for the vice presidency in the 1928 election, at the same time that both Nick's and Bill's names came up for the presidency.

I was flattered and interested for about five seconds. Then I came to my senses.

"Can you believe this? I'd rather be a trapeze artist in Barnum and Bailey's than be vice president," I told Nick in the kitchen one June evening, the scent of peonies wafting in through the window. I worried every day that he'd confront me about Cissy's columns, but he'd just returned from a weekend in Aiken, South Carolina. (Golf, he'd claimed, which was code for spending time with one of his established mistresses, Laura Curtis.) Now he was home and had rolled up his sleeves to try his hand at baking with Paulina, meaning that every counter—and the floor—was covered in drifts of flour and sugar. She and Nick wore matching red-and-white-gingham aprons, although they'd forgone traditional mixing bowls in lieu of more unconventional cooking methods. "The thought of giving all those campaign speeches makes me want to break out in hives."

As did opening the newspaper every morning these days. For nestled between reports of a stock market transformed into a golden calf giving triple cream was bound to be another of Cissy's columns.

"You and I make a pretty pair," Nick said as he allowed Paulina to make a powdered sugar pie atop his bald head. "I have a horror of the presidential bee; it's ruined too many good men."

"Really? I recall a young congressman wooing me with talk of taking the White House one day."

"Better that I content myself as Speaker and Kitz's daddy." Nick swung Kitz—his nickname for Paulina—around and blew raspberries on her cheeks amid a sugar snowstorm. She, of course, laughed uproariously, and he looked at her as he always had, as if she was a small miracle.

I felt a pang of guilt as I wondered where Bill was at that moment, whether he and Mary were enjoying a quiet evening at home, while his daughter giggled and played across town. Cissy's accusations were laughable, for these days Bill and I only saw each other on our shared Sunday afternoons under Mary's watchful eyes.

"Well, I won't run either," I said to Nick.

"It's a deal. By the way, Alice . . ." Nick didn't glance my way as he set Paulina on the floor when her nanny came to get her ready for bed. "While I was in Aiken, I saw the columns Cissy Patterson has been writing about you."

Batten down the hatches, old girl. Here comes the storm of the century . . .

But Nick didn't demand that I explain myself, only brushed the powdered sugar off his head. "I called and told her if she wrote about you again, I'd sue her for libel."

And that was that. Just as he had so many years ago with Fräulein Kroebel's slander, Nick stood by me, no questions asked. Our marriage had been far from perfect, but at the end of the day Nick was my white knight, my most loyal and trusting friend.

The sort of friend I wanted to strangle every once in a while, but nonetheless . . .

"Thank you," I said. "Gagging Cissy Patterson may be the most thoughtful gift you've ever given me."

"If only I'd known that when I was plying you with taffy and violin sonatas." He winked. "I'd have trussed up Cissy in heartbeat."

I batted my eyelashes at Nick. "No wonder you're so popular with the ladies."

Nick blinked, for that was the first time I'd made light of his philandering. He shook his head slowly and kissed me on the cheek, his lips lingering on my hairline. "I don't deserve you, Alice. But I'm thankful that you chose me all those years ago."

I laughed. "Don't go giving yourself airs. We chose each other."

"Indeed we did," he said as Paulina ran into the room in her gingham nightgown, brown curls bouncing and chubby arms outstretched for him to toss her in the air. Suddenly, Cissy's columns seemed terribly unimportant. "I'd do it all again if given the chance."

"So would I," I murmured, watching Nick play rough-and-tumble with Paulina just as my father had once done with all of us children. "So would I."

Chapter 20

Plummeting stocks.

Fortunes evaporated.

Crushing unemployment.

Hoovervilles and the Dust Bowl.

Breadlines and soup kitchens.

Starvation and suicide.

The Great Depression shrouded America in black as thick as mourning. While our accounts had taken a hit during the financial crisis, thanks to Nick's careful investments we were still afloat while others floundered. I even heard rumor that Maggie Cassini, whom I rarely thought of since she'd long ago married and relocated to Florence, had to close her ready-made dress business. Still, there was little happiness to be had, as if we'd all been tried and found wanting. Even politics, my old friend, abandoned us.

The 1930 midterm election saw Nick lose his position as Speaker of the House, for America was fed up with Hoover and replaced enough Republicans with untried Democrats to switch the majority.

Bill narrowly kept his seat and all his committees, but in the face of America's suffering he took a sharp turn into shadowland, writing to me from Idaho.

Dearest Alice,

I find myself afraid for myself and yearn to talk to you of politics. We face
so many threats from within, but I think also from without. Germany,
too, is mired in a deep depression and I worry that they'll soon drag the
rest of the world into yet another war.

Thank you for the recent letter from Paulina. It cheered me greatly,
and I'm impressed to see her handwriting has already surpassed her
mother's.

Hello,
Bill

I smiled, for he was right about Paulina. Our almost six-year-old
darling had surpassed my dreadful penmanship and was learning
how to read. Despite the horrors of this new decade, it was nothing
short of magic to witness her grasping the keys to whole new worlds
of knowledge and imagination as she sounded out words during story
time each night before bed.

She was a girl after my own heart and Nick's, too, as he studiously
chaperoned her to every French lesson and piano practice. Whereas
I delighted in Paulina's newfound reading, Nick reveled in her musi-
cal talent, often calling for impromptu concerts in our parlor where I
was the single—yet extremely enthusiastic—audience member. Paulina, always eager to please her father, would have played all night if
he'd let her.

"Kitz and I are great pals," he hollered as he lifted her giggling
onto his shoulders to commence an imaginary bear hunt one night,
the oil lamps flickering to conserve electricity. He reached up to tickle
her and she shrieked with laughter. I knew I should probably protest
the unladylike play, but I recalled my father's letters about how Ted's
and Quentin's enthusiasm for playing bear never flagged even though
one of them would inevitably be injured. I wished Father had lived to
meet my daughter, to romp with her as he had with Ethel's children.

Paulina and Nick had my blessing to rough-and-tumble for a year of Mondays. In fact, Nick had confided that his one consolation in having to relinquish his Speaker's gavel was that he might be able to spend all his spare time with Paulina before she was grown up.

"Faster, Daddy!" she called and they galumphed off in search of the ever-elusive Arctic polar bear.

It was bittersweet to watch Nick address the Seventy-First Congress from the Speaker's rostrum for the final time. He'd woken that morning with a head cold, but now he grinned as both sides of the aisle gave him a standing ovation. This was Nick's true gift, that he loved his friends and found something to love even in his enemies, so that everyone found him a gregarious and lighthearted leader. Even I, once his most dedicated enemy, now cheered wildly as his staunchest supporter. I lost count of the number of cabinet officers, senators, representatives, capitol messengers, and even scrubwomen who filed forward to shake his hand after the applause died down.

For this was Nick Longworth, the man who knew all the milkmen in Washington by their first names. My husband had served his country well and he'd continue to do so in Congress, even if he was no longer Speaker of the House. And I was proud of him.

Nick was in good spirits until the end of his farewell luncheon, once his colleagues had filed out at the conclusion of an impromptu piano concert and the reporters had departed to type their articles about his legacy.

"I think I'll head down to Aiken to play golf for a few days," he said to me, his eyes tight with pain as he rubbed his temples. The hair there, like the little bit left around his crown, was tilting from gray to white. At sixty-one, he sometimes used his gold-handled walking stick in earnest now, instead of for show. "And try to shake this head cold."

Aiken meant a visit with Laura Curtis, who was famous for her wringing wet parties, but I liked her and couldn't begrudge Nick a good time with his mistress after he'd been forced to give up the Speaker's gavel. Not only that, but Bill and Mary were due back to Washington in a few days; perhaps Bill and I might arrange a rare interlude while Nick was gone.

"Try not to have too much fun." I leaned on tiptoes and kissed Nick's cheek. "Tell Laura I said hello."

Nick was gone a week when the telegram came during tea with Mary Borah and Paulina.

Merry hell, but I'd learned to loathe those yellow slips of paper.

I set down my teacup after reading the terse message, no longer hearing Mary and Paulina debate whether kittens or puppies were the ideal pet. Paulina was drawing an orange cat with oil pastels to demonstrate her vote, the tip of her tongue pinned between her lips in concentration.

"Paulina, darling." I was careful to keep my voice level. "Mother has to go to South Carolina to see Daddy. That means you get to go to Rookwood. You'll be fine on the train with your nanny, yes?"

Paulina nodded as she added whiskers to her masterpiece. She protested when I hugged and kissed her, hard.

"Is everything all right?" Mary asked, but fell silent when I shot a meaningful glance at Paulina and motioned for her governess's attention.

"Nick's cold has turned to pneumonia," I answered once the nanny had shuffled Paulina from the parlor. "It must be serious for Laura to have asked for me."

Mary paused long enough to murmur a brief prayer for Nick. "Let Billy and me know if there's anything we can do."

"You're a dear friend, Mary," I said, but my mind was already hundreds of miles away in South Carolina. Surely Nick would be playing the violin when I arrived, hale and hearty from his week spent playing golf.

Still, I caught the first train to Aiken and brought along a nurse from Georgetown University Hospital, just in case. When I arrived at the Curtises' winter home, a graceful old colonial mansion set back amid flowering magnolia trees, it was to find a whole hive of doctors and nurses already there. And Nick in a desperate condition.

"We've kept the situation quiet." Laura wrung her long pianist's fingers. "The doctors agree it's quite serious, what with Nick's years of drinking and all the burdens of the last years as Speaker."

"I'll send a statement to the press that it's pneumonia." I'd also have to telegram Paulina's governess to keep the news quiet to avoid frightening my daughter. "It will mean dealing with hordes of newspapermen on your front lawn, but this *is* the former Speaker of the House."

"I know," Laura said. Her lip trembled and I might have offered her words of comfort, but right now I needed to see Nick.

I'd experienced much already in life, but I'd never stared death straight in the face. I hadn't been present when Quentin or Father or even my grandparents had died. Yet when I walked into the guest room, I sensed that was about to change.

Gone was the dashing young bachelor who'd rolled up his sleeves to whip up a midnight batch of almond pudding, and even the father who'd gone on bear hunts with his daughter. Nick was unrecognizable, his ravaged body dwarfed by the great four-poster bed. His chest rose and fell with an awful gasping sound, eyes closed and his skin a terrible, unnatural hue.

"Is he comfortable?" I whispered to the nearest doctor at hand, one with a pug face and matching pug eyes who introduced himself as Dr. Wilds. His expression told me the prognosis was grim.

"He's holding on," he said. "He's been asking for you, Mrs. Longworth."

"How long?"

"I fear the crisis will be reached within the next twenty-four hours."

The crisis? Why couldn't physicians speak plainly?

Nick was going to die.

I swayed on my feet, then somehow forced steel into my spine. There was much to do, and plenty of time to grieve later.

I could do this, if only because I had no choice.

The doctors and nurses filed from the room so I might have a moment alone with my husband. I recoiled at first when I touched Nick's hand, unnaturally clammy and hot at the same time, but then his eyes fluttered open.

"Alice," he rasped out, the cords of his neck straining as he struggled—and failed—to sit up. "You came."

"Of course." I settled down next to him and pretended to be put off. "You could have fetched me here with a far less dramatic scene."

"I finally managed to match you"—he interrupted himself by wheezing—"for theatrics."

"Oh, Nick." I bit my lip, hard, so I'd have a new pain to focus on. "I don't suppose it would do any good for me to order you out of this bed?"

He shook his head, his eyes sad. "Would that I could, Bubbie."

Bubbie.

It had been ages since he'd called me that. We'd celebrated our twenty-fifth wedding anniversary just last year, surrounded by a sea of friends and family. I'd resurrected a yellow satin dress with brilliants on the waist I'd worn on the Far East trip and teased my hair into its old pompadour, amused at what an illusion it gave of twenty-five years earlier. Surely our time wasn't up so soon?

"You can't leave Paulina or me," I said, blinking back the stinging in my eyes. "You just can't."

It was low of me to use our daughter to keep him tethered to this life and I knew it, but I couldn't imagine life without Nick any more than I could imagine a childhood without my father. Nick had driven me to distraction more times than I could count, but he'd been a constant for almost three decades, one of my greatest allies.

"I think of Kitz all the time. You gave me a great gift when you gave me her." He reached for my hands, an effort that cost him dearly. His voice grew suddenly soft. "I need your forgiveness, Alice. Please."

"Forgiveness?" I couldn't imagine what he was getting at, and worried that perhaps he was losing lucidity. Yet, despite his obvious pain, his eyes were clear as ever. "For what?"

"For stealing her." His breath rattled in his chest. "From you and Bill."

I drew a sharp inhale. "What are you talking about?"

"I know that Bill is Kitz's father."

It took a long moment to make sense of his words, to reassemble the world as its very plates shifted in front of me.

"You knew?" I finally whispered.

His eyes sought mine. "Since the moment you told me. I'm no fool, you know, although I put on a good act." He rubbed the skin between my thumb and forefinger. "But I'm her father too."

"You knew she was Bill's?" I stood, suddenly needing to move. "And you don't hate me?"

Even as I said it, part of me wanted to hate *him* for the lie I'd lived these many years, but that wasn't fair, not as the enormity of this truth finally unfolded in my lap. Nick had been as greedy as I'd been, thirsty for happiness and a family to share it with.

And we *had* been happy together with Paulina.

He coughed, the sound phlegmy and painful while I waited help-lessly for his answer. "Never," he finally said. "I could never, ever hate you."

"Or Bill?"

"When he gave me Kitz and brought back your smile?" He paused to catch his breath. "No, Alice. I only ever wanted you to be happy."

Despite all the debauches and all the women, I knew he spoke the truth. Nick was what he was, and although it had taken me years to understand that, I accepted it now just as he had accepted me.

And my daughter. *Our* daughter.

He reached for me for what I knew was the last time, and I clung to his hand like a drowning woman. "Tell Paulina I love her."

He closed his eyes, suddenly struck by a storm of coughing so that the doctors pushed into the room again. "Our apologies, Mrs. Long-worth," one said while the other pressed his stethoscope to Nick's chest.

I wanted them to leave so I might linger by Nick's bedside. But that was selfish.

If Nick had taught me anything, it was that I must be generous. I backed out of the room, my eyes lingering on his gray face and his body racked with pain.

Keep moving. Hold the blackbirds at bay.

"Send a telegram to Alice Dows," I told Laura, for she was Nick's other long-term mistress. I thought of Mary Borah's many kindnesses toward me; surely I could emulate her in this moment so Nick might have all the women he loved at his side. "And contact Nick's sister Clara. I think she's in North Africa somewhere, but her household can pass along the message."

Laura gave a mute nod. Yet another reason I'd always approved of her; she was levelheaded and reasonable, even as her lover died in the room next door.

"He should have violin music," I said. "Do you have any recordings?"

She shook her head. "I'll send a maid out for some."

Together we held hands and some small shred of hope, until the doctors emerged stone-faced. Laura clutched hard at my palm and I squeezed back.

"I'm sorry, Mrs. Longworth," the pug-faced doctor said. "But the Speaker has slipped into a coma."

Keep moving.

"Nick's baggage must be packed up," I said to a waiting servant. "Ship it via motorcar to the train station, and then we'll take it to Cincinnati." Five minutes passed, then ten, and twenty. I shivered to watch the truck rumble through the gates to the rear door to pile Nick's trunks and bags and hatboxes inside, the accoutrements of a successful man who'd enjoyed easy living to his final days. The press already milled about on the lawn, cameras and notepads ready as they waited in the dark for word about Nick's condition.

Alice Dows arrived shortly after dawn with tear-swollen eyes and took up her place at Nick's bedside, along with an oxygen tent sent directly to Aiken, a gift from Cissy Patterson.

"Too little, too late," I muttered. I could afford to be magnanimous to Nick's mistresses, but I drew the line at Cissy Patterson.

President Hoover sent a message too; now that the news of the coma had broken, there was an outpouring of messages from his fellow politicians and constituents, and rallying cries from the lawn for Nick to overcome this illness. I shut the doors and windows, unable to take it.

Finally, as the nurses were sent home, I called Ethel.

"Oh, Alice," my sister said after I informed her in a monotone voice of the situation, still surprised at my own fortitude. "What can I do?"

"Can you go to Paulina?" I asked. "She's at Rookwood. She can't hear about this from anyone but me."

"You mean . . ."

"There's no hope." The words tasted of ash.

"Of course I'll go," Ethel said on the other end of the line. "And I'll ring everyone. You just be with him."

"Thank you, Ethel."

I sat with Nick all that morning, flanked by Laura and Alice Dows. Hastily purchased violin music played on a scratchy gramophone dug out from Laura's attic. Every few minutes she would get up and replace the needle at the start to keep the silence from suffocating us.

I hoped Nick could hear the music, that his last awareness was a thing of beauty that he'd held so close to his heart.

One moment Nick was still with us, and the next . . . he was gone.

At 10:49 a.m., Dr. Wilds went to the window and raised his hand in one slow gesture to the waiting newspapermen, a signal to the world that Nick had slipped away.

Looking around the spacious room with its thick carpet that muffled every sound and hearing his well-dressed mistresses sniffling into their lace handkerchiefs, I realized that my husband had passed in a mansion surrounded by luxury, where sport and laughter and ease reigned, mourned by the women he'd loved. All that was missing was the sound of ice tinkling in Waterford goblets and a bottle of Dom Perignon being poured.

"Right." I swiped at my eyes as I stood. In my mind I heard a door being slammed. I was a widow now, and nothing would ever be the same.

Keep moving.

First things first. I had to bury my husband.

Yet one thought brought me to my knees as my world crashed down upon me.

How on earth was I going to tell Paulina her father was gone?

I donned widow's black and directed plans for the funeral in Ohio, which would be held in two days' time. Wreaths were placed on our train engine at every stop, and we slowed for groups of silent citizens who gathered along the way to pay their respects.

I remained stoic through it all, until a message was delivered in Union, South Carolina, that threatened to undo me.

A message not for me, but for Paulina.

Dear Miss Longworth,

The three thousand school children of Union by rising vote today expressed their sincere sympathy for you in your sorrow in losing your pal.

Her *pal.*

I choked on the sudden wave of tears, the twist of scalding pain in my lungs. Right now my daughter was playing at Rookwood, unaware that she would never go on another bear hunt with her beloved pal. I'd asked Ethel only to tell Paulina that Nick was ill. The whey-blooded weakling in me wished that Ethel had told her the truth when we arrived in Cincinnati.

Goddamn it, but a mother should never have to break her own child's heart.

"Mommy!" Paulina cried and launched herself into my arms on the platform, her hair gathered into two braids tied with somber black ribbons. I was grateful to my sister that there were no reporters on hand to capture the image of Paulina reaching for me while Nick's luggage was unloaded amid the engine's billowing gray smoke. "Where's Daddy?" She glanced at the train car. "Is he better now?"

Ethel's expression urged me to be strong, but the words I'd planned to say bunched in my mouth like a woolen rag. Instead I moved to block Paulina's view of the coffin as my brothers directed its removal from the car. "No, dear," I said. "He's still ill."

It had been almost three days since I'd slept and now Ethel shot me a worried glance as I swayed on my feet with the knowledge that I had to find a way to tell Paulina the truth. "I'm here for you, Alice," my sister whispered, her arm braced around my shoulders. "We're all here for you, and for Paulina."

It took me until the next day to gather my courage, while Nick's casket was briefly opened for a private family viewing in Rookwood's parlor. Paulina would stay home with her governess during the funeral, but no matter how much I wished to avoid it, I couldn't deny her this last opportunity to say good-bye to her father.

For Nick *had* been her father.

"Paulina." I knelt beside her in Nick's study—studiously avoiding looking at his violin where it sat forlorn and abandoned on its stand—and drew a deep breath. She was wearing a new black velvet dress and patent leather shoes hastily purchased for the occasion. "Daddy's in the parlor."

Her eyes widened, so loving and trusting. "He is?" She ran to Nick's desk and withdrew a slightly rumpled paper from the top drawer before bringing it to me. "I drew him a picture." She smoothed the paper, a smiling bald man and his brown-haired daughter on one side, and on the other . . .

I traced the misshapen white creature, its sharp teeth carefully drawn in with crayon. The question lodged in my throat and my eyes stung. "Is that a polar bear?"

She nodded proudly. "We're hunting it."

Of course you are.

She craned her neck to look past me. "Can I see Father now?"

How to explain to a six-year-old innocent that her father was in the next room, while he was also gone forever? That he could never look at her drawings or listen to her play piano again?

"Of course," I said, leading her into the parlor where Nick's casket lay waiting. The entire family was there, Mother sitting with Ethel while both dabbed their eyes. The room fell silent as we entered, but I halted Paulina at the door. "There's something you have to understand, Paulina. Daddy's spirit has gone away, and we won't see him again after today. Do you understand?"

Paulina cocked her head at me, like a curious little bird. "But I can see him now? And give him my picture?"

"You can, Kitz," I said, keeping alive Nick's pet name as I hugged her fiercely. "But he looks like he's sleeping, all right?"

Her little hands patted my back, as if she was the one consoling me. "I promise I won't wake him up."

God above, but how am I going to endure this day?

Paulina was too short to see over the raised casket, so I held her while she said good-bye, bolstered by Mother's and Ethel's gentle hands on my shoulders. My heart fractured into a hundred thousand pieces when Paulina leaned over to touch his head and I remembered the time she'd used it as a plate for powdered-sugar pies. "Good night, Daddy," she murmured, placing the picture on his chest. "I love you."

There was no stopping the tears then.

Archie and Kermit served as pallbearers, carrying Nick's coffin to its resting place in the Spring Grove Cemetery, to a plot beneath the limbs of a gnarled oak tree covered with spreading ivy near the center of the Longworth plot. I might have requested national honors for my husband, but I knew Nick had wanted to be buried here, among his family.

Instead, the Capitol had made the trek west to pay homage to its beloved former Speaker.

I smiled weakly to see President Hoover mingling with Republicans and Democrats—all party ties obliterated in honor of their leader and friend—while strains of Mozart's *Violin Concerto No. 1* and

Hayden's "Adeste Fideles" played in the background. I supposed it was inevitable that violin music would forever bring back memories of Nick serenading me in his shirtsleeves on board the *Siberia*, or playing a duet of "Twinkle, Twinkle, Little Star" in the parlor with Paulina.

Only two weeks later, his coffin barely closed, a reporter called to ask whether I'd considered running for Nick's open seat in the House. Appalled, I refused, and now I held the day's newspaper above a roaring fire.

"How you'd have laughed at this," I said to a photograph of Nick sitting on the mantel. He didn't answer, only stared ahead into eternity, his eyes smiling as they always had.

MRS. LONGWORTH URGED FOR VICE PRESIDENT: It is certain that President Hoover and Governor Franklin D. Roosevelt of New York will be the presidential nominees, and the Roosevelt name should be on the Republican ticket, too, through Mrs. Longworth . . .

I threw the paper into the fire and watched the words burn.

"I'm so sorry, Alice. Truly I am." Bill spoke in a hushed voice, his gaze never leaving Paulina, who was idly drawing on a sketchbook at the library window seat. Every other room in our Dupont Circle town house was crammed with vases of half-wilted Easter lilies so that their sickly scent of condolence chased me no matter where I went. I worried for Paulina, for she'd become silent and withdrawn since our return to Washington, as if she'd finally realized that the days of cooking and bear hunts and impromptu concerts were lost forever.

The house echoed without Nick, as if he'd held up the four walls with the force of his dash-fire and good cheer. I found myself longing for the sounds of his laughter and violin music, for the way things were. Yet none of us could go back to those days.

Why was it we never appreciated what we had until it was gone?

Bill cleared his throat, bringing me back to the present. "He knew the truth all this time?"

I only nodded, the pain still fresh. "He knew his faults," I said. "And accepted them in others."

"So what does this mean?" Bill asked, his attention finally on me. "For us?"

I rubbed my temples. "For us?"

Bill cocked his head toward our daughter. I knew what he asked, for Bill had allowed Nick to assume his role all these years, all for Paulina's sake. Now the world was topsy-turvy, the rules being rewritten. For once, though, I didn't have the desire or energy to break any rules.

"Paulina," I said. "Please go practice your piano in the parlor."

She ducked her head and abandoned her sketchbook, hair hiding her face as she wended her way disconsolately across the hall. I waited until I heard the morose notes being plucked out; since Nick's death she'd lost interest in her instruments, too, but I still forced her to practice in the hope that her delight in music would return.

"Paulina is fragile right now, Bill," I said. "She's scarcely strung two words together since we've returned to Washington and cries herself to sleep most nights. I won't burden a six-year-old who just lost a parent with the knowledge that he wasn't her father after all."

Bill's brow furrowed, and the sadness that flashed deep in his eyes made me wince. "I would never suggest that we denigrate Nick's memory. Only that I'd like to be a bigger part of her life, if I can."

I held up a hand. "I know. Perhaps one day she'll be ready for the truth, but not today."

He gave a tight nod.

"Come for dinner on Friday," I said as a peace offering. "Bring Mary, too, if you'd like."

For we still had tea with Mary most Sundays. Surely, Friday dinners with all four of us wouldn't cause too many tongues to wag.

"I'll see you Friday then," he said, before standing and kissing me on the cheek.

I listened to him bid farewell to Paulina. She merely slowed her lackluster playing; I couldn't tell whether she bothered to say good-bye. Probably not, considering how little she spoke these days.

I'd have to remind her of her manners. Later, perhaps, when I wasn't so tired.

When you're at the end of your rope, Sissy, you tie a knot and hold on.

As a distraction, I picked up the guide for modern single women that Ruth had recently sent me, with a note attached that read, *When you're ready for a laugh.*

"A laugh wouldn't go amiss right now," I muttered as I lit a cigarette.

A woman who lives alone should retain a healthy spirit of defiance, I read, *take up a hobby—become a communist, stamp collector, anything to avoid becoming dull—and always have breakfast in bed.*

I already had plenty of hobbies—no communism necessary—and I preferred coffee to breakfast. But a spirit of defiance was a mandate I could rally behind.

Keep moving.

Nick was gone, but business in Washington continued as it always had and always would. Despite the pressure from the GOP and the press, I refused to use my husband's coffin as a springboard to launch my own political career and instead threw myself into the election of 1932.

Unfortunately, this year's choices were appalling: Herbert Hoover again for the Republicans, or worse, old Feather Duster, who I'd once believed would become a long-winded lawyer.

I'd always wanted another Roosevelt in the White House. Just not *that* Roosevelt.

I didn't care what his last name was; it still rankled me that many Americans mistook Franklin for one of my brothers. All the Oyster Bay Roosevelt women took up the cause against him—it was our right considering that Eleanor had destroyed Ted's political career before it began—starting with a garden party hosted by the White House.

I wasn't so much for Hoover as against Franklin and Eleanor, in a nasty way. Yet that didn't mean I swooned in rapture for Hoover either.

"A Hoover vacuum is more exciting than the president," I muttered to Ethel during the garden party, smoothing my black-and-white dress worn to symbolize the two irreconcilable sides of our family. "Of course, it's electric, so it has that going for it. Whereas Herbert here . . ."

My sister laughed under her breath, careful not to draw Hoover's attention. "What sort of chance do you think Frank has against him?"

"None if I can help it," I muttered, trying to imagine polio-crippled, philandering Franklin and horse-faced, awkward Eleanor in the White House. I'd have had more luck imagining the pope in a back-alley cockfight. "I've an article coming out in *Ladies' Home Journal* that will lay everything on the line and clearly establish Franklin as our *fifth* cousin. Hopefully about to be removed."

Ethel raised an eyebrow. "I didn't know we had another writer in the family."

"'Speak softly and carry a big stick.'" I quoted one of Father's favorite maxims with a wry twist of my lips. "Since it would be frowned upon to bludgeon our cousins with a club, I'll use words to ruin them instead." So long as I didn't have to say them aloud on a stage, that was.

"Good," Ethel said with a rare bit of savagery. "Let them have it."

I published the article, the first of many. Which then led to my agreeing to speak on a live radio show.

So much for not saying them aloud. Stupid, stupid Alice.

"This was a horrible idea," I said to Ruth, moments before the broadcast went live from Cincinnati.

"It's a wonderful idea," she retorted as she adjusted my pearls. "Why, just yesterday you gave the longest political speech of your life."

"Ruth, it was thirty-one words."

"You always said you'd try anything once."

"Someone should have washed my mouth out with soap."

Still, despite my suddenly itchy hands, when the On Air light turned green, I let Franklin and the entire Democratic Party have it. I felt like I was chirping away in a tumbril, but my speech was highly acclaimed by the entire Republican Party. Yet in November 1932, despite my best efforts, cousin Franklin was elected to the highest office in the land.

I was so angry I could have ground my teeth into powder and blown them out my nose.

In an attempt to cheer Paulina, I took her to the White House on Hoover's last day, but I couldn't persuade her to speak or to play the piano, and it was grim to see the Hoovers sitting on their sofa like stiff and bruised waxworks. I imagined the celebration we'd be having if it were Ted coming into the White House instead of my turncoat cousins.

I vowed then to become Washington's gadfly in chief, always buzzing in Frank's and Eleo's ears, and daring them to swat at me. While I waited for Paulina to heal, this would be the new torch I took up.

Eleanor invited me to a White House reception shortly after her mollycoddle husband abandoned sound economic principles by moving the entire country off the gold standard. I accepted her invitation and came to the reception in a blue velvet gown, draped in every karat of gold I owned: a green-gold Chiriqui Indian frog pendant, white-gold bracelet watch, amber-golden hair combs, and huge gold eardrops shaped like horns of plenty. I rarely wore jewelry—save my Cuban pearls—but I was making a statement.

"If FDR could take you to the treasury and deposit you, the deficit would turn to a surplus," joked one guest while in Franklin's hearing.

I wiggled my ears as I lit a cigarette, making my earrings dangle and jump. "What I have on is a mere drop in the bucket to what my cousin is costing the country. Isn't that right, Frank?"

Whereas we'd once danced and laughed together, now Franklin only glared from his chair as if I were a veritable Brutus. I heard him whisper to Eleanor a moment later, "I don't want anything to do with that woman!"

I only smiled as I sidled past, flicking my black cigarette holder as I had in the days with Maggie Cassini and Cissy Patterson. "Remember, Frank, that you and Eleanor started this game with that teapot stunt. It's too late for you to back out now."

Poor Feather Duster's strategy was to ignore my very existence while Eleanor attempted to drown me in kindness. "You should really bring Paulina to play with her cousins at the White House," she said as Franklin turned his back to me as if I hadn't called them out on their sabotage.

Silly Eleanor. It will take far more than that to kill this gadfly.

It might have done Paulina good to play with her cousins, even if they *were* on the wrong side of the family. But to accept the invitation would have been a betrayal of Ted and all my principles. Eleanor might not have understood family loyalty, but I did.

So I only shrugged. "I'm sure we have better things to do."

A bolt of pain lit her face, but I pushed my guilt down deep. After all, Eleanor should thank me for teaching her to grow thicker skin, a trait she was going to need if she thought to survive the next four years in Washington.

And me.

"Mama." Paulina stood in the door, sleepy-eyed in a lavender nightgown as I tore another half-finished page from the typewriter and threw it to join its compatriots in the wastebasket. "Wh-what are you d-d-doing?"

I cringed at her stutter, a newfound consequence of Nick's death. When she had finally started speaking in earnest again, it was in these broken and fractured sentences.

"Writing about my life, sweet pea."

"For your b-b-b—for your book?"

"Yes, dear, for my book."

I ran my finger over the front page. *Crowded Hours*. The title was a secret salute to both my father's name for his campaign during the Spanish-American War and Bill's note to me before Paulina's birth. The economic downturn of the Great Depression and the savage estate taxes I'd had to pay after Nick's death meant it was a godsend when Scribner's had asked me to write my memoirs. Yet this was no vulgar tell-all like Cissy Patterson's novels: I refused to spill any salacious secrets about my own life, Nick's, Bill's, or Paulina's, nor did I mention my father's death for fear it would detonate the carefully constructed dam inside me.

"Which . . . which . . ."

"Which part?" Ruth and Ethel had both told me to stop completing Paulina's sentences, but I couldn't see how indulging such a shortcoming could possibly fix the problem. I'd never hit a blind lamb on the nose, but it was better to be clear and concise, to train Paulina to speak quickly. Perhaps then she'd have better luck making friends. Otherwise I feared she'd soon become the target of ridicule at school.

"The part where I met the empress dowager of China," I said. "Do you remember what she gave me?"

"Manchu," Paulina said, smiling and nudging her way onto my lap. "T-t-tell me."

So I let her climb into my lap and retold the story of receiving my beloved bundle of black fur. Then I kissed her atop her head. "To bed with you."

"Yes, M-mama. Love you."

I watched her pad back toward her room, my heart swollen with love and frustration. I'd do anything for Paulina, but I didn't know how to help her. Perhaps only time could heal her.

I finished my memoir—which became a bestseller—and then signed on for a syndicated column picked up by the *Washington Star*, the *Los Angeles Times*, and the *San Francisco Chronicle*, among others.

"Is no one safe from your pen?" Bill asked one day as we walked arm in arm through the veritable peace of Mason's Island. The former neglected and overgrown farmland was slated to be transformed into Theodore Roosevelt Island, replanted with wild trees and fitted with a colossal bronze statue of my father. As a northern mockingbird flitted from shrub to shrub, I felt as if my father himself had given his stamp of approval to the project.

"I happily skewer everyone I disagree with," I said. "Democrats, Republicans, and everyone in between. Someone needed to properly take up the Roosevelt mantle, and it may as well be me."

In fact, I wrote about the full gamut of newsworthy political issues from the rise of Hitler to Edward VIII's abdication in Britain to the way Franklin's New Deal programs resembled a pack of playing cards thrown helter-skelter. Readers responded well, and I especially relished a recent fan letter that said I was hitting them between the eyes just as my father had.

"You do tackle more controversial topics than Eleanor does in her column."

I snorted. "Watching grass grow is more interesting than reading *My Days*. Does anyone honestly care about Eleanor watching Frank swim in the White House pool or taking schoolchildren to the Smithsonian? America would be better served if Eleo retired as First Lady and instead became a Washington tour guide."

Bill chuckled and paused to straighten the collar of my wool jacket. "No one makes me laugh like you, Alice. I'll miss you and Paulina something fierce while you're gone."

"It's only for a couple of months. We'll be back before you know it."

"Do me a favor while you're abroad?"

"Anything."

"Try not to push Paulina too hard."

"Push her?"

"I worry that she takes after me. She's sensitive and I don't want her to fall into shadowland."

I bit my lip. "I feel like she's slipping further and further away, and there's nothing I can do to stop it. Did you know she asked the other day if she could go to boarding school?"

"She's growing up, Alice. That's what children do."

"Well, that's not allowed. She hasn't asked my permission."

"Yes, because you always asked your parents' permission for everything." Bill rolled his eyes. "Try to forget about politics while you're gone and just enjoy yourself, and Paulina. That's an order."

For I'd decided that perhaps the best thing for Paulina would be a trip to Europe for her tenth birthday. We'd avoid Italy and that brute Mussolini, and Germany, too, what with Hitler's seizure of power from the Reichstag, but I itched to show my daughter Big Ben and the Eiffel Tower.

"Do p-people go to the top?" she asked, gaping up at Paris's famous tower. I'd hoped that the trip would spark a shared love of traveling in Paulina while also soothing her irritating stutter, all to no avail. Instead, she'd asked every day since we'd arrived when we were going home, and continued to garble her words as if she had a sack of marbles in her mouth.

"They do indeed," I answered. "I'll go with you if you want."

She looked as if she was actually considering it, but then shook her head.

"It's time to face your fears, little one." I wrapped an arm around her shoulder and directed her to the elevator, ignoring her nervous protests. I'd survived the countless times Father had made me dive into Oyster Bay as a young girl; this was just what Paulina needed. A few moments later we had our tickets and were zooming up for a bird's-eye view of the City of Light.

It would have been glorious, the sharp wind taking our breath away and the Seine shimmering in the distance, had it not been for Paulina clinging to me as if she might faint dead away at any moment. We didn't even step out of the car at the top, for she only buried her face into my side. "N-no, Mama. Please, n-no."

I relented, and afterward, Paulina sat on the grass in the shade of the

Eiffel Tower, still ashen-faced and trembling. All around us, happy families picnicked and tossed bread crumbs to well-fed pigeons, but my daughter looked as if she'd just faced a firing squad.

"A few bites of chocolate croissant will cheer you up," I said, trying to cajole her back into good humor, but not even her favorite pastry managed to bring color to her cheeks. I crumbled the paper package into my fist; I loved my daughter to my very bones, but I honestly didn't know how to handle a child so unlike myself.

I was contemplating the best way to broach the topic when a young man across from us opened his newspaper, displaying a black shout of headline. My self-taught French was serviceable, but Paulina was fluent after years of private lessons.

"Darling." An acrid taste grew in the back of my throat as I nudged Paulina. "What does that say?"

She took a moment to read, then spoke in English the sentence I dreaded.

"*German Military Buildup Violates Treaty of Versailles, Luftwaffe Formed.*" Paulina looked at me with wide eyes. "What does that m-mean, Mother?"

I shuddered, remembering an earlier war with Germany that had cost my brother Quentin's life and, indirectly, my father's too. I hugged Paulina close, as if I suddenly couldn't hold her tight enough. "It means history is about to repeat itself."

In fact, soon my brothers, my family, and all of America would find ourselves repeating the most terrible of histories.

A second world war.

Chapter 21

JANUARY 1940

The world had thought the Great War was the war to end all wars.

The world was wrong.

First, Hitler annexed Austria and then the Sudetenland. Then, in September of 1939, he doused the whole world with gasoline and lit it on fire with his invasion of Poland.

I was firmly against America's involvement, for there was no doubt in my mind that if we joined, all my brothers—and even their children—would volunteer to fight in this second war. Fortunately, Bill was too old to enlist and his duties to the Senate would keep him home, but I couldn't countenance another heartbreak like Quentin's death.

Other people had no such qualms.

Franklin told the American people that he sought to keep us out of war, but then he waved the despicable Treaty of Versailles under Hitler's nose like a bombastic matador with a red flag. I suspected as I listened to Feather Duster's well-oiled sound bites on the radio each week that he secretly yearned for the opportunity to lead the country into war, for his chance at glory and the opportunity to outshine my father, whose face was currently being immortalized at Mount Rushmore.

You'll never outshine my father, Frank, I thought as my fingers flew over my typewriter keys. *Not so long as I draw breath.*

In January of 1940, I warned America via my column that, reminiscent of other dictators across the pond, Franklin would seek an unprecedented third term. And I listened from the Senate gallery as Bill railed against my cousin seizing businesses under the excuse of war emergencies. I stood and clapped when he finished, stomping my feet for emphasis.

His eyes sought me out and he grinned to find me, the same slow smile that I'd fallen in love with from this very gallery so long ago. The silver token of Saint Paul flashed in his palm, a reminder to keep fighting the good fight and also the signal that he'd come by to see Paulina tonight for our regular Friday dinners.

I never missed Bill's speeches. And he never missed a dinner.

But he didn't come the night after that Senate speech.

The next morning, the downstairs phone rang. The clock on my bedside table said it was only eleven o'clock, which meant the servants weren't in yet. I ignored the first few rings, but by the tenth I slipped into a dressing gown and hurried downstairs, the winter gloom casting everything in dreary shades of gray.

"Hello?" I said.

"It's Bill," said the voice on the other end, yet it wasn't Bill at all; it was Mary Borah, her typically singsong voice wrung out. Mary paused, as if gathering her strength, and then spoke the words that scraped my heart hollow. "He's had a brain hemorrhage. The doctors say there's no hope."

No. I shook my head violently, refusing to speak, refusing to let her words penetrate my mind. Surely I wouldn't have to relive this, not now, not after Quentin and Father and Nick. There was *always* hope.

But Bill was seventy-five years old.

Bill, my better angel, my intellectual twin who had saved me and gifted me with such happiness. Bill, who had given me my daughter and sacrificed his chance at being a father.

Bill . . .

"I'll be right there."

"No."

Such a simple word. Yet it was one I'd never heard pass Mary Borah's lips.

"What?"

"I've shared him all this time," she said quietly. "I won't share Billy now. I can't, Alice, and you can't ask it of me. You won't."

My world cracked beneath my feet like rotten floorboards. I'd always known Bill would go before me—he was nineteen years my senior, but so too had I always held the conviction that I'd be by his side when the time came. Now Mary was denying me that.

Mary, whom I'd sought to emulate when I'd asked Nick's mistresses to share my vigil at his side. Mary, who had never asked anything of me before tonight, nor all through the years I'd shared her husband.

"Then why did you call?" Pain streaked my voice, for suddenly this was worse even than Nick's passing. *I* was the love of Bill's life and I wasn't even allowed to say good-bye. Instead, I was the other woman. Common and tawdry.

"Because I thought you should know. That Paulina should know."

Paulina, who was about to lose the father she didn't know she had. And now it was too late to tell her. How could life be so cruel?

"I could come anyway." I threw my shoulders back to do battle, but slumped into the leather wingback at Mary's next words.

"You won't. The scandal died long ago, Alice. Don't revive it, for Paulina's sake, if not for mine."

Then the line went dead.

I didn't go to see Bill. Three days later, he was gone.

A tiny brown package arrived from Mary that same day, addressed to Paulina. Inside was his silver Saint Paul medallion. When I handed it to Paulina she only hugged me, then tucked it into her pocket. "He was a good friend to us, wasn't he?" she asked.

Friend. Lover. Companion. Father.

I nodded, choked by all the things I might have said. I could have told her the truth then—*should* have told her—but I couldn't steal a second father from her, not when losing the first had damaged her so irrevocably.

Oh, Bill . . .

I felt his absence deeply, every dark moment of every dark winter's day, and I regretted not stealing more happiness with him while he was alive. A gaping hole had been torn in the fabric of my world that nothing could mend.

No more late-night political arguments.

No more letters.

No more *hellos*.

My best friend and confidant, the father of my child, was gone.

Father, Nick, and now Bill.

One by one, my men had left me behind.

Fortunately, we women are made of strong stuff. And I had many women to lean on.

Once again it was Ruth who anchored me, sitting by my side during the state funeral in the Senate gallery where I'd so often watched Bill's fiery speeches, where she had once urged me to seize some small measure of happiness with him.

We *had* seized our happiness. So much happiness.

And in that happiness we'd made our daughter. Our precious Paulina, who wasn't at the funeral so her name didn't land in the gossip columns, and who was oblivious to the fact that her true father was lying in state on the Senate floor.

Bill's vacant desk was draped with a lily wreath and black crepe, and Mary Borah could be heard wailing down the hall, cloistered in a Senate antechamber as grief overcame her. I struggled to keep my composure, refusing to bleed in public.

I almost fell over when Eleanor entered the gallery during the reading of Paul's letter to the church in Rome and walked straight toward me, dressed in black. She only took my hand and clasped it to her heart.

"Bill Borah was a good man," she whispered. "He will be greatly missed."

I was shocked into silence as Eleanor stood beside me, and both she and Ruth took up the first bars of "Amazing Grace." I don't know how Eleanor had guessed the depth of my feelings for Bill. Perhaps some family member had let it slip or she'd discerned it for herself, but to this day I'm thankful that she understood.

Not long after, the bombs fell on Pearl Harbor, obliterating American battleships and aircraft and all my hopes of keeping what remained of my family safe.

"We are now in this war." Franklin's voice crackled through the walnut-paneled Philco radio that Paulina and I huddled around. "We are all in it—all the way. Every single man, woman, and child is a partner in the most tremendous undertaking of our American history."

I clicked the radio off, fear pooling in my belly as I stared hard at the photograph of my family on the White House lawn, wondering which of them I'd lose next.

Despite their disabilities from the first war, Ted and Archie both enlisted again. Hoping to keep one brother close, I was secretly thankful when Kermit was discharged from the British Army for a combination of alcoholism and a resurgence of the malaria he'd picked up while mapping the River of Doubt with Father, but then Franklin thwarted me again by agreeing to allow my brother to travel to Alaska and help protect the territory after the Japanese invaded its Aleutian Islands.

I was alone and adrift, constantly fearing the midnight trill of the telephone or the delivery of a Western Union telegram. Worse still, while lost in my own grief, I'd finally succumbed to Paulina's requests to attend boarding school. So I kicked the tent pegs until dawn in my empty, echoing house, alternating between reading every book I owned and writing Paulina letters she never answered.

"She's becoming a young woman," Ruth said one night after I'd begged her to come over to keep me company. "She's just learning to stand on her own two feet. Wait until Christmas and she'll come around. You'll see."

So I had the house decorated for Christmas, although with war rationing it was difficult to get everything I wanted to make the holiday memorable. There would be no glazed ham, but I'd saved up my ration coupons for a chicken and ordered a lovely dress for Paulina made from the silk Empress Cixi had given me eons ago. Pine garlands Mother sent from the trees of Oyster Bay were draped over every surface that would hold them, stockings were hung on both fireplaces, and a Douglas fir filled the parlor with its heady scent. The boxes of ornaments awaited Paulina's return—it was tradition that we'd string popcorn and decorate the tree together while singing Christmas carols.

Yet, when Paulina arrived, bundled from head to toe and her nose red from the cold, she didn't even glance at me or the tree before stomping upstairs, her boots leaving a messy trail of dirty snow. My new chauffeur, Turner, only shrugged when I asked what was the matter.

"She seemed fine in the limo, but then I don't know much about teenaged girls." He bent to set down her luggage, his hands dark against the pale leather. I'd recently purchased a beautiful new Packard limousine, and while I could drive it myself, I'd engaged Turner's services to guarantee built-in conversation. I glared overhead as I heard Paulina's door slam; my daughter's rudeness to me was disobedience that would be dealt with, but rudeness to Turner, who fully appreciated the beauty of a fifty-four-horsepower engine and always knew when all the best boxing prizefights were being held, was inexcusable.

"Thank you, Turner. Take the rest of the day off if you'd like. I'll drive if Paulina or I need to go somewhere."

"Thank you, Mrs. L," he said, doffing his hat at me. "But you be careful out there. This snow is piling up fast."

I smoothed my hair and prepared for battle as I walked upstairs, somehow feeling as if I were readying to defeat my younger self on the other side of my daughter's door.

I tried the handle only to discover it was locked. "Paulina, open the door."

No response.

"Paulina." It was the tone that meant business.

"I don't even want to be here." Paulina's voice boiled over with so much anger that I was taken aback. What had happened to my demure mouse of a daughter who skittered away at the sight of her own shadow? "And I certainly don't want to talk to you. Not now, not ever!"

Merry hell. What had gotten into her?

I crossed my arms over my chest. "Paulina, if you won't come out, it's a simple matter to call the fire department and have them break through your window."

Angry footsteps pounded on the other side before she flung the door open, still in her gray school uniform and dark eyes flashing. "Why don't you call the press, too, while you're at it! You've had them—and everyone else—wrapped around your little finger all your life. You managed to cavort about under everyone's noses and they lapped up all your lies!"

I didn't recognize this harridan that had replaced my silent wraith of a daughter, but it was obvious that some sort of festering, poisonous anger had transformed her into someone I no longer knew.

"What in Lucifer's reach are you talking about?" I asked.

Paulina whirled upon me, her face red and tear-splotched. "I know about you and Bill Borah! I know that he's my father and that you lied to me all these years!"

Her words cut me open, exposing my scarred and still-beating heart. The stillness grew bigger and bigger until I thought my eardrums might burst from it.

"Paulina—" I started, but she cut me off.

"Don't you dare dissemble and shove me aside as you've always done." Her fingers twitched into impotent fists while tears spilled from the corners of her eyes. "You lied to me! I heard you tell my governess the truth before I went to school!"

Oy vey. I truly was a miserable excuse for a mother.

It was shortly after Bill's death and I'd been going through a scrap-book of memories, including some of the headlines that hinted at Paulina's true parentage. The governess had laughed about the press's insinuations that Bill was Paulina's father, but I'd only shrugged as she'd walked away, feeling more than a bit sorry for myself. "Not in-sinuations this time," I'd said, wanting to give Bill his due out loud, just that once. It seemed a terrible travesty that no one could acknowl-edge Bill's most lasting legacy: his daughter.

The very same daughter who was now falling to pieces before me and was justified in loathing me until the end of her days.

"All these years," Paulina said, choking on her rage, "you let me believe that Nick Longworth was my father! We loved you, and you betrayed us both! Did you lie to him too? And what about Mary Bo-rah? Is there anyone you haven't tainted with your lies?"

In all the times I'd rehearsed this scene in my head, I'd envisioned myself apologetic, sympathetic, understanding. Never before had I been trembling with fury, for although I was the one in the wrong, sunspots of anger exploded within me at her tone.

I stepped so close that Paulina instinctively moved back. "Paulina Longworth, I am your mother and you will not speak to me in that manner. I have only ever done what I thought best for you. I lied to you, yes, but so did everyone else, for your own sake. Nick knew the truth, but he loved you as I loved you. So did Bill, and Mary, too, for that matter. We all loved you and wanted only your happiness."

Paulina stepped back with her hands up as if I might somehow con-taminate her. "I won't stay in this house another moment with you."

"Oh? And where will you go?"

"Back to school."

"We're Roosevelts, Paulina," I said. "We never concede, and we certainly don't run from our problems."

She turned and threw herself on her bed, face buried in her pillow. "As if I could ever run away from the likes of you."

I wanted to scream, to rage at her until she saw reason, but instead forced myself to walk out of the room even as my legs trembled. Surely Paulina would come to her senses and see reason, if only I gave her the time and space to do so?

It turned out I knew my daughter even less than I thought.

That Christmas was the bleakest I could remember, with Paulina only deigning to leave the sanctuary of her room for meals without so much as an acknowledgment of my existence. After that, I allowed her to return to school before New Year's so she might think rationally and realize that everything I'd done had been for her own good.

"I love you, Paulina," I said as I placed a package of her favorite cookies on the seat beside her in the limo. Turner was going to drive her back to school without me; the thought of spending hours in confined quarters with only seething anger for conversation held little appeal. For any of us.

Paulina said nothing, only kept her eyes on the back of Turner's head even as I closed the door and watched him ease the Packard out of the driveway and onto the street.

First, Paulina. Then, one by one, my loved ones left me.

Kermit died the farthest from home, alone in Alaska's frozen wasteland. My poor broken brother put a gun to his head, a result of years of alcoholism and depression.

Then Ted. Dear, wonderful, brilliant Ted.

My favorite brother's heart gave out while he was resting in a converted sleeping truck captured from the Germans, one month after he helped liberate Utah Beach from the Nazis and one day before Eisenhower promoted him to major general. His posthumous congressional Medal of Honor was cold comfort for those of us who would never see his smile or hear his laugh again.

I realized as I stared numbly at Ted's empty casket during his somber stateside funeral that this was what it meant to grow old, to watch people I loved die as each passing day brought me another step toward my own grave. This goddamned war had only accelerated my losses.

Despite the letters and the gifts I sent, the funerals for my brothers that we attended together and the amends I tried to make, Paulina refused to forgive me. As the months turned to years, I insisted that she attend college—yet another thing we argued about—so she reluctantly enrolled at Vassar. I had high hopes for her scholastic achievements, but Ruth quickly disabused me of that.

"She's spending all her time with Alexander McCormick Sturm, a distant relative of mine," she told me over the phone. She'd rung me, so I knew this was serious.

"And you're going to tell me that he's deeply intelligent and charismatic? That he's incredibly kind to puppies and walks little old ladies across the street?"

Silence on the line. Then: "If I was feeling kind, I'd say he's passably good at playing polo for Yale," Ruth told me. "Although I'm not sure what else he's good for. Driving fast cars and charming the ladies?"

So he was my daughter's version of Nick Longworth.

I sighed, rubbed the bridge of my nose. "Thus does history repeat itself."

"Paulina can do better, but she's young. We all had flirtations at such a tender age."

Yes, but my flirtation had ended with a wedding ring on my finger and a tumultuous marriage. I had no wish to saddle Paulina with such a future, even if Nick and I had made it work.

"I wish you were here," I said to Ruth. "Perhaps between the two of us we could talk—or beat—some sense into her."

"Since when do young girls take advice from two old biddies?" Ruth laughed on the other end. "Sometimes you have to let them make their own mistakes, Alice. You'll always be there to help her pick up the pieces, right?"

"Of course," I said. "I'd crawl on my hands and knees through hell for that girl."

"Then let her live."

"Far be it from me to contradict my benevolent despot," I said. "Thank you, Ruth."

She only laughed at the old moniker. "Anytime, my dearest friend. Anytime."

Then, just after Paulina's nineteenth birthday, I received a call from Vassar.

"We regret to inform you that Paulina has been expelled," the chancellor said.

"What?" I set down my coffee mug. "How is that possible?"

"The infraction was an overdose of sleeping pills, which we believe was a failed suicide attempt. My apologies, Mrs. Longworth, but we cannot tolerate such behavior here at Vassar."

The words were so cold, so final.

I slipped into a dark shadowland and almost did myself real harm.

Had Paulina inherited Bill's dangerous streak of melancholia? Was Paulina still so upset over my deception that she'd thought to hurt herself?

Distraught, I had Turner drive me to pick her up, expecting to find my daughter tormented or hysterical. Instead, Paulina coolly denied their charge. "It was an accident, Mother," she said as she slid across the limo's leather seat, her ankles crossed demurely and her skirt perfectly pressed, as if I were picking her up for tea instead of expulsion and attempted suicide. "A simple misunderstanding."

"You've been expelled, Paulina. You almost *died.*"

She only shrugged. "You never went to college, and you lived to tell the tale. And I didn't die, so everything is fine."

What could I do? I accepted her repudiation, and when she asked if we could stop by the F Street Club for a luncheon a few days later, I accepted, for she hadn't invited me to anything since before she'd gone to boarding school. I held out hope against hope that she'd finally decided to forgive me.

Silly, silly Alice.

My mind ricocheted as she held fast to the stranger seated next to her, his suit even more immaculately tailored than the majority of the F Street members who were enjoying their aperitifs in the sitting room with us. Alexander Sturm had been waiting for us in the club, handsome in an indoor sort of way and perfectly at home among the club's many priceless antiques and faded portraits, except for the ridiculous beret atop his head. To my chagrin, I already detected in him a dangerous penchant for drinking, as the current tumbler of scotch in his hand and the pre-noon hour could attest to. But Paulina was blind to his faults, just as I'd been with Nick at her age. "I don't care what you think, Mother," Paulina said coldly. "Alex and I are getting married."

Now I understood why she'd asked to meet somewhere public, where she could avoid my causing a scene. For the briefest of moments I wondered, too, if she'd arranged her own expulsion from Vassar to clear the way for this announcement. Now she was hitching her star to the first man available, just as I'd done at her age.

I've lost her. Yet that didn't mean I wasn't still going to fight for her.

"Please excuse us a moment, Alexander," I said.

"If you wish, *Alice.*" His lazy drawl of my name made it apparent that he didn't care one whit for what I wished. I didn't like this impertinent little boy, not one bit.

"My dear Alexander," I said. "The truckman, the trashman, and policeman on the block may call me Alice, but you may call me Mrs. Longworth."

I half expected Paulina to follow him out into the hall, but she only sat across from me, aloof and untouchable. I wanted to shake some sense into her, even though I suspected a subtle approach would be more effective.

Unfortunately, subtlety had never been my strong suit.

"You're too young to get married." It was the flimsiest argument in my arsenal, but worth a try before I commandeered the heavy artillery.

Paulina brushed away an imaginary thread from her sleeve. "Only a few years younger than you were. Girls get married at nineteen all the time."

"How long have you known this boy you plan to spend the rest of your life with?"

"Long enough to know that he's not in awe of you, unlike the rest of the world. That he'll protect me from you."

I lurched back as if she'd slapped me. "To *protect* you? What sort of monster do you think I am?"

"The sort for whom I'll never be good enough, despite your own colossal shortcomings. The sort that lies to her own daughter for her entire life."

Her words torpedoed through my defenses, but I wasn't ready to abandon ship. Not yet.

"You barely know Alexander," I said, my words coming fast. "What are his vices? Does he gamble? Have other women on the side? Spend money like it grows on trees?"

"Alex doesn't do any of those things."

"No?" I arched an eyebrow. "Just how much scotch does Alex drink each day?"

Paulina fluttered her eyelids in disdain. "I don't know, and I don't care."

I threw up my hands in exasperation. "Of course you don't. And I'll bet you never thought to pay attention to that little detail, either, did you? Because I shielded you from your own father's addiction to the bottle!"

Now Paulina lifted her gaze to mine, but her eyes narrowed. "My father? I'm sorry, Mother, but I don't know to whom you're referring. Do you mean Nick Longworth? Or Bill Borah? Or is there yet another man I don't know about?"

Back to this. Nick and Mary Borah had forgiven me; I'd always assumed they would be the ones to hold me accountable for my mistake. I'd never have guessed my punishment would come at the hands of the daughter I'd tried so hard to protect.

My laugh was a sharp and unpleasant sound. "You're a child, Paulina, a petulant child who knows nothing of this world. Right now you're sitting in a club founded by Laura Curtis, a lovely woman who also happened to be one of your father's many mistresses." I continued blithely on, noting the shock that flashed deep in her eyes. "Didn't realize that, did you? All this time you've held me solely responsible for what you perceive to be the great tragedy of your life, but the truth is Nick Longworth cheated on me. *And I forgave him*, just as he forgave me."

Paulina gave a tiny shake of her head, as if she was incapable of digesting this new bit of information. "That doesn't change anything."

I sagged into the couch then, realizing I wouldn't budge her. Then I forced myself to sit straighter. "I fear that you're going to gain plenty of firsthand knowledge about life if you become Mrs. Sturm, and you're not going to enjoy much of it."

"I'll become Mrs. Sturm a hundred times over if it means getting away from you."

I heard myself in Paulina's threat, for forty years ago I'd leaped at the chance to marry Nick and escape my own overbearing parents. It had taken almost a decade for Father and me to stitch up our relationship. I didn't want to wait that long to have my daughter back.

I held my hands up in surrender. "Fine," I said. "You want my blessing? I'll give my blessing. When is the wedding?"

Paulina blinked. She obviously hadn't expected my acquiescence. "The sooner the better."

I recognized the Roosevelt stubbornness—*my* stubbornness—in her then. If I entrenched, there was no doubt I would learn the flavor of my daughter's wedding cake from the society columns.

"Fine." Not for the first time I found myself wishing that Nick or Bill were still at my side. Surely I deserved such a headstrong daughter after being such a terror to my own parents, but right now I wished I wasn't the sole member of my regiment. "You can wear my pearls."

Her expression softened, but she quickly schooled her features back into their frigid mask. "Thank you, Mother."

I closed my eyes as she rose to rejoin Alex. When I opened them it was to glimpse my daughter slipping her arm into Alexander's and letting him lead her out the door onto F Street, her heels clicking on the parquet floor with the sound of finality.

One month later, with Mother and Ethel at my side and two hundred guests at my back, I watched as Ted's son gave away my daughter. Paulina made a beautiful summer bride, dressed in elegant white satin with a Russian lace veil the Romanovs had sent me for my own wedding and my string of Cuban pearls at her slender throat. There was no denying that my daughter thought herself in love as she gazed up at Alexander while they repeated their vows.

But love was no guarantee of future happiness. I'd learned that the hard way.

After today, Paulina would leave Washington to settle in Connecticut near the Sturm family. She'd been gone before, first to boarding school and then to Vassar, but this felt like a door slamming shut. My heart cracked anew when her entire body stiffened as I hugged her before she left for her honeymoon.

"Good-bye, Paulina." I breathed in her scent and remembered holding her for the first time as a baby, soft and downy and filled with so much promise. Now she was all hard edges, the hope and softness leached out of her.

"Good-bye, Mother," she said, her face dead and remote as some distant star.

Then she was gone.

I've failed you, Paulina, I thought as I watched her go. *Failed to protect you, failed to make you happy, failed to keep you from repeating my same mistakes.*

I'd lost her. After losing so many others, I'd let my daughter slip away, had in fact pushed her away with my own two hands. And now I was alone.

So terribly, horribly alone.

The house on Dupont Circle echoed with my lonely footsteps and the whispers from so many ghosts. Everywhere I turned I saw Paulina and Nick, Bill, Ted, and even Father. My grief over Paulina was a raw wound on top of too many unhealed scars.

Is it any wonder I denounced Franklin and Eleanor when the presidential election ramped up only weeks after my daughter walked out of my life? My cousins were convenient scapegoats, punching bags for decades of pent-up grief and anger.

I said so many terrible, awful, contemptible things . . .

I'd rather vote for Hitler than vote Franklin in for another term.

The Republican Party hoped to elect a president and not retain a dictator.

A constitutional amendment limiting the number of presidential terms is long overdue.

FDR really stands for Fuehrer, Duce, Roosevelt.

When Franklin wants to punish America he puts his wife on the radio.

Eleanor is a Trojan mare afflicted with preachy saccharine do-goodism.

Detached malevolence became the armor to keep my grief at bay, especially when Ruth—my beloved benevolent despot—died from pancreatitis less than two months after Franklin was elected to an unprecedented fourth term. Drowning in an ever-expanding sea of grief, perhaps I might have curbed my tongue if only I'd known of Franklin's failing health. But I lashed out even harder, and he died of a massive stroke mere months before the war finally ended.

I wrote my condolences to Eleanor, hoping that she might one day find a way to forgive me. God knew I could scarcely forgive myself.

For so many things.

Chapter 22

NOVEMBER 1951

The lone bright spot in the years after the war was the birth of my granddaughter.

Joanna Mercedes Alessandra Sturm.

Was there ever so sweet a name?

With so few family members left—Mother had passed in her sleep in 1948 so only Ethel, Archie, and I remained—I wanted nothing more than to be close to Paulina and her daughter. Yet I was only allowed to see little Joanna for Christmas and Easter, and not a day more. I'd shown up for her most recent birthday with armloads of beribboned picture books and even the pink-and-green dollhouse Papa Lee had given me when I was a child, only to be informed by Alex that Paulina and Joanna weren't home. I felt like Sisyphus as their laughter rang out from the next room, doomed to push the boulder of my regret up a hill for all eternity.

Until another fateful day overshadowed by still another death.

"Mother?" My daughter's voice on the other end of the telephone was disjointed and frantic.

"Paulina?" I'd fallen asleep sometime around three in the morning with a dog-eared copy of *A Tale of Two Cities* on my chest. It fell to the floor like the thud of a grenade with its pin pulled. "Paulina, what's wrong?"

"Mother, he's dead. Oh, God, he's dead!"

I came fully awake despite the November predawn darkness, heart pounding in my ears. I made my voice as commanding as possible to slice through Paulina's panic. "Slow down and tell me what's going on."

"Alex . . . he's dead. Viral hepatitis." Her words were punctuated with wild hiccups and sobs. "I didn't know who else to call . . ."

My daughter had finally turned to me, which should have made me triumphant, but instead I felt only a deep well of despair. Paulina was too young to be a widow, and she had a small child to raise.

"Where are you?" Shrugging into a loose black housedress, in my mind I was already mapping the fastest route to Connecticut.

"At the hospital. It's been ten days and we thought we'd go home soon. But then . . ."

She broke off sobbing. I staggered, horrified that my daughter's husband had been ill for so long and she hadn't called until now. But she *had* called, and I'd rearrange the heavens to help her.

"I'll be there as soon as I can." I held the receiver between my shoulder and chin as I shoved my feet into a pair of black kitten heels. "Think of Joanna. You have a little girl who needs you."

Yet Paulina didn't seem to hear me. "Alex was only twenty-eight," she said between gasps. "What am I going to do?"

I'd have cut off my right arm to be able to give her an answer. I'd been widowed at forty-seven, which had been far too young, but Paulina was only twenty-six. If there was a God—which I doubted—I'd demand an explanation for this fresh tragedy when I met him. Right now, I had a daughter and granddaughter to care for.

"Go home and wait for me, Paulina. I'll help you through this. I swear it."

A phone call roused Turner from his bed, and soon we were winging our way to Connecticut in the Packard, driving so fast the street signs were blurs of black and white beneath the ugly dawn that bruised the horizon.

"Thank you, Turner," I said when we finally pulled into the drive. Paulina's house was a modest brick two-story set away from the street, but already its bare-limbed trees seemed to droop from the weight of the grief within. "I'll call you when I need to be picked up. I imagine it will be a few weeks at least."

"Of course, Mrs. L." Turner retrieved my bags from the trunk. "But ring if you need so much as a ride to the grocery store, you hear?"

"That would be a long drive for a loaf of bread."

His dark face was somber as he followed me up the walk. "You just say the word."

"You're a good man, Turner."

I knocked on Paulina's door. And knocked again.

"Paulina?" I tried to peer in the windows but couldn't see beyond the drawn green curtains. Paulina's car—a new Ford Victoria in an awful shade of turquoise—was parked outside, so I doubted she was still at the hospital. I pounded harder and tried the handle, then jumped back in surprise when the lock scraped and the door cracked open.

"Grammy?" Joanna looked up at me with eyes so like her mother's, her hair a mess of tangles and a pair of snakeskin cowgirl boots on her feet. "Did you come to help Mama?"

"Yes, sweetheart. Where is she?"

Joanna opened the door the rest of the way and took my bony hand in her tiny one. As we mounted the stairs to the second floor the stale air was replaced with a smell I remembered from ages ago, from my honeymoon and swaying train rides in Cuba.

Paulina lay passed out on her bed, eyes closed and skin clammy to the touch. An empty whiskey bottle lay overturned on the floor by her bed.

"Mama won't wake up," Joanna whispered. "I even tried shaking her."

With a horrorstruck gasp I pressed my fingertips to Paulina's neck to find a pulse, my cheek to her face to feel her breath.

She was still alive. But barely.

Still unconscious, my daughter made a terrible gurgling sound and vomited all over herself. I turned her head so she wouldn't asphyxiate herself, trying not to breathe as the acrid mess stained the bed's embroidered cherry quilt.

"What can I do, Mrs. L.?" Turner had followed me and stood at the door, the epitome of calm.

"I need a basin or a wastebasket," I said. "Anything."

Joanna tugged his sleeve. "There's one in the bathroom. I'll get it." What was left of my heart disintegrated at her stoic expression, for it seemed her mother had inherited the worst of both Bill's tendency toward depression and Nick's love of alcohol. But this was worse than either of them had ever been.

Far worse.

Joanna returned with a plastic garbage bin, which I placed on the floor near Paulina. With Turner's help I removed the fouled quilt, and the new Maytag washer roared to life a few moments later, the same time I felt a small hand slip into mine.

"Will Mama be all right?" Joanna asked.

"Yes, sweet pea. She will if I have anything to do with it." I guessed from Nick's episodes that Paulina would wake in a few hours with a sour stomach and a wicked headache, which I planned to make worse with a scalding lecture. Dead husband or no, Paulina could *not* do this to her daughter.

I pressed a fierce kiss onto Joanna's forehead. "Have you eaten yet?"

She shook her head, tangled brown curls brushing her cheeks. "I'm not hungry."

Of course she wasn't, not after her father died and her mother had done her best to follow him.

"Have you ever played War? It's a card game." A shake of the head. "I'll teach you. In fact, I'll treat you to a banana split at the soda fountain I saw on the way here if you can beat me."

Joanna's eyes lit up. "A banana split with whipped cream?"

"And sprinkles," I said. "I'm particularly fond of the rainbow kind."

"Me too. And a cherry on top."

"Good girl. There's a deck of cards in my gray bag. Go get them and I'll meet you in the parlor."

I had one last task while Joanna found the cards: emptying every bottle of wine, beer, and hard liquor I could find down the kitchen sink. Yet another echo of history repeating itself.

"Oh, Nick," I whispered as I poured out the last of it, staring at the kitchen ceiling as if for divine guidance. "What am I going to do? Bill, how in merry hell am I going to help her?"

I almost picked up the phone to call Mother or Ruth to hear their reassurances, but they were both gone, and Ethel had never dealt firsthand with this sort of problem outside of our brother Kermit. In another life I might have called Eleanor, whose own father had succumbed to his addiction to the bottle, but our relationship was too far gone for such confidences.

I was on my own.

So I settled down to play cards with Joanna, who trounced me solidly. "I declare W-A-R," she announced, laying down her cards before gleefully claiming the last of my pile. I laughed, but the angry lecture I was rehearsing for Paulina in my head made it difficult to fully enjoy myself. It was late evening when my daughter finally woke, just after I'd scrounged a makeshift meal of canned mushroom soup for Joanna from the empty cupboards. "God, Mother," Paulina snuffled into her sleeve after I'd fed her aspirin. "I'm so sorry."

For once I didn't have the heart to berate her, not as she sobbed a full ten minutes into my shoulder about Alex. But I refused to whitewash the issue.

"No more drinking," I said, placing in her lap a silver-framed charcoal sketch of Joanna as a baby from the mantel. I recognized my daughter's talent in the portrait; in fact, the house was full of her landscape drawings and still-life paintings, many of Joanna. My granddaughter, still flush with her first win at cards and a promise of a banana split after dinner, was entranced by an episode of *I Love Lucy* on the television in the next room. Occasionally her laughter would spill out into the hall, sweeter than birdsong on a spring day. "Promise me."

Paulina nodded, reminding me of a much younger version of herself, so eager to please everyone, especially her father. Despite my best intentions, I'd been a mediocre mother, but I was determined to put things right as best I could.

If Paulina would allow me.

"I'll stay as long as you need." I waited for her protest, but she only laid her head upon my lap.

"Thank you," she said. "I'll go to church in the morning, before I meet with the funeral home . . ."

She broke off into ragged sobs again and I held her, running my fingers through her hair. "Shhhh . . . ," I said. "Whatever happens, I'll help you through this. I'm here for you, Paulina."

And I would be. Come hell, high water, the damned Apocalypse, or anything else life could throw at us.

Paulina did go to church the next day. And the day after that. And almost every day after.

I was relieved that she seemed to be finding solace somewhere, while also frustrated that she'd once again withdrawn behind the protective walls she'd so studiously constructed.

Well, Rome wasn't built in a day and neither had it toppled in a day. I could be patient.

Paulina, it seemed, could not.

"You don't need to stay any longer," she said one morning only a week after Alex's funeral, her face drawn and pale. I was washing Joanna's dishes while Paulina sat at the breakfast table, a cup of tea cooling between her hands. "Joanna and I can manage on our own."

There was no hiding my dismay. "But I'd planned to stay at least a month, longer if necessary."

"There's no need." Paulina waved a hand. "We're moving back to Washington. Maybe to Georgetown."

My heart swelled at the prospect. Georgetown was hardly three miles from my own home on Embassy Row—close enough that I sometimes went there on my daily walks—but Paulina's dour expression tamped down my elation. Paulina had only Alex's family and me to help her now, and from the look of things she was choosing me, if only under duress. "Then I'll stay and help you pack."

"Don't bother," she said. "I'll hire movers." Then, as if an afterthought: "I'm going to convert to Catholicism. I thought you should know, if we're to be neighbors."

There hadn't been a Catholic in our family as far back as I could remember, but I'd always felt a person's religion, like sex, was their own business. So long as they didn't practice in the street and frighten the horses, it wasn't my place to judge. Paulina could have told me she planned to join a cult that spoke only in tongues and I wouldn't have cared, so long as she and Joanna truly moved to Georgetown. "I think that's fine, especially if you think it will bring you comfort."

"It will."

"And you'll be fine alone with Joanna until you move?"

"Yes, Mother. I promise not to lose control again."

I could only hope she meant that, and her behavior these past weeks made me optimistic.

And perhaps a little daring.

"You know, we could arrange weekly visits for Joanna and me once you've settled, to give you some free time once in a while." It was difficult to ask my daughter for something I wanted so badly. Every moment with Joanna was precious; just yesterday she'd persuaded another banana split from me when she'd won her first hand of Go Fish while dressed in pajamas and a miniature Stetson. (I'd thought of teaching her to play poker, but Paulina would probably have a conniption.) I couldn't bear the thought of regressing to only seeing her on the occasional holiday. Life was fleeting and childhoods more so. I wanted to drink up every spare moment with my granddaughter.

Paulina didn't stamp down the idea immediately, which I took as a good sign. "I'll think about it."

"I promise I won't spoil her." I grinned. "Not too much anyway."

"I said I'd think about it, Mother."

So I almost squealed like a girl on Christmas morning the first time Joanna *did* come stay with me, for an entire weekend. We spent hours building a secret hideaway on my fourth floor, complete with all manner of secret pillow nooks and blanket crannies. And I'd lied to Paulina, for I *did* spoil her, because that was my job as her grandmother, damn it.

"We are rebellious hedonists, Joanna," I said, lying on my bed and trying unsuccessfully to talk around a mouthful of sticky taffy.

"What's a hedonist, Grammy?"

"Someone who stays up far too late past her bedtime, gorges on books, and devours an entire sack of peppermint taffy."

Joanna upended the empty bag and shook it, then gave a dramatic sigh. "You're right," she said, stifling a yawn. "We *are* rebellious hedonists. Can I read *Horton Hears a Who!* again?"

I glanced at the clock; it was one o'clock in the morning. "Of course, my dear." I handed her the volume from the special revolving bookcase I kept by my bed. "In fact, I demand that you read until you fall asleep. That's when you have the best dreams, you know."

Her warm back pressed against mine was paradise on earth, especially as her breathing evened out into sleep, and I soon followed her into dreamland.

As the years passed, Joanna's choices in literature changed from Dr. Seuss to *Charlotte's Web* to *The Hobbit*, and I was tickled at her penchant for memorizing poetry as easily as other children recited nursery rhymes. My entire staff adored her visits, especially Turner, who kept the limo's glove compartment stuffed with peppermint taffy just for her.

I was determined that Joanna would grow up surrounded by love and also knowing the importance of her family, especially her great-grandfather.

So it was that Turner drove us to New York for the dedication of Sagamore Hill as a national historical site. No matter how I turned it over in my head, it still seemed odd that my childhood home was about to become a monument, a *museum*, to my father and my entire family.

Ethel was there to greet us as we rounded the drive, the daisy-strewn lawn already spotted with suited politicians and newspapermen and most of the town of Oyster Bay. Any other woman expecting the president of the United States—Eisenhower was due to arrive in just a few hours—might have been frazzled, but Ethel was the eye of the storm, just as Mother had been before her.

"I'm so glad you're here, Alice," she said to me. "Perhaps you can entertain some of the guests while we wait for Eisenhower. Tell them a story or two about Father, maybe about the teddy bear?" She turned to Joanna. "Have you heard that one, darling?"

She nodded. "Grammy told me. Did he really refuse to shoot that bear?"

Ethel laughed. "Indeed, but only because it was a poor, ragged thing the hunting guides had tied to a willow tree. Your great-grandfather enjoyed showing off whenever he had the chance. Just like your grandma here."

I beamed. "He'd have sent you home with at least a puppy and a kitten. Maybe a badger and a one-legged rooster too."

Joanna giggled. "I don't think Mama would like that."

"Probably not." I tweaked her nose as we headed toward the towering copper beech tree my family had planted almost sixty years prior, where a knot of well-dressed politicians waited in its shade. "But you never know. Sometimes your mama surprises even me."

Still, even as I chatted with senators and President Eisenhower after he arrived, I worried about Paulina, who was at the moment home with a recurring migraine. I wasn't quite convinced that she'd fully quit drinking, and she'd confided that she sometimes had trouble sleeping and often spent her nights in prayer, having followed through on her conversion to Catholicism. She'd been on her knees when I'd picked up Joanna, lips moving silently while her fingers slipped over well-worn rosary beads. Over the past months, I'd invited her to all manner of political events: my salons, Republican fund-raisers, and even today's dedication of Sagamore Hill. Paulina only ever waved me away.

I'd have done anything to heal her many wounds, but Ruth's advice rattled in my head, reminding me that Paulina would have to find her way in her own time.

I only wished she'd hurry up about it.

I was dressing for one of my salons late one afternoon, thoroughly looking forward to listening to—and perhaps baiting—rabble-rousers Richard Nixon and Joseph McCarthy among the crowd of politicians and statesmen I'd invited to my dinner table that evening. *We'll see who lasts the longest*, I thought gleefully as I slipped my arms into my blouse sleeves, *the vice president or the disgraced senator from Wisconsin.*

It was as I buttoned my blouse that I found it.

A lump in my breast.

Suddenly, my very existence narrowed into one mass of flesh, so that I could concentrate on nothing else. I canceled the salon and tried to distract myself with reading after I made a doctor's appointment for the following day, but the words scrambled into tangled knots of letters as I wondered whether this was the beginning of my end. A glance at a photo of Joanna on my bedside table only served as a reminder that life's precious moments were numbered.

The next day, an office radio down the Georgetown hospital's hall was broadcasting news about the Montgomery bus boycott when the physician delivered the verdict.

"A radical mastectomy," the doctor said. "I'm afraid it's the only solution, Mrs. Longworth. The good news is the cancer is only in one breast. We'll remove the tissue and a portion of the muscle beneath . . ."

The doctor droned on about the length of the surgery and the weeks of recovery I could anticipate. I could only think of all the walks I would miss, the visits with Joanna I'd have to skip. But this would be a—hopefully—very temporary setback.

I was seventy-three. I didn't have time for health issues, but I liked the alternative even less.

"Fine, fine," I said, interrupting the doctor's tirade. "Chop it off and let's be done with it."

Easy to be blasé when the only other alternative was to die.

I told no one of the cancer, not even Paulina. Only Turner knew, and that was because he had to drive me home after my release from the hospital.

And he *did* drive me home. Because I survived the surgery, just as I'd survived polio, two world wars, and countless family tragedies. I wasn't going to let a little cancer lick me.

So it was that a few days later I was recovering at home with a numb chest and a stiff arm, trying to grow accustomed to the flashes of phantom pain and the new lopsidedness of my body—now a stranger to me—when Turner knocked on my door.

"Mrs. L." He was hesitant as he dared to broach the threshold of my bedroom. I was dressed in a set of Chinese silk pajamas and had sent the nurse home after I refused to take any more pain medication since it was too damn difficult to get any reading done with my brain awash in opiates. I had a stack of books picked out for at least the next week and had purchased a miniature refrigerator to keep by my bedside, stocked with all manner of peach cake and Roy Rogers cookies for my late-night reading sprees.

"This better be important, Turner," I said churlishly, setting down an inscribed volume of Ezra Pound's poetry, a gift from the poet himself after I'd once visited him in his sanitarium.

"I'm sorry, Mrs. L," Turner said, then stepped out of the way. The last thing I expected was a uniformed police officer from Washington, DC, to fill my doorway. Standing behind the officer was ten-year-old Joanna, her eyes red and her face blotchy from crying.

"What's going on?" I struggled to sit up. "What's the meaning of this?"

The officer ignored me to kneel down next to Joanna. "You've been a brave girl today, Miss Sturm. You can wait outside if you'd like."

Joanna turned those huge eyes to me. "Can I sit with you, Grammy?"

Despite the pain and the sudden throbbing in my chest, I made a place for her next to me. Only when she was snuggled into my good side did the officer finally look at me. "Mrs. Longworth, I'm afraid your daughter's had an accident."

So many times I'd heard terrible news from the mouths of strangers.

My father's near assassination.

Quentin.

Archie.

Ted.

And now my own daughter.

". . . a fatal mix of alcohol and sleeping pills," the officer concluded. "It's being investigated as a suicide."

Was it possible to simply die of despair? Because in that moment I wanted nothing more than to die. Sometimes pain was worse than death.

I shook my head vehemently, unwilling—and unable—to believe in a world where Paulina no longer existed. But if it was true . . . still worse would be to believe that my daughter had taken her own life. That I could never endure.

Yet I recalled her expulsion from Vassar and wondered if perhaps the school had been right all this time. This was my brother Kermit all over again, only a million times more gut-wrenching as little Joanna burrowed into my side and wiped her eyes with her sleeve. Some accidents happen only when one is courting death, but still, I held fast to the belief that Paulina would never have abandoned her daughter like this.

Surely Paulina hadn't felt so hopeless and lonely as to kill herself.

I refused to believe it. For my own sanity, I *couldn't* believe it.

"Paulina would never do such a thing," I said to the officer. I found myself clutching Joanna, hard, and forced myself to relax. *Everything for her now, Alice.* Everything.

"Of course, Mrs. Longworth," he said kindly, if not exactly convinced. "You have my most sincere condolences."

Turner showed him out, leaving me alone with Joanna. My granddaughter, now an orphan, clung to me.

She had me. She would *always* have me.

"Grammy," she whispered. "Did Mother want to die?"

"No, darling. Surely not."

"But she took all those pills." Joanna pressed her head against my shoulder, staring at the wall. "She was still breathing when they took her away."

I swallowed the strangled cry that threatened to burst from my throat, envisioning the terrible scene, knowing it would forever be seared into Joanna's memory.

Oh, Paulina . . . What have you done?

"Your mother would never, *ever* have left you on purpose." I held Joanna tight as her hot tears soaked through my sleeve. "This was a terrible, awful accident. Do you understand?"

Joanna dragged a sleeve under her nose and nodded mutely, then laid her head in my lap like a broken rag doll. "Is that how your mother died?" she finally whispered. "In an accident?"

"Yes," I managed to say. "I was too young to know her except through other people's stories."

My instinct then was to bury my grief as I always had, to lock it away and never speak of it as I'd learned from my father. To withdraw even from Joanna, for to love meant to hurt, to grieve. But it was too late. I loved this little girl fiercely, and I owed her more than silence.

"You had ten years with your mother." The words threatened to choke me, but I refused to let them. "And I had thirty-two. Do you know what that means?"

Joanna shook her head, more tears falling.

"We have so very many memories of her. And we're going to share them all. We'll never stop talking about your mother, all right?"

Joanna nodded, even as her entire body shuddered with more silent sobs.

And I let her cry, my own tears freely mingling with hers.

One day, I would tell Joanna everything about her mother: how Paulina had played piano concerts in our parlor, stuck her tongue between her teeth while drawing masterpieces of kittens in oil pastels, and laughed her way through imaginary bear hunts with her father. All the things I'd wished my father had told me about my own mother.

We wouldn't talk today, but we *would* talk. Joanna would grow up knowing her mother, if only through pictures and stories. We'd touch the things she'd touched and turn the pages of her life together, her daughter and I, and together we would remember her.

That was one gift I could give them both.

Chapter 23

❧

Six months after Paulina's death, two letters sat on my desk, one a new arrival from Ethel and a second that was creased and well-worn after many months of rereading. My sister had kept up a steady stream of letters designed to distract me since Paulina's death, yet today's arrival was different in that it didn't skirt the tragedy, but aimed an arrow straight at its heart.

Dear Alice,

Are you yet able to listen to the wind and watch the shadows and love it at all? I am sure Joanna is busy and happy, which is good for grandparents. Are you yet able to sing on your charred limb? I keep thinking of you and your agony of spirit over what is past and gone—and I hope that is lessening. Such terrible blows take time to bud up the wound—it never heals of course. But some people's bandages seem wonderfully durable. Mine aren't, but I think yours might be.

Always yours,
Ethel

"Ha," I muttered under my breath. "I'm not durable; I only fool the world while I bleed out underneath."

"Who are you talking to, Grammy?"

"Just myself," I said to Joanna, who was curled on the window seat with Ted's old first-edition copy of *The Jungle Book*. She was dressed in her best frock and cowgirl boots, her hair tamed into two smooth braids. "It's the only time I get to enjoy an intelligent conversation. Except with you, of course."

Joanna winked and returned to her book, glancing up every so often as she kept a lookout on the street, and I stared back at Ethel's letter. There was no denying the limb I sat on *was* charred, but I refused to focus on the bleak landscape. Instead, I reserved my attention for the little bird who perched shivering on the limb next to me.

Except she wasn't shivering so much anymore. Why, she'd even laughed the other day at a joke Turner had told, a full peal of golden giggles that spread until both Turner and I were bent over with laughter.

Such simple joy. That was all I sought now in a life that had been fraught with complications for too long.

Before Ethel's letter had been another—the second on my desk—that had come from an unexpected quarter. It was written the very day after Paulina's death, with hothouse forget-me-nots pressed between its folded pages. I'd read its crisp sentences at least a hundred times so I had it memorized by now.

My dear Alice,

I am shocked that this great grief has come to you, and I am glad you have the small grandchild. If there is anything I can ever do for you, please let me know.

   With my deepest sympathy.

                              Affectionately,
                              Eleanor

In the aftermath of Paulina's death, I'd taken custody of Joanna and moved her into the loft of my house on Dupont Circle. Together we would live as free spirits together, for despite the sixty-four years of difference between us, Joanna and I were kindred souls.

Still, a ten-year-old girl couldn't number her white-haired grammy as her only friend. It had taken me months to gather my courage to answer Eleanor's letter. In the end I only managed it because of Joanna.

Dear Eleanor,

For months after Paulina died, whenever I tried to write I simply crumpled. I do hope you understand, because I want you to know how touched I was by your thoughts, the spring blossoms on your letter. Joanna is with me now. We leave soon for a ranch in Wyoming. Perhaps sometime when you are in town you would let me know and we could have a "family" moment together. I should so much like to have Joanna know you, and for me it would be a pleasure.

Affectionately,
Alice

And Eleanor, rather than slamming that door in my face as she'd have been justified in doing, graciously promised to bring her grand-children to visit.

Today.

"Grammy," Joanna said, shutting *The Jungle Book*. "They're here!"

The doorbell rang and Turner's footsteps sounded across the wooden floor downstairs. He'd asked to stay today so as to meet my legendary cousin, and I listened with suddenly itching hands as they exchanged pleasantries. I stood and brushed imaginary lint from my sleeves. "I suppose there's no putting this off any longer."

I offered Joanna my hand and together we walked down the stairs. I bit my lip; the Dupont Circle house might seem shabby to Eleanor after the splendors of the White House, for I hadn't had the rugs and upholstery replaced in ages, so some were frayed as to be hanging together by mere threads. Yet, a huge Flemish tapestry that had once been in the White House still hung on the wall, along with the grand piano Paulina had once played, covered with a tumbledown of yellowing scrapbooks and sheet music and bits of memorabilia. In a life filled with so much change, I liked to keep some memories close at hand. "Be on your best behavior, remember?" I whispered to Joanna as we reached the landing.

It had been years since I'd seen Eleo in the flesh; the woman standing in my hall had grown stout and jowly, whereas I seemed to thin out more every year. Yet her smile as she shook Joanna's outstretched hand was as wide as ever, as if she'd finally grown into it.

"I'm so very pleased to make your acquaintance," Eleanor said after introducing the army of well-dressed young cousins who all seemed to share Eleanor's formidable teeth. "You look very much like your mother. She was a good, sweet girl."

"Thank you," Joanna said. I was proud of the way she looked Eleanor in the eyes instead of averting her gaze as most children would. They spoke for a moment about our upcoming trip to Wyoming— Joanna was an avid horsewoman and could chatter for hours about tack, horses' withers, and the like, a fact that would have made Bill proud had he lived to meet his granddaughter. I could see that she wanted very much to go play with the other children who waited by the door, and was reminded of all the lazy summers Eleanor and I had spent together at Sagamore Hill, our swimming lessons with Father and late nights out giggling under the stars.

"Run along and show your cousins to your loft," I said to Joanna. "I'll have some éclairs sent up."

She was almost to the stairs before she ran back to give me a peck on the cheek. Then she was off, the herd of little feet pounding on the stairs overhead growing fainter as they all climbed giggling to the fourth floor.

"She seems a dear girl," Eleanor said as she took a cup of Earl Grey tea from the tray and added one sugar cube. My own porcelain cup was full of its usual piping black coffee. "I'm so glad of the chance to meet her, and to finally sit down with you."

"It's been a long time," I said.

"Too long. I wish I'd known the havoc I was wreaking when I made that damnable singing teapot."

How had I ever thought Eleanor a drab wallflower? She'd charged right into the heart of our age-old quarrel before she'd even had the first sip of her tea. Her years as First Lady and ambassador to the United Nations had refined the steel in her backbone that she'd first made known during Ted's bid for the governor's mansion.

"You'd have done it all again, and rightfully so." I gave a chuff of laughter. "That stunt paved the way for Franklin to become governor and then president."

She echoed my laugh. "You're probably right."

My gaze fell on a family portrait of my siblings and me with Father on the White House lawn, his stern expression admonishing me even now. I sighed. "I should never have compared Franklin to Hitler. That was below the belt, even for me."

"God, how Frank raged about that!" Eleanor sipped her tea. "But your quips always caused us to reflect on our actions. I used to pester the hell out of Franklin about labor, welfare, and all manner of issues; it was good to have someone keeping us both in line."

And just like that, we were each of us forgiven. Suddenly, all those years spent at each other's throats seemed a terrible waste. "I think we could have had a lot of fun," I said. "If only the damn old presidency hadn't come between us."

Eleanor gave a wry smile, showing off those awkward teeth of hers. "At least we can look back and laugh at it all now."

"One of the few gifts of being in our dotage."

She raised her cup in salute, her hand spotted and gnarled with age. When on earth *had* we become such old gray mares? "Hear, hear."

We chatted while the children played upstairs, reminiscing over old times and talking about Eleanor's current work in the United Nations and who we thought might run for president in the new decade.

(I hoped for Nixon, she preferred some Democratic junior senator named John F. Kennedy whom no one had ever heard of.)

Finally, when the lazy afternoon sun had started to sink toward the horizon, Eleanor lingered on my doorstep, her gaze straying to where Joanna waited in the hall beneath the ratty skin of a Siberian tiger that Father had shot eons ago, her apple cheeks flushed from playing a rousing game of tag with her cousins.

"You've saved that darling girl," Eleanor murmured to me as she poked me in the ribs. "Bully for you, Alice. And Joanna too."

"She's my second chance," I answered. "I'd face a firing squad for her."

"And you're *her* second chance," Eleanor said. "I think you two will get along just fine."

I was reminded of Ethel's letter as I waved good-bye to my cousin from my front steps.

Yes, the branch I sat on *was* charred, but I refused to let the black-birds of shadowland turn my world bleak and bitter. Voltaire had once mused that life is a shipwreck, but that we must not forget to sing in the lifeboats. Well, I would sing on my charred limb with this scrap of a girl at my side, loudly and probably terribly out of tune, until my dying breath.

And I loved her all the more for it.

Chapter 24

AUGUST 1965

I should always have been a grandmother, never a mother.

Joanna went to school each day and spent her afternoons doing algebra homework and riding horses with Ruth McCormick's grown daughters before Turner picked her up. Our trip to Wyoming became an annual ranch vacation, even after I broke my foot when thrown by one particularly cantankerous horse. And this year, at the ripe old age of eighty-one, I had taken Joanna to the Far East during a summer break from college, starting in Honolulu before retracing the path to China and Japan that the congressional junket had taken almost six decades prior. Everywhere were ghosts: Nick, Willard Straight, Uncle Will, and even Manchu. Nick had said once when we danced in the Philippines that we should return when we were old and gray to see how things had changed.

Things *had* changed, it was true, but even more so, *I* had changed.

This time I was more impressed with the monkeys in Japan than the emperor, for I'd met enough stuffy heads of state in my lifetime. The trip was a riot of pleasures, and I was up before dawn, for at my age I knew I wouldn't return to these countries again.

"You're a fire horse dropped into a harness." Joanna yawned in her traditional futon bed one morning in Japan. "What have you done with my grammy? She never cracks an eyelid before noon."

"It's better that we run the risk of wearing out rather than rusting out." The adage was something Father had once said, although I couldn't remember exactly where or when. Memories were like that these days; I still had my marbles, more or less anyway, but sometimes they did rattle around my skull in the most unorganized manner.

Joanna covered her head with her pillow. "I hardly consider sleeping past dawn to be rusting out."

"You don't sleep when you travel." A kimonoed maid nudged open the sliding door and padded in thonged socks across the tatami mats of our room before placing a lacquered breakfast tray on the low table. "It's a rule. I want to see every monument, temple, and cherry tree I can possibly squeeze into the schedule."

Joanna peered out and filched a rice ball from the tray as the maid bowed and padded back out. "You might have warned me of that before I agreed to traipse to the far corners of the globe with you."

"Ah, but then I might have only had Cat to bring with me," I said, for I'd recently purchased a haughty Siamese to keep me company while Joanna was off at college. His every gesture was a small reproof, and I adored him all the more for it, yet cats made for terrible traveling companions.

Joanna scoffed. "Cat would never follow your orders."

I lifted my bony shoulders in a shrug. "I'm a powder-puff sort of general. Not at all like Don John of Austria."

"'Don John laughing in the brave beard curled,'" Joanna plunged right into the middle of Chesterton's poem "Lepanto," one of our many shared favorites. "'Spurning of his stirrups like the thrones of all the world . . .'"

I picked up where she left off, reminded of cozy evenings at Sagamore Hill when Father and my siblings had whiled away the after-dinner hours in the library by reciting poetry. "'Holding his head up for a flag of all the free.'" We both raised our fists like triumphant soldiers to finish in unison. "'Love-light of Spain—hurrah!'"

I grinned. I supposed Eleanor was right; we *had* saved each other.

I'd sworn I'd sing on my branch for Joanna, and I had. And I'd continue until I drew my last breath. But I wasn't ready for that, not by a long shot.

As I entered my ninth decade I was surprised that people still clamored for me to lend my influence to their myriad causes. I'd never been one for causes—except perhaps my father's—and wasn't about to start now.

Still, I took it for granted when presidents and political hopefuls sought out my salons and the chance to be seen with the *other* Washington Monument, as the press had dubbed me. I thoroughly enjoyed that moniker, perhaps even more than when they'd called me Princess Alice. I had been heartily sad to see Nixon defeated in 1960, but my sadness was short-lived, for I enjoyed the entire riotous Kennedy clan, especially Jackie, who dressed in elegant clothes designed by Oleg Cassini—Maggie Cassini's mustachioed son—and invited me to the White House for cello concerts and historical lectures.

During one of their highbrow seminars meant to stimulate great thoughts, I listened to noted historian Elting Morison disseminate on my father's life. It was odd to realize that my father's entire presidency was considered *history* now. "Not so," I muttered under my breath, feeling a bit malicious as Morison made a false claim about my father and committed the further sin of calling him *Teddy*, which my father had always hated. "Not so."

From her place next to me, Jackie poked my leg and gave me a mischievous smile, looking resplendent as usual with her chestnut hair swept up and diamonds glittering at her throat. "You know, you should be giving this talk, Mrs. Longworth," she murmured in that soft voice of hers. "I can kick Morison off the podium if you'd like."

To which I only chuckled. "Ack, let the little man feel important."

I liked the Kennedys very much, but of course, that didn't mean I'd vote for them. After all, they *were* Democrats.

I missed cousin Eleanor then, for she and I might have had some real humdinger conversations regarding all the bright-eyed political hopefuls. But Eleanor had died from tuberculosis some years back—hard to remember how many as the decades were a hodgepodge now. President Kennedy had ordered all American flags lowered to half-staff in her honor, and he earned several more official Alice approval points when he signed a bill dedicating a congressional office building in Nick's name, now officially the Longworth House Office Building.

Like the rest of America, I was devastated when he was assassinated among the great rancid masses in Texas, even more so for poor Jackie and their young children. I immediately took up my pen to write her with my heartfelt condolences, and wished I could rescue her after Bobby Kennedy, too, was gunned down.

So I met with the former First Lady one wintry afternoon in 1969, scarcely a year after Bobby's death. Jackie had invited me to her childhood home of Merrywood for lunch, which I accepted, hoping I might be able to bring some levity to her life, if only for a little bit.

But Jackie might have been a Minoan frieze, so stiff and numb compared to her usual smiling and graceful self, as if the life had been leached from her after enduring so many tragedies, despite her recent marriage to shipping magnate Aristotle Onassis. It was a feeling I understood after seeing so many of my own loved ones to their graves. However, she perked up when her children ran into the well-appointed sitting room, dressed in woolen coats and mittens while clutching the necessary accoutrements for building a snowman.

"You can stop pretending, Jackie," I chided gently after the little ones had pounded outside, giggling gleefully when their mother had produced a scarf for their project. "It's just you and me, and I'm well-acquainted with how uncomfortable that mask you're wearing can be."

She gave a weak smile. "One must not let oneself be overwhelmed by sadness. Right?"

Her words said one thing, her eyes another.

So I dared to sit beside her on the sofa, and wrapped an arm briefly around her shoulder. "You're wise beyond your years. And I'll swear on whatever altar you want that those two moppets of yours will make this life worth living. Take it from someone who knows."

"You're right." She still looked pale beneath her stylish mink hat, but her eyes held a fresh sparkle, which I took as a good sign. "Of course you're right."

"At my age, I very often am," I said, reaching into my handbag and retrieving two Lucky Strikes from my ancient silver cigarette holder. We lit up together, relaxing as only two widows could. "And one thing I know for certain: we women have to go on with the business of living, even after our men abandon us."

After all, I'd learned that lesson firsthand.

Following the tumult of Paulina's death and the maelstrom that was politics in the 1960s, it would have been far easier to sit home reading every night or writing checks to my favorite environmental organizations, but after all, I *was* Washington's *other* Monument.

If I let the dust gather, I'd soon find myself reduced to the stuff.

So I trotted up to New York in 1966 for Truman Capote's famed black-and-white masquerade ball to rub elbows with Frank Sinatra, Claudette Colbert, and Lauren Bacall. The guests had spent enough on their costumes to finance several third world countries for the year, but I showed them all up with my dime-store black mask, its only accent the elastic band that held it in place. I laughed and smoked and posed for pictures, just like the old days.

And returned to Washington to a house with its front door hanging ajar from its hinges.

"Hello?" I called as I entered, for I'd let the staff off while I'd been gone.

Inside, vases had been overturned, books pulled from shelves, and chaos reigned supreme. I cursed my idiocy as I hurried from one ransacked room to the next, for Capote's guest list had been published, so the thief had known he'd be able to take his time ransacking my valuables.

I riffled through my jewelry box as Turner called the police, but the diamond bracelet from Kaiser Wilhelm, a gold necklace from Empress Cixi, and so many more priceless pieces from days long past . . . they were all gone.

My hand fluttered to the Cuban pearls at my neck—I rarely took them off these days—and I heaved a sigh of relief as my fingers lit upon the one treasure in the jewelry box that mattered. Discarded in the corner was the simple golden locket that I'd once loaned to my brother Ted, less impressive at first glance than the rest of my glittering jewels.

And inside the locket, the precious clip of my father's hair.

Things didn't matter, but memories did. And holding that little piece of Father brought back so many memories.

The illustrated letters he sent me while I was on the Far East junket.

Him adjusting my wedding train before he walked me down the aisle to Nick.

Both of us revising his speeches for the campaign of 1912, laughing over steaming tubs of coffee.

The thief could keep the rest of the shiny trinkets and baubles, but I'd have hunted the criminal to the ends of the earth if he'd made off with this treasure.

Still, just to be safe, I planted poison ivy outside my house after that, to ensure that no one else tried to make off with my memories.

I wanted an outrageous old age, but my body refused to cooperate.

First came the emphysema—a lifetime of smoking finally caught up with me, I suppose—and then the cancer returned, this time in the other breast.

At eighty-six I might have let it get the better of me, but I'd never been a quitter. So I'd signed the release forms for my second mastectomy and shown up to be butchered again.

Given the choice, I'd have preferred a sudden heart attack in the Senate audience gallery to this mundane death by surgery.

I squinted in vain against the garish hospital lights, the walls a phosphorescent white that blurred painfully into the nurses' sterile uniforms. Perhaps even something as dull as dying warm in my own bed would have sufficed. But the villainies of age continued, and I found myself instead subjected to the injustice of a scratchy hospital gown and the impending threat of a scalpel.

"Are you comfortable, ma'am?"

I waved away the nurse's inane question with a hand so spotted and gnarled it might have belonged to a Pharaonic mummy. Sometimes I scarcely recognized the white-haired biddy I'd become. Where was the hedonistic hellion who smoked foul-smelling cigarettes on the roof of the White House, feted mustachioed German princes and an iron-fisted Chinese empress, and inspired the rage for the color Alice Blue in the spring of 1902?

"I'm fine," I lied to the nurse. "After all, I'm about to become Washington's only topless octogenarian." My voice trembled with age, and if I admitted it, a hefty dose of fear even as my pulse thudded in my ears.

But this time I wasn't alone, and that made all the difference in the world.

A warm hand in mine banished most of my fear. "I'll be waiting outside, Grammy." Joanna's brown hair was loose around her face, so like mine when I was her age. "I'd sit with you in the operating room if they'd let me."

I patted her hand. "I know you would, darling," I said as a nurse gave the IV needle an efficient tap and swabbed the inside of my elbow with a cool pad of alcohol. "And if this is the end . . ."

"I'll have you buried wearing your Cuban pearls, in the plot you picked out right next to her. I swear it."

Right next to Paulina. I might have chosen a plot next to Father or Nick, but instead I'd made arrangements to share a headstone with my only child. It wouldn't alter the fact that I'd been unable to save her, but it was the only place I wanted to spend eternity.

Joanna's lips were warm as she kissed me on the forehead. "But that's not going to happen. Not today."

"If you say so."

My mind wandered to more macabre thoughts then, to all those who'd gone before me.

My delicate mother holding me as a newborn and drifting into a deadly fever.

Cousin Eleanor's reaction when she learned of the tuberculosis that would eventually kill her.

A pretty young girl who'd downed a lethal concoction of alcohol and sleeping pills . . .

Not that. Anything but that.

When I closed my eyes, I couldn't help but think of my brothers in their last moments.

A plane shot down over France.

A gun held to the head.

A heart attack in a sleeping truck outside Normandy . . .

Each so brave, in his own way.

Inevitably, I thought of my father then, barrel-chested and booming-voiced even after being shot by a would-be assassin, brandishing the bleeding, undressed bullet wound to a worshipful crowd. Of him returning from the Amazon years later, his body broken and racked with malaria, but still hoping to join the European front as the Great War broke out.

My earliest memory floated to the surface, of trying to clamber onto his lap, me frocked in a pink dress while he still wore leather chaps that smelled of the dusty Dakota Badlands. Train whistles shrieked and engines roared as he'd brushed me off and handed me back to my aunt.

"I can't," he'd said to my aunt even as I reached up empty arms for him. "She has *her* eyes . . . I just can't."

Oh, Father . . .

For a girl who grew up terrified of loving anyone, I had loved and been loved. And paid for it. But as I looked at Joanna, I knew it was worth every moment of heartache, just as I'd promised Jackie Kennedy it would be.

The surgical theater was terrifying, with its glaring lights and swarm of white-garbed physicians. "We're going to start your anesthesia in a moment, ma'am," one said to me. "Can you count backward, starting from ten?"

I scoffed, for I wouldn't waste my final moments with counting. Instead, I counted memories from my most interesting life—burying a bad little idol of Nellie Taft in the White House gardens, calling President Harding a decaying emperor, and comparing cousin Franklin to Hitler—until the world blurred from a heady mix of sedative and memories.

I had no regrets, but damn it all, I didn't want to die on this operating table.

I woke feeling like someone had drugged me, which I suppose they had. For the first few seconds, I could blink, but little else. The blinds were drawn, dulling everything in the sterile hospital room to shades of gray.

Ha. I didn't die.

I felt even better when I saw my favorite brown-haired imp sitting on the couch, legs tucked under her with a book on her lap. Probably *The New American Poetry*, the volume that she'd been carting around for days.

"'*And he smiles*,'" I managed to croak out, "'*but not as Sultans smile, and settles back the blade.*'" The tiny movement made me aware of the thick bandages that straitjacketed my chest. I'd forgotten how sore everything felt upon waking up. At least I'd never have to do it again, for I didn't have a third breast for them to plunder.

Joanna replaced her bookmark and closed the volume with a smile, the last line of "Lepanto" ready at hand. "'But Don John of Austria rides home from the Crusade.'" She came and perched on the edge of my bed, brandishing a foam cup of water. "How do you feel?"

"Alive," I said as I sipped the water. "This old fossil will live to see a few more years."

"You'd better." Joanna set down the cup and produced a brightly wrapped package from under the bed. "Ruth's daughter brought this by."

I was still attached to a jungle of IVs so Joanna had to help me open the present. Inside was a settee pillow embroidered not with the usual humdrum flowers or birds but a saying that would become my new motto.

"'*If you can't say something good about someone sit right here by me,*'" I read aloud with a rabid grin. "I love it. I really, truly love it."

"I knew you would, Grammy." Joanna laughed and gently tucked it behind my back. "I knew you would."

Chapter 25

JULY 1976

That pillow was still sitting on my floral salon couch six years later as I absently petted Cat and checked my reflection one final time, just as I had ages ago before descending the stairs for my White House debut. The woman in the mirror—snowy hair in a loose chignon, slightly stooped back, with a string of Cuban pearls around her neck—looked like an aging Eurasian concubine. That is, until she stuck her tongue out at me. My black-and-white long-sleeved matron's dress and simple diamond earrings were a far cry from my debutante's ensemble, and there was no denying that time had left its calling card all over my face. Still, I supposed it would have to do to meet the queen of England.

Because, for the record, I'd already met the queen of England. That just happened to be a different queen, from a different generation. Several generations, in fact.

"Are you sure I can't wear my hat?" I grumbled to Joanna. "I'm naked without it."

"You can do whatever you want. You always do."

"Bah." I stuck my tongue out again. "Silly girl. You can't wear a day hat to a state dinner. It just isn't done."

Joanna rolled her eyes and handed me the diamond-trimmed

clutch that Edward VII had given me as a wedding gift back in 1906. Its glamour was out of place in my cluttered house filled with dusty pelts from Father's hunting expeditions, pyramids of dog-eared books, and a lifetime of faded photographs. "Promise you'll behave tonight?"

"Not a chance. I never make a promise I don't intend to keep." I took the proffered arm of Joanna's serious sweetheart, Robert Hellman. The devil only knew if they were ever going to get married, but I didn't care. Robert's easy smile and the fact that he addressed me as Mrs. L felt like echoes of Willard Straight, and he looked rather dashing in his tuxedo, reminding me of several other men who had offered me their arm for an evening at the White House.

Nick.

Bill.

Father.

How I missed them. But at the crumbling old age of ninety-two years, it wouldn't be long before I saw them again. And oh, the stories I would tell then!

I turned at the door and gave Joanna a cheeky grin. "What time shall we be home, my dear?"

She gave a mock frown. "Midnight, or pay the piper."

"We'll do our best." Robert kissed her on the forehead. "But we both know Mrs. L here is a wild one."

Joanna winked at me, ever my silent accomplice. "Well, get on with it. Remember your curtsy and tell the queen I said hello."

I'd scarcely visited the White House since Nixon's disgraceful resignation and had considered skipping tonight's state dinner celebrating America's bicentennial, but Joanna had insisted I attend, claiming it would be good for me to get out and see the old house again.

And there it was . . .

I realized as Turner guided the old Packard up West Executive Avenue how much I had missed the great white mansion these past years.

If I craned my neck, I could make out the spot on the roof where I'd smoked illicit Lucky Strikes and below it, the bedroom that looked out onto Lafayette Square where I'd spent my rebellious teenaged years. I wondered who lived there now, whether perhaps it had become a guest room or storage closet for the mansion's extensive art collection. And there was the lawn where Quentin had trotted about with his calico pony, Algonquin, where we'd used mirrors and sunlight to blind Father's Secret Servicemen until he had them use coded flags to order us to cease and desist.

Despite all these years, the White House—my father's White House—still remained.

I'd haunted the congressional galleries for decades because of Nick and Bill, but it was this old house that contained so many of my fondest memories, everything from my debut and wedding day to basking in Father's attention while I recovered from appendicitis.

I might have been a million miles away when Robert opened my door. "You coming, Mrs. L?" The corners of his eyes crinkled with his smile. "I'm a greenhorn when it comes to White House parties, but I suspect the party's in the garden, not on the curb."

I allowed him to help me to my feet. "Lead the way."

To which he scoffed, "I think you'd better do the honors. After all, you probably know more about this house than anyone else here tonight."

"You're right," I said, preening. "I *am* an expert when it comes to this house."

We retraced the path I'd walked so many times for presidential teas and luncheons, and I could almost see a young Paulina at my side in her patent leather shoes and Sunday best, round cheeks dimpling with a shy smile as we visited Grace Coolidge. If I closed my eyes, it might have been Bill at my side instead of Robert, rendezvousing after a meeting with Herbert Hoover and on our way for a stroll through Rock Creek Park.

But it wouldn't do to linger in the past, not when I'd been granted the gift of the present.

"It doesn't seem to make much difference who the occupants of the

White House are," I murmured to Robert. "The parties are always the same."

For upon our arrival in the Rose Garden, a marine in a blue dress uniform swept us past the stately pergola draped with white concord grapevines, and beyond the crabapple and magnolia trees to the front of the receiving line to greet Queen Elizabeth and Prince Philip. Elizabeth was young—fifty, but that was still spry to my ancient eyes—and quite statuesque in a yellow gown and glittering diamond ensemble that reminded me of my own debut. A veritable storm of flashbulbs went off as I was presented to her. To my surprise, she commented on my clutch.

"It was a gift from your great-grandfather before you were born," I said. "I was quite put out when my father didn't allow me to attend his coronation."

"I believe they referred to you as Princess Alice then, didn't they?" Her eyes sparkled merrily. "I do wish we'd been contemporaries—I'd have enjoyed a friend like you growing up."

I gave a high yip of laughter, ignoring President Ford's and everyone else's shocked stares. "I doubt your mother would have allowed us to be in the same room together. Few parents approved of me in those days."

"That makes me even more pleased to make your acquaintance."

"And I you, Your Majesty," I said.

Robert and I moved to allow the people behind us to take our place. It was only then that I noticed his awed expression.

"Did you swallow a fly?" I asked.

He shook his head as if to shake something loose. "You never cease to amaze, Mrs. L."

"How's that?"

"Oh, just your lighthearted banter with the queen of England."

"That was nothing," I said. "You should have seen me with Empress Dowager Cixi. She had men cowering at her feet."

We laughed and made pleasantries with the president until I spotted Lady Bird Johnson at the far end of the line. I waved and she started to wend her way toward us.

I leaned closer to Robert. "Shall I ask her how Lyndon is?"

"You can't do that," he whispered back.

"Why ever not?"

"He's dead."

"Oh." I tried to remember when that had happened, and failed. "Then I shall ask her how Lyndon *was*."

Robert instead allowed me to introduce him to the former First Lady. We had a splendid time toasting and eating and talking, but the real treat came at the very end of the night, when a liveried White House servant tapped me on the shoulder.

"Excuse me, Mrs. Longworth," he said. "But we have a guest who worked at the residence when you lived here with your father. Do you have a moment?"

"Of course." I broke into a grin as he ushered forward an impeccably dressed African American servant with silver hair and a parish pickax of a nose I could never forget.

"Mrs. Longworth," he said with a bow. "Do you remember me?"

I did, despite the many decades since I'd seen him last.

"Of course, Ike." I rose on creaking joints to give him a hug. "Do you still provide lunch trays to the president's children and show them the best staircases for sledding?"

"These old bones of mine shudder at the very thought," he said, knocking his knees with a polished mahogany cane. "No child who has lived in this house since you Roosevelts has enjoyed stair-sledding the way you and your brothers did."

I laughed. "Father once said that no family enjoyed the White House more than us."

Ike nodded sagely. "I suspect he was right."

He led me to an empty table, and together we sat and reminisced about when the world was young, Robert patiently listening and waiting. We laughed together and caught up on all the old staff—who had died or moved on, who had children working as White House aides now—and I told him about my own family. Ike revealed that although his sister Rose had long since passed on, he was here tonight because his son was retiring after thirty years of working in the White House. Finally, as the uncomfortable wooden chairs were being carted away, he and Robert rose and escorted me to where Turner waited with the now-ancient Packard. I caught the final trembling strain of the orchestra's violin playing Mozart's *Violin Concerto No. 1* as we walked across the lawn, as if Nick himself had arranged the perfect score for my final adieu.

"It's been a real pleasure seeing you one last time, Mrs. Longworth," Ike said as Robert tucked me into the back seat. "You've been a fixture in this old town for almost a century."

I shook a knobby finger at him. "I'm only ninety-two. And we moved to Washington when I was seventeen. That's seven and a half decades."

He winked a sagging eyelid. "Don't stop your old capers, you hear? You always did keep us—and the entire country—on its toes."

"And I intend to keep doing so," I said. "Scout's honor."

Daughter of one of America's most beloved presidents, cousin and antagonist to another, wife of the most debonair Speaker of the House, mistress to the most famous senator of the century, mother and grandmother . . .

Yes, indeed, I'd become a power in my own right, the *other* Washington Monument.

Yet as Turner eased the limo down the drive and I craned around to take in the view of the White House lit up at night, I knew that this was truly good-bye.

But at my age, I'd grown accustomed to good-byes.

Of course I heard Father's words in my head as I left this house that had once been his.

And I said the words aloud, just so I could hear them one more time.

"'The credit of living belongs to the one who is actually in the arena,'" I murmured, "'whose face is marred by dust and sweat and blood; who strives valiantly; who errs, who comes short again and again, because there is no effort without error and shortcoming, without great enthusiasms and devotions.'"

I'd been marred time and again by dust and sweat and blood, and the devil knew I'd erred and come up short again and again. Would it have been easier to live a calm, sedate sort of life, the kind that included the occasional yawn? Of course. But that was never my way.

I'd made more than my fair share of mistakes, but I'd also lived enough to last several lifetimes.

I couldn't ask for anything more.

So I raised a frail and age-spotted hand to bid a fond farewell to the precious lifetime of memories, mistakes, and triumphs I had made in this great white house and beyond.

Farewell, to a life valiantly and strenuously *lived*.

AUTHOR'S NOTE

Alice Lee Roosevelt Longworth was marvelously irreverent until her final moments at the ripe old age of ninety-six, wearing her Cuban pearls and sticking her tongue out at Joanna's beau, Robert Hellman. Her last words were, "I'm an old fossil, a cheerful fossil." There was some disagreement over what to list as her occupation on her death certificate—how does one categorize a woman who was a president's daughter, wife to a Speaker of the House, mistress to a senator, and a Washington fixture for so many decades? After one authority ludicrously suggested "housewife," it was instead decided to list Alice's official title as "gadfly."

When I first decided to jump from writing about ancient history's forgotten women to the twentieth century, I was shocked—and more than a little delighted—to discover that no one had novelized Alice's story. I've been an unabashed fangirl of Theodore Roosevelt for as long as I've been teaching United States history, but I first came across the antics of his eldest daughter when I traveled to Washington, DC, and purchased the children's picture book *Mind Your Manners, Alice Roosevelt!* for my then four-year-old daughter. I knew of T. R.'s famous quip regarding controlling the country or Alice, but had no idea that Alice had carried a garter snake named Emily Spinach around in her handbag or cut her wedding cake with a saber borrowed from a military aide. From there I bought every book I could find about Alice—to join a bookshelf already bursting with nonfiction about her father—and spent many months chortling over her outrageous escapades. Many of those antics made their way into this book, from her scandalous motor trip in Lila Paul's Valentine-red roadster to smoking *atop* her father's White House roof instead of *under* it, and her affair with Bill Borah all the way to her knock-down-and-dragout feud with cousins Franklin and Eleanor.

Alice was also America's first media sensation, and there were times when newspapers and other sources contradicted her own recounting of certain events, including the idea that she jumped into the *Manchuria*'s swimming pool with Nick (she recorded it was Bourke Cockran) and was married in a gown of Alice Blue (she said it was white, which photographs confirm). While this book is certainly a work of fiction, I tried to include as many lines from Alice's diaries, letters, and autobiography as I could, including her ultimatum letter to Nick in the Far East and the troubling letter she received on her honeymoon. (Most shocking was Cissy Patterson's note asking Alice to look for her garter in the chandelier!) In addition, all of the characters in this story are based on real historical figures, with the exception of the White House staff, Rose and Ike, although there *was* a former White House servant from T. R.'s tenure who asked to sit and talk with Alice after she met Queen Elizabeth, which seemed to me a perfect sort of bookend for her very long life.

While I endeavored to make this story as factual as possible, there were times when I bent history to better fit the narrative, which means it's confession time . . .

All research points to the idea that Alice was staying with friends when the Roosevelts discovered that her father was about to become president and that she traveled to Washington to take up residence in the White House later than the rest of the family. However, I wasn't going to let my fictional Alice miss out on so dramatic a moment, so I had her present in her family's cabin when the Adirondacks ranger arrived with the news of President McKinley's impending death.

In a novel of this scope (ninety-six *very* full years!) there were a number of events and characters that needed to be condensed, including bringing Nellie Taft along on the Far East junket and merging her with another historical figure, a congressional wife named Elsie Parsons who constantly needled Alice for her inappropriate behavior during the trip abroad. (Since Nellie Taft needled Alice during the Taft presidency, the two seemed a natural fit.) I freely admit that I collapsed several unwieldy timelines, including the arrival of wedding gifts, especially Alice's pearls and Nick's buffalo skin and the fact that Nick died a month after giving up the Speaker's gavel, instead of a week. Finally, the tumultuous years before Paulina's marriage were also condensed. Paulina did overhear Alice tell her governess the truth about Bill Borah, but it was before she attended Vassar, not before she went to boarding school. I moved that critical moment forward a few years for better narrative flow.

In order to expand on Alice's marital troubles and allow her an early scene alone with Bill Borah, I changed the statement from Alice's memoir *Crowded Hours* that Nick rode with her on the train back to Washington after the disastrous 1912 convention. I also relocated a dinner party that Eleanor attended at the Longworth home in Washington to Rookwood to provide additional drama after Alice discovered Virgie Newcastle canoodling with Nick under the tree in Cincinnati. And while Alice wrote that Nick took one of Ruth's many phone calls immediately after T. R. was shot in Milwaukee, I had him absent so poor, distraught Alice had to deal with her mother-in-law instead.

There is no evidence that Eleanor Roosevelt actually drove the infamous Singing Teapot that ruined Ted's political career, but she was directly behind the trick and later called it a "rough stunt." Of course, regardless of whether she was behind the wheel, Alice considered this the moment when their family feud began. (Eleanor, of course, blamed it on the comments Ted made against Franklin during his campaign for vice president.)

There is no shortage of quotes said by or about the entire Roosevelt clan, and I took some purposeful liberties with a small handful of them. For example, Alice's comment that death had to take her father sleeping or there would have been a fight was actually said by Vice President Thomas Marshall, but as he didn't make an appearance in this novel, I attributed it to Alice. Her quip about the truckman, trashman, and policeman being allowed to call her Alice wasn't said to Alexander Sturm, but instead to the infamous Joseph McCarthy.

To keep this from becoming an eight-hundred-page novel, there were many other great scenes from Alice's life that I had to trim, including her meeting with the Wright brothers and a time when she cussed out a white taxi driver for yelling racial epithets at Turner. (On a related side note, I extended Turner's tenure in Alice's employ as it was unclear from my research how many years he worked as her chauffeur, but it surely wasn't from the days of World War II to Alice's final visit to the White House.)

This book took almost twice as long to write as my other novels, due in part to the immense amount of documentation of what sometimes felt like every moment of Alice Roosevelt's life, and I owe a slew of people my eternal gratitude for their cheerleading over the last few years. My early readers, Renee Yancy and Jade Timms, gave me the oomph to keep writing a time period that exchanged horse-drawn chariots for automobiles, and Vicky Alvear Shecter helped me get inside young Alice's head. Kate Quinn earned a special debt of gratitude for reminding me that Alice's leading men still needed sex appeal despite the early twentieth century's penchant for outrageous facial hair. (I'm looking at you, Nick Longworth.) An additional thanks goes to Kate, Stephanie Dray, and Sophie Perinot for stealing me away from the Library of Congress when I came to DC to research Alice's letters and diaries. I'll sneak out for soufflés with you ladies anytime!

A huge thank-you to my agent extraordinaire Kevan Lyon, who plucked Alice's story from the slush pile and hasn't stopped cheering for it since, and also to my fabulous editors Kate Seaver and Sarah Blumenstock, for loving Alice as much as I do.

I am truly thankful to all the readers and bloggers who take the time to read my novels and love to learn about women pulled from the shadows of history. You're my kind of people! Also, to my teacher friends, Claire Torbensen, Kristi Senden, Megan Williams, Cindy Davis, and Nicole Ayers, who keep me sane by dragging me out for hiking and wine (sometimes at the same time) while I juggle the insanity of teaching and writing about history.

To my family, Tim and Daine Crowley, Hollie Dunn, and Heather Harris, who get excited (or at least fake it really well) about book contracts or cover art, I owe you.

Most of all, thank you to Stephen and Isabella. Always.

FURTHER READING ON THE LIFE AND TIMES OF ALICE ROOSEVELT

Burns, Eric. *The Golden Lad: The Haunting Story of Quentin and Theodore Roosevelt*. New York: Pegasus Books, 2016.

Cordery, Stacy. *Alice: Alice Roosevelt Longworth, from White House Princess to Washington Power Broker*. New York: Penguin, 2007.

Hagedorn, Hermann. *The Roosevelt Family of Sagamore Hill*. New York: Macmillan, 1954.

Longworth, Alice Roosevelt. *Crowded Hours: Reminiscences of Alice Roosevelt Longworth*. New York: Charles Scribner's Sons, 1933.

Millard, Candice. *The River of Doubt: Theodore Roosevelt's Darkest Journey*. New York: Broadway Books, 2006.

Morris, Edmund. *Theodore Rex*. New York: Modern Library Paperbacks, 2002.

Peyser, Marc and Timothy Dwyer. *Hissing Cousins: The Untold Story of Eleanor Roosevelt and Alice Roosevelt Longworth*. New York: Doubleday, 2015.

Phillips, Doug, comp. *The Letters and Lessons of Theodore Roosevelt for His Sons*. Profiles in Fatherhood. San Antonio: Vision Forum, 2005.

Seale, William. *The White House: The History of an American Idea*. Washington, DC: White House Historical Association, 2001.

Teague, Michael. *Mrs. L: Conversations with Alice Roosevelt Longworth*. New York: Doubleday, 1981.

Ward, Geoffrey C. and Ken Burns. *The Roosevelts: An Intimate History.* New York: Alfred A. Knopf, 2014.

Ziemann, Hugo. *The White House Cookbook.* New York: Houghton Mifflin Harcourt, 1996.

AMERICAN PRINCESS

A NOVEL OF FIRST DAUGHTER
ALICE ROOSEVELT

*Stephanie Marie
Thornton*

A CONVERSATION WITH
STEPHANIE MARIE THORNTON

1. What inspired you to write about Alice Roosevelt?

I've taught American history since my days as a student teacher, when my first nerve-racking solo lesson was about the presidents of the Progressive Era: Theodore Roosevelt, William Howard Taft, and Woodrow Wilson. Theodore Roosevelt's gumption and zest for life caught my attention even then, and one woman immediately jumped to mind when I was asked whether there were any American women I might be interested in writing about. Because, honestly, who *wouldn't* want to write about the hellion that was Alice Roosevelt?

Writing *American Princess* meant that I had the opportunity to walk in Alice's shoes, to reimagine moments spent with her father, Franklin, and Eleanor, not to mention all of Alice's other interesting acquaintances. (And I'm convinced by now that Alice knew everyone who was anyone during the twentieth century. Richard Nixon? Check. Queen Elizabeth? Check. The Kennedys? One check each for Jackie, Jack, and Bobby.) Cliché as it sounds, for someone who loves American history—and especially the Roosevelts—writing this book was a dream come true.

2. Being such a fan of Theodore Roosevelt, was it difficult to write about him from Alice's point of view? After all, they didn't always see exactly eye to eye, especially in her younger days.

There were definitely scenes that made me cringe, most especially the one where T. R. called her a "guttersnipe." (Which actually happened!) However, I told myself that the election of 1912 would change things as he and Alice finally learned to work together, so there was hope for both of them. (And honestly, there were times I wanted to wring teenaged Alice's neck, so I sometimes empathized with T. R.) Of course, there was one particular scene in 1919 that absolutely gutted me every time I had to reread it for each round of edits and revisions. It's incredibly telling to me that Alice completely skipped over her father's death in her autobiography; I wanted to do the same myself.

3. Alice Roosevelt was a trailblazer for her era, but she seems to have held a rather blasé attitude toward women's suffrage. Why wasn't she more of an agitator, seeing as how she cut her teeth on politics and it seems logical that she'd want other women to have more say in politics?

I think Alice was lukewarm about women's suffrage because it didn't impact her in a direct manner. Over the course of her life, she held the attention of a former president, a congressman and eventual Speaker of the House, and one of Washington's most powerful senators, in addition to all the other politicians who sought access to her salons and dinners. She wasn't called the *other* Washington Monument for nothing; Alice Roosevelt Longworth was a political force to be reckoned with, which meant that casting a vote in a ballot box seemed like a small contribution in comparison. That said, she recorded in *Crowded Hours* that she always believed women should have the right to vote, and was pleased that Nick cast his vote in favor of the women's suffrage amendment.

It should also be noted that Alice supported other progressive political causes including the civil rights movement and gay rights. In fact, although the quote was originally attributed to English stage actress Mrs. Patrick Campbell, Alice borrowed her statement that she didn't care what people did (referring to a male homosexual relationships), so long as they didn't do it in the street and frighten the horses!

4. Did you travel to research this book?

I spent time in New York and Washington, DC, and I could have happily pitched a tent in the yard of Sagamore Hill for at least a week, but instead I contented myself with scribbling pages of notes as I toured Alice's pink bedroom and T. R.'s study (where there are so many wonderful books!). I was also able to visit the Theodore Roosevelt Birthplace National Historic Site in New York City, where they have on display the very shirt T. R. was wearing when he was shot in 1912. It sounds macabre, but the story of T. R. giving his speech in Milwaukee after being shot is one of my favorites to tell my students, so seeing that shirt was actually a bucket-list item.

Also, you can imagine my glee when I discovered that a large collection of Alice's papers are now housed in the Library of Congress. It was surreal—and I got a little teary-eyed—to thumb through diaries she'd written as a young woman, even though her handwriting was so atrocious that the librarians wished me good luck deciphering them. I still can't believe that all it took was a library card and I was allowed to touch—with *bare hands*—letters written by Alice, her father, and cousin Eleanor. Talk about a history-nerd fangirl moment! (I'm not ashamed to admit there might have been a little hyperventilating.)

5. Do you have a new story you're working on?

I'm excited to say that the subject of my next novel actually makes a brief cameo toward the end of *American Princess*. I've jumped from writing about Alice Roosevelt—one of America's first trendsetters and media sensations—to the challenge of telling the story of America's most iconic

First Lady: Jacqueline Kennedy. I've been surprised to discover how many similarities the two women shared, and I was delighted to discover that Jackie invited Alice to horse races, history lectures, and other events during her time in the White House. I'm hoping that I'll be able to get the two of them together for another scene in Jackie's book!

READING GROUP QUESTIONS

1. In a country without royalty, the press dubbed Alice Roosevelt with the title *Princess* Alice. In what ways did she use the press to her advantage, and how did this sometimes backfire?

2. As portrayed in the novel, how would you describe Alice's relationship with her father? Was Roosevelt a good father? Did he change as a father over the course of the novel? Was Alice a good daughter?

3. Alice struggles with forming lasting female friendships throughout *American Princess*. Her falling-out with Maggie Cassini happens early, and she is good friends with Cissy Patterson before they fall out with each other later. How do Alice's friendships with these two, along with Ruth Hanna McCormick, Mary Borah, and Eleanor Roosevelt, transform over the years?

4. Throughout her early years, and even beyond, Alice craves attention and will go to great lengths to get it, most especially from her father, but also from her friends, Nick Longworth, and even the press. Yet there are some societal rules even she isn't willing to break. How does this juxtaposition affect her relationship with Nick throughout their years together?

5. What did you think of Alice's choice to marry Nick? Why did she make that decision? What viable alternatives did she have?

6. Cissy's marriage to Count Gizycki serves as a warning to Alice throughout the story, and both women engage in affairs after their own marriages fall apart. How was divorce looked upon in those days, and how did Alice's views differ from Cissy's?

7. Alice is constantly at odds with her parents during her teenaged years, yet she also struggles as a parent herself after Paulina is born. What lessons did she learn from her parents, and what mistakes did she make? How did she learn from those mistakes after she takes custody of Joanna?

8. *"Blackbirds rarely sit behind the shoulder of one whose pace is fast enough."* Over the course of her long life, Alice experiences many terrible losses. How did her father's attitude toward the loss of her mother—Alice Lee—affect her own ability to grieve? In your opinion, is this a good way to deal with loss?

9. Alice was famous for her caustic wit, and her embroidered couch pillow—*If you can't say something good about someone sit right here by me*—is well-known. When was that wit put to good use? Are there times when Alice should have curbed her tongue?

10. Alice Roosevelt Longworth lived a very full ninety-six years, from 1884 to 1980, to become the *other* Washington Monument. What most surprised you about her very long life? What did you learn about her that you didn't know before?

Photo by Katherine Schmeling Photography

Stephanie Marie Thornton is a high school history teacher by day and lives in Alaska with her husband and daughter.

Ready to find
your next great read?

Let us help.

Visit prh.com/nextread